THE MARCHMAN

Bothwell frowned. "The crown can make or unmake appointments, my lords. It is the fount of all temporal authority. And I have been made chief warden."

"Then we must see Her Grace, and inform her of the true position," John said.

For moments there was silence, the earl tight-lipped. Then he jabbed an accusing finger.

"Whatever you may say, you are failing in your duties as wardens. Robbery and reiving, rape and assault, burnings and slayings, go on all along the border. These make a mockery of all law and order, and you appear to be unable to check it. Or do not."

"There is much of strife, yes, my lord," John admitted. "But as I said, the Borders have their own laws, the Leges Marchiarum. You must know that, your sire having been lieutenant before you. These we seek to uphold. Other relevant laws where we can. What are offences elsewhere may not be such here –"

The Marchman

Nigel Tranter

CORONET BOOKS
Hodder and Stoughton

Copyright © 1997 by Nigel Tranter

The right of Nigel Tranter to be identified as the Author of the Work
has been asserted by him in accordance with the Copyright, Designs
and Patents Act 1988.

First published in Great Britain in 1997 by Hodder and Stoughton
a division of Hodder Headline PLC
First published in paperback in 1997 by Hodder and Stoughton
A Coronet paperback

10 9 8 7 6 5 4 3 2 1

British Library Cataloguing in Publication Data

Tranter, Nigel, 1909–
The Marchman
1. English fiction – 20th century – Scottish authors
2. Scottish fiction – 20th century
I. Title
823.9'12 [F]

ISBN 0 340 65995 5

Printed and bound in Great Britain by
Mackays of Chatham PLC, Chatham, Kent

Hodder and Stoughton
A division of Hodder Headline PLC
338 Euston Road
London NW1 3BH

Principal Characters in order of appearance

John Maxwell: Second son of Lord Maxwell, Warden of the West March.

Dod Armstrong: Body-servant and friend of above.

Agnes, Lady Maxwell: Stepmother of above.

Agnes Herries: Eldest daughter of the Lord Herries.

Catherine Herries: Younger daughter.

William, Lord Herries: Deputy Warden of the West March.

James the Fifth: King of Scots.

Oliver Sinclair: King's favourite.

Robert, Master of Maxwell: John's elder brother.

Sir William Kirkcaldy of Grange: Keeper of Edinburgh Castle. Veteran soldier.

Cardinal David Beaton: Archbishop of St Andrews, Primate and Chancellor.

Sir John Kerr of Ferniehirst: Warden of the Middle March.

Alexander, Master of Home: Warden of the East March.

Lord Seton: Great Scots noble.

Patrick, Earl of Bothwell: Lieutenant of the Border.

Archibald, Earl of Angus: Chief of the Red Douglases.

James, Earl of Arran: Regent and later Duke of Chatelherault.

Sir David Lindsay of the Mount: Lord Lyon King of Arms.

George, Earl of Huntly: Chief of the Gordons.

Archibald, Earl of Argyll: Chief of the Campbells.

Sir George Douglas: Brother of Angus. Noted diplomat.

Sir Thomas Carleton: Cumbrian magnate and raider.

Sir Thomas Wharton: English Warden of the West March. Later Lord Wharton.

Queen Marie de Guise: Widow of James the Fifth. Regent.

Lord Hunsdon: English Warden of the East March.

Sir John Forster: English Warden of the Middle March.

John Johnstone of That Ilk: Chief of the West March clan.

Archbishop John Hamilton: Primate. Half-brother of Arran.

Lord James Stewart: Illegitimate eldest son of James the Fifth.

Master John Knox: Reformist priest.

William Maitland, Younger of Lethington: Secretary of State.

Thomas Kerr, Younger of Ferniehirst: New Warden of the Middle March.

Thomas, Duke of Norfolk: Great English noble and Earl Marshal.

James, Earl of Bothwell: Son of Patrick.

Mary Queen of Scots.

René, Marquis d'Elboeuf: Uncle to Mary.

Anna Throndsen: Norwegian mistress of Bothwell.

Sir John Gordon of Findlater: Second son of Huntly.

James, Earl of Morton: Chief of the Black Douglases. New Chancellor.

Henry Stewart, Lord Darnley: Son of the Earl of Lennox.

PART ONE

1

The young man on the spirited, splashing horse yelled with triumph as he raised his long spear high, with its gleaming, twisting trophy impaled thereon, a fine salmon, flapping urgently but securely held, heavy as it was to hold up, taxing on his muscular arms. But he was a determined character, tall and powerfully built, open-featured, keen-eyed, his long fair hair blowing free in the breeze. With a fierce effort he flung the spear round in an arc, so that its shaft fell across his broad shoulder, and this took the weight largely off his arms. The fish would weigh twenty pounds at least. Reining his mount round, he kicked it into a canter through the wavy shallows, in a shower of spray, back to the sandy beach where, beside an isolated rock, two other fish lay, fair-sized both but not so large as this one. Lifting the spear from his shoulder, he shook it, without dismounting, until his catch fell off beside the others, and pulled his beast's head round again, to send it plunging back into the tide.

This was a favourite sport of John Maxwell's, spearing salmon in the shallow waters of the Solway Firth, where the tide receded further than anywhere else on that coastline, going out for miles, but at its present stage leaving these shallows of no more than two or three feet, where the salmon were apt to lurk, especially here near the mouths of the Nith, Lochar and Annan Waters, where the fish came to spawn. It was a challenging sport, demanding much skill and expertise, as well as strength – but that young man was ever the one for challenge. The fish moved swiftly and unpredictably, particularly when alarmed by the splashing of the horse's hooves, and the refraction of the water had to be allowed for also, so that the spear-point had to be aimed not directly at its target but at where the salmon would be in the split seconds later, this demanding instant calculation of the degree of light deviation through the water, as well as compensating for the confusing effect of surface dazzle. But it could all be effected with practice and swift reactions, once a fish was spotted.

John knew the likeliest places to search, where conditions were favourable, where there were eddies and swirls caused by hollows and deeper ridges in the sand, which the fish seemed to like. It had been a good morning, with three salmon already. Some days he got none at all, and had to be content with leaving his horse on the shore and, taking off his boots, pacing through the nearer shallows in bare feet, feeling with his soles and toes for moving flatfish, flounders, which wriggled just below the surface of the sand, and then spearing down to try to transfix them, watching heedfully not to skewer his toes in the process; fair sport, but nothing compared with the salmon. Next to roe-deer stalking, and shooting the flighting wildgeese with a crossbow – and these Solway marshes were excellent terrain for these also – he loved salmon-spearing.

He had made only one other stab, and missed, when a hail from the shore turned him in the saddle. There, nearly four hundred yards off, a figure stood waving, beckoning, Dod Armstrong, his body-servant and friend. That one would not come to interrupt the sport unless there was good reason. John reined round and headed for the beach.

"The countess would speak with you, master," the other young man shouted as he neared. When they were alone, Dod did not normally call the other master; perhaps it was the shouting of the name that did it, or the fact that he came at the behest of John's stepmother. "The countess has tidings. Ill tidings I'd say, by the looks of her. She sends for you."

"Now? At once? What's to do, Dod?"

"I do not know. She did not tell me. But yon Pate Liddell from Blackshaw came, on a hard-ridden beast, one of your father's men . . ."

John nodded. "Very well. I will go to her. Bring the fish, Dod – three there. A good catch." He kicked his mount into motion again.

He had no long ride, a bare two miles. Indeed he could see the three towers of Caerlaverock Castle rearing ahead on slightly rising ground behind the level marshland. He wondered what was so important as to have his stepmother, no fluttery woman, send for him like this in mid-forenoon.

Presently he was clattering through the castleton of Caerlaverock, quite large, all but a village, cot-houses, shacks, sheds, barns, even a mill, where folk waved to him, for he was popular, friendly towards all, unlike his over-serious and seemingly stiff elder brother, the Master of Maxwell. The castle was not far off, beyond orchards, imposing with its vivid red-stone high curtain walls and higher towers, these last each flying the Maxwell banner of a black double-headed eagle on silver in the breeze, all within what was more than any moat, a small loch indeed, the walls rising straight out of the water. As a boy John had fished from the parapet walk along the tops of those curtain walls, tiny as the fish were that he had caught.

He rode through the orchards and pleasance to the north end of the loch, where it narrowed notably or, at least, where the castle had been erected close enough to the shore to create only a gap which could be spanned by a drawbridge. But before that, he had to cross an outer removable bridge over a deep ditch, which ensured that cannon could not get into practical range of the castle. The Maxwells had always considered their security.

His mount's hooves drumming on the drawbridge timbers, John rode in under the gatehouse arch between the two great drum towers, where the iron portcullis hung, ready to drop down to bar all entrance, waving to the guard

5

on duty, and so on into the large open and paved triangular courtyard.

Dismounting, he handed his horse over to a second guard and entered the pedimented doorway on the right-hand or western side of the great range of buildings, this containing the private apartments of the family, the eastern side holding the kitchens, larders, stores, laundry and the like, the stabling under the banqueting-hall at the southern side. He ran up a twisting turnpike stair to the first-floor landing, to enter the private hall and reach the withdrawing-room beyond, where he expected to find his stepmother.

She was there, sitting beside a well-doing log fire, for it was the end of October, and chilly within those thick stone walls, doing needlework, with his sister Margaret. Agnes Stewart, widow of Adam, Earl of Bothwell, and second wife of the Lord Maxwell, insisted on still being known as countess rather than Lady Maxwell, a strange conceit which the family had to put up with, for she was a strong-minded and determined woman, who had brought John's father great lands as well as a handsome person. Probably it was her royal Stewart blood which made her cherish this style, for she had been the illegitimate daughter of the Earl of Buchan, himself a natural brother of King James the Second. The young Maxwell trio, if they scarcely loved her, did respect her, and alleged that it was her bastardy which accounted for this countess appellation.

"Ah, there you are, John," she greeted him. "You have taken your time! There is more pressing work for you to do than catching fish! You are to be off forthwith, on your father's orders. First to Herries, at Terregles. And then to your own Maxwell lairds. And others. To warn and rouse them."

"Herries? Rouse?" he wondered. "What is this, of a mercy?"

"Trouble," she said succinctly. "Battle, indeed – of a sort. You know that your father and brother are gone to

6

Edinburgh at King James's command, with a force of men to repel English Norfolk, who has been harrying the East March and the Merse at Henry Tudor's orders, James assembling his main array on the Burgh Muir of Edinburgh. Well, they moved south to Fala Muir, under Soutra Hill, on their way to the border, when word reached them that Norfolk had retired, gone back into England, down to York. This because he was unable to feed his army, on account of the Merse having been burned before him by Home and the others to deny him grain, mutton and beef to eat, and forage for his horses."

"That is excellent, at least!"

"Wait you. The king, my kinsman – or his friend Oliver Sinclair leastways – saw opportunity to strike a counter-blow against Henry Tudor. Not through the East and Middle Marches, ravaged as they are, but here through the West March. To invade England on the west, thus, at Carlisle, and show that the Scots can hit back. But most of the nobles assembled with the king have failed him. They will not march to invade. They say talk peace with Henry now that he has suffered a setback, not further rouse him. Fools! But they do not like James's fondness for Sinclair, who urges this course. Beaton, the cardinal, is against it also. So most of the lords have turned back from Fala Muir, taking their twenty thousands of men with them, and leaving the king with only eight thousand. Your father, needless to say, is leal, supports James. But more men are needed, many more. So you are to go rouse Herries and the other West March lairds. Forthwith."

"Now? Go now?"

"Aye, now. There is no time to lose. The king and your father will be on the way now. In four days, five, they will be here. Herries and the rest will require every hour they can have to raise the men. So do not linger. Say that you order it on the command of your father, the Warden of the West March."

John looked at his sister, who shrugged, as their stepmother flicked a countess-like hand.

So he repaired to his own bedchamber on the upper floor to change into more suitable gear than that for salmon-spearing, and then ran downstairs to cross to the kitchen wing to collect some provision for the journey. Dod Armstrong was just coming into the courtyard with the fish, and John shouted to him to ready himself for some considerable riding and have the horses prepared.

That young man nodded, and grimaced.

So, not two hours after he had been at carefree sport in the shallows, John Maxwell was riding on his first mission on the nation's business, and wondering at the wisdom of it all. He was by no means against having a hand in teaching the English invaders a lesson; but if two-thirds of the Scots nobility were against this present project, and more particularly Davy Beaton, the Chancellor and Primate, a shrewd operator if ever there was one, then there could be reason to question. King James was perhaps not the wisest of monarchs, and certainly he was no war leader. And this upjumped new favourite of his, Oliver Sinclair, a grandson of the last Earl of Orkney, they had heard little good about; a pretty boy they called him, scarcely inspiring confidence. James had always been known as a woman's man, the Gudeman o' Ballengeich, who had sired innumerable bastards, if no surviving legitimate offspring. Now that his queen, Marie of Guise, was expecting any day to bear a child, an heir to the throne, had the king changed his preferences? It hardly seemed likely, at his age – he was just thirty – but the Stewarts were a strange breed.

Terregles, the Herries castle, lay a score of miles to the north, not far from the town of Dumfries, in Nithsdale. John had been there before, but not for some time. Lord Herries was apt to come to Caerlaverock if he had to see his superior, not Lord Maxwell, the warden, go to him, the deputy warden. Herries was an elderly man who had married late in life and had three daughters. His appointment as deputy warden had been the king's, not Maxwell's. They were not particularly friendly. But

Herries could field four score mounted men at reasonably short notice.

The pair rode up the Nith by Glencaple and Kelton to the Netherwood ford, where the Cargen Pow stream came in, and they could cross the major river. Then on up the Cargen to Terraughtie, into higher ground now. Although they were passing sundry lairds' seats, John was concerned to visit Terregles first. At a mere twenty-two years, John's word might be questioned, warden's son as he was, and Herries's authority was advisable to reinforce him.

Terregles Castle, not nearly so big as Caerlaverock, but strongly sited above a bend of the Cluden Water near where it joined the Cargen, was a typical L-planned tower-house within a courtyard, with stair tower and angle turrets. A Sir John Herries had been granted the lands here by the Bruce's son, David the Second, back in 1365; and a descendant became first Lord Herries, and his village created a burgh of barony in 1510 by James the Fourth, three years before Flodden. The present lord was the fourth.

John and Dod rode up the brae to the castle gatehouse, saw no sign of guards and proceeded into the courtyard. The sound of girlish laughter came to them from somewhere behind the main house, but they went to dismount at the doorway under its carved heraldic panel at the foot of the stair tower, the door standing open. John rasped the tirling-pin thereon, and waited.

Nobody came to answer his summons.

He stepped within, and halloed. Still no reply. This fortified house seemed less than well guarded.

They decided to leave their mounts tied to a tethering-rail and go round to the back of the castle, where there was a pleasance space of turf and fruit trees flanking the steep drop, all but a cliff, to the Cluden Water. And here they found five people, all female, two buxom women of middle years hanging out washing to dry on a line, and three younger, one only a girl in her early teens. These three were practising archery of all things, the youngest being instructed by the eldest, being shown how to hold the bow and position the arrow, urged to draw back the string sufficiently, using more strength. Even as the visitors watched, the girl let fly, to no very effective result, for the arrow flicked off sideways for only a short distance and lodged itself in the lower branches of an apple tree, to much mirth.

John was brash enough to clap his hands. All turned to gaze at the young men.

It was perhaps three years since John had seen these girls, and the change in them was noteworthy, at least to him. Not so much the youngest, who had been little more than an infant then. The middle one, perhaps seventeen years, was now good-looking, sonsy rather than beautiful, of burgeoning figure and reddish hair. But the eldest, another Agnes if he remembered aright, was enough to hold the eye indeed, tall, long-legged, shapely, and of a dark and striking loveliness, almost to hold the breath as well as the eye of this watcher. John had an eye for women, yes; but this one was exceptional.

He stepped forward and sketched a bow. "I am John Maxwell, ladies," he announced. "From Caerlaverock. And the better for seeing you!" He bowed again. "I had not known that you were archers! Myself, I use the crossbow rather than the long."

"Much easier to aim and handle, sir," the elder beauty returned. "But less challenging sport, no?"

"I think that I met you once, at Dumfries. I am seeking the Lord Herries. As to challenge, lady, I would deem shooting flighting wild geese with a crossbow sufficiently challenging for anyone! Although I can use a longbow against the deer."

"Ah, but perhaps I am less keen on the killing, sir, than on the accuracy of my aim at a butt, weak woman as I am!" That was said with a lift of an eyebrow and a slight flick of the dark hair, which somehow informed John that here was a young woman who was not to be taken lightly, if taken at all.

"It may be that you are right," he acceded. "But I have no doubt that you can *eat* wild goose, however shot, without compunction!"

"How nimble you are with your wits and tongue, John Maxwell," she said. "Let us see whether you are as able with your arms and muscles and eye!" And she took the bow from her younger sister and held it out to him.

So there was more than one kind of challenge, it appeared, even though this sort was not what he had come to Terregles for. Inclining his head, he moved to take the bow and an arrow proffered. He noted the girl's dancing eyes.

The target, despite the alleged objection to killing, was not the usual shield-like archery butt of circles and a central eye, but a painted replica of a roebuck, life-size, on padded canvas. Testing the tension of the string and then of the bow's yew wood by bending it slightly against the ground, he fitted the three-foot arrow's notch to the string, and positioned the shaft between his left-hand fingers and the curved yew.

"I would suggest the eye, sir." That was gently put.

He pursed his lips. She was a termagant, this one. At one hundred and fifty yards the eye was the most difficult part of the target to aim for. An inch above it and the head itself would be missed. Two inches below it and he would be beneath the jaw.

"I would prefer the heart," he observed. "More . . . killing!" And he took aim – but it was on the eye that he focused.

Testing the tension again, he drew a deep breath and pulled string and shaft slowly, carefully back and back, as the bow bent, one eye closed. Then, with a grunt, he let fly.

The whistle of the arrow ended in a thud. The shaft stuck quivering in the upper neck of the deer, just behind the ear.

It was the young woman's turn to clap, although in a deliberate fashion, smiling. She reached out and took the

11

bow, picked up another arrow, fitted it, almost casually took aim, and loosed off. The bolt flew, to strike the butt exactly at the small black circle which marked the deer's eye.

Gurgles of laughter came from the two other girls, but Agnes waved a hand.

"I am used to this bow and its pull, to be sure. You are not, sir," she declared.

"M'mm. You are the expert, I see. Skilful indeed. I stand humbled! Who taught you the archery?"

"My father's chief huntsman. But he has not persuaded me to the hunting, the killing."

John nodded, and changed the subject. "Your father, my Lord Herries. Is he here?"

"You wish to see him? He is down at the river, the Cluden, not the Cargen Water. At the mill of Halmyre with some of our people. The storm of two weeks back sent down spates, which carried away the dam which leads the water to the mill-lade. So the mill is not working. Father interests himself with the like. Not a concern for such as the Maxwells of Caerlaverock!"

"No? I do not see why not. Where is this Halmyre Mill? For I must see my lord at the soonest. I have tidings of some moment."

"You say so? Know you the Tofts? No? They lie between the two waters. See you, I will show you, take you to the mill."

"No need, lady. I will find it."

"If there is need for haste, as you say, better that I take you. It is no trouble. You come from your father, my Lord Maxwell?"

"At a remove, as it were. He sent the commands from the king's army."

"Ah!" She handed the bow over to her sister. "Catherine, I take our friend to Father. I should not be gone long. One hour perhaps. Teach you Janet better bowmanship." And to John, "Come. I will get a horse saddled up."

"No call for that," he said. "If you insist on guiding

me, mount you behind me. My beast can carry two well enough."

"Very well. That will be speedier. Is the word you have grievous? You say from the king's army?"

"Yes. There is trouble ahead, I fear. Disagreement in high places. All but revolt, it seems. I will tell you as we ride."

So, back at the horses, John mounted first and reached down while Dod assisted from the ground and together they hoisted Agnes Herries up on to the rear of the saddle, which involved some little agility on her part and quite a display of white leg, her skirts inevitably disarranged – not that she seemed concerned in any way, nor reluctant to sit close to the man, pressed against him indeed, as was necessary owing to the size and shape of the saddle.

Off they went, then, the young woman's arms around John's middle, out through the gatehouse vault and down the brae, Dod in the rear now, a proceeding hardly visualised for this errand on the monarch's behalf – not that the courier complained.

Down at the waterside they turned southwards to circle a small hill, with quite steep and higher braes to the right, the west, which the young woman named Clunie Hill, and then moved on down to lower ground eastwards, marshy this, all helping to provide Terregles Castle's defence. Adhering to what proved to be a stone causeway through the bog, twisting and hidden, John saw why he was being thus escorted and guided. As they rode, he told his pillion rider of the military situation which was behind this visit, a national emergency.

Half a mile beyond the marsh they came to where the burn draining it joined a bend of the Cluden Water; and just below this was Halmyre Mill, where a score or so of men were at work rebuilding a dam, with timber, stones and soil, the Lord Herries superintending.

He was a fine-featured man in his early sixties, slenderly built and slightly stooping. If he was surprised to see his eldest daughter approaching thus, he did not show it;

13

perhaps he was used to her unconventional behaviour. He greeted John civilly as they dismounted.

His expression changed as he listened to the tidings and requirements. He was no born warrior, this lord, despite his lands' proximity to the border with England and all the raiding and clash associated therewith. But he was a loyal supporter of the monarch who had appointed him deputy warden, and agreed, however reluctantly, to having his men marshal to aid the royal cause, while expressing his doubts as to the necessity and wisdom of the projected invasion into England.

He said that he would send messengers to inform and raise his lairds and their men, in properties scattered over quite a wide area of Nithsdale and the Haugh of Urr. But it occurred to him that John would be calling on Maxwell lairds and landed men, some of them in approximately the same districts, so time and effort could be saved by John apprising some of the Herries ones also. For instance, Terraughtie, only two miles to the south, was a Maxwell place; but Tregallon and Goldielea nearby were of Herries. Arnmannoch on the Bogrie was his also, whereas Shawhead on the Old Water was Maxwell. And there would be others. John agreed that this made sense, but wondered whether the Herries lairds would accept his word as sufficient authority for such a major command; after all, he would be but little known, if at all, to most of them; and Border landholders were not apt to be easily ordered around. Herries acknowledged this, and wondered whether a written and signed authority from himself would be helpful – for such as could read – but his daughter suggested that the problem could be solved by herself going with this young man. All the Herries people knew her, and would accept her as speaking for her father. This, however surprising to John, was accepted by her sire, at least for this day's calls.

John Maxwell appeared to have acquired an associate.

There was a difficulty however. The pillion was all very well for a short while but less than comfortable, or suitable, for longer riding. Nor would it look so well, arriving thus at lairdly houses. This was got over by giving Agnes Dod Armstrong's horse and he being sent back to Terregles on foot to collect another mount and come on after them to Terraughtie. So all was agreed, and the places to try to visit that day compiled, for so long as the October light lasted.

So the pair rode off, soon forded the Cargen Water, a larger stream than the Cluden, and crossed a cattle-dotted vale, with much soft and waterlogged ground, to the slopes of a higher terrain, no lofty ridge this but prominent in all these mosses and levels, with the remains of a Pictish fort visible on the skyline. Terraughtie Castle, a modest tower-house, stood on a terrace of the slopes.

Unfortunately they found that Maxwell of Terraughtie was not at home, gone to a cattle market at Dumfries. His wife, however, agreed to send someone to inform of his lord's demands. It occurred to John that such market and sale might well be attracting other cattle-rearers, and that time might be saved by asking the laird to tell others there of the warden's orders to rally and muster their men. The lady of the house, a plain-faced but practical female, said that she would herself go to Dumfries, to ensure that her husband understood and acted upon the instructions.

Dod had not arrived when they departed to head west-wards, and they left word for him to be sent after them to the smaller Herries property of Arnmannoch, up the Bogrie, another tributary of the Cargen, some four miles away. Here again they found the laird gone to the cattle sale, and John began to wonder whether he himself would have been better going there to make contact with these cattle-rearers. But a younger son remained at the farmery, and at Agnes's urging he agreed to ride to Dumfries and tell his father and others, although, by the time he got there, the sale might well be over and many of the various attenders retired to the town's alehouses and howffs for refreshment before returning home.

Dod Armstrong caught up with them here.

Riding on and trending northwards now for Shawhead, into the hills known as the Glenkins, Maxwell territory, John found Agnes Herries to be excellent and amusing company, with her own views on life and affairs, but not asserting these in any way dogmatically. Her comments on their liege-lord, the king, were to the point, shrewd without being over-censorious, and thankful that he had Cardinal Beaton largely to manage his kingdom for him. She voiced her concern over this present emergency, if it was indeed against the Chancellor's advice.

At Shawhead they found Maxwell thereof just returning from a day's hunting in the Glenkin Hills, and so there was no delay here, he agreeing to gather his men, a dozen of them, to bring to Caerlaverock in two days' time.

Thereafter it was up the Old Water to Scaur and Skeoch, a couple of miles, more Maxwell holdings, where, with the October daylight beginning to fade, they recognised that they could go no further – but which also had the effect of bringing their people in from their outdoor activities and so being available for the instructions. These properties being nearer the Crocketford marts than the Dumfries ones, their owners were apt to attend there with their surplus beasts which they did not want to have to feed over the winter months when fodder was scarce.

They had some nine round-about miles to return to Terregles, for John would not hear of Agnes going off alone through the gloaming and the dusk, as she offered to do; and in consequence he found himself invited to spend the night with the Herries family, which he was nowise loth to do, Dod being looked after by the women they had seen earlier at the washing. Terregles was very much a female-aligned household, its lord having no sons nor male kin, and was none the worse for that, as far as John was concerned.

They passed a pleasant evening by the fire, after a very adequate meal, with the girls proving that they were proficient at more than archery, playing on the lute and the clarsach and singing Border ballads during intervals in the converse and chatter, all very enjoyable for John, who was unused to this sort of family entertainment, Caerlaverock evenings tending to be otherwise, with Lord Maxwell the somewhat stern parent, and having all the turbulent West March rule preoccupying him, his countess scarcely the convivial sort, and John's brother on the sober and studious side. National affairs were but little discussed that evening.

When yawns sent young Janet off to bed, John took the hint and declared that since he must have an early start in the morning, he probably ought to be seeking his couch also. Lord Herries asked him of his projected round of visits for next day, and hearing of it, agreed that a good night's sleep was probably wise. Agnes rose to escort him to his chamber.

They mounted the narrow turnpike stair two more storeys to the attic floor, where the young woman ushered him into a bedroom where a log fire blazed on the hearth and a tub of hot water steamed, in indication that the serving-women had had their instructions also. No doubt Dod was being well cared for likewise.

Agnes waved to all the conveniences, including a garderobe in the thickness of the walling, with drainage-chute, for sanitation purposes, and wished their guest a comfortable and undisturbed night.

"I thank you," he said. "Not only for the hospitality and kind caring here, but for your help and company this day. I had no notion that the duty my father had laid upon me would turn out to be so much to my taste. Thanks to you. What could have been a trying and unwelcome task became a pleasure and a joy."

"Ha, you are a speech-maker as well as a cross-bow master – if none so ill with the longbow also, John Maxwell!" she replied. "I have heard that the Maxwells were ... otherwise! The lordly ones, that is."

"We may not all be painted in the same colours," he suggested. "These are black and silver. Our two-headed

17

eagle is black, but allow us something of the silver background! If you will?"

"Did I not say it? The silver tongue, sir! However you may be two-headed, but not two-faced, I hope!" And she trilled a little laugh, with that hint of mockery, as she turned for the door.

He had not contemplated anything of the sort, but something of the seeming challenge of the laugh spurred him and, following her, he reached out and drew her round, to stoop and kiss her. It was a very brief salute, rough rather than lingering, but very definite.

The young woman drew back a little, and eyed him levelly. "So!" she said. "That is the way of it? I am warned, am I not!"

"A goodnight to you," he jerked, and shook his head, as if in doubt.

She nodded, silent, and turning again, passed out on to the landing, to close the door quietly behind her.

However much riding he had put in that day, John Maxwell did not sleep immediately that night.

In the morning, the visitors gained no impression of displeasure from any of the Herries family, early as their rising was. But after a hearty breakfast, when John had taken leave of his host, the girls escorted him to where Dod had the horses ready. Agnes assured them that she would go northwards that day, in her father's name, to the Herries lairdships of Irongrey, Dalquhairn, Laggan and Killyleoch. And since the Maxwell property of Dalswinton was in that area, she could call there also, if he thought that they would accept her word? It would spare him that visit. John was glad to agree, and thanked her.

"You are very good," he said. "I will not forget. And . . . you forgive me for last night?"

"Forgive? Ought I to?"

"Of your kindness, I seek it."

"I do not think that I am a kind creature! But, if this

18

should be to my credit, and you wish it, then accept my forgiveness.''

Their eyes locked for a moment. Then, mounting, John led Dod off westwards.

One of the longest days riding in the young men's lives followed, north-westwards out of the shire of Dumfries into Kirkcudbright as far as Crocketford, then north to Maxwelton and Moniaive, then east through the Closeburn hills to Kirkmichael and the Johnstone country, until finally, with the dusk, they turned southwards, down the east side of the widening Nith, to Kelton, their last call, and so on to Caerlaverock, duty done. On the whole, reception and response had been good, although there had been questions, grumbles, objections, but no actual refusals of the warden's commands, whatever it was thought of the royal plans. Lord Maxwell's authority and reputation ensured that.

For John it had been a notable endeavour and experience, by no means the least of it his association with Agnes Herries. That was something to preoccupy his mind and senses. At twenty-two years he was not ignorant of women and their ways; but this was different from anything he had known before, the challenge, the testing, the need to prove himself. But, more than that, his concern. He would have to watch this. He was his own man, and must remain so . . .

2

Sooner than anticipated, the royal host arrived in the West March, and almost inevitably came to Caerlaverock, the warden's seat, needless to say making a mighty impact on all concerned, and demanding a vast amount of attention and provisioning, a horsed force of over eight thousand men, with the monarch and such of his nobles and magnates as had not deserted him. Lord Maxwell was even more urgent and demanding than was his normal.

King James the Fifth proved to be quite unlike John's preconceived picture of him, a tall, good-looking man of thirty years, amiable, very approachable, casual in manner, anything but autocratic. But despite all this there was something reserved, hidden about him, some inner citadel which he kept secret, but which could be sensed. And he gave the impression of being in less than good health, the usual explanation therefor being over-much womanising. He certainly paid very gallant attention to his hostess the Countess Agnes and even to sister Margaret Maxwell, who was scarcely a beacon of beckoning femininity, at least in John's esteem.

Nevertheless, the new favourite, Oliver Sinclair, was ever at the king's elbow, a slenderly graceful-seeming young man, much of an age with John, not exactly effeminate but certainly lacking in vibrant masculinity, despite something of arrogance. What James saw in him was hard to perceive, for John and many another. The lordly line of high St Clair was reflected in his bearing, if in little else, not to everyone's delight.

The countess entertained the royal company, while John and the Master of Maxwell, his brother, were sent out to see that the army was as well camped and provided for as was possible, forage for the thousands of horses being all but the major priority. Robert was a withdrawn individual, not aloof but not good at communicating, all but shy indeed, which was scarcely fitting for his father's heir and the chief-to-be of the warlike and dominant clan of the Maxwells, his sire saying sometimes that he would have made a better priest. The brothers were good enough friends even though so different in character. There was little priest-like about John.

Robert told him, during the superintendence of the host's welfare, something of the royal aims and intentions in this foray. The need was to teach English Henry that his ambition to emulate his remote ancestor, Edward Plantagenet, and become Lord Paramount of Scotland was not only insufferable but unworkable, impossible; and that the Scots were more than a match for him, and would remain free and could strike back. Norfolk had been repulsed and had had to retire to York, from the East and Middle Marches. A Scots assault over the border to Carlisle, the capital of Cumbria, would speak louder than any ambassadorial protests. No major invasion was planned, merely a swift strike at the city, as warning to Henry Tudor of what to expect if he continued with his aggressions. If the majority of the lords had not turned back at Fala Muir, of course, then a more ambitious strike would have been envisaged. Robert was less than happy about the entire conception, needless to say; and their father also had his doubts. But as Warden of the West March he had to obey the royal commands. Only the Earls of Cassillis and Glencairn, and the Lords Somerville, Oliphant, Gray and Fleming, with the heirs of Erskine and Rothes, had come on.

John wanted to know for when this affray was planned. He was told that it was to be attempted right away, the very next day indeed, a start to be made. The king was concerned that word did not get over to the English side of the border in time to give warning and produce a force either to counter the invasion or to defend the walled town of Carlisle. So no time was to be lost. John, seeing all his hard riding of the previous days being wasted, said that the Maxwell, Herries and other levies might well not have arrived here in time if a start was made next day. And surely the extra men to increase the force would more than outweigh any slight delay?

Robert did not know. The king was taking Oliver Sinclair's advice, and that fancy fellow was all for advance and haste.

They were late bedded that night.

In the morning, Lord Maxwell did prevail upon the monarch to wait another day, to allow the West March reinforcements to arrive, although Sinclair was much and assertively opposed. But in that Maxwell house, James could hardly refuse.

Fair numbers did come in all that day, and by nightfall fully seven hundred were added to the host. And these were mosstroopers, in the main, tough Border cattlemen and reivers, mounted on wiry garrons, the sort who would much enhance the fighting strength of the army in the wild terrain of marshes, moorland, scrub forest and river-crossings, even if not perhaps in the assault on the city, though they appeared to be a rough and unruly lot.

A start would be made in the morning.

There was a major debate, almost a war of words, in the private hall of Caerlaverock that night, with Maxwell and the other lords urging that King James remained at the castle and did not venture out with the attacking force, not yet at any rate; if they met with trouble and he was captured, then Scotland's cause would be dragged into the dust indeed. Sinclair advised otherwise, a royal lead was what was required. In the end, the king agreed to remain behind for a day or two, and then to bring on any further reinforcements which might arrive.

Caerlaverock, between the estuaries of the Nith and Lochar rivers, was some ten miles west of Annan town, where that other great water entered the Solway Firth. And from Annan to the Sark Water and the border another dozen miles. Beyond that, still another dozen miles, lay Carlisle, near the Eden mouth in this land of rivers draining the uplands. So the host had perhaps thirty-five miles to go, two days' riding for a large body of men. They would halt for the night, then, at Kirkpatrick-Fleming, four miles from the borderline, and cross into England early the following morning, and hope that word of their approach, inevitable as it would be, had not given time for any large-scale mustering of the enemy.

In no very marshalled order the force of around nine thousand men left Caerlaverock, John and his brother riding towards the rear with the Maxwell contingent, their father in front with the lords and Sinclair. The king accompanied them for a mile or two before turning back, saying that he would join them before Carlisle.

On the way along the Solway shore sundry other bodies of troops caught up with them, including not a few Herries men. John's efforts, and Agnes's, had not been in vain.

As they rode, John was not a little concerned, listening to the local lairds' talk, to hear how they were all in fact against this invasion project and only supporting it because of their loyalty, not so much to the monarch as to Lord Maxwell, the warden. Their attitude was understandable, for this assault might well provoke retaliation, whatever the immediate result, in which case it would be the West March denizens who would suffer most, that was for sure. Private raiding over the border was one thing; but major warfare was altogether another.

At Annan town they picked up no notable accession of strength, indeed the citizenry eyed them distinctly askance. England was just too near for warlike enthusiasm. They turned inland here, north by east for Kirkpatrick-Fleming, to camp for the night, six miles from enemy soil.

That evening Lord Maxwell told his two sons that he wanted them to take a few of the mosstroopers in

23

the early morning and scout ahead over the border to discover whether the way was clear and no enemy forces massing. They had to decide which route to take to Carlisle, the coastal or the inland. Much would depend on their report.

So it was another short night and a dawn rising for the Maxwells. With a mere dozen men they rode off from the sleeping camp eastwards, aiming to keep to the higher ground where they could oversee most of the wide levels of the coastal plain yet remain inconspicuous themselves amongst the scattered woodland of the hilly slopes. They crossed the Sark Water into England near Greenwoodie, avoiding the Sark Hall area where there was a small community.

Three miles ahead was the major River Esk, rising in Scotland but flowing into the Solway some eight miles west of Carlisle. This presented crossing problems for all concerned, for it meandered through miles of marshland before reaching salt water and in consequence was wide and boggy as to its banks. So there were only the two fords, the best one at Longtown, seven miles in from the mouth, and a more doubtful one at the Lyne Water junction, nearer Solway. Travellers to and from Carlisle usually used the first.

The scouting party was concerned to keep well north of this Longtown ford, but yet where they could see it, and all the bogland plain, from the higher ground, having to make almost a semi-circle of it to remain on the wooded slopes. They had reached the ancient Scots Dyke when cries and pointings had them all reining up. There, a couple of miles away, was a quite large body of horsemen, obviously making for the Longtown ford from the Carlisle direction. It was too far off for any accurate assessment of numbers, but John reckoned three or four hundred at the least.

Here, then, was trouble. The English had indeed been warned, for it was highly unlikely that a company of this size would be heading for Scots territory at this hour of the morning purely by coincidence. Probably it was but the advance guard of a larger host, sent forward to hold the fords and so hold up any Scots advance. Lord Maxwell had been well aware of the dangers of this. The borderline tended to be a sort of no-man's-land, indeed it was known as the Debateable Land, where loyalties were vague and optional, for the sake of mere self-preservation, and residents could be as pro-English as they could be pro-Scottish; and the mustering of the Scots army would not have gone unnoticed.

The watchers waited for a little, to see what the company down there would do. They saw them crossing the Longtown ford, but coming on westwards thereafter, not halting to hold the ford. So, either they were aiming to hold the further Sark ford, or they were pressing on to challenge the Scots host itself – in which case they could be only a fast-riding vanguard with a much larger force coming, or to come, behind, no doubt from Carlisle.

The Maxwell brothers turned their party round to head back at speed whence they had come.

They met up with their main body approaching the Sark in the Westgilsyke area, their news creating a major impact. So far they had seen no sign of any advancing English, such hidden by the scrub thorn, bushes and reed-beds of the great Solway Moss.

There were mixed reactions amongst the Scots leadership. Lord Maxwell was for waiting this side of Sark and holding the crossing. Others were for making for the higher ground where John's party had just been, this offering the strategic advantage. But Oliver Sinclair said that the king had commanded that they cross on to English soil, whatever happened, as the vital gesture. They must go over Sark, and then possibly circle round to the north of the moss on English ground, and thereafter drive down between this English company and their main array which was presumably coming on behind. Doubts were expressed, but it was agreed that the moss itself would make a very defensive site for a stand, Sinclair pooh-poohing this defensive concern. Attack was the spirit, not defence. Lord Maxwell insisted on leaving a small defensive force nevertheless, to hold the Sark ford behind them, just in case . . .

They crossed the river into England, only Sinclair raising a cheer, a lengthy column.

Not far beyond, into the moss itself, the horses already beginning to plouter in the soft boggy ground, Sinclair suddenly called a halt. He announced that he had a royal proclamation to transmit. Dismounting, he summoned a number of the men-at-arms to create a sort of platform from their spear-shafts and shields, a curious requirement; and when such was contrived, he mounted it and was raised up high thereon – but no higher than if he had remained in his own saddle.

Standing there, he drew out a paper from the breast-plate of his St Clair painted armour, and made his announcement.

"Here is a written and signed decree from the King's Grace appointing myself, Oliver Sinclair of Aldhamer, to be in sole command of this array, expedition and invasion, here on English soil, in His Grace's absence. All will now obey my orders, by royal command."

An appalled hush greeted this declaration, quickly followed by shouts of disbelief, anger, fury. None there who heard him needed to be told that this was ridiculous, utterly wrong, infamous, contrary to all custom and usage – and as foolhardy as it was unacceptable. In warfare on the border, the warden commanded, by age-old right. And there were two earls present, not to mention sundry lords and veteran knights. Sinclair was not even a lord, and knew nothing of warfare or high command in the field. The thing was all but laughable – although none laughed.

The uproar increased and continued, Sinclair looking surprised, upset, and waving his paper. Men cried that he could lead himself, and to deepest hell, but not them! To go back to Caerlaverock and tell King James what he could do with his decree. Did he think that they were all bairns, to be cozened by suchlike nonsense, not with their lives as the stake! And so on.

Lord Maxwell, who was scarcely of the conciliatory and peace-making sort, did seek to calm the situation, urging quiet, reasoned consideration, a council. Even he was shouted down.

Sinclair had been all but dropped from his makeshift platform, and was looking agitated indeed, voice raised but unheard.

John and his brother, arriving towards the rear of the long column, at first could not grasp what was to do, so utterly extraordinary, scarcely believable was the scene, an army in shouting chaos, leadership for the moment non-existent. Staring bewildered, they looked for their father, saw him in argument with the Earl of Glencairn and the Lord Somerville, and knew not whether to go to him or to keep away.

It was Dod Armstrong, as ever close behind John, who saw it, something worse than disarray and mutiny, saw menace, possible disaster. He spurred forward, grabbed John's arm, and pointed. There, not half a mile away, amongst the hawthorn and scrub, was movement and the glint of sun on steel. Quickly there was more than that to stare at. Movement developed into a line of horsemen, two lines, three, and these advancing at the canter despite the soggy ground, long spears levelled, three banners flying above them.

The Maxwell brothers joined in the shouting and calling now, pointing, gesticulating. But in all the uproar, indignation and confusion, few perceived or heeded. No doubt many of the ordinary folk, the mosstroopers and men-at-arms, saw what Dod had seen; but they were not only without orders but their leaders were otherwise preoccupied.

By the time that the enormity of the situation became apparent to the arguing lords, lairds and knights, it was too late for any concerted or meaningful action. They had to remount and seek out their own men, and these, in the main, and sensibly enough, were not waiting there to be ridden and cut down by that hurtling, yelling English charge. In the circumstances it was every man for himself. Most turned to flee – and one of the first to do so was Oliver Sinclair.

John, Robert and Dod swung round to beckon to their Maxwell following. John automatically took charge. Pointing, waving and shouting, he sought to form up as many as would heed him into a roughly V-shaped formation, himself at its head. It was hardly a successful effort, for there were not only Maxwells and Herries men there, mixed, but various others who saw flight as the obvious course; and panic was infectious. John was given no time to assert his command. The English were thundering down on them, spears pointing, swords drawn, and near now, near.

He saw his duty as the rescue of his father. That first. Then to save as many as he could of his people. Clearly more than that was out of the question. Lord Maxwell, remounted and about one hundred yards off, also appeared to be seeking to marshal the lords and magnates around him into some sort of order, whether arrowhead, like his son, or other. He seemed not to be concerned with flight. If John and his V could join him, they might make a group large enough to cut their way through any enemy, which was, after all, only three ranks deep.

John gestured to his people to pack closer together behind him, riding all but knee-to-knee, Robert and Dod at his back, the other thirty or so of them in threes and fours and fives. Then, sword out, he slashed it down to point towards his father's group, and dug in his spurs, crying, 'A Maxwell! A Maxwell!' How many of them heard him was doubtful, in all the uproar, but what was intended was evident enough.

But not to Lord Maxwell, apparently, for he was waving his own party in the other direction, westwards, not towards John's formation. Admittedly the driving English line was shortest there, so perhaps, heading thus, they could avoid the charge, turn past it, even get behind it. If they did so, John could still join them. He veered slightly to the right.

The enemy, however, headlong as was their onslaught, must have had some swift-thinking and experienced leaders, for their extreme left-wing files, now barely two hundred yards away, abruptly managed to swing off westwards at an angle to intercept the Scots leadership group. No doubt these were easily distinguishable by their helmet plumes, heraldic-painted armour and the like, and made an obvious target.

John was put in a quandary. To follow his father's party could end with themselves being cut off and, moreover, being struck in flank where they were most vulnerable. To change course in this V-formation was not easy, the arrow-tip being pressed on by the men so close behind. No sudden alteration was possible, only a gradual swinging round practicable.

John had to think fast. The English detachment represented perhaps one-third of the whole, possibly over one hundred men. And they had the drive and the impetus. He could not hope to outfight them, more than three times his number. His father's group were in like position. Joining them in rear or flank would be no help. He could not, at present, effect a rescue.

What, then? He had only seconds to make up his mind. The detachment of the English had left a gap in their line, inevitably. Through that, and then swing round behind the enemy? That would give them advantage, unless there was another force coming on in the rear. It was a chance, at least. From behind, they could plough through the enemy. Then see what the situation was.

So John led his V on and, with the speed of the English charge, the gap almost came to them. None of the enemy peeled off to challenge them, intent on the greater quarry.

There appeared to be no sign of a back-up force behind.

Pulling round now, however gradually, to maintain the spearhead formation, John was able to point to the backs of the Englishmen with his sword, an eloquent enough gesture. Spurring hard to gain as much speed as the soft ground would allow, they plunged on after the foe.

But it was not to be so simple a rearwards attack as John had visualised, for by the time that his little troop did catch up with the enemy, it was also into complete chaos that they were engulfed. For the English had reached what remained of the vastly larger Scots force, such of it as had not already fled, and all resemblance to an orderly and massed assault had gone. Individuals were now battling, swiping and stabbing and thrusting, circling this way and that in an extended mêlée, horses rearing and bolting and falling, many already riderless. Into this John's V plunged, smashing into friend and foe equally, confusion, turmoil, horror and bloodshed.

Or not quite all confusion. For the Scots, although still the more numerous, were without commanders and in the main intent on escape; whereas the English still had the spirit of attack, and did look to leadership. And this told.

John with his men, ploughing through the ferment of fighting and dying men and beasts, also had leaders on his mind, his father's company, however little leading they were able to effect. If he could get out of and beyond this utter rout and tumult, he might still be able to attempt a rescue of the Scots lords, if they had not themselves managed to avoid assault and capture. For the present, it was impossible to see past the masses of battling combatants.

So he drove on, sword slashing right and left in a figure-of-eight motion, scarcely able to distinguish Scots from English, much slowed down as they were now. Nothing of the knightly skills and training which he had been taught had prepared him for this. But purpose he retained: to get through this rabble of desperate men and seek out his father and the others, and if possible restore some semblance of command and order to this grim day.

It was not to be. When at last that tight little spearhead, the only seeming ordered and compact feature of that dire affray, managed to win out of the press of battling and they could gain some field of view, it was to see, well to the west, a tight and stationary group of mounted men, above which two banners fluttered: and John knew enough of Borderland heraldry to recognise these as showing the arms of Dacre and Musgrave, Cumbrian magnates, indeed the former the English Warden of the West March. And the fact that these all stood immobile, in a solid phalanx, while this fighting was going on so nearby, could only mean that they had gained what they had aimed for and were confident enough of their followers triumphing in this conflict to leave them to it, no doubt with other veteran leaders active in the fray. The Scots lords, or such as had not made their escape, must be held within that assured detachment. And it was much too strong in numbers and serried formation for John's group to attack.

At a loss now, that young man had to make difficult and swift decisions. The day was lost, and hopelessly, that was clear. And his father was almost certainly captured and securely held. What was his duty now? What the right, the best course possible? To save themselves, this little group? Flee the field? To plunge back into the rabble of battlers? To seek to aid more of their fellow-Scots to escape? This last, surely. But how? In all the bloody confusion, what was possible? And would his men obey what he decided on? They had accepted his direction thus far; but the temptation to bolt for safety now would be strong. He must try . . .

Turning in the saddle, John called to his followers. "Shout! Shout!" he cried. "A Maxwell! A Maxwell! Keep shouting it. On and on. As we stand here. Give our people that. A hope. To rally on us. Then make escape. Save what we can. Shout it! Shout!"He raised his own voice still higher, to its strongest pitch. "A Maxwell! A Maxwell!"

31

He was obeyed in this, at least. Possibly relieved that shouting was all that was being demanded of them, for the moment at least, his party took up the slogan, at the pitch of their lungs, achieved a chant of it, and persisted. There was noise enough on that marshland, to be sure; but the steady rhythmic shouting rose above the din and clash. Over and over again the war-cry was maintained, and quite quickly it began to have its effect on the struggling mass of men. It spoke of order, command, challenge, not defeat. The struggling Scots heard, and began to react, to seek to detach themselves from the fighting and make for the source of the chanting.

No doubt it had some effect on the English also, some suggestion that the disheartened and unnerved enemy was recovering – and, of course, these still outnumbered their attackers. The intensity of the fighting slackened.

John kept looking westwards to that detached group. What would be the reaction there? It could possibly change all again.

Once again this questioning of the situation was interrupted by the keen-eyed Dod Armstrong leaning forward to jerk John's arm and point. Away behind the fighting, from the depths of the moss, new lines of horsemen were emerging, long lines, many more than the first force, more banners flying.

John groaned. So this was the main English array. The previous attackers had been only the vanguard. He had wondered that so comparatively small a company was invading Scotland. This was it, then, the end of the road. No more choices. It was flight, capture or death.

He looked round at his brother and Dod, his shrug eloquent. They nodded. Raising his arm, he waved his sword round and round above his head, a very different signal from the former and downward slashing which had indicated advance. None would mistake it, whether or not they had observed the new oncoming host. Slogan-chanting died away.

With a last head-shaking glance towards where his father

presumably was held, John pulled his horse's head round, as others of his group were already doing. His duty, now, was scarcely to lead the flight, but to help as many of his fellow-Scots to get away as was possible, but, to be sure, not to delay overlong at it for his own escape. Time would be short.

It was no orderly retirement, needless to say. Men detached themselves who could, and fled, in northerly directions, in ones and twos and groups, none waiting for other. Robert and Dod did wait for John, not hiding their anxiety, urging him to be off. He was waving others on, and pointing, yelling. But soon he realised that this was no longer of any effect. And the enemy, now aware of massive backing near at hand, grew the more determinedly aggressive. It was time to be gone.

They joined the other escapers leaving that dire and humiliating field, not of battle but of shame and folly, while still they could, spurring hard. It still lacked an hour until noon.

3

They were back to Caerlaverock by nightfall, their only pausings being when they allowed their mounts much-needed drinking at the fords of Annan and Lochar. So far as they could see they were not pursued however.

They were by no means the first back with the appalling news, and found the castle in a state of alarm, defences being prepared to withstand a siege if need be. The countess appeared to be not so much distressed as angry, allotting blame indiscriminately. What fools were all concerned – and she clearly included her stepsons in her condemnation, probably even her husband. As for that Oliver Sinclair, she was almost beyond words, save to declare that being captured rather than cut down was too good for him; apparently some of the earlier arrivals from the moss had seen him seized, while fleeing, by a band of the English.

The young men found that King James had left Caerlaverock for Lochmaben Castle the previous day, this the former Bruce stronghold, now crown property, some ten miles to the north-east of Dumfries, this to try to rally more of the Dryfesdale, Eskdale, Ewesdale and Liddesdale clans to his standard, Johnstones, Riddells, Armstrongs, Jardines, Liddells, Wauchopes and the rest, folk notoriously unruly and difficult but stout fighters if they could be enrolled in the royal cause. These were a law unto themselves, but James had been hopeful, even if the countess was not. She declared that not only was it likely to be a fruitless quest, but that the king was a sick man and in no fit state to go riding round these remote and harsh upland dales.

John declared that in the morning they must go seeking the monarch with their tidings, grievous as they were. The king must be informed.

That night the young Maxwells sought to assess the grim day's results, costs and likely consequences, how many had died, how many captured, what the English would do now. Would major invasion of Scotland follow? They thought not. Even with that additional force they had seen arriving at Solway Moss there would be scarcely a large enough host to advance in a full-scale assault on the West March. It had been really only a defensive move, they judged, to seek to save Carlisle; and the total victory which it had won was probably as much a surprise to the Cumbrians as it was an unlooked-for disaster for the Scots. It seemed unlikely, therefore, that in the circumstances the enemy would press on northwards at this stage – although that might follow at some later date. Caerlaverock ought not to have to withstand siege, they thought.

Next day, then, the three young men rode off almost due north, by the Lochar Water, flanking its own three mosses, a dozen miles to the village of Torthorwald, well east of Dumfries town, and on another five miles to the extraordinarily sited castle and township of Lochmaben in mid-Annandale. No fewer than seven lochs were grouped here, so that this community was all but lost in a welter of waters, which, of course, made its stronghold strong indeed, however islanded and inconvenient of access for the local residents. The castle occupied a peninsula jutting into one of the lochs, and was further defended by a series of deep and wide water-filled ditches, only crossable by drawbridges, breaching the narrow isthmus thereto. Any other approach had to be by boat; and the lofty walls, parapets and towers ensured safety from all such. Caerlaverock was strongly sited, Lochmaben more so.

The trio themselves had difficulty in gaining access to the fortalice, which seemed to be all but deserted, giving little impression of housing the King of Scots, although, of course, James's and the keeper's people would probably

35

mostly be away seeking to mobilise the dales clans. When eventually they did win entry, it was to find the monarch with the elderly Johnstone castellan and his wife, at table. Bowing, John was struck by the ravaged appearance of their sovereign-lord. James did not exactly look old nor frail – he was, after all, only thirty years – but somehow tired, dispirited. The countess had declared that he was a sick man, to be sure.

He recognised the Maxwells at once, however, and his quite handsome features lightened somewhat. "Ha – tidings!" he exclaimed. "So soon? You bring me news, my friends? From my Oliver."

The brothers eyed each other. Robert left John to do the talking.

"Sire, I fear . . . I fear that the word is not good," he said, anything but assuredly. "Ill tidings. There has been failure. Disaster, even. Your Grace's host is . . . dispersed. Scarce defeated, but scattered, put to flight. At Solway Moss."

"Flight? Dispersed? No! Not that! Not that! It cannot be!"

"Highness, it is so. We were there. There was disunity. Dispute. The leaders in disarray. And a force of English struck. We were all unready, taken by surprise. In no formation to fight. It was rout!"

"Rout!" The king was on his feet now, clutching at the table as though for support. "Rout! And . . . Oliver? What of Oliver?"

"He fled, Sire. Early on. With . . . others."

"Fled! Oliver fled! Fye, Oliver fled! No! Not that. Where is he? Where is my Oliver?"

John swallowed. James's concern appeared to be for his favourite rather than for his army and people. "He was captured, they say. While fleeing."

"Dear God, Oliver fled! Captured." The king slumped down on his seat again. "Of a mercy – no!"

"I fear so, yes, Your Grace." Without realising it John was frowning at the way their liege-lord was taking the news. "Captured, yes, Sire. And others amany. Including our father. And the earls and lords. Only – *they* did not flee!"

James buried his head in his hands.

The keeper had also risen, with his wife hurrying from the chamber. "What happened, man?" he demanded. "How came this about? Here is folly, unbelievable folly!"

"Folly, yes, sir. Dispute. Surprise attack. None in command. Men unready. Disaster, no less. We sought to save whom we could. Not many. All leaders taken. How many died, I know not. Some sought to fight, but most fled. For lack of leadership."

"Oliver . . . !" James groaned.

"What now, then? Where is all the host? There were thousands, I heard. What is to do now? And who are you?"

"I am John Maxwell. And this is my brother, the Master of Maxwell. Our father, the warden. Who should have been in command, and was not!"

Johnstone eyed them, lips pursed. "He, the warden, and others, are held, you say? By the English? And the rest?"

Robert found his voice. "Dispersed, as my brother says. Fled in all directions. We saved whom we could. More English were coming, many more. I saw the banners of Wharton and Dacre and Musgrave."

The keeper of Lochmaben looked down at the head-bowed monarch. "What is to be done now?" he demanded. And got no help from the king.

John, glancing at his companions, shook his head. "Your clans, here? The Johnstones, Jardines, Armstrongs and the rest – they are being raised? If they can be mustered. To form a barrier, a defensive screen to prevent further English advance into our March while the others who fled are rallied again. That surely is what should be done. And in the king's name!" And he stared down at the stricken monarch.

The older man nodded, looking in the same direction. "Sire, we must act. This grievous situation must be righted, as best we can. On your royal authority. In your name."

The king looked up, still distraught, scarcely aware of what was being said, most evidently.

"Where are your dalesmen to rally?" John asked.

"Here, at Lochmaben," Johnstone told him. "But it will take time. Two days, three . . ."

"Better, surely, if they headed for the battle area right away? To be there so soon as may be, to present a front against any enemy advance. There may be none such, but it is possible. They, your folk, will have their chiefs, Larriston, Mangerton, Gilnockie, Stonehouse and the others. Hard fighters. That is the first need. Lest we have an invasion. The deputy warden, the Lord Herries, to be put in command. His is now the responsibility."

"First, I say, His Grace should be off to the north. Out of this threatened March. If Your Highness was to be captured, all would be lost indeed. Go north, Sire, and there ready the lords who failed you at yonder Fala Muir. They may not have been prepared to invade England, but they will unite to repel any invasion of Scotland, imperilling their own lands!"

James wagged his head, wordless.

"Yes, I see that," John acceded. "Has His Grace folk here, to escort him northwards?"

"No. All are gone to raise the dales. I have two or three servitors only left."

John looked at his brother. "You, Rob, you could see to that. Escort the king. Dod with you. Get His Grace to Edinburgh while I go to see Herries. No? We must act quickly, in these straits. Myself to Terregles. You with the king. The dalesmen to be sent on to Herries."

Robert Maxwell looked doubtful, but did not refuse or protest. In such circumstances as these, he was not so strong a character as his brother, whatever his abilities of mind.

The need for haste obsessed John. The king's departure was less urgent, to his mind, than the improving of the military situation. It was Terregles and the deputy warden for him, forthwith, Johnstone agreeing.

He left a somewhat distracted Robert, and the reliable and practical Dod to assist, bowed briefly to the sovereign, and took his leave.

Terregles lay about a dozen miles west of Lochmaben, but not direct miles, with the rivers of Lochar, Nith and Cluden to ford as well as many lesser streams, so that it was dusk before John reached there. He found no muster of men taking place, no indication of crisis, no major alarm. Some knowledge of the débâcle at Solway Moss had been brought, of course, by escapers, but these had not been in a position to know the full situation and losses, or at least had not informed of them, probably nowise eager to emphasise their own unheroic parts therein.

Lord Herries had not realised that he was now forced to act as full Warden of the West March, the king's commander in that great and vital area, with Lord Maxwell a captive. Clearly shaken, he as clearly did not know where to begin, what his priorities were to be, just for what he was responsible. The situation was quite outwith his previous experience, for the masterful Maxwell had called but little upon his deputy's services. Bewildered, bemused, he sat and scratched his grey head.

His daughter Agnes was of more use, John assessing that *she* should have been the deputy warden. Listening, she promptly asked for all the important details of what had happened, who was missing, how John judged the situation likely to develop and the steps to be taken to cope with it all, her father heeding, silent.

John related, explained and offered his assessment, his views on what required to be done, these distinctly urgent. He said that he had told Johnstone at Lochmaben to have the men of the upland dales sent here to Terregles, this causing Herries to blink somewhat; but reckoned that they would not be here for at least a couple of days. Meanwhile, he proposed that the survivors of the disaster should, as far as was possible, be rounded up, also to assemble here, so that there could be quite a major force to lead. He himself would aid in this rallying, but in the process head south-eastwards to the Sark area to discover, if he could, what the English were at. His guess was that they would probably have returned to Carlisle meantime, with their prestigious haul of prisoners, such as had not been taken in centuries, not even after Flodden Field, although they might well have left part of their force at the Sark to threaten further the Scots, or to prevent any possible counter-attack.

"You are suggesting a Scots assault on Carlisle, a rescue?" Agnes asked.

"No, no. That would demand far more men, and leadership, than we could mount at this present," John said. "And my guess is that they will hurry their captives away deeper into England, to ensure that there is no such attempt at rescue. They have not only our warden but two earls, five other lords and a number of knights and lairds, not to mention the king's sorry favourite, whom they will want to hold secure and probably ransom, enough to fill many a Cumbrian coffer! No, I see our task as showing an armed presence, ready, holding the borderline, to discourage further attack and invasion. While, it is to be hoped, the king persuades his northern lords to do their duty in the defence of the realm."

"And myself? What do you see as my course in all this?" Herries asked, extraordinary as it might seem for the deputy warden to be demanding the like of this young man.

"To be there, my lord. Leading the West March force remustered, and facing England." He did not use the term figurehead, but that is what he meant. "The Johnstones, Jardines, Armstrongs and Elliots chiefs should be there, it is to be hoped and expected, for they will no more welcome an English invasion than we do. They are wild men, but veteran fighters. They will play their part. Would that they had been there two days ago, and we might have been spared this calamity."

Herries did not look greatly comforted.

"In the morning, then, we will do what we did before, John? Or much of it?" Agnes said. "Go round the lairdships and properties and summon their men back here. If they will come! At my father's orders!" And she raised a knowing but affectionate eyebrow at her unwarlike sire.

"Yes. Only I will go further south, for the Sark borderline, to see what the position is there." He looked grim. "Unless we learn more ill tidings still. Then to Caerlaverock, to rally the Maxwells."

"And the king?" Herries asked. "Will he be sending down an army, with its seasoned commanders, to take over the defence of the land?"

"That is what is intended, yes. King James was very shaken by it all. But no doubt he will recover, and use his royal authority." John sounded more confident than he felt on this. "My brother, the master, is with him and will urge haste and strong action."

"It was all the king's fault, was it not?" Agnes said. "In appointing the man Sinclair to command, instead of your father and the earls?"

"That is true. A great folly. He has been on the throne since 1513, near all his life. He should have known better. But he appears to be a sick man."

Weary with much riding and stress, and with a prompt start required in the morning, John sought his couch there early that night. As before, Agnes escorting him to his room, the same that he had occupied previously.

"I fear that my father is scarcely the one for these duties," she said, as they climbed the stairs. "He is too gentle a man. Will you hold close to him, John? When he must take command. He will be glad, I know, of your help, advising – you who seem to be born to it."

"That I will do," he agreed, as they paused at his door.

"I do not know about being born to it, although I have a warlike sire. But . . . I do know that I would hold close to more than the Lord Herries, see you!" And he touched her arm.

"Ah, but perhaps I am not of such gentle sort!" she said, but she did not shake him off.

"I was thinking, back there, that it is a pity that there are no women wardens of the Marches!"

"So! You deem me one of those, a contentious, aggressive female? I am sorry if that is how I appear."

"It could matter to you how I deem you?"

"Oh, yes. We women have our vanities. I would not be thought to be a, a dragon-smiter!"

"You might smite *men*, I say. Where they are weakest. And not only with the longbow!"

"But not John Maxwell, of the silver tongue but eagle's talons and double heads! Two heads must be a convenience for a man? Doubling his prospects!"

"It could enable me to see the clearer, the more fully. See the beauty, the fairness, the goodness, the kindness . . ."

"I told you, I am not one of the kinder sort."

"Yet you were kind enough to forgive me my lapse of last time that we stood here!"

"Any man may make a lapse, once!" she said.

"But . . . twice?" And he reached out, to grasp and draw her to him, kiss her, on brow and eyes and lips, and slightly open lips at that.

She did move to free herself, but only after a moment or two, a breathing-space perhaps. "Inveterate!" she got out, the breathing evident in her rounded person. "You try and test a woman, do you not?"

"Not every woman. Will I be forgiven? Again?"

"I will tell you in the morning, sirrah!" She moved away, to descend the stairs to her own chamber. But looked back over her shoulder as she went. "Sleep well, nevertheless, two-headed one. As well that you have only the one pair of lips!"

42

At her tinkle of laughter, he took a threatening step after her as she disappeared down the turnpike.

In the morning he had to assume that he was forgiven, for in fact it was Agnes bending over his bed and gently shaking his bare shoulder which awakened him.

"Sloth is another deadly sin!" she informed him. "You will require to make prolonged confession, John! Time that you were astir. Breakfast on the table."

Sitting up, yawning, he reached out to her, but in his only half-awake state she eluded him easily.

"Hasten you," she told him. "Or the warm water yonder, for your washing, will be cold." And she left him, smiling.

Early as it was, all the Herries family were at the breakfast table, and there was much female chatter as to where the two couriers were going that day. John said that since it was thirty-five miles to the Sark, south by east, he had better not delay long on the way, for he wished to be back at Caerlaverock by dark, and knowing what the situation was regarding the enemy. He and Agnes could ride together as far as Terraughtie and Carrochan, whereafter she could head westwards for Arnmannoch, Shawhead and the rest, while he made for the Nith ford at Kingholm and on to Kelton, before heading due east for the borderline. Catherine, the middle sister, volunteered to help in this task of informing the lairds that their men were needed again, but her father drew the line at that. She was only seventeen, and young for her years; none, he feared, would take her very seriously, and this was a fell serious matter.

So without delay the pair set off, John seeking to school his thoughts to matters of men's arms rather than women's, while being very much aware of Agnes's delectable presence at his side.

The lady of Terraughtie scarcely welcomed them, for her husband, Maxwell thereof, had been one of the lairds captured with his chief; and they had lost a number of their men. But she promised to gather as many as was possible to send up to Terregles, while asking of John what was likely to be the fate of her spouse. He told her that ransom would probably be the answer to that, but as for how much, he had no notion. Not entirely happy about that either, with Agnes's sympathy, they left her.

At Carrochan, a smaller establishment, they again met with no enthusiasm, and John judged that this could be the reception everywhere, and scarcely to be wondered at. But the warden's calls had to be obeyed – that was the long-established rule in the Borderland, however unwelcome.

The couple parted company after Carrochan, John declaring that he hoped to be back at Terregles two nights hence, and adding that he wished that they did not have to separate thus, Agnes shaking her head over him.

After crossing Nith and making his unpopular call at Kelton, it was just a matter of hard riding southwards and eastwards. John did halt at Annan, to ask whether there was any word of the English, and be told that nothing had been heard thereof, or anything of invasion after the battle. He pressed on the remaining ten miles or so.

It seemed strange to be approaching that grim area again, so soon after the shame and horror of it all, now with no sign of threat nor danger. He reached the Sark without anything to concern him save the memories. At that water's reedy edge he halted, facing England and the Solway Moss. Nothing moved over there save for a few cattle-beasts, no men, armed or otherwise. He could not see far, of course, level as it all was, for thorn trees, scrub and tall reeds. But would it be likely that any enemy force would be lurking in all that wet and unpleasant wilderness? Surely not. If the English were indeed guarding their border – and they did not appear to have pushed on into Scotland – then the place to do so was here on the south bank of Sark, a defensive site.

John rode up and down that riverside for a mile or so to ensure that he was missing nothing, all the time wondering how many of his fellow-Scots had drowned in this water two days ago. He did see the bloated corpses of two horses, half in the water, and a helmet and a broken lance, that was all. So much for man's woes and agonies.

Presently, fears allayed meantime, he turned to ride back whence he had come.

It was dark before he reached Caerlaverock, too late to do more than summon the immediate men of the castle and castleton to be ready to ride in the morning. The countess, who had been awaiting possible siege, was relieved to hear that there was no danger of this at present; but scornful as to the monarch's likelihood of achieving much with his lords further north, and also of anything Robert might be able to effect, with James, or otherwise. John felt rather that way himself, although he did not say so.

In the morning he set off round the Maxwell lairdships on his less-than-popular calls, speaking in his father's and the deputy warden's names, and ordering all men capable of bearing arms, and horsed, to report at Terregles at the earliest. He had many visits to make, for the Maxwells held wide lands all over the area west of Dumfries and into Kirkcudbrightshire of Galloway, in a score of parishes. He could not reach them all in one day, but he could and did command messengers from those he did attain to, to carry the summons to the others. He gained little satisfaction from his day, but was sustained by the thought that he was determined to get back to Terregles that night, however late, and could see Agnes again.

In fact it was the many twinkling red gleams of campfires which welcomed him to the Herries establishment, hours after dark, where he discovered a large gathering of men, many hundreds, mainly dales mosstroopers, already assembled, regaling themselves heartily on Herries beef and mutton, washed down by vast quantities of ale, the noise reaching John at quite some distance. The castle itself, when he reached it, seemed to be full of their masters, as loud-voiced and scarcely polished as to manners, Johnstone, Armstrong, Jardine, Liddell,

Riddell and Elliot landholders, against whose advances the Herries sisters had to be continually on their guard, the serving-women of the household being less successful at this, perhaps less exercised in the matter. But at least the dales had not failed the warden's summons.

Lord Herries played a somewhat distracted host, and was clearly much disburdened when John showed up, more or less resigning control, such as was possible, into his hands.

Agnes, fairly well able to look after herself as she might be, made no bones about welcoming him warmly, asking him as to the situation at the border, and urging him to make some sort of announcement and statement to these obstreperous lairds, for they clearly were volubly unsure of what was being demanded of them, and her father had been less than explanatory.

Nodding, John had a word with Herries, and climbed on to the hall dais platform and banged a tankard on the table for quiet – which took a while to be effective.

"On behalf of my Lord Herries, deputy warden, I, John Maxwell, speak," he called. "We are here, not to invade England, but to ensure that the English, after the recent folly at Solway Moss, do not invade Scotland. I have just returned from the borderline at the Sark, and at that time there was no sign of an enemy presence. But there was no distant view, and it is possible that they might be massing beyond the moss, nearer to Carlisle. They may not be, but it is necessary that we discover. They may well be content with their easy victory meantime, and all the important prisoners they took, and plan no assault over the border. Not yet. But Henry of England wants to rule in Scotland, and sooner or later he will strike."

Growls and shouts from his hearers greeted that last, fists shaken.

"So it is necessary that we show him that we are not his for the taking! I say that we ride tomorrow for the Sark, and will be joined by others from Caerlaverock and thereabouts. My Lord Herries agrees that we should halt our force at the Sark, lining the border from, say, Tower of Sark to the lowest fording-place before Solway, some four miles. This in groups of two score or so, to show a presence. But also send a party forward, over into England, across the Solway Moss, as far as the Esk, possibly to Longtown, this to show the English that we are there and to be reckoned with. No further, but enough to leave Carlisle in no doubts that we are roused and resolved. Bide at the Sark for two days, it may be, and then return here, leaving a small company to patrol the borderline for a while longer. The English will not fail to know of it. How say you?"

It was not easy to hear the various answers to that, but clearly none there was expressing reservations about it going too far. Satisfied, John jumped down.

It was late before they got to bed that night, with the visitors in no hurry to rejoin their men out in the chilly night; but Agnes waited up, although her sisters did not, playing hostess. When at length the last of the dalesmen departed, she and her father heaved sighs of relief, Herries declaring that these might be good fighters but made demanding guests. He was thankful that John seemed to know how to deal with them. Agnes added her commendation as to his announcement of the morrow's doings and his seeming assurance. Also hoped that he could and would remain close to her father on this enterprise, for he greatly needed the support and guidance – this while she escorted him aloft to his tower chamber, as before, adding that she wished that she could accompany them all, although recognising that this was impossible.

"That would be my wish also," he told her. "Although not that you should run into any danger. There may well be none, no battle. But it cannot be, I fear. However, you will be here to come back to!"

"And is that so worthy a prospect?"

"To me, it is."

She fell silent.

At his room door, she found her voice. "More than you can be concerned over danger, John. If, as I deem likely, *you* lead the forward company into England, promise me that you will not risk yourself, do no more than show a presence, restrain yourself, you who are so much the leader. If I am here to come back to, back you must come!"

"Is my return so important as all that? To you?"

"Say that I want my father back safely, and for you to ensure it!" But she pressed his arm as she said it, and left him there to open his own door.

Lord Herries led quite a sizeable force, a new experience for him, to cross Nith to Dumfries and then turn eastwards, the sisters waving them off. They had some thirty miles to go, four hours' riding for seven hundred men – over one thousand when the Caerlaverock contingent joined them at Annan. The dalesmen and the lower-country men rode very much apart, and John made a point of leaving Herries's side frequently to join the others, who seemed to eye him with reasonable acceptance.

As they neared Sark, he rode ahead with a couple of others to spy out the land. This Debateable Land hereabouts was deserted country, too soft the ground and liable to flooding for useful farming, as well as dangerous from raiders, with no villages and only the occasional cowherd's shack and a few cattle-beasts. Scouting, the trio saw nothing else.

At the borderline they waited for the main body to come up, and the business of dividing the host into parcels of a score or so each commenced. John reckoned that they were some twelve hundred men; so they could make between forty and fifty groups to spread along the four miles, each within no great distance of others, and so to present a formidable barrier to any enemy attempts to cross the river. The dalesmen automatically took the northern, higher section. Herries situated himself in the centre. It was just after noon, and all dismounted to make camp. They were going to be here for two days at least. Fires were lit; there was no seeking to hide their presence.

After a rest for the horses, John selected a party of about five score of his Caerlaverock and other Maxwells to go with him across the nearest ford and head on eastwards, Herries urging him to be cautious and not to be away for long.

Deliberately he led his company on to the site of the disaster of those days before, some of his followers having been thereat, none eager to talk about it. All too readily found, the ground was still strewn with bodies, men and horses, carrion-crows flapping up therefrom as they approached. Shaking his head, John said that they must, on the way back, at least seek to give the dead Christian burial; fortunately, with the ground so soft, it ought not to be difficult to scoop pits for graves.

They rode on.

It was a couple more miles to the great River Esk from the battle scene, opposite the Longtown ford, and they saw nothing on the way to concern them. This, the first village they had seen since Annan, more than a dozen miles, was no large community, with a church, a couple of mills and a huddle of houses and barns, the Esk wide here but with an underwater causeway through the shallows, this part of the direct route from Carlisle, nine miles further east, into Scotland.

John did not lead them over that ford. There was no point in crossing. They would be seen perfectly plainly from the village, no doubt alarm already aroused there. He did suggest that they shouted "A Maxwell! A Maxwell!" just to emphasise the situation; and the chant was kept up for quite some time. No corresponding cries came from Longtown.

Their challenge made and their objective achieved, with no evident reaction, whatever panic there might be in yonder village, after perhaps fifteen minutes of it the Scots turned and headed back whence they had come.

At the battle site, the crows returned, they all dismounted to bury the dead, using whatever they could to dig into the boggy ground, swords, dirks, even dead men's helmets and breastplates, a sorry task indeed. John went to seek out some dead hawthorn wood, and used tethering-rope to bind a cross-piece to a longer, if twisted, shaft, to form a rough crucifix; and when they had filled in the wet soil and mud on top of the dead, thankful to be done with it, he planted this over the spot and said the Lord's Prayer, the best that he could do. They would send a priest from Annan to better them, in due course. They left the dead horses to the crows.

It had all taken them some time. Lord Herries was distinctly anxious before they got back.

Some of the dalesmen, born reivers, had not wasted their time in the interim, and had purloined and slaughtered a few cattle-beasts, whose they cared not, and these, chopped up and distributed, grilled over the fires of dead hawthorn, made a meal of sorts to add to the oatmeal which every horseman carried in a pouch at his saddle-bow. Thereafter, with the early dark, sentinels posted, they made up for the previous late night by wrapping themselves in their horse-blankets and wooing sleep. At least it was not raining, however chilly.

John, aware of his responsibilities as effective leader there, rose twice during the night to check that all was well and the guards awake.

The following day was uneventful, save for those who rode off prospecting for more cattle. Herries and John recognised that there was no point in forbidding this, however deplorable; these reivers would so behave whatever was said, looking on it as, if not their right, certainly their privilege, and the responsibility for the beasts entirely on the owners.

They had relays of scouts out, now, permanently, beyond the Solway Moss tracts, to warn of any enemy reaction or approach. None developed that day. They waited for another night, and still no sign of opposition.

By noon on the third day, they decided that there was no need to remain there any longer, nothing to be achieved. John hoped that they had made their point.

So it was turning back and dispersal, anticlimax as this might seem. In fact it was what not only Lord Herries had hoped for, significant gesture made, without actual fighting. All groups and companies were warned, however, to be available and ready for further mustering, and at short notice.

There was no real need for John to accompany Herries back to Terregles, when his own men were heading for nearer Caerlaverock, but he did so, nevertheless, for his own reasons, the older man nowise dismissive. On the way, they discussed the situation on the national scale which was likely to evolve. It was to be hoped and presumed that the king by now had sent out summons to his lords nationwide, to rally to the defence of the realm. How long it would take for such army to assemble, and whether it would march south-west thereafter at once, or wait at some central point to see if English attack developed, or indeed assail the enemy itself, and on what front, this they debated. Whether an attack over the East or Middle March might be considered more effective? Robert Maxwell, it was presumed, would send word back to Caerlaverock as to what transpired, might already have done so. In King James's state of mind, and health, he might well be something of a broken reed; but Cardinal Beaton, the Chancellor, was a strong and resolute character, and would no doubt ensure prompt and suitable action.

They reached Terregles in the gloaming, to a warm and relieved welcome from the Herries sisters, Agnes throwing her arms around her father, to whom she was clearly devoted, and then eyeing John a little uncertainly before gripping his arm and giving him a chaste kiss on the cheek. For his part, the man restrained himself from seeking to improve on this, other than by holding her close for a moment, before all the exclamations, questions and plaudits started. One little and odd intimacy did occur, however, and was nowise resented, with the young woman declaring that they both smelled in need of washing, after four days of living rough and a-horse, and she would have hot water from the kitchen into their bedchambers forthwith. She also said that they would have much to make up for in the way of eating, and that she would endeavour not to disappoint.

They did eat heartily thereafter, the icehouse raided for salmon, fowl and venison, with supportive sweetmeats to follow, wine to wash it all down, so that, by the withdrawing-room fire afterwards, it was not long before John was yawning, his disturbed nights checking the sentinels beginning to tell. This did not go unnoticed, and soon he was being told that he ought to be abed. Lord Herries declared that he too was weary and would retire thus early. John was a little concerned at this, tired as he was, as they rose together, Agnes with them; but was relieved when the older man said his goodnights at the first-floor landing and entered a room on that floor, while his daughter and guest went on higher.

On the next floor, the young woman did not pause at her own chamber, saying that she was not for sleep quite yet, with some matters to see to for the morrow, but continuing on upstairs to John's attic room. He took her arm.

"I hope that I smell better now?" he told her. "I have sufficient shortcomings with you, without that!"

"Shortcomings? What mean you?"

"I am a Maxwell, for one. How was it you put it – two-headed? I am a killer of God's creatures, and less than expert with the longbow. A lapser of lapses! I must seem over-assertive, ever seeking to take charge. And you named me a trier, a tester of women, once."

"Did I? Ah, but I also told you that I had my failings, sir. As we all have!"

"Does that mean . . . ?"

"I leave you to decide that! Perhaps you will have discovered some that I am scarcely aware of myself?

52

And leave you to your slumbers also, my weary friend! A good night to you, well-earned."

"I am scarcely so weary as all that!"

Shaking her head, she came into his inviting arms, face upturned – even though more briefly than he might have wished.

He made the most, however, of what was available.

In the morning, John took a reluctant leave of the Herries family, promising a fairly speedy return, and headed off for Caerlaverock.

There he learned little of significance. No word had yet come south from Robert, nor any rumours as to the king's activities. The English appeared not to have initiated any hostile moves meantime. The Border Scots were licking their wounds after Solway Moss, the Countess Agnes declaring that they deserved all that they had got.

John Maxwell found himself acting chief of the Maxwells, and busy indeed in keeping in touch with all their branches and lairdships, especially concerned with those which had sustained casualties, either slain or captured, and in seeking to maintain morale.

He had little time for salmon-spearing, wildfowling or roe-deer shooting; nor indeed for social visiting, but Terregles was never far from his mind.

4

It was late November before Robert, Master of Maxwell, and Dod Armstrong returned home, with strange tidings. King James had been acting oddly indeed, it seemed, even for him, and less responsibly than was expected from a monarch. From Lochmaben that silent man had gone to Edinburgh, where he had seen Cardinal Beaton and more or less handed over all care and answerability for the realm to the Chancellor and Primate. Then, of all destinations, he had headed eastwards, Robert and Dod still in attendance, for the fortress-castle of Tantallon, at the mouth of the Firth of Forth near North Berwick, this because, close by, rose the little red-stone tower of Hamer of Whitekirk, Oliver Sinclair's house where his wife was presently providing lodging for the king's latest mistress. Not that James was in any state for extra-marital activities at present, a depressed and sickly man indeed, his mission there undoubtedly to acquaint Lady Sinclair with the sorry fate of her husband and to offer to present all necessary ransom monies for his release.

From there, after a couple of days, the king had returned westwards, passing Edinburgh and on the extra eighteen miles to Linlithgow where, exhausted as he was, he remained for only the one night, this in his wife's company. For here, in the royal dower-house of Linlithgow Palace, the queen, Mary of Guise, waited to give birth in only a few days' time. She, a capable Frenchwoman of character, had had two previous deliveries of sons, but sadly both had died in infancy. Of James's innumerable other progeny, none was legitimate. So now an heir to the throne was awaited.

Not that James Stewart appeared to be greatly interested nor concerned, his mind all on Oliver Sinclair. It was Robert Maxwell who told the queen details of the Solway Moss débâcle, to her head-shaking reception and Gallic shrugging. She asked about Cardinal Beaton's reactions, and obviously looked to that able individual to maintain the realm's defence and control, in her husband's present state. Robert said that he had got the impression of her as a strong-minded and purposeful woman, such as the king so evidently needed at this crisis in his strange life and reign.

Nevertheless, next morning James was for off, physically exhausted as he appeared to be and with his child expected any day. He was for crossing the Forth at Queen Margaret's Ferry and on to Hallyards Castle in Fothrif of Fife, there to visit Sir William Kirkcaldy of Grange, Lord High Treasurer of the kingdom. Uncertain whether or not to remain with him, Robert had decided that probably he ought to do so, and with James appearing to expect it.

So it was farewell to the queen in the morning, and a dozen miles to the ferry across the narrows of the firth, and another dozen beyond north-eastwards, to Hallyards near Auchtertool. Sir William Kirkcaldy was a man of vigour and integrity, and obviously concerned for the monarch. James was fortunate in his councillors and advisers, at least – this as well for the king's sake, as a man of curious and uncertain character. It transpired that the visit here was largely to ensure that sufficient funds were available from the treasury to meet any demands for Sinclair's ransom, whatever the amount.

The monarch's ultimate destination, it now appeared, was Falkland Palace, also in Fife, the royal hunting-seat below the Lomond Hills in the county's central vale, the Howe, a favourite haunt, where many of the royal bastards had been conceived, only another dozen miles. There, in that handsome establishment, with James taking to his bed and seemingly prepared to stay in it now, and with an ample staff of servitors, under the keeper, to look after him, Robert had reckoned his duty done, and had sought royal permission to leave, granted with a weary nod.

So it was back to the ferry and to Edinburgh, where they learned that the Chancellor had summoned, in the king's name, Scotland's lords and lairds to be ready for promptest muster in full force, should there be word of English aggression over the border, or preparedness therefor. Robert and Dod were thankful to head off south-westwards for Dumfriesshire and home.

All this, recounted at Caerlaverock, evoked mixed reactions; almost incredulity as to their liege-lord's behaviour and state of mind; concern for the queen; satisfaction that the cardinal-archbishop appeared to have matters in hand; and wondering as to what now? So much depended on the English, and Henry the Eighth's decisions.

There was, of course, the important matter of the almost certain demand for Lord Maxwell's ransom to be considered. None at Caerlaverock had any doubts that this would not be long in coming, and substantial, for the Warden of the West March. Resources and rentals had to be assessed, possibly even some properties sold, the Countess Agnes much displeased, and critical of all concerned.

For his part, John decided that his prime duty was to go and inform the deputy warden of the situation, and to offer his help and co-operation. Presumably he, Herries, was now warden, however unsuited for the task. With the king in his present state and affairs of the realm in turmoil, any new appointment was unlikely for the time being. John foresaw his assistance being in some demand – not that this depressed him.

He could not complain of his reception at Terregles a few days later, all clearly glad to see him, even though Lord Herries looked almost apprehensive as to what might be his tidings and their impact upon himself. Agnes greeted him with a kiss, but of the friendly rather than the amorous sort – but her sisters were present, and, laughing, she proceeded to do the same. They declared, almost reproachfully, that they had expected him back sooner. He explained that he had had adequate excuse despite his desire to come, and with much to see to at Caerlaverock in his father's absence. But now he had much to tell.

So around the withdrawing-room fire, beaker of wine in hand, John reported on his brother's account of the king's doings and behaviour, to their wonderment and exclamations. There followed the inevitable speculation as to what would be the consequences, and the effects on their own lives. Agnes was particularly astonished and critical of the king's neglect of his pregnant wife, especially after the deaths of the queen's two previous children.

Herries was, of course, preoccupied with his own position in these circumstances. What likelihood was there of him being replaced as deputy warden, or acting warden, while Maxwell remained captive? John anticipated none. The wardenships were very much royal appointments, and in his present state the monarch was unlikely to be much concerned. How long Lord Herries would remain responsible would depend largely on how soon the expected ransom demand came from England for his father, and for how much. For if it was some great sum, it might take time to collect, calling for possibly some sale of properties, this involving willing buyers, the times not very propitious for selling land so near to the English border. So it could be months before his father was home and able to resume his duties.

The older man sighed. "I feared as much. Let us hope that there will be little wardening having to be done, little of war and struggle, leastways." He reached over to tap John's arm. "My daughter says that, if I am acting warden, I am entitled to have an acting deputy. She suggests yourself, my friend."

"You have already acted the part," Agnes said. "You might as well have the style of it."

John looked from one to the other, wondering.

"It is a royal appointment," Herries went on. "But in the circumstances . . ."

"That could be confirmed later," the young woman declared. "What is important, what is required, is action now, no? Not some time hereafter, depending on a weakly king's whim. You would do it, John? You are, after all, the warden's son."

"If my lord would have it so – yes." But it was at the girl he looked.

"Good! My father will be much beholden to you."

"Indeed I already am. I do not doubt that the king will accede to it, coming from myself," Herries said, his relief obvious. "Already I have problems to face. From the dalesmen – the Armstrongs, Johnstones, Liddells and the rest. They were useful back there, in time of need. But now they exact their price! From the low country. Cattle-reiving, sorely. Complaints come to me. What can I do? These are a law unto themselves. And we need them if the English attack."

John frowned. "A warning. Of royal displeasure. The cardinal assembles an army. If that comes south, a few such reivers could hang. They will not have forgotten Johnnie Armstrong of Gilnockie, whom the king hanged those dozen years back, with his friends. Give them a warning, just."

"Would *you* give it? Go round Eskdale, Ewesdale, Liddesdale, Wauchopedale? Tell them. In my name?"

"If they will heed such as myself, yes. They may not."

"They did before. At the Sark."

"That was different. You were there, my lord. Plainly I was acting for you. It was *you* in command. But now, myself?"

"I will go with you," Agnes said. "My father's daughter they will perhaps accept."

John swallowed. This was more than he could have dared hope for. Would her father object?

"I should myself go," Herries admitted. "But I fear

that I get over old for this riding of Marches. My Agnes should have been a son!"

God forbid! John thought. But the girl smiled. "Sore disappointment that I am, I do my best! John will have to make do with me."

"Could not I come also?" the interested Catherine put in. "I am a fair horsewoman."

"I do not see why not," her father said – although John saw otherwise.

Agnes cocked her eyebrow at the young man. "Perhaps two Herries daughters would be more effective than one? With these wild dalesmen?"

There was nothing that the visitor could say as to that.

The talk became general.

So in the morning it was a trio that set out from Terregles eastwards, to cross Nith into Dumfries town and on for the higher ground by Torthorwald and Lochmaben, where the king had halted, and thence to Lockerbie in Dryfesdale where the real hills commenced. Needless to say, John would have preferred to be riding with Agnes alone; but Catherine made cheerful, laughing company, clearly excited over her involvement in this mission.

They decided that they should head for Langholm in Eskdale first. They could not possibly go round all the dales and their lairds – Wauchope, Kirtle, Milk, Tarras, Ewes, Hermitage, Liddel and their lesser valleys. But Langholm was the largest community amongst them all, and its castle was seat of the most powerful of the Armstrongs since Gilnockie and Mangerton had been put down those years before. It lay some eighteen miles north-east of Lockerbie, where the Wauchope and Ewes Waters joined Esk, an important and defensive position. That meant a thirty-mile ride, over rough country most of the way, enough for the first day, in late November.

In that company it was hard for John to concentrate his mind on the gravity of his task, holiday mood more natural, the hilly scenery contributing.

Down Wauchopedale they came to Wauchope Castle, a small square tower-house on a mound. Here they made their first call. Wauchope of that Ilk was a burly man of middle years, whom they found superintending the felling of birch trees to make stockading for cattle pens, which caused John to wonder whether such extra fencing was considered necessary for a possible accession of low-country beasts. With the appearance of the young women, the laird obviously looked on it as in the nature of a social visit, and haled the trio into the tower for his wife to entertain. John had some difficulty in emphasising the purpose of their call and the possible consequences for the dalesmen if their raiding continued, the older man obviously looking on such talk as scarcely apt for the occasion. Agnes sought to support John, indicating her father's concern, but no impression of major impact was forthcoming. The assumption was that the visitors should spend the night there, and John had to declare that they were going on, as it was only early afternoon, to Langholm to see the Armstrong chief, this leaving the Lady of Wauchope much disappointed. Feeling that their first effort had not been very effective, they took their leave.

Wauchope was only a couple of miles from Langholm, which was quite a township surrounding the castle at a bend of the large River Esk, a strong position. Here they found Armstrong absent, gone up the tributary White Esk apparently, on unspecified business. His wife was less hospitable than at Wauchope, and a son a surly character, less than friendly although eyeing the young women up and down assessingly. John was therefore able to deliver his warning remarks more sternly, urging that they be passed on to husband and father, as coming from the king's warden, the same king who had made an example of Gilnockie and the others. They left in no congenial atmosphere, Catherine somewhat upset.

It was now late afternoon and would be dusk shortly, no time for heading up long Ewesdale for Kirkstyle and

Arkleton. They decided to return to Wauchope for the night, where they would still be reasonably welcome, they thought.

They were not disappointed, Watt Wauchope and his wife prepared to overlook their previous declining of hospitality. A quite pleasant evening was passed, with reiving not discussed, although traditional tales of Borderland forays and frays were recounted.

When the lady of the house conducted the two young women off to their chamber, John had to forego any bedtime exchanges other than conventional goodnights.

Next day, crossing Esk into Langholm again, they set off up Ewes Water for five twisting miles, to Kirkstyle, under the lofty Bauchie and Wrae summits, where rose another typical square tower within a courtyard, seat of one more Armstrong, this one at home, and more tractable without being actually friendly. Warning conveyed, they pressed on up a subsidiary stream, the Arkleton Water, for the Elliot house of that name, whose laird they met branding cattle, stolen or otherwise, in a hollow of the hills, the smoke of the fires leading them thither. As elsewhere, the presence of the young women had its effect, with Arkleton all heavy gallantry. But he heard John out without comment, but also without evident umbrage, and indeed was helpful in directing them on their way to their next destination, the dale of the Tarras Water, still deeper into the high hills eastwards, actually sending them on with a guide over a cattle drove-road around a shoulder of Auldshiel Hill, the highest point in their travels so far, and which would be inaccessible in a month or two's time when the winter snows came. Their escort pointed them down beyond, and southwards now, into the deep and steep valley of the Tarras, to where they could see more blue smoke arising, whether cattle-branding or other, and where apparently was Tarras Tower, another Armstrong holding – this the most numerous and powerful of the dalesmen clans.

Neither John nor the girls had ever been in these

uplands, empty in the main save for a scattering of wiry, shaggy cattle, some blackface sheep and all the chuckling grouse, no villages nor communities, only the occasional herd's shack. It was a world unto itself, and scarcely to be wondered at if its folk, few as they appeared to be, devised their own laws rather than heeded the realm's. The trio rode through it all much aware of its wildness, with that awareness constant.

The smoke at Tarras Tower proved to be brushwood burning, from clearance made in the riverside haughland, presumably to create better pasture. Armstrong of Tarras, directing, was sufficiently impressed by his unexpected visitors to provide them with a meal. He had been at the Sark, and recognised John.

Now they were to head for Liddesdale, eastwards, the nearest major valley to the actual borderline, the upper dale Elliot country, the lower mixed Liddells, Nixons, Scotts, Beatties and more Armstrongs. The apparently obvious route for travellers would be to proceed down Tarras to its junction with the Esk again; but this, they were informed, was inadvisable, since the lower end of this dale opened out into Tarras Moss, which was all but impassable for those who did not know its secret and twisting passes, it being, indeed, the Armstrongs' main security barrier. So the recommended route was due eastwards over the hills by another drove-road, rising high, by what were seemingly known as the Black Heights, over Hazelhead Hill and down the Badda Cleuch. Tarras himself saw them on their way, assuring them that it was only eight miles to Whithaugh, where they would find Elliot thereof, a scoundrel but good with sword and lance. They would have to be careful where the track lipped Burrowstoun Moss.

It was more climbing for them, then, steep to win out of the dale itself then a more steady ascent into the great, vacant hills. John was somewhat concerned over having brought the sisters to such country of which he had not fully realised the wildness and inaccessibility; but the girls made no complaints, seeming to enjoy the remoteness and challenge of it all. They explained their surprise that such territory should exist, only a score or two of miles from Terregles, without them ever having known of it.

Heedfully they circled the Burrowstoun Moss which filled a sort of plateau between Tinnis Hill and Loch Knowe, raising scores of wild duck, their drove-road thereafter crossing the Black Sike which drained the moss, however inadequately, and continued over the heathery shoulder of the Black Height itself, a major peak indeed. Whereafter it was downhill all the way, by a long wedge-like corrie, presumably the Badda Cleuch, for the remaining three miles or so to the Liddell Water, where, guarding a ford, they found another tower-house, Whithaugh, not far above the community of Newcastleton.

They had to go on to Newcastleton, for they learned that the Elliot chief was there attending a wedding, of all things. So thither they rode, and well before they reached the village they could hear the noise, shouting, laughter, singing, presumably nuptial celebrations.

Newcastleton proved to consist of one long street of cottages, shacks, sheds and alehouses, no fewer than four of these, plus a small church; and end of November as it was, and by no means warm for the season, much of the wedding revelry appeared to be taking place in the open. No doubt the festivities had been going on for most of the day, and the alehouses busy, for clearly rejoicing had reached the stage of fairly general intoxication for many, indeed not a few bodies lying at the roadside and embracings going on right and left. John looked somewhat askance at all this, questioning its effect on his companions; but they seemed interested, even amused at what they saw and heard, and nowise alarmed.

Nevertheless John was thinking of advising a return to Whithaugh Tower when the sight of the little church and the comparatively substantial house beside it gave him the notion that the parish minister might well be the one to approach in these circumstances. They made for the manse, amidst wavings and cries of tipsy welcome, especially for the girls.

They found the Reverend Patrick Elwood – he explained that it was the same name as Elliot – helpful and cordial, not exactly apologising for all the carousal but explaining that it was a very special occasion, with Will of the Park marrying Meg of Redheuch, and all the Elliots emphasising their goodwill, some perhaps more vehemently than was advisable. He had conducted the service some five hours previously, so probably the rejoicings would be subsiding soon. It was all very well meant.

John still wondered whether they should leave the village, but when the minister told him that Whithaugh and other Elliot landed men were all down at Canny Jock's tavern, it occurred to him that he might be able to save themselves some journeying by calling in at this alehouse and seeing a group of the lairds together. The Reverend Elwood offering to conduct him there, John left the young women advisedly with the clergyman's motherly wife, and the two men went on foot down the noisy street, to further greetings.

Presumably Canny Jock's tavern was in some way superior to the other three since it was so selected, but even so considerable noise emanated therefrom. The minister's arrival was greeted with cheers from the fairly crowded main apartment, and tankards of ale were thrust at the newcomers. Master Elwood declining, but nowise sourly, pointed out to John a thickset youngish man with fiery red hair and square features as Elliot of Whithaugh, and informed that he was sitting with the Elliots of Redheuch, Larriston, Park and Braidley – all in fact on John's list of calls. Undoubtedly they were all drink-taken, but none looked actually drunk.

John, now faced with something of a dilemma, wondered whether he had indeed been wise to come thus. This festive occasion was hardly one to interrupt with his wardenly warnings. Yet now that he was here, just to beat a retreat would seem feeble. How would these tough characters receive what he had to say, in their present state and in a group?

The minister bent to tell Whithaugh that this was John Maxwell, son to the Lord Maxwell. So now there was no avoiding the issue.

John, eyeing them all, thought that he recognised two faces which he had seen at the Sark, but could not put identities to them. He accepted the proffered ale and sat down in a space made for him on a bench.

He had to raise his voice in the din. "I am well pleased to see you all, on this occasion," he said, choosing his words carefully. "I wish you all well. But I come from my Lord Herries, warden while my father remains captive. He has had complaints not a few, from landed men as well as farmers and herdsmen, of the low country, their cattle stolen. By dalesmen." He glanced round the somewhat flushed faces. "Know you of any who might be responsible?"

No reply was forthcoming, although eyebrows were raised and hands drawn over mouths and beards.

"My lord is anxious not to lay blame on innocent folk," John went on. "But such reiving must stop, and reivers be punished. So, my friends, I urge you to spread the word. You understand?"

"*You* say so!" one of the group said, all but snorted. "Think you that we need take such talk from the likes o' you? A young Maxwell pup!"

"I hear the ale speaking there, I think, not the Elliot lairdie!" John said, but with half a smile. "I am acting deputy warden to Lord Herries."

There was silence, at least from this group.

John himself did not speak now, to let his message sink in.

It was the same man who found voice first, slurring his words a little. "*You* say so! Why should we heed the likes o' you?"

"Send and ask the Lord Herries if you doubt. His two

daughters are with me here, in the manse. But I would advise speed in so doing, friend. For the king's army is being mustered at Edinburgh, to march here to warn the English. And to warn others who offend against the king's peace, including even dalesmen! And with a rope, belike! His Grace used a rope none so far from here once, you will recollect. So, spread the word, I counsel you." And he took a sip of the ale.

"We are Elliots, not Armstrongs or Johnstones and the like," Whithaugh said, after a moment or two. "Honest folks."

"To be sure. But you will have neighbours who are perhaps less so. I say serve them. And the warden. And the King's Grace. With *your* warnings." John took another sip, and rose. "I thank you, my friends. And bid you farewell." And nodding to them all, he turned away.

"That was featly done," Master Elwood said, as they left the tavern. "Heed not the one who crossed you. That was Steile, in his cups. He is none so ill a man."

Back at the manse they found the young women relaxed, at ease, indeed settled in, for apparently Mistress Elwood had invited them to stay the night, and they glad to accept. John offered to seek a couch in one of the taverns, but the minister said that if he did not mind occupying a bunk bed in the walling of their living-room he was welcome to it. The alehouses might well be rowdy and less than comfortable on such occasions for hours yet.

So after eating plainly but amply, and chatting around the fire, it was fairly prompt retiral for all. The noise from outside had to some extent died down.

Much beholden to the Elwoods, the three of them left Newcastleton for the lower, southern end of Liddesdale in the morning, there being no need to proceed further up, where most of the Elliot lairds had their seats. John did not anticipate much trouble amongst the lower-reaches holdings, for although possibly even more lawless, these were comparatively small folk, not exactly broken men but members of scattered clans and families, Liddells,

Nixons, Irvines, Beatties, Bells and the like, and unlikely to challenge the warden's spokesman openly, even though they might not heed his admonitions.

With the borderline just across the river now, they called briefly at Mangerton, Kershope and Dinwoodie, leaving the message; and at Penton, with the dale opening out to the mossy low ground, crossed some modest heights westwards back to the lower Eskdale, where they made their final calls at Irvine Tower and Auchenrivock, Irvine seats where the lairds were less likely to be lawless, but who could influence the folk of less respectable habits. Reasonably well received, and as reasonably satisfied with their efforts, they left the high ground to head for Lockerbie, Dumfries and Terregles, still lengthy riding but presenting no problems other than a thin, chill rain, which they were thankful had held off until now.

John congratulated his colleagues, saying what excellent company they had made, how well they had borne the toils and trials of the journeying, and how valuable had been their contribution to the mission, which last was laughingly rejected as nonsense. But no regrets were expressed as to taking part in it all.

At Terregles Castle Lord Herries was glad to see them, not exactly loud in his praises for he was not a loud man, but grateful, and proud of his daughters. John, in giving his report, emphasised that some official and written authority would be advantageous if he was to go on acting deputy, to impress such as Elliot of Steile, and Herries agreed. He would write a letter to the king, recommending John, and asking for royal confirmation.

Weary but not dissatisfied, they all made an early retiral for that night. On their way upstairs, John took Agnes's arm.

"See you, this is the first time that we have been alone together in three long days," he told her.

"And is that so important?" she asked.

"To me it is, yes. Do not tell me that you did not know it! Catherine is good company, but . . ."

"But you prefer women one at a time?"

"I prefer *you*!" They had reached her room's door, and he opened it for her, but in so doing managed to convey himself over the doorstep, and so stood so that she had to squeeze past him if she was to enter. She did not remain outside.

Needless to say, she was captured into his arms, and held, and kissed on hair and brow and eyes and lips, his hands not inactive either.

"I have been aching for this . . . these three days!" he got out.

"Poor John," she murmured, which meant her lips moving under his. "You felt . . . deprived?"

"More than that."

"Is your need of womankind so great?"

"Need of *you*, woman!"

"I am . . . so different from . . . others you have . . . fondled?"

"What others?" But he did not allow her to answer that, her mouth fully bespoke, her person pressed hard against his, sufficiently for her breathing to be affected – at least, the heaving of her bosom seemed so to indicate. If in consequence he relented a little, it was only to enable his hand to slip between them, to cup one of her so active breasts, while the other moved down behind to her hip.

Agnes allowed this fore-and-aft enfolding to continue for a few breathless moments, and then used her own hands to push themselves apart some way, gently but firmly, backing her head to free her lips.

"Needs . . . discharged!" she said. "At least, met. If not satisfied. Even a weak woman has to . . . say enough . . . on occasion."

"A weak woman – *you*!" Gripping her arms he all but shook her. "I, I need you, lass!"

"Your need . . . is noted. Mine, mine is to preserve some modest security!" She patted his shoulder. "Off with you, needful one. Aloft. To your couch. And leave me to mine."

"I would that . . ."

"I know it. But you will sleep none so ill, nevertheless. A goodnight to you, John. You must warden more than the West March, no?"

He forced himself to leave her then.

In the morning, Lord Herries had a letter for John, signed and sealed, addressed to the King's Grace, recommending the appointment of John Maxwell as Acting Deputy Warden of the West March, in the present circumstances, as a necessary assistant and aide. He was to take this north to wherever the king was to be found, with the minimum of delay, and they would hope that in the meantime there would be no critical situations developing.

John took his leave when he could devise no further excuses for staying, and was seen off with kisses and embraces – of a sort.

5

He left Caerlaverock the very next day, with Dod, to head for Edinburgh, with a change of horses, on a hundred-mile journey, by Nithsdale to Moffat, then Ettrick to the Tweed and Lauderdale, passing the night at the great monks' hospice of Soutra, founded four centuries before by Malcolm the Fourth; major riding. They were at their first destination, the walled city, by noon the following day, and there, at its castle-fortress, learned the dire news. King James was dead.

Strangely enough they were told this by none other than Sir William Kirkcaldy of Grange, whom Robert Maxwell had met at Hallyards in Fife, and who it seemed was keeper of Edinburgh Castle as well as Lord Treasurer of the realm. He was there for an urgent meeting of the Privy Council, to be held on the morrow, to consider and decide on the nation's destiny in this crisis.

As Kirkcaldy recounted it, the king had never left his bed at Falkland, appearing to be utterly exhausted, physically and emotionally, the keeper there and servitors mystified. Then, a week after his arrival, the word came from the queen at Linlithgow. She had been delivered of a daughter, whom she was proposing to name Mary, with her husband's agreement, the child well formed and with no signs of the sickliness which had killed the two previous infants. James's reaction to the news had astonished those present; no satisfaction, no relief, but the reverse. Raising his fists he had cried out, "It cam wi' a lass and it will gang wi' a lass!" And he had turned his back on those by his bedside and his face to the wall, and had not spoken thereafter. He had been referring, of course, to the royal Stewart line, how the throne had come through Bruce's daughter Marjory to her son by Walter the High Steward, Robert Stewart. Now, after seven generations, it had come to this baby girl, Mary Stewart, for there was no other legitimate heir. If one day she passed the crown on to *her* offspring, it would not be to a royal Stewart.

Less than one week later James Stewart had died, seemingly having lost all will to live, aged thirty years.

So now Scotland was in something of a state of shock. They had a ten-day-old monarch, queen-regnant, something unknown hitherto, since the Maid of Norway, Alexander the Third's grandchild, had died on her way to the kingdom, aged seven years. All sorts of problems and uncertainties faced the ruling classes, particularly the council, the lords and the parliament. A regency would have to be established; but that was perhaps one of the least of it all; there would have to be at least eighteen years of regency. A realm with a baby queen to reign was something unknown, and a recipe for troubles on many fronts. The morrow's Privy Council would be a crucial one indeed.

John, shaken like everyone else, was also concerned over what was to be done about the West March situation and Herries's letter. The council would be all but overwhelmed with much more important and urgent matters. What was he to do in these circumstances?

The other was helpful. The only man whose office entitled him to supreme authority at this moment was the Chancellor, Cardinal Beaton, first minister of the crown. And he was a fellow-Fifer and former neighbour of the Kirkcaldys. He was in Edinburgh for the council also, resident down in the Abbey of the Holy Rood. He, Kirkcaldy, would escort Maxwell thither and introduce him.

Grateful for this kindness, John was taken down the mile-long spine of Edinburgh's Lawnmarket, High Street and Canongate to the abbey, set directly below the towering peak of Arthur's Seat, where their late monarch had added a tower for his own use. The cardinal-archbishop was, however, lodging in the abbot's house.

Beaton, when they reached him, past guards, proved to be a fine-looking man of nearly fifty years, of a commanding presence but with little of the looks of a prelate, as suited his character, for he was anything but a typical churchman. Indeed, despite the heights to which he had risen, he had come to clerical status comparatively late in his career, unusual as this was, seventh son of a Fife laird, Beaton of Balfour. He had married and had children, then gone to France on an embassage, to return there a dozen years later as resident ambassador; and while thus acting, for reasons best known to himself, despite his marriage, had taken holy orders and been promptly given the French bishopric of Mirepoix. He had served in France for six years, aiding the French authorities as well as the Scots, until King James recognised that he could use his undoubted talents better at home, and he had been recalled, and given the rich abbacy of Arbroath. Rising swiftly in power and prestige, two years later he was appointed Archbishop of St Andrews and Primate of the Church in Scotland – this largely because the Reformation initiated in England by Henry the Eighth was creating reactions in Scotland, and reforming tendencies, or heresies as the churchmen called them, fell to be put down with a strong hand, and Davie Beaton was considered the most effective for the task; moreover he had become Chancellor in the meantime. So largely thanks to him, Scotland remained Roman Catholic where England was not, however much the would-be reformers sought otherwise.

The cardinal, although clearly busy, received them affably enough, eyeing John shrewdly and saying that he knew the Lord Maxwell and regretted his capture at the shameful Solway Moss disaster. He took the Herries letter, scanned it briefly, and handed it over to a clerk with instructions to write "Agreed and acceded" thereon, and then took the clerk's pen to sign it, and handed it back –

all as simple as that. For better or worse, John Maxwell was now Acting Deputy Warden of the West March, at least until the appointment might be reviewed by whoever became regent.

Bemused by it all, he and Dod took leave of both cardinal and Kirkcaldy, and with nothing to detain them in Edinburgh set off on their return home forthwith.

So much for affairs of state.

Arrival back at Caerlaverock presented John with a new concern and responsibility, anticipated as it might have been although it had come rather sooner than expected, namely the demand from the English Lord Dacre for the ransom moneys for the Lord Maxwell: one thousand marks sterling. The Countess Agnes was furious. This was twice, at least, what she had feared, a great deal of siller. For sterling marks, English coinage, then were worth three times the value of the Scots merk. So this represented two thousand pounds Scots, the value of many quite substantial farms and holdings. Like the rest of the Scots nobility, Lord Maxwell held much land but comparatively little actual currency, coins being but seldom required in their mode of life, where goods, services and farm stock were the normal means of exchange.

So Robert and John had to set about the difficult and humiliating task of raising the required sum, in silver, if they were to get their father home, no easy or simple matter, especially with the realm in the state it was, and the Borderland under threat. Few, they feared, would wish to invest already scarce coinage in lands within half a day's ride of England. Yet land sale was the obvious, indeed the only, means of collecting the large ransom demand. Much debate and argument and head-shaking ensued.

Clearly the most suitable course was to try to sell lands to their own Maxwell lairds, of whom there were at least a score of some consequence; but three or four of these had been captured with their lord, and their families faced with the same problem. Then there were the great West March landholders such as the Douglas Earl of Morton and Sir James Douglas of Drumlanrig, and the nearby Kirkcudbrightshire lords, the Gordons of Kenmure, the Dunbars of Mochrum and the Maclellans of Kirkcudbright itself, all these the sort who might wish to extend their possessions. And, to be sure, as it had to come up, there was Lord Herries himself, their nearest great neighbour, obviously one of the most hopeful for buying, however little John Maxwell might wish to approach him – for of course he was the obvious one to do so.

Therefore John found himself in the odd position of deliberately delaying his return to Terregles while he and Robert rode the country around seeking other buyers, in the hope that they might find a sufficiency to make it unnecessary to approach Herries. That they did not was a sorry comment on the situation, in more ways than the one.

When the visit to Terregles could no longer be delayed – for there were important tidings to deliver there, apart altogether from John's desire to see Agnes – it was with very mixed feelings that he set out. To be seeking to trade on their friendship to persuade the young woman's father to purchase land was against the grain indeed for John.

Cravenly, on arrival, he put off the sorry part of it until later, not to spoil his warm reception and the welcoming gestures. He had rather feared some reproaches for not having come sooner, but such did not eventuate, since the family had not realised how speedy had been his return from Edinburgh, and the brevity of his negotiations there. So, assuring Lord Herries that he now had an officially appointed deputy, John launched into his account of what Kirkcaldy of Grange had told him, to exclamations at the death of King James, the birth of the infant princess, now indeed Queen of Scots, the national upheaval and uncertainty which must follow as a consequence, word of all this not having reached Terregles. Many were the questions and comments which followed, wonders over the dead monarch's behaviour and

74

fate, concern for his widow and the child, misgivings as to the rule of the realm, and doubts about English reactions. John was unable greatly to reassure them. It was going to be a worrying Yuletide and 1543 for Scotland.

When in due course the visitor did come to the matter of the demands for his father's ransom, John weakly evaded the question of difficulties in raising the necessary money, sympathetically as his host expressed himself.

Herries had no grievous wardenly problems to recount, in the interim, and no new complaints as to dalesmen's reiving; so it looked as though the young people's tour around the dales had had effect.

It was not until bedtime, and Agnes and Catherine escorted the visitor upstairs, that John, for once not privately wishing the younger sister to be elsewhere, brought himself to the point of mentioning the vexed subject of the sale of lands, not exactly putting forward their father as a possible purchaser but indicating the need for such. Agnes, however, took his obvious discomfort over the subject otherwise.

"You should seek loans, John," she declared. "No need to sell land. I am sure that Father would be glad to help."

John blinked. The idea of borrowing had never occurred to him, to any of the Maxwells. They were much too proud for that. Selling was bad enough for their dignity; but seeking loans was like begging, not to be considered.

"No, no!" he exclaimed.

Again she took him up wrongly, assuming that he judged that her father would not lend. "He will, I am sure," she said. "He feels greatly in your debt. For all that you have done for him. Some small return. We will put it to him in the morning."

Catherine made encouraging noises.

That "we" in Agnes's assertion registered strongly with

the man, even if the idea of seeking a loan did not. It indicated collaboration, collusion, a joint purpose with the young woman, which he much relished whatever the subject behind it; so he did not correct her as to his meaning.

"The sale of land is more . . . honourable, perhaps," was all that he said.

"A nonsense!" she averred. "A loan is only for the time being. A sale is a loss, for always."

They were now on the second-floor landing, off which both girls' bedroom doors opened. So there was no opportunity for private exchanges on this occasion, and Catherine was the recipient of a hug and kiss only slightly different from her sister's, before John proceeded on upstairs to his accustomed chamber. Despite this, he had much to occupy his mind before he slept that night.

Agnes was as good as her word, and prompt about it, at the breakfast table next morning broaching the subject to her sire.

"John tells me that the English require a large sum, three thousand merks no less, for his father's ransom," she announced. "The Maxwells talk of selling lands to help find the monies. But we think that a loan would better meet the need. We hope that you would help in the matter, Father?"

"A loan?" Herries did not look nor sound either surprised or alarmed. "Three thousand merks is a large sum, yes. I feared that the demand would be great for the West March Warden. The English are ever strong on ransoms. Yes, to be sure, I will help in this. How much do you need, my friend?"

Scarcely ready for such speedy and specific enquiry, John hesitated. "I . . . ah . . . I am grateful, my lord. But do not wish to cause you any concern. We have gathered in, or had promise of, some two thousand merks siller. But, given time, no doubt we can find the remainder."

"Time, while your sire languishes a prisoner! I can aid you shorten that time. Aye, and so unburden myself of the full wardenship! I can make up the missing one thousand merks for you, given a week or two."

"So there you are!" Agnes said. "You can win your father's freedom now."

"M'mm. You are kind, generous. But ... I cannot accept without some, some acknowledgement on our part, some promise. We had thought to sell more lands. My lord, you must accept some of these, in token assurance of repayment. They are properties, farms, near to here, Maxwell land. We had thought to sell them. On the Old Water. Barnsoil, Larbreck, Crochmore, aye, and Midrig. These, near your own Cluden Water, you could hold. Take the rents meantime as yours."

"I ask none such, John. I have a sufficiency. Your father was captured fighting on the nation's affairs, not his own. I was not there; perhaps I should have been. This way I can repay in some measure. Although it should be the realm's treasury which pays such ransoms."

"That it will never do! But, for the Maxwell honour's sake, our pride, you must hold these lands, in name, until the debt is repaid. Or I cannot accept it. My father would not have it otherwise."

Herries shrugged. "If so *you* would have it."

"If you will it, we can ride there this day. It is not far, six or seven miles. You can see them, and I can inform the tenants as to the situation."

"Very well. But it is not necessary."

So that forenoon they all rode westwards, for all three sisters insisted on accompanying them. The four holdings that they visited were not exactly hill farms but very much cattle-steads, set in the braes between the Cluden, Cargen and Old Waters, with, in this mid-December, the beasts mainly gathered down to the infields and so available for inspection, well-fleshed stock, testifying to the worth of the lands. Their owners received the visitors respectfully but forbore comment on the situation. It would make little difference to them as to whom they paid their rents in cattle, meal and service. One had lost a son at Solway Moss. Herries left the explanations to John, and did not act the lord.

Back at Terregles that night, Catherine, who now appeared to look on herself as part of a trio, again chose to accompany John and her elder sister upstairs at bedtime – the other sister, Mary, being still young enough to be sent off earlier despite her complaints thereat. But on this occasion, Agnes took a pleasing initiative, to John at least, by announcing at the second-floor landing that in this cold weather she wished to assure herself that there were extra blankets laid out for John's attic chamber bed. Catherine could hardly claim that she also was needed for this, even though she pouted her lips and received a smacking kiss on them by way of consolation as the others went on higher.

Actually the chambermaid had seen to all adequately, logs blazing on the hearth, washing water steaming in a tub and blankets piled on a chest. So there was no need for Agnes to do anything. But, needless to say, John was not one to let this opportunity go unacknowledged, and went to clasp the young woman to him eagerly. She could hardly expect less than her sister.

She received considerably more, and suffered it without real complaint, even though she slapped a venturesome hand once or twice. His lips she did not deny, however, her own parting.

When she could, she spoke. "Your Maxwell pride costs you dear, John? There was no need for all that, today. I wonder that you are prepared to . . . associate with us thus!"

"I would do more than associate, lass!"

"Ah, no doubt. But I am thinking of the Maxwells and Herries, and your pride. We are very different families. We have been less than two centuries here, ennobled only sixty years ago. Whereas your father is head of a great and ancient clan, and high in the land. As well as warden, he is a Lord of Session, is he not? And was ambassador to France. Father says that he could be in the necessary council of regency for the child queen; for he was on such when King James went to France to find a wife, no? Oh, you have reason for your pride. But . . ." She left the rest unsaid.

"What mean you by all that?" he wondered. "When I spoke of my Maxwell pride, I meant only honour, good repute, not vainglory and arrogance. What mean you?"

"I felt . . . I feel . . . that I should know. We are seeing much of you, and may see more, with this of the wardenship. I would know whether I am to be on my guard!"

"Guard? Against what? Me?"

"Your posture, your attitude. Born of your pride. It could be, shall we say, unacceptable. For a woman who has her own pride!"

"Aye, and you have that, I swear! But I claim that you misjudge me. Are you now assured, lass?" That was quite urgent.

"More assured, yes. Weak women have to be careful, see you."

"You called yourself weak before. And you must know that you are not! Is that not dishonest? A kind of pride?"

They had drawn apart in this exchange, and were searching each other's faces in the flickering candlelight. For long moments they gazed, until abruptly she turned and all but ran from the room, and out, without anything more said, not even a goodnight.

She left the man with much to think about thereafter, to wonder and to question.

In the morning, all seemed to be normal, no constraints nor avoidances. But when it was time for John to mount and away, he was favoured with an embrace which amounted almost to a shaking, and this without a word spoken, although there were plenty of farewells from the other two sisters and from their father. John went, unsure whether he should feel encouraged or the reverse. He was little the more certain on the matter by the time that he reached Caerlaverock.

Despite his questionings of mind, much as John would have liked to have spent Christmastide at Terregles, he could hardly have considered it on such a family occasion; moreover, he was not so invited. But fairly soon thereafter a messenger arrived from Herries, to announce, not a request to appear again, but that by the Chancellor's orders there was to be a meeting of the three March wardens, this at Ferniehirst Castle near Jedburgh in Teviotdale, the seat of Sir John Kerr, the Middle March Warden, on St Kentigern's Day, 13th January, this to discuss the realm's security; and the Lord Herries, being less than well, wished his deputy warden to attend in his place, if this was not too inconvenient. Needless to say, John could by no means refuse, even though January was scarcely the time of year for journeying through the Border hills across the spine of Lowland Scotland.

With Dod Armstrong for company, he set out three days later on the quite lengthy ride north-eastwards, of just over one hundred very rough miles. They went by Lockerbie and up the Dryfe Water, into the heights, to Boreland, and then up the White Esk. This involved hard riding, for the days were short and there was no suitable overnight halting-place before Roberton on the Borthwick Water, some sixty miles. They ran into their first snow of the winter on the shoulder of Ettrick Pen, but fortunately this did not last for long, and they were able to start on their downward drop to the Borthwick Water before dusk. It was dark before they reached Roberton in its wooded valley, where there was a change-house of sorts.

By mid-forenoon next day, in hard frost now, they were

in Teviotdale, and riding through the quite large town of Hawick, the first such they had seen in those eighty miles. From then on it was merely a matter of following the Teviot down its wide vale, past Minto Craigs and the Dunnion Hill, to the Jed Water's confluence, and the Kerr castle of Ferniehirst in Jedforest.

Sir John Kerr and the Master of Home, the East March Warden, were there, awaiting John and the Chancellor's representative who was being sent down to inform and consult with them. If the two wardens were surprised to see only this young deputy instead of Herries they did not show it – and in fact the Master of Home, son to the Lord Home, was not much older than John. The Home family looked upon the East March wardenship as theirs by right.

The cardinal's emissary, who arrived presently, proved to be the Lord Seton, a personable man in his early thirties but of ancient lineage. He had much to tell them before ever they got down to the matter of the defence of the Borderland. The Privy Council, of which he was a member, had had much discussion, debate, argument and discord over the appointment of the necessary regency for the infant Queen Mary. There was a strong party seeking reform of Holy Church, much more concerned with the detachment and parcelling-out of the vast Church lands than with religious details, this prominently represented on the council. The late King James had never paid much heed to this, not being very religiously minded. But now these had seen their opportunity, with many of them resentful at the over-great influence of Cardinal Beaton. Led by the Earls of Angus, Dunbar and Lennox, these had vetoed a regency council composed of Beaton himself and the Earls of Huntly, Moray and Argyll – this, Beaton claimed, the late monarch's own wish, they saying that the cardinal had persuaded the dying king to it while mentally deranged. Also they were against the appointment of Queen Marie of Guise as regent for her daughter, claiming that as a Frenchwoman and a bigoted Catholic she was unsuitable. So, as a stop-gap, the council had nominated James Hamilton, Earl of Arran, to the position, as nearest legitimate kin to the late monarch, a son of the Princess Mary, Countess of Arran, sister of James the Third. But he was a weak man, when the country needed a strong one, a recipe for trouble. Fortunately Beaton was strong, and so long as he remained Chancellor, and supported by both Church and parliament, he could probably guide Arran, and serve the realm as so evidently required.

So they came to the reason for this meeting. The cardinal judged that there should be a unified borderline defence. Henry Tudor had been trying to win control of Scotland ever since he came to the English throne. Now, with an infant monarch and considerable disarray, he would be the more eager to seize his opportunity. He would seek to undermine the northern kingdom by every means in his power, and to impose Protestantism, by stealth, intrigue, bribery and division; but there could well be armed invasion also, as in the past, over the border. So, whether this came by Berwick-upon-Tweed, by the Reidswire or the Deadwater, or by the Solway shore, or by all of them together, it was important that he should be met by a strong and unified defence, if possible under a single command. How thought the wardens as to that?

John did not require the expressions on his present colleagues' faces to tell him how this suggestion struck them. The wardens of the Marches were ever notably proud of their appointments and concerned for their status and independence. The idea of having someone set over them, be it even one of themselves over the other two, would by no means appeal.

"Why this, my lord?" Kerr demanded. "We wardens are perfectly capable of acting in concert without requiring some incomer to act the leader!"

Home growled assent.

"It is not so much to lead as to co-ordinate," Seton said. "To act as link between you all. The borderline is long, over one hundred and twenty miles, I am told.

Attack could come anywhere. Each of you could have stern and urgent demands on you, suddenly. You would not know whether there were also attacks on the other Marches at the same time, or threats thereof. Some other, concerned with the overall position, assessing the dangers, from Tweed to Solway, and seeking to inform, to marshal, to guide, would be valuable, the Chancellor judges."

"We do not need some other to come and tell us our duties," Home declared. "*We* know the Borders, and our own folk. And where the English can strike, with any hope of success. We have our methods of swift passing of news. Beacons on hilltops and prominent towers. In minutes of an assault anywhere, beacons lit, smoke by day, fire by night, the word can cross the land, and faster than any man can ride."

"There could still be need for one concerned for all three Marches, a marshal, to ensure that the fuller threat was understood and dealt with. Each warden responsible for his own March, yes – but one to weigh, estimate, plan overall. A Lieutenant of the Borders."

The frowns did not clear away. In the circumstances, John held his peace.

Seton went on. "I do not know the distances of each March, the bounds. But if the full border is one hundred and twenty miles, you may each have forty miles of territory to oversee, much of it wild country, hills and bogs, rivers and valleys, much empty land. Do not tell me that one linking you all would not be of value?"

"If he did not know our Marches, as we do . . ." Kerr said.

"Ah, but the Chancellor has thought of that. He proposes as lieutenant Patrick, Earl of Bothwell, lord of Hermitage in Liddesdale, who so well knows the Borderland."

That had them blinking, John included. For Patrick Hepburn, Earl of Bothwell, was a shrewd choice, and not only for his knowledge of the area. His father had been a friend of James the Fourth, indeed had died at that king's side at Flodden Field. He had been given Hermitage Castle, the greatest stronghold on all the border, with upper Liddesdale. Now it was his son's. And that son's mother, the Countess Agnes, was now married to the Lord Maxwell, and was John's stepmother. Moreover Bothwell's own wife was Mary Home, cousin to this Master of Home.

There was silence then.

Seton used his advantage to good effect. "My lord of Bothwell would not be coming in any way as your superior, but only your associate, my friends. Not a chief warden but one to assist you in your joint tasks. And one who knows the English and their ways! The cardinal believes that he could serve the realm well, and yourselves also."

Bothwell had been banished to England for a time, for suspect activities including dealings with the Earl of Northumberland.

John wondered what the Countess Agnes would say to this. And what his father might say, when he returned.

The two wardens seemed now to be reasonably reassured that their standing and independence were not to be undermined.

Seton informed that the Chancellor was planning that, in case of invasion, there should be a more or less standing force ready to come south at short notice for the lieutenant to use as reinforcement for any or all of the wardens' mosstrooping arrays, this under himself and the Master of Lindsay. Being based in eastern Lothian, this should be able to reach the Borderland in half a day's riding. This was welcomed, so long as it was clear that once committed to action this force would be under the command of the warden involved, unless it was an invasion on all three Marches.

That more or less concluded the matter and discussion and, with Kerr hospitality generous, a pleasant evening was passed before the fire in the great hall of Ferniehirst.

Still with frost gripping the land in the morning, a start

at first light was made in three different directions by the visitors.

John and Dod called in at Terregles on the way home, needless to say, and found the Lord Herries's reluctance to travel to the wardens' meeting had been excusable indeed, for the claim that he was unwell had been no exaggeration. He was, in fact, confined to bed and clearly a sick man, his daughters worried. He could not keep food down, vomiting it, and inevitably weak.

John, at the bedside, made his report; but the older man was but little interested.

The sisters urged John to stay the night. Agnes said that their father had had attacks like this before, but never quite so severe. It was, of course, a grievous problem that he could not retain his food and so was not recovering his strength. They had tried different sorts of provender and drinks, also herbal remedies, but his stomach seemed to reject them all. They were much concerned.

The young woman was interested in what had transpired at Ferniehirst, more so than was her father indeed. She knew about the Earl of Bothwell, declared him untrustworthy, and said that John should be on his guard over him, whatever the cardinal's regard. And she pointed out that, in the present situation, he, John, was in effect Warden of the West March, a strange development. She judged that he would serve in the office well. He had shown himself capable of it, and she believed that the rough mosstrooping lairds and dalesmen would accept his authority.

Later, when Catherine again waited to ascend the stairs with them, and goodnights were perforce less comprehensive than the man would have desired, there was an unlooked-for development. Unclad and ready to have his bedtime wash, there came a light tapping on his door. Presuming it to be the chambermaid, a cheerful, motherly soul, John went as he was, to open – and there stood Agnes, still fully dressed. Finger on lips, she slipped into the room and quietly shut the door.

"Forgive this intrusion, John," she said. "I do not want Catherine to hear." She carefully kept her glance above his waist.

Surprised indeed but far from disconcerted, he searched her face.

She moved over towards his smouldering fire. "I had to speak with you," she said, a little breathlessly. "Alone. After, after last time you were here. When we were in this room. I wanted you to know what I was at, then."

He had gone to the water-tub to pick up a towel there and wrap it round his middle. Strange that he had not thought this necessary when he had expected it to be the chambermaid; but it was somehow different with Agnes. She did not comment on this provision.

"I was concerned, then, when I spoke about your pride, your Maxwell pride. That you understood my position. I had gone about with you, near and far. Accepted you as companion. To aid my father and yourself both. We had been much together. I wanted you to know that I had my pride also. That I was not . . . an easy woman! That you might think me loose, over-free. And accepting your, your salutations! Your attentions! You understand? That is why I spoke as I did."

He wagged his head. "I wondered, yes. Had I been arrogant? Presuming? I was to have a care!"

"No, no. It was not that. I want you to know how I feel."

"How do you feel, lass? For me?"

"What am I to say to that so that you do not take me wrongly? I like you, John. Or I would not be here."

"Like! That is a word which can mean much. Or little! I would that you could better like!"

She stooped to poke the fire's embers. "You are a demanding man, John Maxwell!"

"Perhaps I need to be, if I am to warden this March!" He reached to take her hand, and turned to lead her over towards his bed. "My – how did you say it? My salutations need to be displayed. However modestly!"

"In this, your bedchamber, they must needs be modest! And you, you unclad!" She went with him, to sit on the bed.

"Would that you were likewise!" he exclaimed. But she ignored that.

His arms went round her, and they kissed.

Inevitably, having her person against his naked skin aroused him the more – and he had to rearrange his towel. When one of her own arms, to keep herself upright against his pressure, encircled John's waist, he burst out.

"This is unfair! Myself thus, and you . . . !" He clutched at her bosom.

"Then I had better depart," she said. "Having said what I came to say." But she did not rise there and then, nor did she shake him off. And her hand remained at his waist.

Whether that was encouragement, or not, he took it as such. The neck of her bodice was not high, and with a slight slit, so that he was able to slip his hand within and down, to cup her warm breast, the nipple firm between his fingers. She took a quick breath, which he felt as well as heard, but she did not speak.

"You are very lovely," he said. "I *need* you!"

"Need? I think that . . . you put it . . . over-strongly, John. It seems that you want, yes. Desire my person. But . . . need?"

He stopped her questioning with his lips.

Then, as those fingers of his grew bolder, probing, she changed her hold on his waist up to his wrist, and drew out that hand, not forcefully but with a quiet decision.

"I have my needs also, see you," she told him. "Modest needs, yes. And one of them is to be alone, with myself, now. In my own room. To consider."

"Consider what?"

"To consider John Maxwell! And what he means by needs and wants." She kissed him then, and detached

88

herself, to rise. "A goodnight to you. And dream, perhaps, of kinder women!"

He hurried after her to the door, careless now that his towel fell to the floor. But she was gone.

John was prepared for some tension or reserve at the breakfast table, but became aware of no hint of such. When he went to take farewell of the girls' father, it was to be told that the thousand merks promised would be sent on to Caerlaverock in a day or two. Leave-taking thereafter was of the normal warmth, with injunctions to hasten back, Agnes her smiling, friendly self.

Dod Armstrong found his companion somewhat silent company for the first part of the homewards ride, despite the former's account of satisfactory progress with the castle's chambermaid Jeannie.

7

Winning Lord Maxwell's release from durance vile was less simple than his sons imagined, once the ransom moneys had been collected. They sent Dod Armstrong to Carlisle to inform Lord Dacre there that the sum was to hand, and seeking instructions for the exchange; but when their messenger came back, it was to announce that there would be delay, for the important captives were now in London, on King Henry's orders. The point of this was uncertain, but perhaps ominous. Dacre would send to inform them when Lord Maxwell was available. The countess was much offended.

Then they had a visit from her son, Patrick, Earl of Bothwell, now come south to be based on Hermitage Castle in Liddesdale as Lieutenant of the Borders. John and Robert had not seen him for years, he having been exiled, a tall, saturnine-featured man in his thirties, who seemed nowise beloved of his mother. He declared that as lieutenant he was concerned that the West March was not in a better state of preparedness and wardenship. He had been to Terregles and seen Herries, whom he assessed as quite useless, frail and sickly. Clearly he did not think much of John as deputy, and said that the sooner Lord Maxwell was back the better. When he heard of the latter's removal to London, he was further troubled, declaring that Henry Tudor would not have ordered this without very definite purpose and that the consequences might well be serious, for Henry was hatching momentous plans. A new warden might have to be appointed, therefore. John had to restrain himself from informing him that the wardens had agreed to his, Bothwell's, appointment as lieutenant only on the assurance that he came as associate and helper, not as in any way in charge, earl though he was.

The visitor had some extraordinary news to impart, apart from all this. Despite himself having been appointed lieutenant on the cardinal's authority, the said cardinal and Chancellor had actually been arrested, on the new regent's orders, and confined in the royal prison-castle of Blackness near to Linlithgow, scarcely believable as this was. The reason for it was correspondingly remarkable, for it was actually done at Henry of England's request. It seemed that the Tudor had swiftly perceived the opportunity presented by the present strange monarchial situation in Scotland. He was proposing that his child-son, Edward Prince of Wales, aged five years, should be married to the infant Mary, Queen of Scots, this to the advantage of both realms. Scotland should remain independent. All wars and invasions should cease and permanent peace be established. Beaton had been wholly against this suggestion, not trusting Henry, and concerned that newly Protestant England should not encourage the reforming faction in Scotland, over-strong as it already was. But the weak Regent Arran, now apt to use his French title of Duke of Chatelherault, himself pro-reform, had acquiesced, supported by the Earls of Angus, Morton, Lennox and other great lords. Whereupon, in captivity as he was, the cardinal had promptly, as Archbishop of St Andrews and Primate of Holy Church, put all Scotland under spiritual interdict. This unique and quite unexampled measure meant that all religious observances, other than in private devotions, were banned and would cease until he was released – that is, if the realm's clergy obeyed, as seemed probable. There would be no church services nor masses, no baptisms, weddings, no anointing of the dying, no funeral rites, nothing. How long the country could bear this was uncertain, whatever the zeal for reform, but few thought for long. Bothwell reckoned that the cardinal might well be released already.

There was much debate at Caerlaverock as to this

proposal of King Henry's anent the marriage of the two royal children. Was it not to be considered, as at first impact? Or were there aspects in its favour? Would it give Henry a dominance over Scotland, despite any assurances as to independence? England would not be the loser, that was for certain. But would Scotland also gain by it? An end to the centuries of warfare and fear of invasion. Trade with the English. And, of course, for those seeking reform of the Church, notable assistance. This last aspect did not greatly concern any at Caerlaverock, but undoubtedly it would weigh with many, especially amongst the nobility, who had long been jealous of the increasing power and wealth of Holy Church.

John had been considering a visit to Terregles to consult, not so much with Herries as with his eldest daughter, as to the implications of what Bothwell had told them, Agnes in fact being more effectual in matters of the wardenship than was her sire, when that young woman surprised them all by herself arriving at Caerlaverock with one of her sire's men. She likewise came with news, and more ill news at that.

The brother of Sir John Kerr had come to Terregles to inform of a new and dire development. Sir George Douglas, brother of the Earl of Angus, had had a meeting with the Lord Lisle, English East March Warden, at Berwick-upon-Tweed, this at Henry Tudor's command. It seemed that Cardinal Beaton had indeed won his release from Blackness Castle and Henry was furious. He was demanding that the Chancellor be rearrested and sent to England; also that certain key fortresses and strong points in Scotland be handed over to English garrisons. Otherwise there would be invasion. Since not even the most pro-English and reformist factions would ever agree to all this, the wardens must be prepared for trouble over the border. Co-ordinated plans must be drawn up.

So John had to make another journey to Ferniehirst in Jedforest, and Bothwell insisted on accompanying him. They escorted Agnes back to Terregles, and proceeded on to Hermitage in Liddesdale where they spent the night, the earl with a retinue of eight men, John with Dod Armstrong.

Hermitage Castle was a great and grim fortalice, in a re-entrant of the high hills, probably the strongest hold in all the Borderland, remote and inaccessible. Just why it had ever been built there John was at a loss to know. It had a history as daunting as was its appearance. Built by the de Soulis family, it was the seat of the traitorous "Wizard Lord" who rebelled against Robert the Bruce. Given to the Douglases, here the so-called Flower of Chivalry, Sir William Douglas, starved to death his friend and colleague the much-admired Sir Alexander Ramsay of Dalwolsey. Here many another had languished in its dungeons.

Internally the place was as unwelcoming as was its exterior, cold and bare. Bothwell, when he was here, roosted in one of the four square angle towers, and, not to be wondered at, this was as seldom as he could make it. His main seat, where were his Home wife and small son and daughter, was at Hailes Castle near to Haddington in Lothian, from which his predecessors had taken their title of Lord Hailes.

Scarely congenial travelling-companions, they reached Ferniehirst the following afternoon, where Bothwell's appearance was less than warmly received, John doing rather better.

They received further details as to the Berwick meeting between Douglas and Lisle. Henry Tudor was determined on his objective of marrying his young son to the infant Mary, Queen of Scots, and was demanding their immediate betrothal; and at the age of six she was to be sent to England for the nuptials. Meanwhile a number of illustrious hostages were to be sent to London to ensure compliance, these to be freed only when little Mary was delivered up. All this under threat of all-out war. And as a sweetener, for Douglas support, Sir George's brother, the Earl of Angus, was being offered Henry's younger daughter, the Princess Elizabeth, as bride. Scotland was to be given only until June of this year, 1543, to comply.

93

So, since even the Douglases could scarcely swallow all this – Angus had married James the Fourth's widow, Margaret Tudor, and so was a brother-in-law of Henry, for some years, and had been a member of the English Privy Council, dwelling in England frequently – preparations were to be made to resist invasion, on Beaton's orders, if not the weak Regent Arran's. Sadly, seldom had Scotland been so divided, endemic as division was in the realm, largely, at this time, on account of the religious situation.

The wardens made their plans, so far as they were able, Bothwell voicing his opinions and counsel, so little heeded that John actually began to feel sorry for him – after all, he *had* been given the duty by the Chancellor. Each March was to have its maximum manpower readied for swift muster, and at all times a striking force was to be maintained prepared for immediate action. The West March was the largest of the three, and with all Galloway to call upon, should produce the greatest numbers of armed men, John was reminded. The beacon system was to be added to and synchronised, so that notice of an invasion anywhere could be sent from east to west within an hour or so, day and night, one beacon per prominence lit for a small assault, two for a larger one and three for major invasion. Group leaders were to be appointed, preferably with experience in warfare, and their duties allocated. Constant liaison was to be kept between the wardens, nothing being said about Lord Herries, John evidently being accepted as warden in all but name until his father's return.

When, in the morning, it was departure, Bothwell elected to head for Hailes rather than back to Hermitage, over which John did not blame him.

Lacking the earl and his escort, John and Dod made considerably better time of it back south-westwards, and in fact managed to reach Terregles that evening, although the last miles were ridden in darkness, there to be received affectionately even though with scoldings as to overlong riding. Lord Herries was no longer abed, but looking frail.

John recounted all that had transpired at Ferniehirst, and the consequences were discussed. Obviously another circuit of the dales was indicated, to inform the lairds there of the need for swift readiness to repel invaders; also to improve the beacon chain and nominate group leaders, which in that company would not be simple. But there were also the low-country men to be given their instructions, especially the Galloway chiefs. The Galwegians tended to be a people apart, although in a different way from the dalesmen, seeing themselves as scarcely in the West March, a harking back to the old days when this was an all but independent Celtic earldom, which had even made its own treaties with the English, the Welsh and the Irish. These chiefs would require careful handling in order to obtain their co-operation and the adherence of their large numbers of men. Fortunately the Maxwells did have their links there, having been judiciously marrying into the great Galloway families' heiresses. It was agreed that a quick tour round Kirkcudbrightshire should be the first priority, since the nearer folk and dalesmen would be more prepared anyway for action. Agnes and Catherine declared their intention of again accompanying John, as hopefully useful aides – for the Herries had Galloway links also – he far from objecting, and their father acceding.

When, fairly early, Herries sought his bed, their guest, weary with hard riding, did likewise, and had his now usual double ushering upstairs, this time with no pretexts as to chambermaidenly feelings put forward, and so goodnights only moderate. John wished that he could devise some means of improving on this situation, much as he liked Catherine. Agnes managed some small gesture of intimacy, but the man was eager for more, however tired.

It was arranged, in the morning, that he should go on to Caerlaverock, to inform all there, and seek to have his brother Robert to assist them on their Galloway expedition

– this to share the task, but also possibly to pair off with Catherine in the visiting, to the advantage of all – the young women to come on in two days' time.

John wondered, as they parted, whether any other Warden of the Marches had been so blessed with female assistance.

Three days later, then, the Galloway mission commenced, on St Baldred's Day, 6th March, and not exactly as John had planned, for although brother Robert was not averse to accompanying them, and as Master of Maxwell might add useful authority, sister Margaret, finding the Herries girls taking part, volunteered to come along also, and in the circumstances could scarcely be refused however ineffective she might prove; she was a quiet and reserved young woman, of an age with Agnes but so very different in character. John hoped that, amongst other things, her horsewomanship would not hold them up. This move of hers surprised her brothers.

Not getting away until almost noon, with three more attendants as well as Dod, they headed almost due westwards for the Glencaple ford across Nith, the lowest such crossing, with the river already broadening out into its estuary into Solway. Once across they were into Kirkcudbrightshire, part of Galloway. They made first for Kirkconnell Tower, a Maxwell place, where they were able to delegate duties over the Criffel, Mabie and Shambellie area to that laird, and so were free to ride on westwards ten more miles to Loch Arthur and Beeswing, and another four to Drumcoltran, another Maxwell tower, where they could spend the night. On the way they were looking out for suitable heights and prominences for establishing beacons, for this was a provision not much developed hitherto in these parts, with English invaders usually and advisedly tending to leave Galloway alone. This was not just a matter of finding high ground, and folk living nearby to tend and light the beacons, but of ensuring that the chosen spots could be seen from far afield in all relevant directions, with no intervening ridges, woodlands or other obstructions to distant views. So this meant considerable prospecting and climbing and gazing around; and quite quickly John decided that this was delaying them over-much, and would best be left for another occasion or to the local lairds.

With the three women to accommodate, overnight lodging was an important consideration, so their destination of Drumcoltran Tower for the first night was selected, quite a large house of a Maxwell kinsman. This Herbert Maxwell could be relied upon to take on the duty of alerting the vicinity. Also his wife was a sister of Gordon of Lochinvar and Kenmure, head of one of the most powerful of the Galloway families, and she could be helpful with advice.

All went well at Drumcoltran, with the laird and his lady helpful, their two sons ready to lead any local armed levies at short notice; also to deal with the beacon situation hereabouts. Their mother said that John could rely on her brother, Gordon of Lochinvar, and actually wrote a letter to pass on to him.

With Robert to share a bed with, and the three young women given a room on another floor of the tower, night-time partings were of minimal privacy.

In the morning they decided to head for the valley of the major River Urr, where a Herries cousin had the castle of Spottes, some ten miles westwards across hilly country with no sizeable lairdships on the way, but very much beacon terrain. It was a day of showers and fitful wind, which made the riding less than pleasurable, but nobody complained.

William Herries of Spottes was elderly but amiable and made much of his kinswomen, urging them to stay the night. But John was for pressing on southwards down to Buittle, another Maxwell place. So leaving their wardenly instructions and suggestions, they took the road again.

Buittle was an important castle, having been a seat of the early Celtic Earls of Galloway, passing, through the famous Devorgilla, daughter of Earl Alan, to John Balliol her son, who became the ill-fated Toom Tabard, King of Scots. After the Wars of Independence, the Douglases got it, like so much else, for supporting the Bruce, but it had come to the Maxwells by discerning marriage. Here the visitors spent the night, well entertained.

Their next day's target was still more special, the great Threave Castle on the River Dee. This was an equally famous place, long the seat of the Earls of Douglas, Stewards of Galloway. When James the Second had personally stabbed to death the eighth earl – the only such assassination by royal hand recorded – and thereafter forfeited the over-strong main line of the Black Douglases, the representation of the illustrious house had passed to the secondary line of the Red Douglases, one of whom had married the heiress Countess of Angus and gained that earldom through her. Threave Castle, however, and the Stewartry had fallen to the crown; and various Stewards of Galloway had been appointed, the present one Sir Thomas MacLellan of Bombie, head of that important Celtic family. There were many branches of that clan, indeed Sir Thomas was probably the most important of the native Galloway chiefs, and so high on John's list of calling. Buittle said that probably he would be found at Threave, the headquarters of the Stewartry.

So still westwards they went, in better weather, up the Buittle Water through more hills to Carlingwark Loch, eight miles, and on another two to the Dee, greatest of all the Galloway rivers. And there, on a small island in the wide stream, soared the massive and stark keep.

As they approached it, Robert told the girls the story of how the Fair Maid of Galloway, a Douglas herself, was married to the eighth earl. She and her husband were enduring a siege by James the Second, foe of the Douglases, and were sitting at dinner when a cannonball came ploughing through the masonry, passed over their heads and imbedded itself in the further wall, the pair proceeding to wipe the dust and grit off their table and continuing with their meal, a ballad having been made of the occasion. That cannonball was namely for more than just failing to interrupt a dinner, for it was the largest then known, which was why it had managed to penetrate the thick castle walling. An enormous cannon had been fashioned by a local blacksmith, for the MacLellans, from Mollance nearby, and this the royal army was trying out. The smith, proud of his handiwork, called it Mollance Meg, after his wife, and the name had become corrupted to Mons Meg when the weapon was installed later in the royal fortress-castle of Edinburgh.

Threave, being built on its island in the river, was inaccessible save by a hidden, underwater zigzag causeway; so the visitors had to shout to draw attention and seek admission. They had been observed, however, and an answering call from the gatehouse demanded their identity and their business. John declared that it was the Deputy Warden of the West March and the Master of Maxwell seeking Sir Thomas MacLellan of Bombie, Steward of Galloway. It came back that Sir Thomas was not present but my lord might see them.

As they waited, they wondered who was my lord.

Presently a horseman emerged from the gatehouse arch and came splashing and twisting and turning across the river to them.

"My lord Earl will see you," he announced.

"Earl? Which earl is this?" John asked, surprised.

"My lord Earl of Angus. Come, you. Follow exactly as my beast goes, or you will be off the causeway into deep water! Single file."

They left their four attendants at the riverside.

Cautiously, Robert in front, John bringing up the rear, they directed their horses across that hazard without disaster, and on up into the castle's courtyard. At the keep's doorway a man of later middle years, handsome in a stern fashion, stood awaiting them. He eyed the ladies particularly.

"To what am I indebted for this visit?" he greeted them.

"We are seeking Sir Thomas MacLellan, the Steward of Galloway," John said.

"I am Angus, now Steward of Galloway," they were told. "By the regent's appointment."

This was astonishing news, even though, as chief of the name of Douglas, the family had held the stewardship for centuries, and Threave with it. This earl, with the so-dramatic past, must be in high favour indeed with the Regent Arran.

"Did I hear correctly?" Angus went on. "It is the Master of Maxwell, Deputy Warden of the March? What is your business, sir, with the steward?"

"*I* am the deputy, my lord – John Maxwell. The master is my brother. Sons of the Lord Maxwell. With our sister. And two daughters of the Lord Herries, Warden. We come on the realm's affairs."

"So-o-o! Then you are welcome. Come you inside."

Up in the great hall, the same the cannonball had traversed, they explained the purpose of their visit, while Angus sent for refreshment. It seemed strange to be putting it all to this man, the security of the Borders against English assault, to one who had been on Henry Tudor's Privy Council and had a pension from that monarch, had married Henry's sister Queen Margaret Tudor after James the Fourth's death, divorcing Bothwell's aunt to do so, then been divorced by the former queen and exiled to England, and was still looked upon as Henry's friend. Was this one to rouse Galloway against invasion?

Angus heard John out without interruption, although his eyes strayed frequently towards the women. At the end, he nodded.

"My Lord Maxwell, whom I saw in London, has worthy sons," he said. "What do you require of me, then?"

"Douglas support, my lord. In readiness for swift action, if need be. You could add greatly to our West

March strength." After all, it was said that the old Earls of Douglas had always kept one thousand men available for eventualities at Threave.

"You believe such attack is likely?"

"We do. Did not your own brother, my lord, Sir George Douglas, learn from the Lord Lisle at Berwick that unless impossible demands on Scotland were met, King Henry would send an army to invade, to gain his will?"

"That, I think, was but . . . persuasion! Henry knows that some in Scotland are against this proposed marriage of his son and our child queen, excellent as such would be for this kingdom, for both kingdoms. An end to centuries of warfare and conflict. Lisle would but prompt, by the threat."

"But this of hostages? And the handing over of Scottish fortresses and castles? Perhaps even this one of Threave!"

"Again but pressure to agree. Henry is like that. But his cause is a good one. For this realm as well as his own."

"You believe that, my lord? Our independence not at risk?"

"I do, young man. I would never see Scotland's sovereignty and freedom endangered. But the two thrones joined in marriage would serve us well. Henry has vision as well as strength and will. He seeks to end all war with the north."

"And this of religion?" Robert put in. "He would have the Church here reformed, as he names it?"

"Who would not? Save Beaton and his kidney! But that is for us Scots to decide, not Henry Tudor."

"As is this of the marriage," John insisted. "If Henry seeks to impose his will, by force . . ."

"In that case I will oppose him, my friend. Never fear, you have my word for it. I will ever fight for our independence."

"Then, my lord, in this we are agreed. We seek Douglas's aid if there is invasion."

"Very well. You shall have it. But not for petty cross-border raiding, see you. That your mosstroopers can deal with. But major invasion, yes." Angus waved a hand. "Now, these ladies have had to listen to such talk overlong. They deserve better courtesies! Soon we shall eat, and to the best that this poor house may provide. Meanwhile, I would hear kinder talk. Of your affairs and concerns, ladies."

"We also are concerned over the affairs of our land, my lord," Agnes told him. "Its safety and well-being. That is why we are here."

"Yes, yes. But all our talk need not be of such. Life is to be enjoyed as well as protected and planned, no? Men are all too much and often concerned with the last and lose sight of the first. That is when womankind has much to teach us. After we have eaten, perhaps you will entertain us? Music? Singing? Dance, even?" Clearly, despite his stern features, the Earl of Angus was a ladies' man.

John debated with himself while the girls responded to their host's challenge. He had not intended that they should stay long at Threave, for they had other calls to make. But it looked as though the earl expected them to stay the night. Should they agree to do so? Their next intended calls were both some distance off and it was now mid-afternoon, Kenmure and Lochinvar to the north, and Bombie, near Kirkcudbright town, to the south, each perhaps a score of miles off. It might well be best to remain here overnight. And this Angus was a highly important man in the realm's affairs obviously, not to be offended. Could they further gain his favour and co-operation?

They stayed on, had an excellent meal, and spent a pleasant evening, with lute and clarsach, of song and ballad and some dancing, with Angus demonstrating that he was as light on his feet as the younger man, and as he was reputed to have been in his loyalties and affections, to the delight of Margaret Maxwell in especial, who was quite unused to such attentions. When it was time for bed, John was quite thankful that there were three young women to share a room on this occasion, not just Agnes, for he would not have put it past this Douglas to invade later a lady guest's privacy.

Sharing a bed, the brothers discussed it all, and also their onward progress. They decided, in the interests of speeding up their mission, that they should split up hereafter, Robert to go south to MacLellan at Kirkcudbright and then eastwards by Dundrennan and Auchencairn and Orchardton and so home, while John went north up Loch Ken to the Gordon country, and thereafter circled round through the hilly Glenkens area, by Corsock and Crocketford and Shawhead, by which time they would surely have done enough for one tour.

So in the morning it was farewells all round, with Angus very gallant in an expert fashion towards the women and John taking the opportunity to ask that he might add the steward's urging to the wardens' as to mustering and readiness for action, since these Galloway folk scarcely saw themselves as Marchmen, and received permission so to say only where real invasion, not raiding, was involved. They had to be satisfied with that.

Robert went off with his sister down Dee. John would have liked Catherine to have accompanied these two, so that he could go on alone with Agnes, but this was too much to hope for.

It was northwards, then, with Dod, the four of them.

The Dee, as well as being the largest of the Stewartry rivers, had the extraordinary feature of widening into a twenty-mile-long lake, part way, Loch Ken, as it were in mid-course, this averaging perhaps half a mile in width, with islands and headlands and bays, and hills on either side, producing much scenic beauty. There were drove-roads up each side, but Angus had advised the eastern. Their destination was Kenmure Castle at the very head of the loch, another former seat of the old earls of Galloway, now owned by Gordon of Lochinvar.

In the spring sunshine and all the prospects opening before them it was difficult to maintain any feeling of the urgency of their mission, especially after that evening's entertainment. When they were on their own, thus, without the escorting men-at-arms, Dod Armstrong became very much part of the little group and a welcome companion, with his own contributions to make. It produced good riding for them all.

Where the long loch narrowed in to a river again, the great castle of Kenmure was set on the crest of a ridge and in a very strong position. Here, it was claimed, had been born John Balliol, son of Devorgilla, who had become probably the most unfortunate of all kings of Scots. The Gordons from the Merse had gained the lands, along with Lochinvar, in due course, and now held sway over much of north Galloway. However, the callers found that Sir James Gordon was not presently here at Kenmure but at his other seat of Lochinvar, seven miles to the north. So on they travelled, into the hills now, following up the Ken Water instead of the lochside.

As its name implied, their new destination was at another loch, a small one only half a mile long, on considerably higher ground, with its castle, like Threave, on a little island. But here they did not have to shout for attention, for there was a sort of gallows at the waterside, with a great bell hanging from it which, when rung, sent its echoes all over the surrounding braesides, and quite quickly produced reaction, not from the castle itself but from the cothouses of the nearby castleton, from which men emerged to seek their business. Whether impressed or otherwise by the identity of the deputy warden or only by the presence of the ladies, these made no delay about escorting the visitors over to the island, in this case by a flat-bottomed boat, which meant leaving the horses, with Dod, at the castleton meantime. It was only a very brief crossing, to be sure, and they entered the stronghold by a sort of water-gate which could be closed by a portcullis, and so reached an inner courtyard and keep, a highly defensive if somewhat inconvenient access.

Sir James Gordon they found to be a stooping, emaciated man but giving no hint of weakness, physical or otherwise, much of an age with Angus, with a friendly, buxom wife and a large family of five sons and five daughters, not all present here. Sir James had his own fame, having been involved in the notorious slaughter of the previous MacLellan of Bombie in an Edinburgh street fifteen years before, but having been acquitted of blame and sufficiently vindicated to be made one of the select company which had accompanied King James to France on his matrimonial quest a year or two later, obtaining then the extraordinary favour of a royal exemption for himself and his followers of answering to the courts for any misdemeanour whatsoever, commanded by them, until the king's eventual return to Scotland. What use the Gordons had made of this dispensation was not recorded.

At any rate, the callers were well received, and John had no difficulty in persuading Sir James to comply with the warden's requirements and instructions, especially when added to by Steward Angus's supporting authority, the younger man not putting too much emphasis on the scale of invasion stipulation. Gordon promised to have some three hundred armed men available, given a couple of days' notice, and said that he would inform other lairds in the neighbourhood and see that the beacon provision was carried out.

Well pleased with their progress here, the four of them set off, eastwards now.

They got only as far as Corsock, on the upper Urr Water, by dusk, another Gordon house where, with Sir James's authority to add to the rest, they met with no problems and reasonably comfortable conditions.

Bardarroch made their next call and then Crocketford where, at Milton Loch with its prehistoric crannogs of artificial islands, which much interested them all, they reached Milton Tower itself, a place with Herries links.

They had thought to spend that night here, but learning that they were only a few miles from Drumcoltran where they had stayed for their first night out, the much more commodious house of John's kinsman Herbert Maxwell, they pressed on, and were there received back warmly.

And there, abruptly, all changed. They had just finished their evening meal, with darkness fallen, when a servitor came to inform the laird that a man had arrived to announce that one of their new beacons, at the Pictish fort on Blairshinnoch Hill, was ablaze.

This news demanded urgent reaction. It might be a false alarm; some fool might have mischievously set it alight; but it could be authentic, and men from Drumcoltran were on nightly guard there. John demanded whether it was just the one fire, or more, to be told that the messenger had just said a beacon. So it was downstairs to question the man, who declared that at Camphill farmery they had just seen a single blaze on the hilltop.

John and his host and sons called for the horses at once, and nothing would do but that Agnes and Catherine came also, to inspect – they were as good horsemen as were the men, were they not? So, dark as it was, off the party rode the mile north to Camphill, at the foot of Blairshinnoch Hill, and well before they reached the farm they could see the red gleam on the ridge, a single gleam, at least from this angle.

As they worked round, it was evident that there was indeed only the one blaze. The farmer told them that his youngest son, on duty that night up there, had spotted a blaze, just one, on Auchenfad Hill some eight miles to the east, this none so far from the Nith estuary, and had, as instructed, set their own beacon alight.

Picking their way in the darkness, the riders mounted with some difficulty to the north end of Blairshinnoch Hill, to the earthen ramparts of the ancient Pictish fort. Before they reached it they saw another blaze, due westwards this one, which their host declared would be the beacon on the Barr Hill of Springholm, five miles off, also in his bailiwick, lit no doubt in response to this one. So the system was working, at least hereabouts.

Up at last on the summit, an excited pair of young men hailed them, pointing. From here they could make out five other blazes, all single, two to the east, two to the south and the one at Barr Hill. Whether it was a genuine alert, or false, a mistake, it gave John some satisfaction, intimation that his orders were being carried out. But the fact that they were concerned that it all might arise from some irresponsible numbskull's prank did reveal the system's weakness.

So now, what? John Maxwell had no doubts, at least. If there was invasion, be it only a raid, the deputy warden's duty was to be where he could be found and informed. In present circumstances that would be at Terregles Castle. He must get there just as quickly as possible, riding by night or not. And on this occasion he was adamant, wishing to accompany him as the Herries girls were, and however excellent a-horse. He and Dod would cover the ground more swiftly alone. The young women could come on in the morning. He was for off, forthwith.

Seeing him determined, Agnes acceded.

Drumcoltran said that his sons would see the young women safely to Terregles, only some dozen miles away, in the morning.

They parted there and then, for this Blairshinnoch Hill was in fact north-east of the tower, and on John's and Dod's way. They would go due north through low hills to Loch Rutten, four difficult miles, then east six lower ones to the Cargen Water near Terraughtie Castle, then north again to Terregles. It ought not to be too awkward, with their night vision developing.

Agnes was concerned, at their farewells, not so much about the dark journeying as about what John might do thereafter, in seeking to counter any English invasion attempt. His promise of care did not seem greatly to reassure her.

As it transpired, the two men made less trying riding

of it than might have been feared, although they could by no means push their mounts, only able to trot here and there. On their way they saw another beacon lit at Terraughtie. The Borderland was being well warned.

It was the early hours of the morning when they arrived at Terregles, to find lamps lit in the castle, Lord Herries abed but awake. Taken to his room, John was much relieved. The word was that there had been quite a sizeable raid across the border in the Kielder area, through the Larriston Fells and into the Hermitage Water valley, none so far from that castle itself, this presumably still going on. The Armstrongs, Johnstones and Elliots of the upper dales, affronted at this intrusion of their own backyard, as it were, had angrily mustered and headed for the scene. That was as far as Herries knew. Whether other forces had joined them was uncertain, but as this was very near the western parts of the Middle March, it was quite likely that there would be equally swift reaction there also.

John and Dod snatched a few hours of sleep.

In the morning, guessing that the independent-minded dalesmen were not likely to think of sending couriers with information as to progress, or the reverse, to Terregles, they took fresh horses and set off, still eastwards, for Lockerbie and Langholm and the dales country, to discover for themselves what the situation was and what was needed of the warden.

They did not, in fact, get as far as Langholm, in mid-Eskdale, when they met a party of Wauchopes nearing home, and in cheerful mood. These announced that they had seen off the English, with the help of others to be sure, in upper Liddesdale, three or four groups of the enemy, over the Steile, Kershope and Larriston area, sending the raiders packing with comparative ease and recapturing a deal of stolen cattle in the process. A few houses and barns had been found burned, and no doubt a few women raped, but that was all, the English discreetly departing for home over the Bewcastle Fells.

Relieved at this news, John demanded details from young Wattie Wauchope, who agreed that Armstrong of Whithaugh and Elliot of Steile had taken charge. Only as a casual comment they learned that one of the enemy bands had been flying the banner of Wharton, this without apparently recognising the significance of it. For Sir Thomas Wharton was Warden of the English West March. If he was involved in this seemingly only token raid, then clearly it was more or less ordered as a gesture, a warning, no doubt by King Henry, to indicate his concern that his demands as to the royal marriage were to be met, and swiftly, a threatening of more drastic action, major invasion, if not. Wharton would scarcely go in for minor raiding and reiving.

Assured that the raid was over and the enemy returned to Cumbria, and with this indication as to what lay behind it all, John and Dod turned their beasts' heads westwards for Terregles again, reasonably satisfied that the first testing of readiness, the beacons, and wardenship, had gone well enough.

8

With no further alarms and beacon-warnings, John still awaiting his father's return from captivity, on getting back from another tour of visits in Galloway, to the southern shire of Wigtown this time, he received a summons from Lord Herries to Terregles, the messenger indicating a degree of urgency. Nothing loth, he did not delay.

Agnes greeted him, on arrival, and despite having been apart for over two weeks, he got the impression that she was less pleased to see him than usual, warm as his own reactions were. Her father was sick again, she told him, and abed; but she allowed Catherine to conduct the visitor upstairs.

Herries, looking almost gaunt and with hands trembling, was more eager in his attitude, dismissing his daughter and reaching out to grip John's arm.

"Sit you," he said, voice weak although anything but hesitant. He scanned the younger man's face intently. "I have awaited you. I feared . . ." He left that unsaid. "John, hear me. I will not live long now, that I know, have known for some time. I do not fear to die. But I do fear for my daughters. I have no near male kin. I fear for them."

John cleared his throat. What was there that he could say?

"I have relied on you, John Maxwell, for much. For all this of the wardenship. You have been good, a stout support. More than that. Now I need, need more of you."

"I am ever at your service, my lord." That was feeble, inadequate, but what to say to a man who declared that he was dying?

"Agnes is a fine young woman. Strong. Able. But she *is* a woman, and cannot act the man. And a man is needed now. For Herries."

"I will do what I can, you need not fear. For her. And the others."

"I prayed so. I want you to wed Agnes."

John all but choked, speech impossible.

"You hear me, man?" The older man sounded almost desperate. "Wed her. Can you? Will you?" The grip on John's arm tightened convulsively. "You have a fondness for her, I think? See you, she is my heir. The lordship of Herries will go to her. I will pen a petition. To the crown, the regency. Seeking royal permission for the lordship to come to *you*, through her. On marriage, and my death. It is my right so to do. You and she will be Lord and Lady Herries. Provision of lands and houses for my other daughters, yes. But the lordship and Terregles to you and Agnes. You will do it, man? Say that you will do it!"

John had heard all that but had barely taken it in. Only those two words really registered – wed Agnes. The rest was immaterial. He was being given Agnes Herries, *given!*

He could only nod his head, however positively.

That seemed to be sufficient, however, for the other, who sank back on his pillow, as with what feeble strength he had drained out of him. "You will? God be praised!" he gasped, and closed his eyes.

"My lord," John got out. "I love Agnes! She is my delight, my joy, my need! I have wanted her, longed for her, dared scarcely hope for her. This, this is beyond all!"

Herries still did not open his eyes. "God be praised!" he said again.

"Yes. But . . . Agnes? What of her? How will she see this? She has some liking for me, yes, I believe. Some friendship. But, marriage? Take me for husband?"

"She will not, cannot, refuse."

"But . . ."

111

"I have spoken with her." Those eyes, which had briefly opened, closed again. "Go, man. Go now."

Wagging his head, John rose, looked down at the frail figure on the bed, and after a pause went to the door and out.

He found Catherine and Janet in the hall, and wondered whether they knew of all this. Almost hesitantly now, he asked for Agnes.

They eyed him curiously. "She is in the orchard," he was told, no questions put to him.

The April sun shone fitfully between the showers as he went out, seeking her, yet all but afraid of finding her. She was standing under an apple tree, toying with a budding twig.

"Agnes!" he said, and could think of no words to meet the occasion.

"Yes," she said. That was all.

He went to her, but, with no turning towards him, he did not reach out to her, touch her. Biting his lip, he eyed her only.

So they stood, at a loss.

"Agnes, lass," he jerked at length. "You are . . . unhappy?"

"Yes."

"I am sorry. Oh, I am sorry, my dear. For I, I have been happy indeed! But I would not have you unhappy. Ever. What am I to say to you?"

"What is there to say? It has, it seems, all been said!"

"No. Not that. If you will not have it so. Then, nor will I."

"It is his wish, his will. My father. And he . . . dying. I cannot say no."

"But I can! Even though it costs me dear. Dear, lass, dear! But I must, if you are so against it."

"Cost you a lordship, yes!"

"That is the least of it. That I have no way deserved nor desired. It is you I have desired, you, girl!"

"Desired! Ah, yes, I have not failed to note your

desire, at times!" That came out brokenly. "And now your desire, it appears, can be granted! That, and the lordship, both!"

"I say no! Not if you would not have it so. *I* can refuse, if you can not. It is a price I must pay. Out of my caring for you. Even at the cost to your father, yes."

"Caring!"

"Aye, caring, Agnes. Think you otherwise?"

"I do not know what to think."

"Could you not come to care, also?"

She eyed him now, searchingly. "There is caring and caring," she said. "But marriage. That is . . . something other. There *need* be no caring in that. A tie, a bond, a taking."

"It need not be that. I could hope, aye, hope. Seek to arouse, to nurture caring in you. That would be my wish, my need, my desire . . ."

"Desire again! Need! Wish! For marriage, I would seek more than that, fool that I am!"

Suddenly he was almost angry. "See you, woman, what would you have more? What must a man offer to win you? You have me, my all. My caring and esteem. My longing, my devotion, my heart and love. My need, yes."

Agnes Herries stared, wide-eyed now, swallowing. Her hand rose, to point. "Love!" she cried, her voice breaking.

"Aye, love, and more than love. My whole being's need . . ."

He got no further, for she sprang forward to throw herself into his arms, all but beating fists against him, wordless.

Astonished, he held her heaving person. "My dear, my dear!" he got out, into her hair.

For long moments she clung to him, and then, shaking her head, pushed herself back. "I, I heard aright?" she panted. "Love! You said it? You said that you loved me!"

"Loved, yes – of a surety I did. What have I been

saying all along but that I love and care and need you, girl? Were you deaf?"

"Not love. You did not say it. Not until the end. Until now. That you *loved* me Love! Love is what a woman needs, must have, for giving of herself. The rest can have some import, yes. But love – that is for the heart! And you have never said it, John. Until now!"

"Could you not tell, lass?"

"Oh, I wondered. I hoped. But you did not say so. I feared . . ."

"Is one small word so important, then? So needful?"

"It is, for me," she said simply. "Because *I* love you, John!"

"You do! Lord, you do?"

After that, for a while, words great or small lost their importance, other means of communication taking over, and eloquently.

But at length they managed to draw apart, at least sufficiently to speak coherently.

"You *will* wed me? Say that you will," the man demanded. "Since we love."

"Yes, my dear, yes. But it is hard, still. Hard. Not as I would have wished it. To be given away! All but bartered for a lordship! And for you to have the care of three females! My father means well by us, but this is not how it should be between us."

"Does it signify, lass? So long as we have each other."

"If you had sought my hand first . . ."

"I had not dared. Myself a second son, with no great properties. And you the heiress of a lord, and with broad acres."

"Have I not shown you that I cared for you? Allowed you . . . freedoms, tokens? And acted your aide in this of the wardenship."

"All that, yes. But such kindnesses did not make me fit to be your suitor. Until now it seems that I become so!" He reached for her again. "When will we be married?"

She smiled, but shook her head. "Do not be hasty! A woman needs time to prepare for such great change in her life. Yet, yes it must be before long. My father will wish to see us wed before, before . . ."

"It cannot be too soon for me!"

They embraced again, and sufficiently comprehensively for them not to notice before a giggling from behind them intimated that the two sisters' patience had run out and that they had come to discover progress or otherwise.

"All is well, I see!" Catherine declared. "We are to have a good-brother! Good, good!"

Moving apart, one pair eyed the other.

"Do not cheer too soon!" Agnes chided, but far from sternly.

"Whom do we congratulate?" came the reply. And to answer her own question Catherine came up to give John a hearty kiss, before laughing to her sister. Janet looked embarrassed.

They went indoors amidst much female chatter.

Presently Agnes and John went up to her father's room, to inform that all was as he had wished it. However, Herries was asleep, and not wishing to disturb him they tiptoed out.

They spent an anything but placid evening.

When it came to bedtime, something of John's new status was demonstrated by Catherine making a point of heading off alone, with knowing looks to complement her goodnights. The other two carefully remained by the withdrawing-room fire for a while longer, eyeing the flickering flames and thinking their own thoughts.

When they rose, John took Agnes's hand to escort her upstairs. Whimsically she looked at him.

"We are not wed yet, you know, young man!" she warned.

"No-o-o. But tonight is especial, surely? It ranks as our betrothal, does it not?"

"You could call it that, yes. However brought about. What does betrothal stand for?"

"A promise! Promise of bliss to come!"

"To come, yes!" But she squeezed his hand.

Up at the door of her room, Agnes paused before opening it. "One day, it seems, this chamber will be yours also!" she said.

"Then, ought I not to see it now? Prospect it? That I be informed!"

"Informed of what, sir?" But she opened.

"Of something of what is to be mine, no?"

"A bed. Tables. Kists. Blankets. A few hangings. Do these concern you?"

"Only in that they are yours. And all of you and yours concerns me." He closed that door behind them.

The fire was lit, for the evenings still were chilly. She went to stand before it, waving a hand around. "Are you satisfied, then?"

"Scarcely that," he told her, and took her in his arms. "It looks all well enough. But it lacks the heart of it. What makes it not just one more room. *You!*"

"I am here, am I not? In it."

"Not yet as you should be. It is your bedchamber. You should be preparing for bed."

"Ah. But I do that alone, see you. Not with a man in it. Not yet, that is."

"What of the betrothal's promise? Some earnest. Some portent." His hands went to the bodice of her gown, gently drawing the neck aside.

She did not answer; but nor did she push him away.

John forced himself to seem very moderate about it, kissing her hair as he loosened the silken fabric, and as the smooth white shoulders were bared, stooping to run lips over the warm and still more silky skin. Down he drew the cloth, to uncover and release her lovely bosom, to her indrawn breath, but to no actual protest.

She was indeed given a breathing-time space then, for these breasts of delight and challenge had to be explored and fondled and kissed most diligently, appreciatively, before he proceeded onward, lower, until the gown

116

slipped away to the floor and Agnes stood in her brief shift, revealed and shapely indeed.

"Is that . . . sufficient promise?" she asked, somewhat throatily.

"I think, not quite." And lest she should voice objection, closed her lips with his own, while his hands continued with their busyness. That shift slid off easily enough and followed the gown to the floor.

Superb in her naked womanhood, she did not shrink nor cower, but nor did she flaunt her beauty of form and line and physical feature, but stood gazing at the fire, proud in its best sense without being prideful.

It was the man's turn to have difficulty with his breathing, as he eyed her, silent.

She turned, to search his face, and then held out her hand to him, in a strangely trusting gesture.

He nodded, acceptingly, and then, with something of a sigh, went to pick her up bodily in his arms and carry her over to the bed. Laying her down on it, he stood back, set of countenance.

"Good John, kind John," she said. "Go now. While you can. While we both can . . . part! Promise enough! Go, John, until, until . . ." She shook her head. "That is right, no? Right."

Without a word he turned and left her. Thanks and needful reaction must needs wait until the morning.

John left for Caerlaverock the next day, a man elated. It was agreed that they should wait a little longer for his father to win home, Herries acceding that this was only suitable, on the understanding that the marriage was assured and that if there was any dire worsening of conditions, a summons would be sent for an immediate return by the bridegroom.

9

Lord Maxwell did indeed get back to his own place and folk three days later. Never one to show much emotion nor to demonstrate feelings, he nevertheless returned more reserved, seemingly, than ever, all but harsh in his behaviour. It took some time before he unburdened himself fully, or as far as in him lay.

His first abrupt declaration to his family was a sore one indeed, announced in a level voice. Robert, his son and heir, was to proceed to England, to London, as hostage.

Appalled, they all stared at him, scarcely believing that they had heard aright.

"It is King Henry's command," they were told. "Only so was I permitted to return here. The others also – Glencairn, Cassillis, Somerville and Oliphant. All to send their heirs."

"But, but . . ." Robert exclaimed. "This is not possible! Beyond belief. You cannot mean it? Me – to go to England! A prisoner! In place of you?"

"I do mean it, boy! Not only you. These others. All the heirs, the masters of lordships of the Solway Moss lords. Henry Tudor's command. On signed bond. Otherwise we none of us would now be out of the Tower of London. After months therein."

"You agreed to that, Father?" John demanded. "To send Robert? Your son!"

"We had no choice. Henry is a hard taskmaster. And we judged that we could do better back in Scotland. Win back our hostage sons thereafter. Better than remaining prisoners there." Maxwell did not sound apologetic, merely factual, grim.

"When? When do I have to go?" Robert, shaken, asked. "When? And for how long?"

"Within the month. For how long I know not. Until we can send Henry the word he seeks."

"And what is that?" the Lady Agnes wondered.

"The agreement that our child queen will marry the Prince of Wales."

"Sakes! And you accepted that?"

"We had no option. That, or remain prisoners in the Tower. Where we could achieve nothing."

"And I have to take your place there? Until . . . ! When there is but little chance of this of the marriage being agreed to. This is not to be borne!" Robert Maxwell had never spoken to his formidable father so before.

"Quiet, you!" he was told. "It will be none so ill. You will be well treated. Hostages, not prisoners. Not in the Tower. And it may well not be for long. For this of the marriage, it is believed, *will* be agreed. It is, probably, for the best. For both kingdoms. An end to war and enmity. Peace between the realms, after all the centuries. The death of King James changed all. We shall have reform of the Church. It is best. Arran will agree to it, I think."

"Cardinal Beaton will not!" John averred. "Nor Queen Marie de Guise."

"What know you of it, boy! Beaton and his like will be silenced. The Queen Marie signifies little. Arran, the regent, is for reform and an end to warfare. I, and the others, will be going to see him in a day or two. There is to be a meeting of the council."

"You speak as did the Earl of Angus, none so long since."

"Angus? He has been here? We saw him in London."

"Not here. But he is now Steward of Galloway. And, it seems, for this marriage."

"Aye. This matter, I think, will all be over and settled shortly. Your stay in London may well be brief, Robert." He turned to his wife. "Come." And shrugging, their father left sons and daughter to eye each other.

119

John and Margaret commiserated with Robert. But perhaps it would be none so hard and sore a trial? An experience, a seeing of new places and folk. In the company of the other lords' sons. A change from the Borderland. That was the best that they could do for him.

In the days that followed before Lord Maxwell went north to attend the hastily called council at Edinburgh, they gathered more of what their sire had had to undergo and suffer, bit by bit. After the Solway rout, he and the others had been taken to Carlisle, and treated none so ill, he moved on to the Lord Dacre's house, of Greystoke, near to Penrith, where the ransom was decided on. Then word had come from Henry that the lordly prisoners were to be sent to London and treated with severity. A sore journey down through England followed, under strong guard, being lodged in gaols, tolbooths and the like, and on arrival in London being chained together, by the King's command, and marched through the streets, to be mocked and jeered at, spat upon and pelted with filth. They were flung into the dungeons of the Tower of London, like felons, earls, lords and lairds as they were, the ransom position apparently forgotten.

Then, of a sudden, all was changed, when word arrived of the death of King James and the birth of the infant queen. The prisoners were taken out of the cells and lodged in fair quarters in the governor's residence. And there, presently, Henry Tudor himself came to visit them, a great burly, flamboyant man of swiftly changing moods, one moment laughing, back-slapping, the next shouting and fist-shaking. He had come to announce his reaction to the new situation in Scotland – the marriage of his heir and the new queen. This, he declared, was the obvious and righteous development for both kingdoms. Peace and friendship instead of enmity and bloodshed. And amendment of religion. The two realms to remain separate and independent, but co-operation and amity to reign. Trade to prosper. Peace and prosperity. If his Scottish friends would return home and promote these fair endeavours, they should go free – but send hostages. If not, back to the Tower with them, there to rot.

It had not taken long, apparently, for the prisoners to come to a decision. The prospects held out by Henry were sufficiently attractive; after all, with suddenly an infant monarch, religious dissension, and no strong hand on the helm of state, there was bound to be a difficult period ahead for Scotland, unrest, strife, possibly even civil war. This, of not a union or taking over but of a marital linking of the crowns and a collaboration between governments, could be the answer, so long as continuing independence was assured. With the promise of that, the doubters were silenced, Maxwell seemingly one of them. So all was agreed, and after six months of captivity it was to be home again. At least Henry had not insisted on their remaining in London until the hostage heirs arrived, saying that he trusted them.

Whatever their father's inmost feelings and reserves – and he was not a man to demonstrate such – his sons wondered whether *they* could trust Henry Tudor, a monarch who had been trying to conquer Scotland ever since he mounted the throne, more actively even than had most of his predecessors. Their expressed doubts were not commented upon.

Lord Maxwell did show some satisfaction, scarcely enthusiasm but at least approval, over John's marriage plans, in that he would become, in due course, Lord Herries, and this would greatly enhance the Maxwell name and power. He had but scant regard for the present holder of that title, and barely knew the daughter concerned. But the wedding had his endorsement, and the sooner concluded the better, before the weakly Herries changed his mind. When he, Maxwell, came back from the Edinburgh council, they could hold it. By that time it would have been decided, with the other lords concerned, as to the arrangements for their heirs to travel south, so Robert might be able to attend the ceremony before setting off.

So much for family nuptial celebrations.

Robert, while supportive, and approving of Agnes, had his own preoccupations to concern him.

John now had, to be sure, ample excuse for another visit to Terregles. Would this of so early a wedding date be acceptable there?

In the event he found no objections voiced to a ceremony planned for three weeks hence, by which time Lord Maxwell would surely be back from Edinburgh and, hopefully, Robert not yet departed for London. Agnes said that she ought to be as ready by then as she was ever likely to be for their union – but she said it with a smile. In her father's state it would have to be a very quiet affair, held in the castle hall, so that he could be present, with the parish priest instructed to keep matters fairly brief, which well suited John. Lord Herries was no better in health, but no worse seemingly, and he had been sufficiently himself to pen the promised letter to the regent, in however shaky a hand, intimating his desire and his right to pass on the lordship of Herries, lacking any male heir, to his daughter's husband, at his death, and seeking the necessary crown assent. This precious document he passed over to John, to give to his father to take with him to Edinburgh, so a prompt return to Caerlaverock was indicated.

Agnes, and to a lesser extent Catherine, was concerned to hear of what had happened with the lordly prisoners in London, and of King Henry's requirements. They were very doubtful over the proposed betrothal of their child monarch to the Prince of Wales. Would this be acceptable in Scotland, beneficial, as John's father and the other captives seemed to have accepted? And, to be sure, that Earl of Angus. Were most of those in power apt to be in favour? Was it not highly dangerous for the security and future of the realm, giving Henry all but a stranglehold on Scotland? It was all tied up with the religious situation, of course, Henry Protestant and so many of the Scots magnates seeking, if not reform of worship, at least dispersal and appropriation of the vast

Church lands so long envied? Cardinal Beaton for certain would be against it all, and was he not reckoned to be the strongest man in the land?

John agreed with all that. But he was influenced by anxiety about his brother's position should the council turn down the English proposals. Not that his attitude would affect the issue, anyway.

That night the betrothed ones went through a similar goodnight programme to the previous one, except for John lingering a little longer over details, and being less abrupt about his eventual exit, Agnes shaking her head over him but patient even though no more permissive, promising, promising, and subtly indicating that she too was looking forward to the fulfilment of the promise. Was it not worth the waiting for?

The man acceded that it might be, but that without much in the way of ardour.

It all had the effect, as before, of him not getting off to sleep very promptly thereafter.

In the morning he was for off again, with that letter, and no lack of instructions and advice as to preparations for the great day. Were women always like this about marriage? At least they surely need fear no English raiding to demand the wardens' attention meantime, although with that Tudor they could never be sure, a man unpredictable. John presumed, now that his father was back, that he himself was still deputy warden, although nothing had been said about that.

10

Confirmation of his position as deputy warden came in unexpected fashion only a few days after John's return to Caerlaverock, by means of a summons by his father for both his sons to repair to Edinburgh forthwith, for purposes unspecified. Robert assumed that this would have something to do with his hostage journey, despite being in the opposite direction; John with no idea why he should be needed.

They set off, at any rate, without delay, Dod as ever accompanying.

Fast riding, with an overnight halt at Broughton, over the heights into upper Tweeddale, brought them to Edinburgh the following evening, to the Earl of Angus's large town-house in the Canongate, where apparently their father was lodged, somewhat to their surprise. They had not thought that the Douglas chief would be on such terms with the Maxwells.

They quickly learned the reasons for their summons. The Privy Council had urgently called for a special meeting of parliament to be held, waiving the normal forty days' notice requirement in the circumstances, and the reformist lords were anxious to emphasise their fullest strength thereat – not that Robert or John would have a vote, but the more of their persuasion on view, apparently, the better. Since neither of the young men was at all sure of their approval of the attitudes recently voiced by their father, this call scarcely gratified them.

There were further reasons for their presence, however. The other hostage sons were to meet and plan their journey to London, it being deemed best that they all went together, with a suitable escort and in some style, to demonstrate that they were no humble captives but free and proud scions of great houses, pledges of goodwill rather than mere hostages. As for John, it appeared that the Regent Arran, having read Lord Herries's letter and agreed to its terms, had decided that, in view of John becoming a Lord of Parliament in due course, and in esteem for his good work as Deputy Warden of the West March, indeed acting warden, he should be made a knight – this last seemingly partly on Angus's recommendation.

To say that John was surprised at this was to put it mildly. It had never crossed his mind that he should be honoured in this way, or deemed himself worthy; and almost equally surprised that the Douglas should have suggested it. This interest in the Maxwell family was something new, and not readily understood. Admittedly the earl was now Steward of Galloway, and so apt to be much in touch, and hopefully working in concert with the warden. But this hardly accounted for these sudden demonstrations of friendship. Lord Maxwell had mentioned that he had seen Angus in London. Was there something more to all this than met the eye?

At all events, next day the two young men were taken further down the Canongate to the great Abbey of the Holy Rood, where the late king had built a fine house contiguous to the abbot's lodging, where the regent was now dwelling, and with the Chancellor-cardinal, his unfriend, staying immediately next door with the abbot. The entire sprawling establishment below the towering hill of Arthur's Seat was alive with activity, important folk everywhere.

Angus won them access to Arran without much delay. James Hamilton proved to be a handsome and amiable man, younger than John had expected, only in his late twenties, with quite a presence about him, yet with something indecisive in mouth and chin. He accepted John and Robert in friendly enough fashion, despite an air of abstraction, and seemed only to remember

125

the object of the visit when Angus reminded him that this was the Deputy Warden of the West March and his brother. Then, nodding, he sent one of those with him, who proved to be Sir David Lindsay of the Mount, Lord Lyon King of Arms, a smiling character, to go fetch a sword. As they waited, he did congratulate John on his activities of wardenship, his eventual advance to the lordship of Herries, and Lord Maxwell on his son. He amended that to sons, and turning to Robert, nodded, a thoughtful touch.

When Lyon returned with the necessary sword, the regent all but casually ordered John to kneel before him, tapped him on each shoulder with the sword blade, mentioned that he should remain a good knight until his life's end, and added, "Arise, Sir John!", giving back the sword to Lindsay.

Distinctly bemused, not to say astonished, disappointed, John got up. Was that all? Knighthood was a major honour and rise in dignity and status, a change in his entire rank and position. Could this brief gesture on the part of Arran be all that was required? Was he really, effectively knighted? Two or three words and taps on the shoulders. And with the regent already chatting to Angus and his father as though nothing had happened. He himself could feel no different, indeed almost crestfallen, which was scarcely the suitable reaction. Sir David Lindsay did hold out his hand in felicitation, whereon Robert followed suit. That was all.

Lord Maxwell indicated to his sons that he and the Earl of Angus had matters to discuss with the regent over the morrow's parliament, and that they should retire. So the Master of Maxwell and Sir John thereof bowed themselves out, the entire procedure not having taken more than five minutes.

"How does it feel to be a knight?" Robert asked interestedly, once in the open air.

"Ask me that hereafter, when I can feel anything at

all!" he was told. "At this moment, I feel somehow less-ened, cheated, perhaps. Certainly not raised in standing and degree. Was that a sufficiency? A man should be knighted by a king, then it might feel aright. Am I truly knighted?"

"Oh, yes. When there is only a child as king, the regent represents him and acts accordingly. Indeed, I understand that any knight could create another knight, although the usage is that only monarchs, regents and commanders in the field do so. So you are truly Sir John Maxwell."

"I may come to believe it, one day!"

Just before the parliament was due to sit, the extraordinary news reached all – Cardinal Beaton had been arrested, on the orders of the regent, and confined in Blackness Castle. The word of it shook the realm, and this just before parliament sat.

That parliament, so important, the first since King James's death, and with chaos in the kingdom after the disaster of Solway Moss and the arrest of Beaton, was held in the great hall of Edinburgh Castle. It was bound to be a difficult and stormy one. The Privy Council had met, and its decisions had to be homologated, or reversed, by parliament. There were three great issues to be settled, with lesser ones – the crown, regency and the succession; King Henry's demands and propositions; and the religious situation, especially with the Cardinal's arrest. All were bound to arouse passions and controversy. The position of the Queen-Mother, Marie de Guise, was also a cause for concern. It was known that she had summoned her brother, the Duc de Guise, to come to aid her in her difficult situation. She was, of course, a strong Catholic, and a strong woman, and would certainly rear her child in that faith. The reformist party was much exercised. It was known that there had been a recent meeting of anti-Rome lords, at Perth, and these would have much to say at the parliament.

All this was why the Maxwell brothers were here in

Edinburgh, whatever their personal views. The great ones of the various sides desired to offer their respective shows of strength, even though when it came to the votes, only lords, prelates, commissioners of the shires and representatives of the royal burghs could register their decisions. But numbers behind the voters could tell.

So the great hall was crowded indeed, and even though they climbed to the great castle-fortress on its rock early, John and Robert had to squeeze themselves into a very indifferent position in a window-embrasure, and this a good hour before the session was due to begin. Even so they were in distinguished company there, for the castle guards were preventing admission to all save those with impressive credentials. John had the Spanish ambassador next to him. It made a noisy gathering, despite its illustrious composition.

The appearance of heralds in their handsome tabards, with their trumpeters, entering by the dais-doorway, at length intimated the start of proceedings. A fanfare announced the entry of Sir David Lindsay of the Mount, Lord Lyon, with his staff-of-office, who went to thump this on the dais-table for silence, where the clerks sat, and to declare that parliament was duly in session, and that the lords temporal and spiritual would take their seats.

Then in due seniority and precedence the nobility filed in, excepting the earls, Lord Maxwell amongst them, followed by the bishops and mitred abbots, moving in procession to their reserved seating. There was a pause and then Lyon announced the earls, save for those who were great officers-of-state, and these came in, including the two ex-captives, Glencairn and Cassillis, and Bothwell, Lieutenant of the Borders.

Another pause, and then to more staff-thumping, the Chancellor entered alone, a fine figure in his scarlet robes, proud, authoritative, the Archbishop of Glasgow, Gavin Dunbar, a notable character and poet, whose uncle of the same name, Bishop of Aberdeen, sat in the prelates' benches. He paced to the dais-table's centre and there stood.

The officers-of-state filed in now, the Earl of Erroll bearing the sword-of-state, as High Constable, the Earl of Argyll, Lord Justice-General, with one sceptre, the Earl Marischal with the other, and the Earl of Atholl bearing the crown on its cushion. Everybody stood, and these proceeded on to the dais, to another, smaller table, set behind the throne, whereon they laid the Honours of Scotland, and there waited.

Another fanfare, and Lyon led in the Regent Arran, to usher him to the throne, on which he seated himself.

Those who had seats could now resume them, Lindsay going to stand behind the throne.

The Chancellor took charge, after bowing towards the throne. He announced the first item on the agenda, the vital matters of the crown, regency and the succession. They all lamented the death of their late liege-lord James, he declared, but hailed the birth of his daughter Mary, heir to the throne. There had been no queen-regnant over their realm previously, unless the Maid of Norway, granddaughter of Alexander the Third, could be so-called; but she had died before ever she could be crowned. This situation presented the nation with a problem, an infant monarch requiring a regent. The council had recognised more than that, the . . .

He got no further, with the Lord Boyd rising to interrupt.

"My lord Chancellor, there need be no problem and no question. The throne of this ancient kingdom has always been occupied by a king, not a woman. Therefore the next *male* heir to King James should be monarch. And that heir sits there!" He pointed to Arran dramatically, his own kinsman. "He should be sitting here as monarch, not as regent. I say that the council chose wrongly in accepting the child-princess as queen. Scotland requires a man on its throne, especially so now, at this juncture. And James Hamilton, grandson of the Princess Mary who was daughter of James the Second and sister of James the Third, is the next lawful heir. The council erred." He sat down.

There were murmurings of approval, and the reverse.

The Chancellor banged the table with his gavel. "The council considered the matter well and at length," he said. "A decision had to be made, and swiftly. There is no statute nor edict which declares that the monarch must be a man. That is only custom and usage. The Princess Mary is the only lawful child of the late king. As such, to reject or deny her right would be wrongous, it was decided. But – it is for parliament to approve or disapprove."

There was a din of upraised voices, which had to be stilled by the beating of the gavel. "Parliament's will must be decided in correct and no uncertain fashion," the Archbishop added. "Does any move that the council's decision be revoked?"

"I do," Boyd cried.

"And I second that." So said the Lord Ruthven.

"I move the endorsement of the council's judgment," Angus declared.

"And I second," Lord Maxwell added.

So, thus early in the session, matters had come to the vote. The Chancellor called for a show of hands for the amendment first, that is, support for the council's decision. There was no need for any count thereafter, as the great majority clearly were in favour of the child-queen's position.

When the noise died down, the Chancellor resumed. "The succession falls to be decided upon. Until such time as the infant queen grows to be able to produce an heir of her own, the Earl of Arran's heirship is evident. Is that agreed?"

No doubting voice was raised.

"Now there is the regency. The council decided that the said Earl of Arran, next heir, should fill that office. Is this accepted?"

"Why not the child monarch's mother, Queen Marie de Guise?" That was the strongly Catholic Earl of Huntly, the Gordon chief, speaking. "I so move."

"And I second," came from the clerical benches, two bishops at once getting to their feet.

Uproar.

When he could make himself heard, the Archbishop commanded order and asked who supported the council's choice. Half a dozen lords, none spiritual, were standing at once.

So now a crucial vote, and not only for the regency but indicating the strength of reformist versus Catholic feeling. The counting of yeas and nays took place amidst much commotion, for this was a difficult decision for not a few, even amongst Church supporters. Queen Marie was very French, and had brought in many French courtiers, artists, artisans and chaplains. A French-dominated regency was desired by few, and was moreover a sure recipe for trouble with England.

The vote, when counted, produced a majority for Arran, although not a large one, some of the clergy abstaining. It must have taxed the Chancellor hard to announce the result equably, John realised.

So that was the first great constitutional issue settled.

The next, however, was even more controversial, the matter of King Henry's demands on Scotland. The Chancellor announced, in a level voice, the Tudor's wishes that his young son, the Prince of Wales, should be betrothed forthwith to the infant Queen Mary; and giving only until June for the agreement, with certain hostages sent to England in token thereof, and with sundry named strongholds and fortresses in Scotland to be delivered over to English garrisons meantime – this, or there would be armed English invasion. That was carefully enunciated.

Pandemonium broke out. The Archbishop let the noise go on for longer than usual, before hammering for quiet. How said parliament, in due orderly session, he demanded, not in such broil and uproar?

Again it was Huntly who led the opposition. "I say that this of the Tudor's insolence is not to be borne!" he cried. "Are we to jump to his command, like whipped curs? Let Henry act the tyrant in his own England, if they will let him. We in Scotland owe him nothing, and will repel any of his armies which dare to set foot on our soil. I move rejection of all his demands."

That met with loud applause from many, but not all. There was no lack of seconders.

Angus rose. "My lord Chancellor," he said evenly. "I judge that almost all in this hall feel as does my lord of Huntly. *Feel*, I say. But are feelings enough? We have to use such wits as God has given us! This of Henry of England's threats arouses us, yes. But the threats are aimed to bring us to agreement with his proposals, which have some good in them. Indeed, I say, of much advantage to our nation. This of betrothal and eventual marriage between the future King of England and our queen. That, provided that we have safeguards, could be no ill development for Scotland. Alliance, instead of enmity. Peace. An end to the warfare which has plagued us down the centuries. Much increased trade and wealth. Our shipping spared from attack on the seas. I say consider this well before you make your decision."

"I say the same," Lord Maxwell supported. "Henry is no fool. He knows that we Scots will never accept English domination and overlordship. But he sees also advantage for both realms. Let us not shut our eyes to these."

A chorus of backing came from not a few, including to be sure the Earls of Glencairn, Cassillis and the other former prisoners.

"What are these safeguards?" Huntly demanded. "We all know that these lords voice Henry's cause, since they agreed to send their heirs as hostages to England. But our realm's weal is not to be bought and sold so, however we may feel for the prisoners! What safeguards can we rely upon, to preserve our nation, if we agree to this of a marriage and alliance?"

That gained considerable backing also.

Angus answered him. "Henry has promised that the two realms will remain separate and independent. In token of which he will offer his second daughter, the Princess Elizabeth, as wife for the Earl of Arran, regent."

That, not hitherto announced, created some stir.

From behind the throne, Argyll, the Campbell chief, spoke. "My lord Chancellor, as token, that could but increase the English grip on our Scotland. I have heard that Henry requires our young queen to be handed over to his keeping, and this by the age of six years. Does that sound like independence? And he is asking that you, my lord Chancellor, be sent to his keeping in London also, until all is settled, you our Chancellor. Is *that* independence? And this of the castles and fortresses. It seems to me that the Tudor would take over our Scotland in fact, whatever he promises in words!"

Growls from all over the hall greeted that.

The Earl of Moray, Argyll's brother-in-law, added his voice. "While this of a marriage may be none so ill, Henry Tudor's other demands are not to be considered, I say. I urge that this parliament rejects."

"My lord Chancellor, these demands are but threats, Henry's threats," Angus asserted. "Voiced, perhaps foolishly, to seek to ensure acceptance of the betrothal and marriage proposal. Idle threats, I judge. But the main overture is good, to Scotland's advantage. Let us not be misled, and put off the greater good by threats of lesser ills."

"You are not proposing, my lord, that parliament agrees to accept all these dire conditions imposed on our free nation, in order to gain the doubtful advantages of a royal marriage?" the Archbishop asked evenly.

"No. I say accept the principal proposal, the marriage, but reject the threats. It is my belief that Henry will agree, and not carry them out. *I* have spoken with the Tudor . . ."

A score of men were on their feet, exclaiming, arguing,

accusing, questioning. The Chancellor allowed it all to continue, probably deliberately, judiciously, to let the heat generated cool itself off, calmer reason and judgment hopefully to take over. At length he banged his gavel.

"This parliament is the governing body of our realm, my lords, commissioners and friends," he said. "It is our duty and responsibility to make decisions in the name and on behalf of the nation. You have heard what has been declared for and against the proposals of King Henry of England. We all now must decide, one way or the other. Motions should be put, so that they can be voted upon. Who moves? And to what effect?"

"I do," Angus declared promptly. "I move that this parliament accepts the proposal of a royal match between our infant queen and the Prince of Wales. With safeguards for our realm's continuing independence. Such safeguards to be debated."

"And I second," Lord Maxwell said.

"And I reject," Huntly exclaimed. "Safeguards or none."

"That I second!" the Bishop of Aberdeen supported.

"My lord Chancellor, should we not decide on the safeguards before voting on the main issue?" the Earl of Atholl suggested.

"I think not, my lords," the Archbishop decided. "If the main issue, this betrothal, is rejected, then there is no need to waste parliament's time on the safeguards to it. You have all heard the two motions, for and against the betrothal. We will take the amendment first. Those against the proposal, show."

There followed considerable murmuring and uncertainty. Some hands went up at once, some hesitantly. Some members even rose to their feet, then sat again. Obviously there was much doubt and indecision. But it was clear that nothing like half the company voted.

"Before the clerks count," the Chancellor said, "let us have the vote in favour of the proposal. It may be that there will be no need to count."

He was right in that. The hands raised showed that a substantial majority favoured, if not the betrothal itself, at least the breathing space which agreement to it in principle would provide. Scotland was prepared to purchase peace with England.

"And now, the safeguards!" the Archbishop said, almost grimly.

There followed a lengthy debate, with many points of view, interjections and arguments, speakers rising from all over the hall. Clearly the safeguards and opposition to the various threats were more important to many there than was the principal resolution. When at length the Chancellor called a halt and summarised the requirements and decisions skilfully, the conclusions added up to this: no fortresses to be yielded up; the hostages to go south, yes, since that had been promised, but certainly not the cardinal; Scotland's identity, name, laws, officers, courts and ministers to remain unaffected; if no heir was eventually produced by the royal marriage, the Scots crown to revert to the lawful successor; the queen not to be sent to England until she was at least of ten years; the regency always to be held by a native Scot; and last, but most vital, Scotland's independence to be assured, any contrary move to invalidate the entire agreement.

So the matter was settled, to the qualified satisfaction of most present, apparently even Angus and Maxwell.

There was a third great issue facing the nation, which was in the forefront of the minds of many there: that of reform in religious matters. But this was not a matter which could be put to parliament's vote directly. Holy Church was, in theory, independent of the temporal power, and the cardinal and lords spiritual would never accept any motion which denied this. So any debate or reform had to be, as it were, indirect, sidelong.

It was the Lord Maxwell who found a way to get round this ban on discussion of Church affairs, much to his sons' surprise, since he had never appeared to be greatly interested in religious observances hitherto.

"My lord Chancellor, I would put forward a motion to improve the understanding and enlightenment of our people at a time of great national difficulty and uncertainty," he said. "Would it not be to the advantage of all if the holy Scriptures, the Bible, were to be permitted to be read not only in the Latin but in our native tongue? Many, indeed most, of our folk do not have the Latin, in which the Scriptures have hitherto been read. This would, I say, much assist our people's knowledge of right and wrong, to the realm's weal, and the assistance of parliament in making its decisions understood and accepted. I so move."

"I second," Angus said, with a smile.

There was a distinct pause. All there saw this for what it was, a subtle step on the road to reform, but one which it would be difficult for the churchmen to forbid. Until now *they* had expounded the Scriptures from the Latin, to their own interpretations, and so greatly influenced religious thinking and behaviour. Here was challenge, however cunningly disguised.

Clearly, Archbishop Dunbar, as one of the heads of the Church, was thus put to the question, whatever his position here as neutral chairman. He rose to the occasion. Turning towards the benches of the bishops and abbots, he actually smiled, even more obviously than had Angus.

"My lords and friends," he said, easily. "I applaud this suggestion. I have long considered that such reading and translation would be for the benefit of many, of most of our fellow-worshippers. The nation would benefit, and so would Holy Church. I would so accept the motion, as I hope would all. Does any say otherwise?"

None could, in the circumstances, even the most dogmatic of the prelates. To much exchange of glances, a gabble of comment, and even some chuckling, the thing was done, passed.

The Maxwell brothers were amongst those who eyed each other. Their father continued to surprise them. His

136

sojourn as an English captive appeared to have greatly changed him.

There evidently being no further unexpected motions put forward, there remained only the formal naming of a group of important lords to be the official Keepers of the Queen's Person, representing parliament, under the regard of the royal mother, Mary of Guise. These were to be the Earls Marischal and Montrose, and the Lords Erskine, Ruthven, Lindsay, Livingstone and Seton.

That concluded the business, and to a brief fanfare of trumpets the Earl of Arran, from the throne, declared the session adjourned, the only words that he had spoken throughout. They all rose as he paced to the dais door, preceded by the Lord Lyon.

John had had his first experience of parliament, and a notable one.

Robert thereafter had a meeting with the other sons and heirs of the ex-captives in an anteroom of the castle, to arrange details of their journey to London, all of them wondering what effect today's decisions would have on their reception and stay in London, some apprehensive.

Then, leaving their father with unspecified business in Edinburgh, next morning it was home to Caerlaverock.

11

Needless to say, John was not long in heading for
Terregles; after all, his wedding arrangements had to be
confirmed for a mere ten days hence. His reception warm,
he found all in order therefor, Lord Herries's condition
no worse, and feminine anticipation rife. He delayed his
announcement of his knighthood for some little time,
not so much in modesty as over a sort of discomfort
about it; he somehow could not deem it quite genuine,
so casual and brief had been the dubbing ceremony, and
the feeling that the Regent Arran was less than adequate
as bestower. But the girls were delighted when he did tell
them, making a great thing of it, bowing and sirring him
regularly, Agnes declaring that she was going to confuse
everybody by becoming Lady Maxwell before, in due
course, becoming Lady Herries, when there was already
an Agnes, Lady Maxwell. But she asserted that Sir John
well deserved the honour, and pointed out that it would
give him the greater authority as deputy warden.

He gave an account of the parliamentary proceedings to
Lord Herries, still bedridden, who showed some interest,
particularly over the decision on King Henry's demands,
and agreeing with it on the whole. He feared, however, that
there would be repercussions from the English, and the
wardens' services might well be required before long.

Agnes's wedding preparations appeared to be well
advanced – John surprised at how much of such seemed
to be required. He was of no great help.

The sisters were concerned for Robert, whom they
liked – as, of course, was John. But there was nothing
that anybody could do about it, with their father having

given his word to Henry. They could only hope that the royal marriage agreement would appease the Tudor, despite those safeguard clauses.

That evening, round the withdrawing-room fire, they discussed future plans. The couple agreed that they should live here at Terregles, where John would eventually be master anyway. His father had settled on him the small properties of Barclosh and Corra in the Kirkcudbright parish of Kirkgunzeon, as his portion; but this was some distance off and less than convenient for wardenly duties, whereas Terregles was. So the south-west tower of the castle would be set aside for them, ample accommodation – even, Catherine declared, with a giggle, when there might be children to house.

At bedtime, John took it for granted that he entered Agnes's chamber with her, to go through the undressing routine; and despite the short time now to wait for comprehensive fulfilment, the bride-to-be had to urge restraint, still more persuasively than heretofore, of those eager lips and hands, the more necessary and onerous as she herself became aroused. Grudgingly the man bowed to pressure, but not so much as to let it spoil the bliss of the occasion altogether.

Only nine nights more . . .

The day following, John decided to make a ride round the nearer dales, in the interests of wardenship, and to give the lairds there some information as to the parliament, and thus help them to feel something of involvement in the realm's affairs and be the more aware of their duties in its defence. Agnes and Catherine, who accompanied him, were consistent in introducing him as *Sir* John, although how much this impressed the tough Armstrong, Johnstone, Irvine and Elliot leaders was doubtful.

That night's bed-going was made less fraught with reservations in that Agnes had to announce that her monthly woman's handicap was upon her – as well, she pointed out, with but eight more days to go.

In the morning it was back to Caerlaverock, to find his

father returned and, surprisingly again, Angus with him. The two seemed to have become very close. The earl, of course, being very much a widower and lacking a family, found Threave Castle on its islet a remote and less than friendly place to steward Galloway from. So perhaps he found Caerlaverock more congenial.

Their father disappointed the young men by announcing that Robert could not attend the wedding, as the hostages were to set off southwards three days hence. So John would have to do without a groomsman.

The brothers' parting, in the event, was less taxing on the emotions than might have been the case, with one heading for unknown exile and the other for marital joy, for quite a cavalcade descended on Caerlaverock, its last call in Scotland, eight young men dressed in their best, with an escort of a score of armed men, with the banners of their several houses, intent on making a suitable impression on the English as they went to their so certain destination but uncertain destiny. In the circumstances, farewells were moderate and feelings left largely unspoken.

The Maxwell party which made for Terregles those few days later still included the Earl of Angus, who declared that he would be interested to meet the Herries family, since his great-aunt, the Lady Janet Douglas, had married Lord Herries's grandfather, whence came young Janet's name. Fortunately the weather was fine, otherwise the Countess Agnes would have been much displeased over the dozen-mile ride, she being no great horsewoman.

All was ready for the occasion when they arrived, the bride very lovely in a handsome pale blue taffeta gown trimmed with gold and silver embroidery, which Agnes herself had made, her sisters also very well turned out, so that John's sister Margaret felt much outshone since she had had to come in gear more suitable for horse-riding. Lord Herries had been brought down to the withdrawing-room, where he reposed on a couch, and where the actual ceremony would take place, since the hall was all set for the wedding feast afterwards. The castle did have an oratory, a small chapel, but it was not large enough for the occasion. The parish priest, looking distinctly agitated in all this lofty company, sought to keep out of the way as much as possible, despite Agnes's attentions.

In the circumstances, the custom of bride and groom not seeing each other until the actual nuptials could not be adhered to; indeed, Agnes had to be in charge of the entire proceedings, acting hostess in addition to all else, and this she did competently as well as pleasingly, a happy and attractive figure, much admired by the guests, even by Countess Agnes, and making John very proud.

All being prepared, there was in fact little delay after the groom's party had arrived, before the service, this in order that the visitors could get sat down to refreshment reasonably soon after their ride, and also that Lord Herries did not get over-tired. John was the last to complain about that, for the sooner they could get the formalities over the happier he would be.

So, after only wine and sweetmeats to sustain the new arrivals, the ceremony commenced, with the priest instructed to make it brief without sacrificing dignity, consequence and significance. The withdrawing-room was just large enough to contain them without undue crowding, with only the two families and Angus involved, the hazard of Lord Herries's health and ability to attend having been a major factor in making all arrangements, and inhibiting invitations for friends.

A small table had been placed at one end of the room to act as altar, and on this were set the elements for the nuptial mass. Before it, the priest took his place, with Herries's couch sidelong nearby where he could see all. John went to stand alone in front of the rest, missing his brother's presence and support. Young Janet played soft music on her clarsach. All remained standing save for her father.

At the signal of a change in the melody, Agnes and Catherine came in from the hall, to join John, who bowed to them, a little stiffly. After a suitable pause, the castle servitors, six of them, came in to stand at the back.

The music ceasing, the priest took over.

In something of a gabble at first he commenced the Latin ritual, but soon moderated it to a more appropriate intoning. Not that John was concerned. The more swiftly all this was got over the better, as far as he was concerned. He was very much aware of Agnes standing so close to him, the rise and fall of her bosom indicating emotion. He wondered if it was permitted that he touch her arm. Probably not.

The flow of words went on, rising and falling also, John making little effort to translate them into anything meaningful, his mind on the woman at his side whom he had thus won, her excellence in beauty and character and abilities, and his great good fortune. What had he done to deserve her? The service – mere words spoken by this somewhat uninspiring little man – was that enough really to alter their entire lives and standing? Make them one in the sight of God and man? It was all, in some fashion, like that knighthood, however much more important, a mere form of words and gestures. Was this truly a changing of persons, a new unity? Or had the real marriage taken place when they both recognised their mutual love? Was that a sacrilegious thought?

John had got thus far when the nearest touch, less than a nudge, from Agnes brought the realisation that the celebrant had reached the vows and ring stage, and his co-operation was called for. Fumbling a little, he produced from a pocket the gold circlet, a family heirloom, and, repeating the vows, slid it on the outstretched finger, and was emboldened to squeeze the soft warm arm at the same time, as they were duly declared now to be man and wife.

Agnes turned and met his gaze with the most beatific smile of love and promise, wordless but sufficiently eloquent. That, now, was union, wedlock, no mere form of phrase and token sign. Now, suddenly,

142

as they knelt to receive the blessing, he felt married indeed.

But they were not finished yet. There was still the nuptial mass, involving the priest consecrating the bread and wine on that table and then summoning the couple to come forward and partake, followed by Catherine and Janet and then the rest of the company, before taking the elements over to Lord Herries on his couch. A final benediction on them all, and it was over. Catherine was weeping, for some reason.

John Maxwell realised that he was an impatient man. Now, all he wanted was to be alone with Agnes and to demonstrate his so fervent feelings. But that was not to be, indeed not for some considerable time. First of all there were the congratulations, which seemed to him prolonged, however well earned. Then, with Lord Herries looking faint, he had to be got off up to his bed, this requiring careful yet muscle-taxing handling to get him up the narrow, twisting, corkscrew and defensive stairway of the castle, this heedfully supervised by the new Lady Maxwell. Thereafter followed the wedding feast, quite a banquet, representing much preparation and raiding of the castle's ice-house, much speech-making thereafter, Lord Maxwell's brief, Angus's more eloquent and flowery, and very complimentary towards the bride and also her sisters, not forgetting Countess Agnes and Margaret Maxwell, he very much the ladies' man. John had to reply as best he could.

Fortunately, in the new husband's regard, the dozen-mile ride back, before darkness descended, meant that the Caerlaverock company could not delay long once this was over, for there had never been any suggestion that all should stay the night at Terregles in the circumstances. So, the countess urging, a move was made reasonably soon, the required well-meant advice given to the couple, with the farewells, John waving them off thankfully.

Agnes's sisters, excited by all the day's happenings, could not be dismissed nor avoided, but presently John

143

contrived to get his wife alone for a brief few minutes by taking her up to see how her father fared, and after assuring themselves that he was all but asleep and requiring no immediate attention, escaping out to Agnes's own room, there to take her in his arms and all but devour her with kisses and endearments. Understanding, indeed co-operating, she voiced her happiness and rejoicing, praising his behaviour thus far and his hard-sought patience, declaring her love, and promising, promising, even as she led him back to the door and out. She was all his now. Only a little more waiting and she would prove it.

So back to the sisters and a strange evening of doing nothing in particular, for they had already eaten more than adequately, and after the day's highlights a settling down before the fire seemed somehow incongruous. Clearly newly-weds should go off on their own without undue delay after the ceremony; but where could these two have gone? Agnes made the best of it by calling for music and singing, which certainly helped to pass the time and dispel the sense of waiting.

Catherine it was who, in due course, pretended to yawn, and suggested that honey wine and some light fare was called for before their retiral, and went off to see to it, to John's agreement and gratitude. That was not all, for when she had returned and they had duly partaken, she and Janet, who had been allowed to put off bed-going on this occasion, announced that they were going to escort the bridal couple to their new quarters in the south-west tower, this with meaningful looks.

So all four rose and proceeded downstairs and along a vaulted corridor and then up into this semi-detached, circular tower of three storeys and an attic, with its own parapet and wall walk which, it appeared, was now to be the married home. It was sparsely furnished as yet as regards the living-room on the first floor, but very adequately and comfortably as far as the main second-floor bedchamber was concerned. This was the first John had seen of it all.

A bright fire blazed, lamps lit all, and a large tub of steaming water invited. Catherine and Janet, with much concern that all was in order and no least detail neglected, at last took themselves off, with their own kisses and giggles.

Husband and wife faced each other alone, the bridal night theirs.

John had had plenty of time to anticipate this and to consider well. Despite his urgency, there was now no need for haste, he had told himself; it would be much better, for them both, to savour this longed-for, incomparable occasion, this fulfilment, not exactly slowly but unhurriedly, with the fullest appreciation, impatience neither suitable nor called for. They had all night ahead of them, and all the joy and desire and longing now available, at least for himself. And he must make it as nearly so for Agnes as he knew how.

So, after a first holding of each other and a gazing into eyes, he took her hand and led her over to stand by the fire, quietly, silent indeed. There, after a few moments he stroked and kissed her hair, but gently, only that.

Taking a deep breath she turned to him. "I am yours now, all yours, John my dear. And, and you are mine!"

"Aye. For now and for ever!" he said. "The waiting over. We are one, one! How I have longed for this."

"Think you that *I* have not?"

"You have, lass?"

"You doubt it? That a woman may love and need and desire less than a man? It is not so. I, I will prove it!" And reaching out, there in the flickering firelight, she began to unbutton his doublet.

Almost he grabbed her, to reverse the process, but stopped himself in time, perceiving the better, fists clenched to keep his hands from touching her and snatching at her gown. But that self-control was needed was in itself a joy, a rapture, promise indeed.

No doubt she was aware of the effect on him and, while not pulling and wrenching at his clothing, did not linger over the business either. He did aid her a little by kicking off his footgear while she unbuckled his belt and slid his breeches down to join his doublet on the floor, even though she had a little difficulty in getting them down at the front. Then there was only his shirt to get off, which was less of a problem, and there he stood before her, all naked and very positive masculinity.

She drew back, to gaze and gaze. Then, reaching up, deep-breathing, began to pull at her own dress.

Quickly now, he moved to stop that, his turn, and to be relished not rushed. He knew the process, of course, from past experience, and was the more skilful; but there was no disenchantment on the repetition, not with the prospects ahead and all the loveliness to uncover anew. He could not prevent her from helping him here and there.

So, at length, they were able to stand as their Creator had modelled them, holding hands but at arm's length, looking, surveying, revelling in what they saw and could now claim. There was no need for words.

But there was a need now, nevertheless, vehement need, probably on both their parts, although it was John who acted. Stepping forward, he swept her up bodily into his arms and carried her over to the bed, ignoring that steaming water-tub – that could wait. Setting her down, he deliberately removed her arms which were clasped around his neck, so that he could look down at her lying there, all warm, eager, beauteous invitation, before he fell on her with lips and hands and person, seeking, exploring, imperative, and receiving no check.

Yet even now he restrained himself, that impatient man, restrained hands and body that is, but not lips, for, pushing her back, he proceeded to kiss her all over, front and back, above and below, a most thorough and all but prolonged process, which had the woman twisting and jerking and gasping, shaking her head so that her long hair had to be lifted aside time and again lest any least portion of her was left unkissed and aroused.

At length his own arousal became too clamant to be

resisted further, and he lowered himself on to her, he seeking, she guiding, and no obstruction encountered. Truly joined together at last, after all the waiting, time no longer signified. In truest unison they consummated their marriage, bliss achieved.

Perhaps the bliss was more complete on the man's side than on the woman's, at least that was the impression, for he was not entirely inexperienced in the matter whereas Agnes was. Her pressure continued for a little after he began to relax, before she sank back, but murmuring endearments and kissing him still, if not satiated, at least greatly rejoiced and moved.

Presently, when he rolled over to her side, hands at least still caressing her upthrust breasts, he remembered that water-tub.

"Come," he said. "They, they say that cleanliness is next to godliness. And have we not much to thank God for this night?" He eased himself out of the bed.

She followed him, after a while, and came to help him wash himself down, but in no very thorough fashion, saying little, but her fingers stroking his skin tenderly. When it came to his turn, John was much more assiduous, going as it were into detail, which had effects other than ablutionary. Soon, with only a token towelling, he was leading her back to the bed.

And now he was able to take his time and give her more fully what she needed and clearly found to her infinite satisfaction, and proving in the process that a woman could be as passionate as any man.

John, rejoicing, went on to his own second fulfilment.

With the night, and all the days and nights ahead of them, they slept, arms entwined.

147

PART TWO

12

Marriage, sadly, not always comes up to expectations; but for Agnes and John it most certainly did, and surpassed them. They were both strong-minded characters, but happily their strengths tended to complement each other, in the main, rather than conflict. Not that they could not disagree on occasion, but they were able to accept the other's right to their own opinions and attitudes without umbrage.

Feelings could be tested, inevitably, especially with the pair sharing a house with the two sisters, although these did seek to leave the south-west tower very much to the couple themselves. And, of course, Agnes having more or less run Terregles for long, could not and did not suddenly resign her duties therein. And with Lord Herries still alive, however bedridden, John could not seem to play the laird. Not that he desired to, even though he did see things that he would have changed had he been fully in charge, not so much about the castle as in the estate.

Joyful as these first weeks of wedlock were, the nation's affairs could not fail to preoccupy and concern the Deputy Warden of the West March, especially with his father as warden, and in some measure involved in the dealings with Henry Tudor, a connection which distinctly worried the son, not only in the impact the situation might have on his hostage brother.

The regent sent south two ambassadors to expound to Henry the decisions of parliament, Sir James Learmonth, the High Treasurer, and Sir William Hamilton of Sanquhar, kinsman of Arran. Their efforts at London were however less than fruitful. The Tudor, while accepting the agreement for the royal children's betrothal, resented the delay in the little queen's being sent into his keeping, and was furious at the safeguard conditions imposed. He sent the envoys home very promptly, they all but fearing for their liberty – and not alone. For with them he sent Sir Ralph Sadler, one of his most trusted courtiers, to be "guardian" of the child Mary, to be ever about her presence; this only for two years, after which she was to come back with him to London, whatever that parliament had said about *ten* years. Not only this, but Henry, declaring himself to be rightful Lord Superior of Scotland, was prepared to appoint the Regent Arran as King of Scotland North of Forth, repeating the offer of the English Princess Elizabeth as wife for Arran's son, on condition that the so-called safeguard clauses were immediately deleted. And just to indicate that he was not to be trifled with, he ordered the impounding and detaining of all Scots ships in English ports, and the capture of any found sailing in English waters.

So the Scots were left in no doubts that neighbourly relations with England were far from set fair, and the March wardens warned to be on the alert for further English "persuasions". It did not look as though the young hostages in London were likely to be released in the near future, nor to have their stay there made enjoyable.

While all this was in train, the Scots were not entirely inactive. Cardinal Beaton, now Chancellor, using the Abbot of Paisley, a half-brother of Arran, as envoy, concluded an agreement with the King of France to make threatening gestures against England, a state of undeclared war already existing; and not only that, but to send an expeditionary force to Scotland, to help the pressure on the Auld Alliance, and to support Holy Church in the northern kingdom. Henry the Second was indeed concerned to keep his English namesake's French ambitions in check, with the threat of war on two fronts.

During all this activity on the three nations' affairs, more local precautions and operations had to be maintained. There were wardens' meetings, which John had to attend in his father's place, to make plans for united action along the borderline in the event of English raids, and how to react should there be full-scale invasion rather than mere forays. Patrols had to be organised more or less constantly on the Marches, and these to gain the dalesmen's co-operation. The Galloway forces had to be roused and encouraged to take a more active part in the West March defence, instead of their long-standing somewhat detached attitude, John acting there in the name of Angus, the Steward, as well as on his own and his father's authority. Angus seemed to spend most of his time at Caerlaverock these days.

In that connection there was an unexpected development, a surprise at least to John. Angus was to wed Margaret Maxwell, an extraordinary union which presumably was contrived for some purpose by Lord Maxwell and the earl. Admittedly Angus was very fond of the opposite sex; but Margaret seemed to be on the young side for a man almost old enough to be her grandfather. Not that she seemed to be in any way loth, for so seemingly shy a creature. John had never been really close to this sister of his; indeed she was hard to win close to. But she appeared to find Angus acceptable. Perhaps she relished being a countess, wed to an earl. Or perhaps the fact that his second wife had been a queen, actually Henry Tudor's sister and widow of James the Fourth, added some sort of glamour to the marriage. Lord Maxwell had never been a fatherly man, and it might be that Angus's attentions supplied some need. At any rate, no complaints were forthcoming.

A couple of months after their own wedding, then, John and Agnes attended another, this on a much more ambitious scale, held in the great St Michael's Church in Dumfries, the Bishop of Whithorn and Galloway officiating, assisted by three other clergy, and large numbers of Maxwells and Douglases present, including the famous Sir George Douglas, Angus's so clever brother, known to have the ear of the English monarch, and used as an emissary by both nations. John would not have trusted him a yard, but perhaps he was prejudiced. Altogether John was uneasy over his father's link-up with the Douglases, which had all come about since his captivity in England.

He and his wife excused themselves from the festivities thereafter at Caerlaverock on the grounds that Agnes did not want to be away from her father's bedside for overlong. He was now failing notably.

In fact Lord Herries died a few days later, as quietly as he had lived, the girls finding him dead in bed one morning. Fond as they were of him, all felt that it was in essence a happy release for him, gone to a much better life than he had had for these last years. The simple but moving private funeral service in the Terregles burial ground two days later was attended only by the family and the local folk, all of whom had reason to think highly of their lord, a kindly master who might have made little impact on the national scene but who would be missed by those who knew him.

John asked himself if there was a lesson for him to learn there.

He also wondered whether *he* was now Lord Herries? The regent had reportedly agreed that, in marrying the heiress Agnes, and no male heir available, he should, through her, succeed to the style and dignity, as was the dead man's wish. Did this now follow without further concern, or was some procedure and ceremonial necessary by the regent or in parliament, to make him a duly authentic Lord of Parliament? Nobody he asked seemed to know, even Angus; for it was not a circumstance which happened very often. Not that it greatly concerned John, for it would not affect his life in any major respect. His wife and her sisters began to refer to him as his lordship, part banteringly; but, oddly, Agnes continued to call herself Lady *Maxwell*, presumably as a compliment

154

to the man she had married and the honour he had won, not merely inherited.

They let it go at that.

Soon after the funeral, in September now, a brief and all but token coronation ceremony was held for the infant Queen Mary at Stirling Castle; but this apparently did not call for any large attendance of magnates, in the circumstances, although Angus did go to it, earls being the successors of the ancient Celtic *ri*, or sub-kings, and essential witnesses for the crowning of the Ard Righ, or High King, or in this case, Queen. Lord Maxwell saw no need to be present, and his son perceived his wardenly functions as more vital; for his father, although still West March Warden in name, having been appointed so for life in 1517, was in fact leaving the duties to John, and his fellow East and West Wardens accepting him as their colleague, while they still resented the Earl of Bothwell being appointed as lieutenant, allegedly senior to them.

John was, in fact, all but beating a trail to Ferniehirst Castle in Jed Forest in the Middle March that autumn and early winter, for the ever-present threat of trouble from over the border was made the more immediate by the reported arrival of two of Henry's experienced commanders, Sir Ralph Eure and Sir Brian Layton, on the south side of Tweed. Word of these came from spies at Berwick, Norham, Wark, Redesdale and other English border strongholds. Whether they represented one more of the Tudor's persuasive threats, or were indeed sent there to lead or prepare for invasion, was the question. But it meant that the wardens had to be prepared for swift and concerted action, for these were veteran campaigners from the south, not just the local Northumbrian and Cumbrian leaders. Reports of their visits to areas all along the borderline were sufficiently alarming as to demand varied but detailed plans on the Scots' part.

So John was kept busy, for the West March was quite the largest of the three, the most scattered and therefore the most vulnerable to attack. Agnes accompanied him on many of his visitations, a great help as well as the best of companions.

Not only John and the other wardens were kept in suspense that winter and the following spring, all Scotland was. Despite the presence of Eure and Layton, no actual invasion took place, although Scots ships continued to be seized and the hostages remained in durance. The Maxwells did not hear how Robert and the others fared; but since Henry was keeping up the pressure, the likelihood was that their conditions would be less than pleasant. It was not until May, in fact, that the news broke – invasion, Henry's very scanty patience run out. But invasion not where was expected, over the border. The Earl of Hertford, Henry's kinsman and Lord Chamberlain of England, brought a great fleet up to the Firth of Forth to land an army at Leith, the port of Edinburgh, and set that town ablaze.

Beaton – for he took charge, rather than Arran – mustering all defences for the capital city, sent word hot-foot to the Borderland to expect a supportive and possibly the main invasion there. So John and his colleagues hastily assembled all their strength to face Eure and Layton at last, all along the marches, or at least at the passes through the Cheviot, Kielder and Bewcastle Hills, where the passage of large numbers of men was possible. Just where the English might strike was anybody's guess; but from all the toing and froing reported from that side, it could well be at several points simultaneously. John took up his main position in Liddesdale, near Hermitage, Bothwell's seat, although he made constant visits up and down his long line, from the Carter Bar where he met the Middle March, to the Solway shore, to ensure readiness and vigilance.

Nothing happened, no secondary invasion developed. But they had to wait and wait, a difficult situation to maintain, to keep their mustered troops alert or even in position, or there at all – for it had become hay harvest time by now, and the oat harvest loomed ahead, vital for most there, nine-tenths of them land workers. The commanders did allow relays of men to go home for brief spells, lit beacons to summon them back in haste, but the majority must always be camped ready, a dire circumstance for such folk, any sort of discipline hard indeed to maintain, idleness leading inevitably to trouble, especially for any local inhabitants, the women particularly.

They got little or no news from the north, only rumours, these mainly brought by wandering friars, and far from detailed or conclusive. The gist of such was that the walled city of Edinburgh had not fallen, thanks largely to the useful arrival of the hoped-for French force under a General de Thermes, which came safely to the Clyde port of Dumbarton in the west. But Hertford was ravaging the surrounding Lothians in savagery, his army burning, slaying, raping.

It was grievous, at least for John and his like, to sit idle there, facing south, while all this was going on behind them and when they might be going to help their fellows. But this could be the English strategy, distraction to aid their principal attack over the border. The so-trying watch and ward had to be kept up.

Then, at last, in late June, firm word came to them from Beaton. The English fleet had sailed off southwards, leaving Hertford and his army, certainly most of it, based on Leith and remaining as harshly aggressive as ever, although still Edinburgh held out. The reason for this was uncertain. The fleet might have gone to fetch reinforcements. Or it might have been no longer required there, with Hertford intending to turn southwards to assail southern Scotland and the Borderland from the rear. This was the most likely explanation, and the Chancellor's instructions were, in effect, for the warden's forces to turn about and face northwards now, prepared to assist the army which Beaton was gathering to assault the invaders, but for them not to abandon their position against possible attack by Eure and Layton, a complicated requirement. There was, the courier told them, another conceivable reason for the fleet's departure. It could be that it had gone to fetch cannon, with which Hertford was not at present equipped, for the battering down of Edinburgh's walls and defences. This was a grim possibility.

The border surveillance had to go on, two-way now and none the easier for that. A large number of John's force were dalesmen, not the most patient and amenable of mortals, essentially independent and scornful of orders, Beaton's, the regent's or anyone else's. Fortunately they had largely developed a respect for John, otherwise he could not have maintained any sort of coherent force in place.

He won back to Terregles now and again, brief visits; but more often Agnes, with Dod Armstrong and sometimes Catherine, came looking for him. He was seeing a lot of Bothwell inevitably, indeed he spent many nights at Hermitage Castle, and came to find that earl none so ill a collaborator even though he was scarcely of a friendly nature, and complained much of non-cooperation by the other wardens.

No attack by Hertford's forces did develop south of the Lammermuir, Moorfoot and Pentland Hills, any more than from over the border. John almost wished that it would, so frustrating was this endless waiting. And with August, the oats fell to be harvested, essential provision for the survival of man and beast. Men were deserting his force daily, in consequence.

Then, as September came in, another messenger arrived from the Chancellor at Stirling, who, despite being a cleric, appeared to be acting commander-in-chief. And he brought extraordinary news. Hertford and his army were cooped up in the walled town of Haddington, besieged. This had been made possible by the belated arrival of a large force from the north, under the Gordon Earl of Huntly, with reinforcements from Atholl and Fife, that and the military genius of the French General de Thermes.

Excellent as these tidings were, there was however an ominous footnote. A small squadron of English ships had arrived again off Leith, possibly bringing the necessary cannon for Hertford; and when these had discovered that the port was back in Scots hands, they had turned and sailed back home whence they had come. But it was inconceivable that Henry Tudor would allow his kinsman, friend and chamberlain to be left besieged in Haddington, or anywhere else, and they must expect a major assault now to free him and subdue Scotland, the time for mere threatenings over.

So it was a still more alert watch to be kept on the border. At least now they ought not to have to face two ways.

They had another couple of weeks to wait before the cardinal's fears were confirmed and the Tudor's anger demonstrated, urgent orders accompanying the news. Part of the Borderers' force was to hasten northwards – not all of it since there might well be a complementary assault by Eure and Layton. Another and much larger English fleet had arrived in the Forth. It had not been able to land its troops at Leith because that place was now protected by cannon brought down from Edinburgh Castle, under expert French gunners. But there were other ports and landing-places on the south shores of Forth, and the English would disembark somewhere, nothing more certain, and probably as near to Haddington in East Lothian as they could win. Such landings must be opposed with their utmost strength. So it was all haste.

John, recognising that his impatient mosstroopers and dalesmen would probably welcome this action, and would not take happily to Bothwell's command, decided himself to lead them northwards, leaving the earl to see to the West March vigil.

Even he found himself looking forward to action at last, whatever Agnes's doubts and fears.

13

At the head of two hundred mosstroopers John rode north for Edinburgh. If the news sent to them was accurate they ought not to encounter any of the English on the way, but they went prepared. Just what their role was to be was not specified, presumably either to try to prevent landings or to attack enemy already landed. They hoped that, horsed dalesmen as they were, they would not be called upon to take part in the static and tedious task of siegery, assuming that Hertford was still penned in Haddington.

Threading the Lammermuir Hills by the Soutra pass on the second day, they were none so far from Haddington in fact; but in that rolling terrain they could not see the town, although, much further away, they could see Edinburgh, because of its towering Arthur's Seat, castle-rock and other prominent eminences, outlined against the blue of the Firth of Forth.

It was dusk before they reached the city, and John left his company to camp in the royal hunting-park which surrounded Arthur's Seat, while he went to try to discover the situation and what was required of them. He found this none so simple, for the gates of the walled city were shut at the darkening, and it took much shouting to convince the guards at the Abbey Gate that he was Sir John Maxwell, Deputy Warden of the West March, with reinforcements for the Chancellor's army, seeking instructions. Presumably, having recently been under siege themselves, the custodians were suspicious, even of a single horseman.

Once within, he made for the only house that he knew, Angus's lodging in the Canongate. Not that the earl would be there, but his brother Sir George used it, and was the sort of man who would know the situation, however doubtful his allegiances.

Douglas was out, John discovered, but was expected back shortly. So he elected to wait, glad of the refreshment offered after his long riding. His men would fend for themselves very ably.

Sir George arrived back shortly, with a lady companion whom he introduced merely as Elizabeth. John was somewhat embarrassed to seem an interloper on such an occasion, and declared that he must hasten back to his mosstroopers once he had learned what the position was. Douglas seemed nowise put out, a handsome man, who bore himself with a sort of habitual flourish. John had met him, of course, briefly, at Angus's wedding at Dumfries. He was now, after all, some sort of connection by marriage.

He proved to be as knowledgeable as expected and hoped for. The situation, he declared, was involved and fluid. Hertford was still besieged, although some small number of his people had broken out of Haddington by night and were said to be roaming the countryside. The large English fleet, held at bay off Leith by superior cannon to their own, had now moved off in small groups up and down the coast, no doubt looking for the best place to make a major landing. De Thermes, the French artillery expert, was put in the difficult position of trying to ensure that his unwieldy, oxen-drawn cannon were, if possible, reasonably near at hand to prevent any such landing, a difficult task indeed. But since the assumption was that the fleet was there to try to relieve Hertford, the preferred landing could be assumed to be somewhere near to Haddington. So the Frenchman was taking his artillery along the East Lothian coast. But even that was no simple solution, for there were a dozen and more miles of possible landing-places east of Musselburgh. Huntly, Argyll and the other northern lords were forming a barrier, with their troops, along that stretch. And the cardinal himself, with the regent, was basing headquarters at that town, Musselburgh at the mouth of the Esk, to oversee all.

John, grateful for this information, took his leave. In the morning he and his people would make for this Musselburgh.

The dalesmen had, to be sure, brought supplies of basic food with them in their saddle-bags; but when John got back to the camp he found fires burning and beef and mutton being roasted on spits over the flames. He forbore to ask how this meat had been obtained, but was not inhibited from partaking thereof.

They rode the five miles eastwards in the morning to the ancient coastal town of Musselburgh where one of Scotland's many Rivers Esk – which merely meant the Gaelic *uisge*, water – reached the firth, a historic place right back to Roman times, when it was called Inveresk, and where the good Regent Moray, the Bruce's nephew, dying, had called it the Honest Toun, meaning loyal. There they found the burgh occupied by great numbers of armed men, and the citizens not looking over-kindly on new arrivals, however loyal.

Apparently the regent and Chancellor were occupying the Town House and Tolbooth, many nobles with them. There John went for instructions.

He did not meet the cardinal, who was in council with various leaders, but he did see Arran, who seemingly tended to leave military matters to Beaton, odd as this might seem. Rather vague as he was, he remembered the man he had knighted and, John noted, referred to him as Sir John, not as Lord Herries, which might or might not be significant. What *was* important was the news that the English fleet appeared to be reassembling off Aberlady Bay, another ten miles down the coast, and it looked as though that would be the landing-place, just four miles north of Haddington. His advice to John was to get his men there just as quickly as possible. De Thermes was already heading there with his cannon, had been since dawn; and the Scots army was to form a great line inland, where there was a long stretch of marshland flanking the Peffer Burn, which the English, if land they did, would have to cross to reach the Haddington area; this, below the modest Garleton Hills, would act as something of a moat.

They caught up with the lumbering oxen-train just as they came in sight of the great V-shaped bay of Aberlady, almost three miles wide at the mouth and half that probing into the land. It formed the estuary of the Peffer, quite a major stream, and apart from the burn's actual course through the mid-bay, the rest actually dried out at low water. This was the situation now, tide out; and sure enough, as they rounded the westernmost headland, there was the concentration of shipping lying off, undoubtedly waiting for higher water to allow them to enter the bay. Eleven vessels could be counted. Craft of that size would require fairly deep water to make a close approach to land.

At the very head of the bay John saw a great castle soaring above the levels of saltings and mudflats and sand, well over a mile inland from the wide sand-bar at the mouth. The castle was obviously strategically sited where it not only dominated the head of the bay but the entry to the Peffer and a smaller tributary, itself a defensive situation. Presumably this would be where the Frenchmen and their artillery were making for. With the tide so far out and the bay shallow, it would be hours before those ships could sail in close enough to make a landing for their troops. They might, of course, send their men ashore in small boats, indeed they probably would have to, there seeming to be no piers or quays reaching out to allow large vessels to tie up. There was time, therefore, for the cannon to reach the castle and be got into position.

John led his party on. Luffness Castle proved to be an impressive place, four-square within a wide water-filled moat of some three hundred yards on each side. High curtain walling rose within the moat, some twenty-five feet, with a wall walk along the top, and at each corner was an angle tower, circular, with, facing the bay, twin drum towers to support the portcullis and drawbridge which guarded the only entrance. Within stood a tall and massive keep.

John had heard of this place, knew something of its story, for it had its own fame. Built in the twelfth century by one of the Earls of Dunbar and March, of the ancient Celtic royal line, it had fairly soon passed to the Lindsay family by marriage, one of whom, Sir David de Lindsay of Luffness, had been regent for the young Alexander the Third – indeed, the present Lord Lyon King of Arms, another Sir David Lindsay, was a descendant. The Lindsays had grown very powerful, married into the royal family, and become Earls of Crawford, gaining lands all over Scotland. So, as time went on, they were but seldom at Luffness, and appointed a family called Bickerton as hereditary keepers. In time the Bickertons managed to buy the property from the Lindsays, and reigned here as its lords. Only a few years before this present, the Bickerton line had ended in a daughter, who had carried Luffness to a Hepburn of Waughton nearby, kinsman of the Earl of Bothwell. It was from that earl that John had learned all this, at Hermitage. Sir Patrick Hepburn was the present laird of Luffness, his wife the last of the Bickertons.

The Marchmen rode past the village of Aberlady and joined the bay thereafter. Ahead of them they saw a small fishing haven and cottages tucked in just eastwards of the castle, where suddenly the salt marsh and mudflats narrowed in and the Peffer became a stream, this little community no doubt serving also as the castleton for the Luffness retainers.

A sense of great activity met the newcomers' eyes, men by the hundred digging earth, sand and mud and carrying it and carting it up to heighten the natural bank which rose above the tidal levels before the castle. Wondering over this, John led his people up the round-about approach to the fortalice.

Everywhere were armed men and horses, over-taxing the limited space in and around the castle, John's two hundred merely adding to the confusion. Leaving his people, he went to try to learn what they could usefully contribute.

Seeking commanders, he was directed to the scene of the sand-and-soil heaping and piling and consolidating, this all under the direction of two men, very different in appearance and stature, one tall and youngish, the other small, stooping and of middle years, but remarkably spry, the latter shouting to the digging and spading toilers in very doubtful English and proving to be none other than the French general, de Thermes. The other was the laird here, Sir Patrick Hepburn.

Announcing the arrival of his mosstroopers, John was told by Hepburn, somewhat coolly, that if these could demean themselves sufficiently to dig and carry soil, they could make themselves of some use in the building of this great embankment and mound. The general required it, apparently, for his cannon, which were reputedly on their way, he having come on in advance to prepare it – for it seemed that the artillery pieces were far too heavy and large to be mounted on the castle curtain walling, so this high base had to be provided for them, however little it did for his property. Hepburn sounded as though he could be an awkward character, and clearly looked upon the Marchmen as but reivers and cattle-thieves.

John went back and told his followers what was expected of them, and admittedly they did not take kindly to the idea of manual labour of this sort. They had come to fight, not to dig and toil like serfs. But, telling them that they could probably injure the invaders more by so doing than by the use of their lances and swords, John set them to work. And all hands were needed, for the bank required a vast amount of soil to raise it to the height and width and solidity de Thermes demanded; and the workers had to go ever further away to win the necessary rubble. Moreover, the tide was coming in, so time was vital.

The noise of clanking and rumbling at length heralded the arrival of the cannon, seven of them, great heavy pieces with barrels up to twelve feet in length, drawn by teams of groaning, slow-moving oxen. These had to be dragged up on to the new earthen bank, which seemingly was still less high than the general would have wished; and getting them up was in itself no light task, with many men having to reinforce the oxen, to push and pull with much puffing and heaving and swearing. Then they had to be positioned to de Thermes's satisfaction, spaced along the mound; and thereafter was more heavy labour in carrying up massive cannonballs by the score from carts which had followed the cannon, these with sacks of powder and braziers and fuel for lighting the necessary fuse-sticks.

All the time the bay was filling up.

John kept watching those ships. They did not seem to have moved, come no closer in, despite the rising tide. Hepburn explained curtly that even at highest tide nine-tenths of the bay was too shallow to take large vessels. These craft would have to follow the course of the Peffer through the mud- and sand-flats, unseen as it would be under the inflowing salt water, this course being considerably deeper than the rest. No doubt the Englishry had managed to pick up some local wretch of a fisherman to inform them, and would wait until the highest water to move in. The Frenchmen had been relying on this to give them time to make their own dispositions.

Now that the digging and carting had to be over, the dalesmen were interested to see the results of their labours, and how the cannon would perform, none of them being knowledgeable about artillery. So, although Hepburn said that John should now take his folk inland to join the long line of largely northern levies under Huntly and Argyll who were forming the barrier beyond the Peffer marshes, he demurred. The toilers should have their reward in seeing the cannon in action. Besides, they could be useful here should the enemy achieve a landing.

It was well into the afternoon before the ships at last

made their move, hoisting modest sail and starting to head westwards at first, in single file. They turned towards the land near the western headland, this causing Sir Patrick to declare that they were indeed well informed and knew what they were doing, for that way the Peffer entered the firth. Soon the vessels were turning eastwards again, coming ever closer.

How close? – that was the question. Would they come just as far as their draught would let them? Or anchor further off and send their men ashore in small boats? With the cannon loaded with ball, primed with powder, fuses laid and tarred sticks ablaze to light them, the French gunners waited. So did all.

On the English came, the watchers now all but holding their breaths. The craft were coming two abreast at this stage, very slowly under very little sail in the south-west breeze, all but feeling their way, one pair close behind another. Six hundred yards? Five? How much closer? Suddenly de Thermes smashed a fist down on an open palm, his wizened small features alight with devilish glee. Presumably that meant that the ships were now within range of his cannon. His gunners were watching him questioningly, but he flapped a hand at them, clearly telling them to wait. He was greedy for results, that one.

Could the Englishmen see what was waiting for them? Surely those long-snouted pieces on this mound would be evident. Hepburn grabbed John's arm and pointed.

"They have them! They also!" he jerked.

John saw cannon being pushed across decks to the bulwarks of the leading ships, smaller cannon, much smaller. Even so, de Thermes nodded grimly and, raising an arm, brought it down in a slashing gesture, to point at the vessels, a quite unmistakable command.

The waiting gunners, their pieces already lined up on targets, needed no further direction. Promptly lighted brands were applied to short fuses, the men then jumping back out of danger.

There was a brief pause as the fuses burned, then a succession of thunderous blasts which battered the eardrums, temporarily deafening the watchers, those nearest the guns staggering back with the shock of the explosions. Not all the bombards went off together, depending on the length of the respective fuses, and one did not fire at all, to the fist-shaking agitation of its gunners. But six did discharge, in clouds of acrid smoke, the pieces rearing backwards on their clumsy carriages, men scattering, hands up to ears and themselves cannoning into each other in the thick and sudden obscurity produced by the gunpowder.

All this reaction tended to prevent the eager spectators from immediately observing the effect of the salvo. When John could see, the haze dispersing, it was at first not to discern actual hits registered, damage done out there, if any. Then he perceived that one of the ship's masts and sail was hanging over the side. On another there was obvious confusion, decking and woodwork destroyed and part of the bulwarks carried away. On still another, John perceived a gaping hole in the side, near the stern. Some of the shots may have missed their targets, but that major havoc had been wrought was apparent.

What became swiftly apparent also, however, was that gunfire could be a two-way exercise. Puffs of smoke from some of the English vessels intimated a return barrage. The bangs were muted – or perhaps it was the watchers' ears were still ringing with their own noise. John, for one, scarcely deemed that they were under fire until a ball whistled past to the left, to smash into the castle's curtain walling behind him, but there just to fall to the ground, not penetrating the stonework, indicating that it was beyond effective range. There were splashes in the water in front of them, near the shore. So far as he could see in the lingering smoke, no damage had been caused amongst the defenders. The ships' cannon were of considerably lesser calibre, and so their range shortened.

De Thermes was shouting in French to his gunners

unnecessarily, for they were all busy ramming balls into the barrels and pushing these down with ramrods, emptying powder into the breech cavities, fixing new fuses and re-aiming. Some were quicker than others, and the resultant fire was irregular, but none the less effective for that, the one piece which had failed to detonate before now leading. The resultant barrage of noise was therefore the more prolonged, and the drifting smoke as obscuring of the view. But the havoc wrought was probably no less, although John did see two spouts of water rise near the ships, indicating misses.

Then he saw two boats being lowered from one of the foremost ships, and filled with men. The general perceived this also, and yelled directions. Two of the hurriedly reloading cannon had their trunnions worked to lower the muzzles slightly, to aim at these, and duly fired. Neither scored a hit at the small targets, but the splashes in the water were near enough to alarm the boat-handlers sufficiently to have them turn back and hastily row to get behind their ship, out of sight.

De Thermes chuckled and all but danced.

More gunfire came from the English, but it was obviously more of defiance than with hopes of damaging effect. Only the odd ball reached the embankment and, so far as John could see, caused no hurt.

The Frenchmen kept up their bombardment, with not a few more hits being scored, another mast coming down and sundry gaps appearing in timbering.

How long it took to convince the English commanders that there was no profit for them in this situation John could not have told, for in these circumstances the passage of time just did not register. But results did, and presently whoever directed the squadron presumably summed up the position as hopeless, for sails were hoisted, fallen masts and gear cut loose and ships' bows turned round to head westwards. The commander would recognise, too, that the tide had turned again, and if they lingered overlong they could be aground. One vessel was so severely damaged that it had to be towed by another, but none was actually sunk.

This retiral brought forth cheers from the defenders, with congratulations heaped upon the gunners, Hepburn actually going to shake de Thermes's hand, John and others following suit.

They watched those eleven ships limp out into the firth. The question now was, what would they do next, go where, try what? This East Lothian coast was all shallow and sandy, save for a few cliff-bound stretches which were equally useless for sea-landings. North Berwick town had a harbour, but it was tidal. Dunbar, further on and facing the Norse Sea not into the Firth of Forth, had a deep-water haven, but it was a long way from Haddington, and defended by a strong castle. Would the invaders try there? Did they know about the state of these harbours? If not, then they would certainly be at something of a loss. They had been held off at Leith, further up-firth, in the first place.

As the defenders watched and wondered, they saw the English ships heading away from the bay, out into mid-firth and continue so to sail, towards the Fife shore, eleven miles away. That Fife coast was quite different from the south one, much less of sand and shallows, with many deep-water harbours, fishing the major preoccupation. The English might choose to go there, to lick their wounds and possibly wreak vengeance on the innocent Fifers; but that would not help the besieged Hertford.

Nobody seemed now to be in command at Luffness, to order what should be done in these circumstances, Sir Patrick being merely the laird and de Thermes only concerned with his artillery. John supposed that, oddly enough, *he* was probably the senior commander there, as a Deputy March Warden. He decided that the best course now was to take his men inland to join Huntly and Argyll, inform them of the situation and take their orders.

So, with the English ships now mere dots against the Fife

shoreline, he took his leave of de Thermes and Hepburn and, mounting, led his dalesmen south-eastwards over Luffness Muir, following roughly the course of the Peffer's windings, with the low green Garleton Hills rising ahead and marking the division between the Vale of Peffer and the Vale of Tyne in which lay Haddington.

They had no difficulty in finding the northern earls and their army, this stretching out for a couple of miles along the marshy vale. The Gordon and Campbell chiefs, they learned, had already been informed of the situation at Aberlady Bay by their own minions posted there, and saw no need to welcome John and his adherents. They were sending on a number of their people eastwards to Dunbar, some fifteen miles, in case the enemy fleet should decide to attempt a landing there, although they thought this unlikely. They had no instructions for John, indeed appeared to look down Highland noses on him and his dalesmen as a lesser breed which could well be dispensed with.

John decided that his best course was to head back the nine miles to Musselburgh, to discover from the regent and cardinal what might now be required of them, his horsemen glad enough to be riding free rather than hanging about either here at the Peffer, at Luffness or over the hill at the Haddington siegery.

At the town by the Esk's mouth they were again not first with the news about the enemy ships' rebuff and departure. The Fife coast was being kept under careful observation. But the Scots leadership was preoccupied with another aspect of aggression. A small party of English had been waylaid and captured as they headed for Edinburgh and Leith area, a courier and his escort, presumably unaware of Hertford's present besiegement; and on this courier they had found a letter, signed by Henry Tudor himself, giving his detailed instructions to that earl and other English commanders. Arran himself showed this document to John, so indignant and concerned was he over its contents. After a brief preamble anent the royal requirements as to the need for vigour, military co-operation and haste, it went on thus:

> . . . you are to burn Edinburgh town, so razed and defaced when you have sacked and gotten what you can of it, as that may remain for ever only a perpetual memory. Sack Holyrood House. Sack Leith, and burn and subvert it, and all the rest, putting man, woman and child to fire and sword without exception when any resistance shall be made against you. Fife also to be sacked, no creature in especial to be left alive in the cardinal's town of St Andrews. In the Marches, order to be taken so that the Borderers be still tormented . . . and brought to such penury that they shall not be able to live.

There was more in similar vein.

John was as shaken as was Arran, and astonished that any anointed monarch, and the self-proclaimed head of the Church of England, could so write and command, all but a madman surely in his lust for power and domination, and over a neighbouring and independent nation.

One aspect of this message did not fail to strike an alarm bell, as well as to create grievous resentment. This courier had ridden north from the border; therefore almost certainly he would have been in touch with the English commanders there, Eure and Layton, and would have shown them this monarchial letter and instructions. Therefore prompt attack was probably imminent, if not already started. So the place for the Deputy Warden of the West March was undoubtedly on his home ground. Sir John should head southward, the regent declared, discover the situation there, and send back word at the earliest.

John was all too ready to comply, and would have set off there and then, dusk as it now was; but he was advised to wait until the morning in case the English fleet made some other attempt on the south coast of Forth, and hasty

172

plans had to be made to counter it. A fast horsed force such as the dalesmen might well be useful.

All were glad to enjoy the facilities of Musselburgh town for the night. Fishing-boats were out in the firth, meantime, keeping watch on the Fife shore for enemy movements.

In the morning there was good news, at least on this front. The English squadron were under sail and heading out of the Forth estuary for the Norse Sea, not apparently making for the Dunbar area. The threat of seaborne invasion appeared to be over, for the time being at least.

The Marchmen could head for their March.

John arrived back at Terregles to much warmth and affection, a joy indeed. Let them have some peace now.

14

It was only months, however, before there were dire tidings. Major invasion over the border was in progress, mainly in the Middle and East Marches under Eure and Layton, although there was a strike into their own territory by Sir Thomas Wharton, the English West March Warden, this along the Solway shore. Lord Maxwell was dealing with this meantime and, Angus thought, containing it, from all accounts. But the word from the east was grim. Jedburgh and Kelso towns had been burned and hundreds slaughtered; and the English were ranging the land in large numbers, killing, ravishing, raping. It was disaster on a large scale, far more than the Scots wardens could cope with.

Much as he had been looking forward to a day or two with Agnes, John was faced with urgent duties, three of them. First to remuster the dalesmen, who had of course returned to their dales, these and any other lower-country levies which his father had not already called up. Second, to send information back to Arran and Beaton, as required, at Musselburgh, or more probably now at Edinburgh, urging powerful help for the Borderland, for this message using Dod Armstrong. Third, to try to contact his father and discover what was required here in the West March.

After a night in his wife's warm arms, he was off at first light next morning for Caerlaverock, Agnes insisting on going with him, anxious to see as much of him as might be.

At the great castle by the Solway they found Angus and his bride keeping company with the older countess, but not Lord Maxwell, who was reportedly somewhere in the Gretna and Chapelknowe area, having managed to drive back Wharton's invaders over their own border again, and was holding them there, although anticipating that they would be summoning reinforcements from Carlisle.

It was a very different Angus who told John this, a man angry, his easy gallantry superseded meantime, Margaret discovering a new husband. It was the word that the Douglas lands in the Middle and East Marches had been harried and destroyed by the English, and the Douglas graves desecrated, despite his former understanding with Henry – Teviotdale and Hawick, Cavers, Timpendean, Bonjedward, Melrose and Mordington. This had infuriated him, his leanings towards the Tudor now gone. When John reported to him the contents of that courier's letter from London, the earl grew the hotter. He had not been a man for battle and war, of choice, but now he was for drawing the sword. And a long and sharp sword the Douglases could draw, if need be, one of the most potent in all Scotland. The Douglas lands, all over, could muster thousands. As well as his mainly Middle March lands devastated, he was worried about his great Lothian properties, Tantallon the principal Red Douglas seat in particular, which could be in the path of an English advance from the East March, especially if there was an attempt to rescue Hertford.

Angus was all authority now, and as though only awaiting John's arrival, one of the premier earls of Scotland and head of the great house of Douglas. There was no question of John going to assist his father – Maxwell could do well enough without him. It was the matter of halting Eure and Layton before they could do any more damage, and punishing them adequately. How best to proceed on this most urgent task, that was the question.

They discussed all aspects of the situation, as far as these were known. Angus had already sent messengers to the Galloway and Dumfries-shire Douglases at Threave and Drumlanrig in especial, and these would be assembling at the latter castle at the head of Nithsdale. Others would be available further north and east. How best to use them, in the circumstances?

John said that since the southern parts of the Middle and East Marches were already savaged, and the English pressing northwards apparently, they had a choice. They could move in force due eastwards into those devastated areas, seek to marshal the angry survivors and then turn north to attack Eure and Layton from the rear, while hoping that the regent's forces would be fronting them from the north. Or they could themselves head northwards to join the said forces, work out a joint strategy and form a united front.

The earl favoured the latter course, to give time for the northern Douglases to join him. From Lothian alone he reckoned that he could raise fifteen hundred without difficulty; and Morton, the Black Douglas earl, could field a thousand from Dalkeith and thereabouts. Beyond Forth it would take longer, from Pittendreich, Lochleven and the like, another thousand, Glenbervie still further, say five hundred. With those assembling at Drumlanrig, he reckoned that he could field four thousand quickly and, given a week, six thousand. Astonished that one man could think to conjure up such numbers at will, John agreed that the best course was to head north, picking up as many men as possible, with himself adding the dalesmen, and join the regent's host, with presumably Huntly, Argyll and other great lords' forces taking part.

John returned to Terregles, agreeing to meet Angus at Dumfries in two days' time, with the Marchmen, Agnes seeking to accept the new departures and their attendant dangers with good grace.

In the event, when they met at Dumfries town, despite the large numbers Angus talked of, John and his dalesmen, plus some new adherents, now three hundred, made the earl's party of a mere hundred from Threave look distinctly feeble. But that would be rectified as they proceeded northwards. Agnes and Catherine accompanied John thus far, the eventual parting having to be moderated to circumstances.

The journey up Nithsdale to Drumlanrig, a score of miles, took them the rest of the day. At that fine castle, seat of Sir James Douglas, Angus's forecasts were substantiated, an assembly of no fewer than fourteen hundred men, all horsed, already gathered.

A lively night was spent, taxing even Drumlanrig's resources.

With these numbers the onward journey towards Edinburgh was slow, by dalesmen's standards, especially as their route lay through the Lowther Hills by the Dalveen Pass and the old Roman Road, and so into upper Tweeddale, with more hills to be faced. They were heading now for the Neidpath and Gala area, more Douglas territory flanking the Middle March, which, it was hoped, had so far escaped the invading hordes.

There, they found, although fears were rife, no havoc had yet occurred, and they collected another three hundred men. They could have had more, but Angus deemed it right to leave a sufficiency able to defend the neighbourhood should the English come thus far west. They had covered fifty difficult miles that day, good going for so large a force.

Now they had a choice of routes in heading for Edinburgh. They could go north, by Innerleithen and through the Morthwaite Hills, making for Dalkeith, to link up with the Earl of Morton. Or up the Gala Water by Stow-in-Wedale. Or still further east up Lauderdale and over the Soutra Pass. But the further east they went the more likely they were to meet the invaders, who were known already to have sacked Melrose and burned its abbey with the Douglas tombs, where Bruce's heart was interred; and while in one way this would have been the rewarding and popular course with most of the host, strategically it was probably unwise. How many men Eure and Layton had at their disposal was not known, but it must be a large array to have inflicted so much damage over a great area. And the central Tweed region would almost certainly be their main base for terrorising both Middle and East Marches, so convenient a joining-place of the rivers of Leader, Teviot, Kale, Jed and Ale. The Douglases *might* be able to defeat the English invaders, in part; but probably it would be wiser, more effective, to join the main Scots army and seek a major victory in all-out battle. And that way, the enemy would not be forewarned.

So, up the Leithen Water, by the Dewarton of St Ronan, to the Morthwaites. John volunteered to ride ahead with a small party to try to discover where the regent's force was now positioned. It might well already be on its way to the Borderland. Angus agreed.

This, as it were back-door entry into Lothian brought them to the headwaters of the River Tyne, the same in whose vale lay Haddington, but that was some score of miles away. If indeed Arran's army was heading south, which way would it take? If starting from Edinburgh or Musselburgh the obvious route was by Soutra and over into Lauderdale, which would bring it to the vital Melrose–Tweed area. So, once emerging from the constrictions of the Morthwaites, John turned north-eastwards in that general direction. And, sure enough, near to Crichton Castle, they saw a large contingent of horsemen following the main highway for Soutra. This could scarcely be the enemy, heading southwards, so John spurred forward to intercept.

It proved to be the Master of Rothes, from Fife, with twelve hundred men, sent by Beaton, largely from his own St Andrews area. He was able to inform that the main Scots army, which he was hastening to join, was ahead, by this time probably halfway down Lauderdale. Whether it had yet met up with the enemy, he knew not.

What then for Angus's force? No point in them coming on northwards; it should be eastwards for the foot of Lauderdale. Wasting no time, John left Norman

Leslie, the Master, and, riding hard, sped back whence he had come.

They reached the Douglas force not far from the head of the Gala Water, and in the hasty conference which followed it was decided that by going back down the Gala and crossing over the high ground to the Allan Water and Langshaw, they could reach the Earl's-Town of Ersildoune. There they would be only some nine or ten miles north of the strategic and ravaged Melrose.

They managed to make Ersildoune, one-time home of the famous Thomas the Rhymer, by nightfall, and found the Fife contingent already there. And not only them, but Scott of Buccleuch with one thousand more men. So the valley was crowded indeed, the Earl's-Town folk less than happy, and wondering whether they had been spared English ravages at too great a cost.

Buccleuch said that the word was that the main Scots array had divided, one section under Arran himself and the Kerr Middle March Warden turning eastwards to go to the aid of the Master of Home, the East Warden, whose father's castle of Home had been destroyed and who was now fighting Eure somewhere in the Merse. The other section under Bothwell, as Lieutenant of the Border, had gone westwards looking for Layton, who was said to be ransacking the area between Melrose and Selkirk.

With a force of now nearly seven thousand, all the leaders agreed that the best course was to join Bothwell, Arran's host being too distantly vague as to position, with Coldinghame, none so far from Berwick-upon-Tweed, being rumoured as where Eure was presently attacking. Angus would have wished to go and liberate Melrose, the Douglas shrine, but it was recognised that this would best be done, or attempted, after an enemy force had been challenged and hopefully defeated, this ravaging host under Layton.

In the morning therefore they all rode south-westwards through the low green hills of the soaring triple summits of the Eildons, the Romans' Trimontium, to ford Tweed at Faldonside.

They found Bothwell and three thousand men at Bowden, a village above its sequestered valley west of St Boswells. That earl was uncertain as to procedure, as indeed was Angus himself, warfare apparently being like that, and not all the dash and glory the balladry made of it. Smoke was rising in great clouds to the south, presumably over mid-Tweeddale, seeming to indicate English activity there; but whether this represented Layton's main array was another matter. Local folk had come to him from St Boswells, south of Melrose, urging him to come to them. A great crowd of refugees and survivors from the devastated areas had apparently congregated there and were seeking not so much protection as vengeance for homes destroyed and dear ones slain. They were armed, after a fashion, not with swords and lances but with hatchets, scythes and knives.

There was some hooting at this information amongst the Douglases and dalesmen, but Angus said that these might have their uses, reminding his hearers of the quite vital part played by the common folk at Bannockburn, two centuries earlier, which had helped to turn the tide of battle at a critical juncture.

But this did not guide them as to the joint force's further procedure. Until they knew where Layton was, with his main force, there was not much that they could do. They might as well stay here, at this Bowden, and send out scouts right and left to try to gain the information they required.

Needless to say, the dalesmen were in demand as scouts. John himself, however, offered to go to this St Boswells, to tell these local people that they would be used if the opportunity arose, and to be ready to receive instructions. He might also learn something of the general situation.

So he rode, with a couple of companions, eastwards along the southern slopes of the Eildons the three miles to the village of St Boswells, which oddly had so far escaped the destroyers' attentions. Here, at the smallish fortalice of Lessudden, he found a great gathering of folk; men, women and children being cared for and fed by the Scott laird and his family, these having come from all over the ravaged Melrose area. Why this village had itself escaped, none knew.

Stories of atrocities came pouring out, with demands for revenge. John told them that the Earls of Angus and Bothwell and others were nearby, with a large host, seeking the enemy; and if a battle ensued there might well be a part for them to play. So to be ready. But meantime, if they learned of any significant movements by large bodies of the English, to send word to Bowden. Or, for that matter, if other Scots forces were to appear in this vicinity, to let them know that a large army was waiting there. He did learn from one little group that there was a quite major encampment settled on the slopes of a ridge called Peneil Heuch, not far from the village of Ancrum about nine miles to the south, said to be under the command of Sir Robert Bowes. John knew Bowes was the Warden of the English Middle March. So here was a new challenge to be reckoned with.

Back at Bowden this last news caused debate. Should they sally out and attack this English position at Peneil Heuch? Their men were spoiling for a fight, after all the cross-country riding. They possibly could get rid of Bowes and his party at least. On the other hand, if this was done, the other English forces, the main ones under Layton, would be warned that there was a large Scots army in the vicinity, and this could detract from any surprise attack such as was wanted, and undo any good that this hiding at Bowden might achieve. Let them wait until they discovered just where Layton might be.

They were glad that they had made this decision when, next day, they had a different sort of news. This was brought by messengers sent by the regent to find them, informing Bothwell that this Arran's section of the host was on its way back westwards from the Merse, having learned that Eure was doing the same further south, leaving the Coldinghame area. Possibly Eure had learned of the Scots army's approaches, and was taking the precaution of heading back to rejoin Layton to form a reunited host. So the regent would do likewise, and the two armies could come to grips.

Angus, with the knowledge about Bowes at Peneil Heuch which Arran did not have, sent the messengers back to tell of this new danger, and urging that they joined up at Bowden at the soonest, but to approach as cautiously as was possible, to maintain secrecy for a surprise attack, advising the St Boswells route.

They waited, inactive save for the scouts.

Two days later the two forces were reunited, to form an army of major proportions, Arran and Ferniehirst much cheered to find the great Douglas contingent there. In the meantime, the scouts had brought word that Layton, who had been basing himself on Jedburgh, despoiled as it was, now was moving northwards in force up over Teviot into the Ancrum area. Perhaps he had heard of the Scots presence at Bowden, or was making to join Bowes at Peneil Heuch, or both. If Eure, from the east, was also making for thereabouts, then indeed the English were concentrating in a significant fashion, and matters might be coming to a conclusion at last.

Sir Andrew Kerr of Ferniehirst, warden, whose land most of this was, declared that if battle there was to be, this Bowden was not the best place for the Scots to form up, however hidden. Already there were far too many men crowded into the confines of the Bowden Water's valley. Much better on the higher ground overlooking Ancrum Muir, five miles to the south, where they could be hidden by the bulk of Gersit Law, yet be in a position to drive down on to the lower ground of the muir. His properties of Sandyknowes and Williamrig would be best, he recommended. They could cover the distance in darkness, he leading them, and so preserve secrecy.

So that very night the move was made, to the thankfulness of the Bowden villagers, a great undertaking indeed to move all those thousands of horsemen over rough country in darkness. But Kerr knew every foot of the way and could foresee the problems. Well before dawn they were all settled down again on the upland farms of Williamrig and Sandyknowes – at least, so they were told, although they could discern little or nothing of their whereabouts.

In the first morning light they saw that they were amongst low, sheep-strewn and grassy hillsides, with the humpbacked ridge of Gersit Law blocking out all views eastwards. Without delay, most of the leaders rode thither, dismounting before they reached the crest of the hill so as not to be apparent on the skyline, to peer over.

Before them, now, were spread vast stretches of the mid and east Borderland, the morning mists rising from the valleys, from the Eildons and the Black Hill of Earlston to the north, to the Cheviots and the English borderline on the south, with the whalebacks of Smailholm and Home to the east hiding some of the Merse, well over one thousand square miles of a wonderfully fair and scenic land greeting their gaze, even though it was spoiled now by the lingering smokes of burning Teviotdale and Jedforest, making the Douglases and Kerrs tighten their lips. Immediately below, but separated by a small and lesser ridge to this Gersit, lay the comparative levels of Ancrum Muir; and just beyond this rose a similar but slightly higher ridge to their own, Peneil Heuch; and even at nearly three miles' distance they could make out the dark shadows which represented masses of men based on its slopes, how many they could only guess at.

Leaving scouts to watch from there, they headed back to their own camp, to breakfast as best they might and to discuss tactics.

Did the English know that they were there? And if they did, in what numbers? And the English numbers? Had Layton joined Bowes? Even Eure, now, perhaps. Who was going to attack, and who defend? Much more information was desirable. Could they lure the English out from their strong position down on to the intervening moorland? Send out a proportion of their strength into full view perhaps, to coax the enemy forward, and then fall on them in flank with their main force? The trouble there was that if no very large company went out, the enemy might well send only a small proportion of their host to deal with it, and the situation be nowise bettered.

Buccleuch it was who came up with the favoured proposal. That lesser small ridge below this Gersit Law. They could use that to provide the answer, making the land fight for them. If they could get some part of their host down into the hollow between them without being seen, then line up the remainder of their people, not too many of them, up on the main ridge in full view, but remaining there and looking as though reluctant to risk a descent into the moorland for battle, this might well cause the English to believe that the Scots were outnumbered, too few to make an attack, and so encourage *them* to make the assault in strength, uphill as would have to be. The men down in the hollow – they would have to be afoot, to get them there unseen and to remain so – once battle was joined above, could mount up the slope behind the enemy and attack from the rear. The English, to avoid climbing the lesser ridge, would have to flank it, right or left, or both. Thereafter they would be caught, from before and behind. In a cavalry battle footmen could well play a useful part, hamstringing the horses, pulling men from their saddles, infiltrating.

All agreed that this was worth attempting. And if the English did not rise to the bait, then they themselves were no worse off than at present.

The problem would be getting the large numbers of men down into that hollow unseen from the enemy positions. Ferniehirst, however, declared that if they went carefully, dismounted, round to the north, there was a burn channel which could give them cover. He would lead them.

John made a suggestion. Those St Boswells folk. If

they could be sent for, to come and provide a distraction, massing on the north edges of the muir without actually closing with the English, it might help?

Angus supported this. It might seem strange that he should assume that he was in command of the entire force, with so many other great ones present, including the regent and Bothwell, Lieutenant of the Border. But it was accepted without dispute. He was the Douglas and had much the greatest contingent of men there, besides being the most senior earl.

So dispositions were made forthwith. A rider was despatched to St Boswells, four miles to the north, to urge a massed appearance of the folk at the edge of the muir. That would take at least two hours to materialise; but it would likewise require that, and more perhaps, to get the thousand or two of men, dismounted and going round-about, down into the dip, without being seen by the enemy.

John elected to go with Buccleuch, Ferniehirst and the dismounted company, and was joined by Sir David Lindsay of the Mount, Lord Lyon, who had ever to be near the regent, a personable and effective character. The other lords stayed with Angus, Arran and Bothwell.

The dalesmen, grumbling about being bereft of their beloved horses, nevertheless dismounted and followed their deputy warden, all leaving their lances behind.

Without undue delay Ferniehirst led the long, coiling column of men northwards through the hillocks until they reached the burn he had mentioned in its quite pronounced channel, and so could turn eastwards down this, unseen from any distance. At one point, where there was a gap in the intervening slope, they had to go very carefully, all but bent double, but that only for a hundred yards or so. Afterwards, the bulk of the lesser ridge hid them, and they were able to turn into the hollow between the heights.

It all took time, with so many men involved; but presently Buccleuch was able to signal up to the scouts, lying watching on the higher ridge, that all were in position and that the next stage of operations could proceed.

This consisted of Angus and the other leaders riding openly, with only a proportion of the remaining host, up on the summit of Gersit Law, and there halting in a long line, in full view from near and far. They waited, some dismounting.

Inaction followed, most strange-seeming in the circumstances.

John said to Lindsay that this must be one of the oddest encounters in the long history of Scots–English warfare, waiting, waiting. For just what, and for how long? The couple crawled up to the top of their own lesser ridge, flat on their bellies, to gaze over. No indication of movement showed from Peneil Heuch.

John was a little concerned, as time passed, that the St Boswells folk might arrive on the scene too soon, before the English made a move, if move they did, and so find themselves exposed to the full fury of a cavalry attack, when all that he had sought was for them to form up and seem to make a threatening diversion. The last thing he wanted was for them to suffer casualties, these who had suffered sufficiently already.

Not only John but others were beginning to despair of any reaction, when the sound of trumpets came over to them, high and thin but clear, from the east. That must mean something, concerted activity presumably.

Waiting over, they saw movement at last over there on Peneil Heuch, the dark shadow, which was masses of men and horses, beginning to change position, to advance westwards, downhill towards the muir. So far, so good.

The watchers, however, became almost alarmed as the movement went on and on, so large appeared to be the numbers involved, squadron after squadron of horsemen, following and swinging into line abreast, succeeded by more and more of the same. All Layton's and Bowes's forces must be there, and probably Eure's now also.

Onward into the moorland levels they came, no longer

acting raiders and ravishers but as a disciplined host, with banners flying, in purposeful strength. To within half a mile of the lesser ridge they advanced, and there halted, the commanders no doubt scanning the opposition, the ground, and assessing.

John, for one, was doing his own assessing, and wondering whether perhaps the Scots leadership had underestimated the enemies' numbers and power.

Then, after a pause, the English lines began to re-form. Soon it became apparent that they were dividing into three distinct groups, two large and one smaller, the latter in the middle. At a single trumpet-blast, both larger groupings resumed their advance, swinging well apart, right and left. The smaller company, of some hundreds, remained stationary, obviously to form some sort of rearguard or for reinforcement if required.

"They are doing it!" John jerked. "Doing what we had hoped. Dividing to climb the law, but on two sides of this ridge we are on. Hoping to assail our people up there in flanking attacks. It is as Buccleuch devised."

"Aye, they reckon that they are strong enough to attack, and ourselves hesitant, afraid. We shall see!" Lindsay said.

Other recumbent watchers worked their way back to join the hidden, waiting force in the hollow, but John and his companion remained meantime.

One element of danger did occur to John, and no doubt to more than himself. With the English horsemen mounting the side of Gersit Law, if any of them turned to glance backward and down, sidelong, they might be able to glimpse the Scots waiting in the valley, or some part of them. But was it likely that any would do so? Men riding into battle, to attack a waiting force on higher ground, would not be apt to look away half to the rear. And only those nearest, at either side, would see into the hollow anyway. The chances were that there would be no sighting and diversion.

But, while they watched, tensely, another problem and

would-be diversion presented itself to them. This was the appearance of figures on the north edge of the muir, the St Boswells people responding to the call, more and more of them coming into view. And, if into view of themselves, into view of the waiting rearguard of English likewise, for the newcomers were not seeking to hide themselves, the suggested diversion indeed – but this rearguard situation had not been visualised.

And, as John feared, presently about half of the enemy company moved into action and swung off right-handed to make for the crowd, which they would be able to see was all on foot.

John bit his lip. What had he let those good St Boswells folk in for?

But anxious as he was for the newcomers, he and Lindsay had to concern themselves otherwise. Shouts from the hollow intimated action there, and they had to hurry down to join Buccleuch and Ferniehirst, who were marshalling the dismounted host. The two main wings of the enemy array were now almost up at the crest of Gersit Law, and Angus and his mounted ranks were withdrawing before them, to lure them further beyond, where more Scots were waiting, hitherto hidden. It was time for the dismounted men to make their contribution. Out of the hollow, in no very ordered or regular files, they began to climb. None of the enemy had turned back in their direction, at any rate.

Hastening uphill over the rough ground was breathtaking, especially for men clad for horseback and mainly wearing thigh-length riding-boots. Some were better at it than others. So it was a panting and not very disciplined rabble which eventually arrived at the crest, to be formed up into some sort of order, while waiting for the less agile.

John was near the front. He stared, like most of his companions, at what met their gaze. For battle had joined, at last, full-scale, savage cavalry battle, two or three hundred yards in front of them, and slightly downhill, the noise of shouting, yelling, screaming men, neighing horses and the clash of steel.

There was no point in forming up in any sort of lines or order for men on foot to seek to harry the rear of a horsed enemy. Every individual must seek to attack as best he could. Buccleuch and Ferniehirst, leaving the last breathless stragglers to come on in their own time, waved on their people, swords and dirks in hand, even a few battle-axes.

In complete surprise they descended upon the English, who, preoccupied with forward fighting and in fairly tight formation, were nowise looking behind them, no slogan-shouting nor cries giving them warning. In amongst the rearing, sidling horses and yelling riders the Scots ran, thrusting, stabbing, smiting with naked steel. The horses, to be sure, had to be the principal targets at this stage, much as the dismounted men cherished horseflesh and hated the savagery on them, for it was not easy to reach up and pull riders from their saddles amongst flailing swords, whereas hamstringing and ripping the horses' bellies could be done from behind by stooping men, and the enemy not able to reach back and down readily. And the hamstrung beasts' hindquarters usually collapsed, toppling the horsemen, who then became an easy target for dirks and blades.

The forward ranks of the double English assault, now more or less joined up again, were too much concerned with their conflict against Angus's long front to be aware, for some time, of what was happening behind them. Cavalry, where it has space and freedom of manoeuvre and movement, has major superiority over infantry, able to ride down, with height and weight on its side. But constricted front and rear into a comparatively narrow belt, as here, horsemen were much handicapped, obstructing each other, hemmed in, mounts jostling. The English fought well enough in the circumstances, but the men on foot were able to infiltrate, dart and dodge and circle, even under horses' bellies, the main danger that of being trampled down under lashing hooves rather than cut down by downward-flailing swords, lances in this crush being of little use. And the Scots concentrated on seeking to bring down leaders.

Angus and Bothwell and the others had changed from defence to attack, and this constricted the enemy even more.

The English, then, found themselves outwitted, out-manoeuvred, possibly outnumbered, and their leadership unable to effect any overall command. It did not take very long for escape rather than assault to become many of the enemy's preoccupation.

But escape was none so simple either, even though horsemen could wheel round and ride down the footmen, for dead and dying beasts, lashing and threshing, now formed a dire barrier between them. They had come from two sides of the hill for their attack; now they sought to flee that way. But Angus's riders were urgent to prevent this.

In all the dire struggle, chaos and smiting, two concerns never left John Maxwell's mind: that enemy rearguard back in the moorland, and those St Boswells folk's situation. The former would not be able to see what went on over the brow of Gersit Law; but once the escaping stragglers began to appear round the sides of the hill, they would realise that all was not well, and might come hastening up to aid their fellows, and so be in a position to ride down the Scots dismounted men. That situation, of course, might help the common folk at the muir's edge if they were being attacked; but they might well be suffering severely meantime. He began to try to gather together some proportion of his busy dalesmen, to find horses and come with him to attempt a rescue.

That was not easy either, although there were plenty of riderless horses to grab amongst all the fallen ones. Once he himself was mounted on an English beast, it was less difficult to make his commands evident. He could not identify Buccleuch nor Ferniehirst, nor even Lindsay, in all the seething mass of men and animals, to tell them what he intended. He just had to do what he could on his own.

When he had managed to muster some sixty or seventy of his mosstroopers and got them mounted, he was setting off back for the crest of the law when he saw Lindsay, and urged him to get Buccleuch to send on more horsemen after them to the muir.

On the ridge, he saw that the rearguard, or part of it, was still waiting down below, presumably unaware of the disaster which had overtaken the main body. Northwards, he could make out scattered fighting going on with the St Boswells people.

John decided that was the priority now. He headed his little force along the ridge and down, in that direction. Possibly the sight of them would further mystify the English rearguard commander. The noise of battle behind soon became overborne by the yells and screams from the conflict in front. At least this indicated that the citizen fighters had not been wholly overwhelmed and cut down.

It seemed like total confusion there, as John's company thundered down on the struggling mass, scattered over a wide area of rough ground, the cavalry dispersed amongst the large numbers of local men – and women also, for John was astonished to see females amongst the fighters. The English were, to be sure, having the best of it, beating down with swords and spearing with lances from their superior height, and trampling down their victims; but a number of fallen horses were evident, so probably hamstringing was being practised here also.

In these circumstances, the arrival of even a comparatively small but concentrated force of cavalry had a major impact, with the enemy spread around, although inevitably John's people did ride down and knock over some of their fellow-countrymen in the process. But quite quickly their coming put an end to this engagement, the English riders perceiving advantage in being elsewhere, and disengaging to go and rejoin their rearguard.

John, gazing in that direction, saw more cavalry streaming down from the law in fairly compact formation, so not fleeing English, but no doubt Buccleuch's men coming to deal with that rearguard. Sending most of his men to assist in this, he dismounted, with a few companions, to see what could be done for the brave folk here.

It made a grim scene to be sure, with many dead, dying or wounded, bodies littering the ground, some stirring, some screaming or moaning, others lying still. There were a few fallen Englishmen also. He found one young woman being acclaimed by her companions for her very effective battling and courage. Calling her Lilliard, they were praising her for fighting on even when grievously wounded about both legs, then kneeling and wielding her wood-axe against the enemy horses' hocks. Undoubtedly these Middle March Borderers had a long and large score to settle with the invaders, and not only for this occasion.

Promising to send help to attend to the wounded and get the dead back to St Boswells, John, thanking all that he could, remounted and turned southwards. Quite quickly however he altered direction to westwards, for he could see that the English rearguard was now in flight and no aid required there.

Up on the high ground again, enemy escapers everywhere in evidence, many now on foot, they found battle over, prisoners being rounded up, dead being identified and counted, booty snatched, the Scots rejoicing. Banners, English banners, were being waved aloft, one of these being Sir Ralph Eure's own, his body found nearby. Sir Brian Layton was also dead, but seemingly Sir Robert Bowes had escaped. Perhaps he had been with the rearguard. Other knightly leaders had been slain or captured, these latter useful for ransom or exchange for hostages. English losses were clearly enormous, Scots comparatively modest.

Presently campfires were being lit and victory celebrated, the Battle of Ancrum Muir won. Some Scots were already heading for Peneil Heuch in anticipation of finding much booty there at the former English encampment.

John took another party of his men down to the muir-end again to assist the citizenry there, as promised, and to escort them, with their casualties, back to St Boswells, where he spent the night in Scott of Lessudden's house, amidst a mixture of rejoicing and mourning.

In the morning he returned to the Gersit Law encampment to find all breaking up, some already gone, including the regent and Bothwell, with other lords, some returning to Edinburgh, others to their homes. Angus was going on north-eastwards to his seat of Tantallon. None feared any early English comeback, too great had been their disaster.

John and his dalesmen saw no point in waiting, and turned their horses' heads south-westwards for the West March.

Henry Tudor had suffered two defeats within a short space of time, and lost two of his veteran commanders. Whether he was in any way compensated to hear that, while the Ancrum Muir affray was preoccupying the Scots, Edward Seymour, Earl of Hertford, his brother-in-law, had managed to make his escape from beleaguered Haddington and hasten hot-foot for the border at Berwick-upon-Tweed, was not reported.

15

It was good to be home again and, surely, with no likelihood of any more English attacks for some time at least, the Tudor having his wounds to lick. Agnes ensured that her husband enjoyed a return to married life to the full; and from that young woman this was no mere figure of speech. John did not look upon himself as any sort of a hero, but accepted what his wife called well-earned rewards with modest satisfaction.

Meantime military action on the Scots part was superseded by diplomatic. For they now had something to bargain with, not only their victories, but the prisoners taken at Ancrum Muir. Moreover, Francis, King of France, was delighted over these blows against his enemy Henry, and demonstrated it by sending more troops and artillery to Scotland, and having his fleet make threatening gestures around English coasts, this at Beaton's suggestion.

Angus, whether with the regent's agreement or otherwise, sent the Earl of Cassillis, the Kennedy chief, one of the former Solway Moss hostages, down to London as envoy to offer an exchange of prisoners for the present hostages, one of whom was, of course, Cassillis's own heir, the master. No doubt Henry would have cared little about the fate of the ordinary men-at-arms taken at Ancrum, but the knightly prisoners were a different matter, and there were almost two score of these. Angus's instructions were that whoever else was released, if not all were, Robert, Master of Maxwell, was to be freed, the least that he could do for his new wife's family. He also, to be sure, claimed ransom moneys for himself.

The Tudor did send the young hostages back, all of them, their usefulness now gone, whatever his feelings in the matter. There was rejoicing at Caerlaverock and Terregles, as elsewhere undoubtedly.

But Henry had other methods of seeking to get his way than by force of arms. After a comparatively uneventful year, Scotland learned of it in May. Cardinal Beaton, the Chancellor, the Tudor's most potent enemy, and holder-up of any Reformation in the northern kingdom, was assassinated, on orders from London.

They heard the details at Terregles on a visit by Robert, who had got them from Angus. The friend, so-called, of Beaton, the Master of Rothes, he who had led the Chancellor's contingent of twelve hundred to Ancrum Muir, was very much involved. The cardinal had been in bed in the sea tower of St Andrews Castle, his principal seat, that early May morning, when a knocking had sounded at his door, which he prudently kept locked. He had called to ask who was there and the answer had come: "A friend." When he demanded which friend, at that hour, he was told: "Friend Norman." That was, Norman Leslie, Master of Rothes. So Beaton had risen from his bed and gone to turn the key in his lock. And in they had surged, eleven of them, including the master, daggers already drawn, reformers all and clergy amongst them. Naked from his couch, the cardinal was quite unprotected, and with many stab-wounds fell to the floor. The Reverend James Melville, a prominent priest in Fife and leader of reform, held up his hand and declared that this should be done in more godly fashion. He led the others to kneel on the floor and pray. Thereafter he himself struck the final blow at their victim, announcing that this was being done in God's service, whereafter they had hung the corpse out of the window of his bedchamber, facing towards where George Wishart, a Protestant martyr, had been executed not long before. This was foolish, for there it was seen by members of the night patrol of the castle, which was well guarded, and, the alarm raised, men had rushed up and captured the assassins. So now they were prisoners in St Andrews Castle and Scotland was without a Chancellor and an Archbishop of St Andrews, Head of Holy Church. Henry had had his revenge, or part of it.

Most of the nation was shocked, and not only at the barbarity of it. The strongest man in the land was dead – and Henry Tudor would not have gone to such lengths for nothing. What now?

That summer there was a series of small raids over the border, all in the East and Middle Marches, just, as it were, to keep the pot boiling; and it was reported that Hertford was back in the north, sent up to Wark Castle in Northumberland, overlooking Tweed, presumably to send scouts to spy out the land, with a view to further invasion. It could be just a threat, for no large number of men were said to be with him, but again Henry shaking his fist. That the West March had escaped the raiding was interesting. The assumption was that this was probably on account of the vulnerability of Carlisle to counter-invasion; that and the celebrated toughness of the dalesmen as defenders of their territory. John could not believe that it had anything to do with the Maxwell wardenship, as Agnes suggested.

As summer moved into autumn, other concerns tended to preoccupy the Terregles household. Agnes announced that she was pregnant. And Catherine fell in love with a young Galloway man, Alexander Stewart, Younger of Garlies.

John was delighted at the thought of becoming a father, but became over-concerned for the mother's health and safety, declaring that she ought not to ride a horse nor risk almost any physical exercise, which Agnes said was nonsense. They had debate over names, John standing out for William, if it was a boy, son and heir; Agnes wanting Elizabeth if it was a girl. Young Janet, now sixteen, sought to emphasise her attainment of womanhood in all this adult elation by asserting that she was about to become an aunt.

As for Catherine's romance, Sir Alexander Stewart of Garlies, down in Wigtownshire, a powerful laird, had been one of the captives at Solway Moss, and his son, in consequence, sent as one of the substitute hostages. Robert had become friendly with him in London, and on their return home had brought him to Terregles. He and Catherine had found each other attractive.

Not to be outdone by Terregles, Robert announced at the Yuletide festivities that he was going to marry the Lady Beatrice Douglas, daughter of the Earl of Morton. Angus had introduced them, no doubt partly with the objective of consolidating Douglas power in the south-west; but she had turned out to be a pleasant and friendly creature, a plump and warm armful, so all were well content, even the Countess Agnes, who had feared that Robert might let down the Maxwells by marrying some lesser-born female.

The two weddings were planned for spring-time.

In the new year, 1547, these familial felicities were somewhat dampened by the illness of Lord Maxwell. He had been rather noticeably lacking in energy for some months, and this had been put down to a wound he had received at the last raid, by Wharton, before Ancrum Muir. But now it appeared to be something deeper-seated, an internal affliction. He was in his late fifties but beginning to look older.

He had never been a man to demonstrate his affections, unlike the late Lord Herries, and his ailment, although it greatly restricted his activities, did not plunge the family into deep gloom. But then, in an unusual display of candour and openness, he declared that he was not going to live much longer and that he was glad that he could go knowing that his heir was going to wed, and hopefully produce a second heir to the lordship; also that his younger son was proving effective in the wardenship, and ought to succeed him as Warden of the West March. He was writing to the regent, to see that this was confirmed, the Maxwells looking on the appointment as more or less hereditary in their family. As it was, John was now in effect sole warden anyway.

The months passed and Lord Maxwell seemed to get neither better nor worse. Since he could not travel the many miles to Dalkeith in Lothian for Robert's wedding, the celebration was held at Caerlaverock, amidst a great assembly of Maxwells and Douglases, this in late April. Then, with Agnes expecting her delivery in July, it was decided that Catherine should marry in late May, a much less glittering affair but none the less happy and effective for that. Alexander Stewart was a good-looking and hearty young man, of high spirits and a certain pride in his descent from the royal Stewart line, somewhat distant as this was. Catherine and he made a lively pair. Garlies was only a good day's ride from Terregles, so the sisters would still be able to see a lot of each other.

The English, meantime, did not assert themselves unduly and spoil things. Perhaps the fact that Henry Tudor married once again, for the sixth time, if true marriage that could be called, had something to do with this?

Then, with Agnes expecting to give birth any day in early July, Lord Maxwell was found dead in his bed one morning. And, in fact, John, hastening back to Terregles from the funeral at Caerlaverock, found his wife in labour, and was thankful to be able to hold her hand during a couple of those painful but momentous hours, before the midwife banished him. Soon thereafter he heard the bleating cry of William Herries Maxwell, and was able to hurry back, summoned or not, to hug the exhausted but smiling Agnes and admire the pink little creature who would one day be the sixth Lord Herries.

It was indeed strange to bury a father and win a son in the same day.

16

In January 1547, all Scotland heaved a mighty sigh of relief and found cause for national rejoicing. Henry Tudor, the man who had for so long menaced the northern kingdom so direly, had suddenly died. He had apparently gorged himself on one of his favourite foods, a kind of eel, had taken a fit and choked to death. A great, gross man, and over-taxing his body continually in more than in eating, he was only aged fifty-six.

So now England had a nine-year-old monarch, a sickly boy. Could Scotland at last look forward to a period of peace, at least from invasion?

They had not long to wait for an answer to that question, just four months to be exact, although rumours were rife before that. Hertford was now regent for his nephew Edward, created Duke of Somerset, and, it was said, had vowed to continue the campaign to bring Scotland under English domination, without waiting for the projected marriage between the young king and little Mary, Queen of Scots. No doubt he wanted revenge for his long and humiliating confinement in the town of Haddington.

At any rate, that September, Somerset crossed the Tweed at Berwick, with a force of fourteen thousand men, supported by a fleet of no fewer than thirty-four ships of war which sailed up the Scottish east coast in parallel, ready to land supporters in the rear of any defensive positions, major invasion indeed. He headed northwards, undoubtedly making for Edinburgh. The Scots had cheered too soon.

This was not the sort of military challenge which the March wardens could tackle, even in unity, and Bothwell summoned all three to make for the capital, or at least to Musselburgh nearby, where apparently Arran would seek to oppose the enemy thereat.

John, now full warden and with five hundred dalesmen and lower-country troops under his brother, now Lord Maxwell, hurried up Nithsdale for the Lowther passes. No doubt the Galwegians and the Douglases would be on their way likewise.

In fact they caught up with a large contingent, under Sir James Douglas of Drumlanrig, in upper Tweeddale, who informed that Angus had ordered them to make for Edmondstone Edge, a long ridge of higher ground lying north-east of Dalkeith towards Musselburgh. Here, rather than at the Eskmouth town itself, the regent was assembling Scotland's army, this because of the English fleet which could sail into the Esk. The two groups continued on in company.

Dalkeith itself lay in the Esk valley some seven miles from Edinburgh; and long before they reached that vicinity they encountered other parties, large and small, heading in the same direction, from Ayrshire and Lanarkshire mainly, Kennedys, Cunninghams, Boyds and the like. None doubted the seriousness of the challenge ahead of them.

The Edmondstone ridge was entirely evident before them at Dalkeith, the latter quite a township close to the Eskside castle of Morton, Robert's father-in-law, no great height but quite a major swelling of the landscape stretching for a couple of miles towards the Forth. And once up thereon, all could see the great assemblage of shipping out in the firth, the English fleet, three times the numbers of the squadron which had attempted to land at Luffness three years before, a waiting menace indeed, lying off the mouth of the Esk at Musselburgh.

The newcomers joined the main army at the north-east end of this higher ground, where it fell away fairly sharply, Edmondstone Edge, perhaps fifteen thousand men already mustered, under Arran, Angus, Huntly, who had succeeded Beaton as Chancellor, Argyll, Atholl, Home and Montrose. Others were awaited, the latest arrivals welcomed. The two other wardens, and Bothwell, were already there, having had less far to come.

The news was that Somerset was not far away, having marched his host swiftly by the coastal route from Berwick, avoiding encounters at the fortified strengths of Dunbar, Tantallon and Hailes. He was now said to have passed his former siege-place of Haddington and had camped the previous night on the Gleds Muir, near to Tranent. That was only five miles to the east, but was not visible from here because of the intervening ridge of Fawsyde, the smallish castle of which stood out on the skyline plain for all to see, however modest in size. The enemy ships were obviously waiting until the Lord Protector, as Somerset was calling himself, came into view, to make a concerted attack.

There proved to be some dispute as to tactics amongst the Scots leadership. They were in a fairly strong position here on the edge, and might be best to wait and let the English do the attacking. On the other hand, it would be unfortunate if the enemy was allowed to take the town of Musselburgh, where there was a haven which the fleet could use, and also where the only bridge across the Esk for many miles was positioned. Holding Musselburgh would much hamper the enemy.

This dispute emphasised a very real Scottish weakness. Who was in command, to take final decisions? Angus clearly thought that he was; but Arran was the regent and, although not an assertive man, some there, notably Huntly and Argyll, jealous of Angus and the Douglases, held that *he* was overall commander. Arran favoured the Musselburgh option and the saving of the good folk of that town from English savagery; whereas Angus was for remaining on these heights and letting the foe face the hazards of an uphill assault. Such was the clash on strategy when John and the others arrived.

Actually it was Lord Home, the East March Warden's father, who defused the situation meantime by suggesting that a company, more than just a scouting party, should head off eastwards for that Fawsyde ridge with its skyline castle, a bare two miles off, and see where the English army was, and whether, if they occupied that ridge instead of this one, they might be in a still stronger position and able to prevent any near approach to Musselburgh. And, at the same time, send down a force to hold secure that Esk bridge, in case the fleet landed troops to take it and get behind them here. Angus, while reluctant to abandon the present strong position, acceded that there was no harm in allowing both these suggestions to be carried out. Arran agreed.

So, the two moves were made, Home himself and about three hundred horsemen heading off down northwards to capture the bridge, while his son, the Master, with a slightly larger number of his Mersemen, rode off due eastwards for Fawsyde Castle. Both would send back reports.

Neither objective being far away, word was not long in being received. The Master's came first, although Fawsyde was slightly the further off. The English main host was approaching in vast numbers from the Tranent direction, along the ridge therefrom, and he and his men had already had a skirmish with an advance party surrounding Fawsyde of that Ilk's castle, vanquishing them. First blood to the Scots.

Lord Home's own report took somewhat longer to arrive. He had been surprised to find the Esk bridge already held by a quite large party of English landed from the ships; but after a quite bloody attack by his cavalry they had managed to recapture it, difficult as this was because of the narrow dimensions of the humpbacked crossing. He was now holding it secure.

This news was scarcely recounted to the leadership when the banging of gunfire turned all eyes northwards. The ships, or some of those nearest the Esk-mouth, were firing their cannon. Almost certainly they would be aiming at Home's cavalry clustered round that bridge.

Presumably these vessels had heavier, longer-range pieces than had the Aberlady Bay ships.

So now, what? If the English were already approaching Fawsyde ridge, it was too late for the main Scots array to move there, they would not be able to get into position before the enemy were on them. So, remain here, Angus said. But Arran still thought that the Musselburgh folk must be protected. Should they not go down to aid Home, protect that bridge, and prevent any landing from the ships? They could mass back out of range of those cannon, and use the River Esk as a barrier between them and Somerset's advancing force.

Angus was wholly against this. They would be throwing away their strong position, for what? They were on the wrong side of the river to save Musselburgh, and with that fleet to help him Somerset could, if he so desired, use it to transport his people, or some of them, *behind* the Scots lines. No, that would be folly. Let them wait here.

Most of the lairds seemed to agree with this. They would stay there meantime.

The cannonade had ceased, so presumably Home was holding the bridge – at least there were no calls for help. It was early evening before the Master's Mersemen came back from Fawsyde, or most of them, but without the Master of Home. They reported that he had been unhorsed and taken prisoner, despite their efforts, by a second English assault on the little castle, and some of their number slain. But the castle still held out, Somerset apparently having no cannon to turn against it with his army, only with his ships.

It was sad tidings about the Master's capture and the Mersemen's loss. But, still sadder presently, when, as darkness was falling on the encampment, a party came up from the Esk bridge, bringing with them the Lord Home himself, in a sorry state, indeed unconscious. A cannonball crashing nearby had caused his horse to shy and throw him, and he was obviously seriously injured, blood oozing from the mouth and ribs crushed.

It had been a bad day for the House of Home, and no good augury for the future.

Sentinels on the alert all round the Edmondstone ridge, the Scots host passed a wary and wakeful night.

In the morning they could see all Fawsyde ridge dark with the enemy. And not only that, but right down to the coast at Salt Preston and Drummore more English could be discerned, these clearly making their way round the shoreline towards Musselburgh.

The injured Lord Home was despatched to Edinburgh for the physicians' attention.

Arran, backed by Huntly and Argyll, decided that they must act to save the town, and in doing so coax Somerset off the heights of Fawsyde, if possible. Angus demurred. Here they were in an excellent strong position. They should wait. Somerset could not afford to. He would be more concerned with attacking and seeking to defeat them, the main Scots array, than in occupying Musselburgh. Bide here, the Douglas said.

But the regent and the others would not have it. Arran ordered all to mount and move. Angus, furious, ordered the reverse, all to remain where they were.

It was deadlock, folly, shame, and bad indeed for the men's morale, an appalling start to what could be a fateful day, divided and opposing commands. But the majority of the lords supported the regent and the Chancellor, Huntly. They instructed their men to move.

John Maxwell, like so many another, was in a quandary. He supposed that he ought to obey the regent, the queen's representative, and the Chancellor, chief minister of the realm. But he agreed with Angus's stance, who was his sister's husband. As, of course, did the Douglases, including the Earl of Morton who was now Robert's father-in-law, and Drumlanrig and the so-clever Sir George, Angus's brother. Robert was for remaining where they were. John decided that he should do likewise.

So the great Scots army divided. About two-thirds of it moved off northwards, downhill, banners flying and fists being shaken at those who remained behind, a state of affairs surely seldom if ever before seen in the nation's turbulent history on the eve of battle.

With the thousands involved, it took some time for the regent's force to move down over the slopes of Whitehill and Craighall to the crossing of the Esk; but those waiting on the high ground knew when the others had reached it by the cannon-fire which recommenced and continued, much more of it than previously, indicating that extra ships had moved into the Esk-mouth and were involved. It was not possible to see the actual bridge area from Edmondstone Edge. Those listening could only hope that the gunfire was not creating dire havoc. That bridge was narrow, and large numbers crossing over would mean long delays and concentrated targets for the ships' artillery.

But presently, what they could see from their present stance was movement on Fawsyde Ridge, much and steady movement. The English were leaving those heights and coming down towards Musselburgh, north-westwards, into what were known as the Pinkie Braes. And their low-ground detachment was on the move also, from the Drummore, Westpans and Levenhall area, obviously intending to join up.

When Angus recognised that this was a continuing movement, a total altering of the situation, he saw opportunity, and swiftly decided to change his tactics. That would bring Somerset and his reunited host into the marshy levels below Pinkie Braes, the How Mire, soft ground and difficult for cavalry. Presumably Somerset did not realise this. If the English could be trapped there, on the eastern outskirts of Musselburgh, and his own force descending upon them from the higher slopes, with Arran facing them from the town area, they could have the enemy at a major disadvantage. Here was a chance offered unexpectedly. His lieutenants agreed with him that their strategy should be altered.

So messengers were sent spurring down after the regent's people to inform them of the situation and opportunity. And orders were given, to move off that edge, eastwards. Action at last.

John reckoned that there were perhaps four thousand of them riding down those slopes behind the one-time Roman fort of Inveresk. Would Arran's larger host reach the chosen How Mire and Pinkie Braes first?

In the event, it was the low-ground English detachment of about five hundred cavalry which were first to approach, these riding along the coast road, Somerset's main array still descending the Wallyford slopes. Seeing this, Angus ordered John to take his dalesmen and some others, perhaps eight hundred all told, and ride swiftly down almost to the shore, to try to drive this enemy force inland, southwards, into the How Mire soft ground, where he could deal with them there, this before Somerset could arrive. The cannon-fire was still booming behind them.

Nothing loth, John led his detachment off, eager for real battle after all the waiting and the purely wordy conflict. They could see their foes about half a mile away, actually riding towards them.

This looked as though it would be a comparatively straightforward battle, two horsed forces to clash on fairly level and firm ground, John reckoning that he had the advantage in numbers. Waving his arm, he shouted for his people to split into three groups, himself leading the centre, Robert and his Maxwells taking the right and Wauchope of that Ilk the left, thus to attack head-on and in flank, typical cavalry tactics. On they raced.

But whoever led the enemy was a tactician also. Presumably recognising that he was outnumbered, he swung his force, not southwards towards the How Mire area but northwards down to the sandy shore of the firth, right to the tide's edge so that, whatever else, he could not be outflanked on that side. Along the shore he headed towards the town.

Faced with this unexpected and unusual situation, John had to think quickly indeed, his three-pronged assault invalidated. Yelling and gesturing, he pointed seawards, and his men, seeing what was happening, responded as best they could, although in no very orderly and co-ordinated change of direction.

On they pounded, the distance between the two forces rapidly diminishing, John calculating, assessing urgently. One group to swing westwards, to cut the English off from the town area. The rest to seek to smash through the now somewhat elongated enemy force, this necessarily so because of the fairly narrow extent of the sandy shore, with some of the riders actually splashing in the shallows. Break up the foe into two or more sections, causing confusion and leadership difficulties.

Leading hundreds of galloping horsemen, it was none so easy for John himself to indicate a change of strategy or to transmit new orders. Rising in his stirrups, his shouting would be unlikely to be heard for pounding hooves and snorting horses, but his arm-waving and pointing might just be understood. Of course, his fellow-leaders, brother and Wauchope, would be looking for directions in this new situation, and his gesticulations welcome, however interpreted.

Wauchope, on the left, got the message, may well himself have decided that this was the course to take in the circumstances, and wheeled his section off half-left, to seek to cut off the enemy from the town outskirts. On the right, Robert was less aware of what was desired; but his group was somewhat separate from the centre anyway, and obviously all were going to charge down on the English line and hopefully cut it up. So his task was fairly evident. On centre and right they drove.

The enemy commander, to be sure, would see the danger, but have his own difficulties in communicating orders, strung out as his people now were. And time was short for all of them. He managed to get a proportion of his men to wheel round, backs to the tide, to face the oncoming attack, spears levelled, although his forward people, seeking to outride Wauchope's men, maintained their westwards dash. So, in fact, part of John's hasty design was fulfilling itself, and, by the opposition itself, the English line divided.

Then, time for plans and devices past, it was sheer clash and shock, collision and combat, amidst rearing and stumbling horses, smiting, stabbing steel, splintering of lances, the howling and screaming of attacked and attackers, riders and mounts falling, bloody chaos, leadership for the time being ineffective, indeed non-existent.

To be sure, hard-riding attack always has the advantage over a less headlong cavalry mass and defence, and the impact's brute force did favour the Scots, enabling them in places to burst right through the enemy ranks.

John, seeking to exercise the only lead left to him, tried to head for where a couple of banners rose above the array, and where presumably was the English command. But the pressure alongside, and especially from behind, of charging riders, forced him straight ahead, and sword swinging in figure-of-eight slashing, he had to drive into the ranks immediately in front, no choice offered. He was aware of the physical shock of a blow, the steel tip of a lance glancing off his heraldically painted breastplate, jerking him aside in his saddle, but not so much that he could not maintain his balance; and rising in his stirrups again, he managed to bring down his sword on the spearman's shoulder with a mighty blow which toppled his assailant over. Then there was another in front of him, aiming his lance also, and somehow John got his sword back and up, to smite down on the lance shaft itself, breaking it, although he all but lost his own seat in the effort as his plunging mount carried him on past this open-mouthed foeman. There was still another now directly ahead, but he was fending off an attack on his left, and John was able to unhorse him with a sidelong swipe. Then, with the density of the enemy thinning in front of him, he realised that his steed was splashing up water. He was in the tide, only the open firth ahead.

Urgently now he sought to pull round, adjusting his wits to the battle as a whole rather than his own modest part in it, deliberately not plunging back into the fray. Right and left, amidst all the confusion of fighting, struggling men and terrified horses, he could see that he was not the only Scot in the water, that others had won through the English lines and were turning back, now in an advantageous position to assail their enemies' rear. Instead of doing so himself, John rode splashing eastwards, towards where he had seen those banners, although they were no longer visible.

As he went, it was clear that almost everywhere the Scots were gaining the ascendant, their foes overthrown, outridden, being scattered. Even as he scanned and assessed, panting, he saw the first of the English spurring away, in flight. That, he knew, would be infectious. The day was theirs, or this part of it, he judged.

Soon there was no doubt of it. Such of the English as could were making their escape, leaving behind a sorry host of dead and wounded, with fallen and riderless horses. John was joined by Robert, unhurt and both elated and shaken, unnerved by the savagery and bloodshed, thankful to have escaped uninjured but proud too of victory. Together the brothers sought to bring some order to the situation, impassioned men apt to be less than amenable to discipline and control. For John had the wider scene to consider. This was only a side issue of the main confrontation, however successful. He had to get his men back to support Angus and the others.

They found the English commander dead beside his fallen banner, and learned from the wounded that he was Lord Grey de Wilton. The Scots had their losses also, but few compared with the enemy. High spirits prevailed.

While the wounded on both sides were being afforded some rough care, Wauchope cantered up with the news that he too had had a measure of success, having managed to head off the group making towards the town, prevented them from returning to join their comrades, and done battle with some, although most had made their escape away southwards, no doubt to rejoin Somerset's main host.

Leaving a few men to look after the wounded, John himself pointed southwards, inland, where their duty now lay.

As they rode, they could see something of the overall situation. The hollow of the How Mire was hidden, but on the slopes to east and west were masses of men and horses, the former in great numbers, the English army, come down from Wallyford but seemingly halted; the latter fewer and presumably their own men, waiting also. There was no sign of Arran's force, coming round from the town; but the boom of cannon continued, so it must still be providing a target for the ships' gunners.

Leading his people on, John, mounting a slight crest presently, could see into the lower ground beyond. It formed a shallow basin, undrained, between the modest green slopes, perhaps half a mile long by one-third wide. It was reedy but not actually flooded, indeed there were cattle grazing amidst it. And not only cattle they could see, but men, many men, and on foot.

As they drew nearer they could see what was going on there. Groups of dismounted men, their horses left higher, were being formed into schiltroms, rough, packed squares or circles, the forwards men kneeling, the inner ranks standing, all with their lances out-thrust at various angles, like huge bristling hedgehogs, a device against cavalry which Bruce had used at Bannockburn, Angus a great exponent of the hero-king's tactics. With the soft ground holding up the horsemen, these would not be able to ride down the schiltroms by main force, and those projecting spears would prevent their mounts from getting close enough for the use of swords. A number of these groups were forming, Angus again using the ground to fight for him.

The question, of course, was would Somerset rise to the bait? It might be that he would have to, for if he avoided these groups and swept westwards towards the town and Arran's main force, then he would have all these foemen left behind him, to menace his rear.

John, avoiding the Mire meantime, led his horsemen round it, west-about, to ride up and join the still quite large detachment waiting on the slopes behind, these with the dismounted men's horses.

As expected, Angus was there, eyeing all keenly. He was, needless to say, heartened to hear John's news, although he had more or less assumed their success, in the circumstances, if not the scale of it. But, his attention not to be distracted from the main issue, he watched for Somerset's reaction to the situation developing.

They did not have long to wait for that. Even as John announced the death of Lord Grey de Wilton, a quite senior commander whom Angus knew, they saw movement eastwards. Somerset's host was dividing again, one section to ride off down towards the How Mire, this as the Scots desired. But even so, Angus cursed. For this looked like perhaps only one-third of the whole. The main mass was remaining where it was. And that force would still far outnumber Angus's company if it advanced upon them. Somerset was no fool – unlike Arran! Where was the regent and the main Scots host?

They sat and watched developments down in the hollow. Whoever was in command of the English detachment was wary, not seeking to rush into the soft ground and attack the schiltroms, but circling slowly round, inspecting, assessing, testing the terrain. In the old days, bowmen would have sought to decimate those dismounted spearmen from a distance, but gunpowder had outdated archery for armies while not yet providing adequate musketry for horsed troops.

Angus cursed the more when it became evident that the enemy down there were not going to risk a direct attack on the schiltroms but merely were encircling them and penning them in, and thus made these men ineffective and prevented them from rejoining Angus and recovering their horses, the Scots strategy invalidated. The earl was the more concerned, if not dismayed, when he saw Somerset's main force begin to move, not down towards the hollow but sidelong, round the slopes in their direction. He was being outmanoeuvred, going to be attacked himself, and by a force still at least four times as large as his own.

Where, in the name of God, was Arran, he demanded. The boom of cannon was his only answer.

There was nothing for it but to retire in the face of that dire threat, leaving the dismounted men down there to fend for themselves as best they could. The earl sent messengers to race back westwards to find the regent, Huntly, Argyll and the rest, and to urge, indeed demand, a swift advance in this direction. The Pinkie Braes were the place to make for, just south-east of Musselburgh, not an ideal battleground but the best they could hope for hereabouts, broken, grassy territory where at least no massed cavalry charging would be effective.

Thither Angus led his force, now just over three thousand. Pray that Arran would comply, and swiftly.

They had less than a mile to go before they were into those braes, and still no sign of aid. What to do? Much further and they would be into the town streets where, whatever else, they could not hope to defeat or even much hold up a large army. It was either make a stand here, or outright flight. Somerset might well be cautious approaching these braes, so perhaps they had a little time.

Angus chose a fold amongst modest hillsides formed by a small burn which had made a groove for its present course, no major barrier but enough of a trench to check any charge of cavalry; and the fold would keep them hidden from any distance. It was the best that they could do.

Angus set his people to dig pits and holes with swords, daggers and hands, further to hamper horsemen. Watchers were stationed on viewpoints to give warning. He divided his strength into three sections, normal usage, to facilitate possible flanking moves. John and his dalesmen found themselves on the left and lower sector, himself seemingly in charge of it, with Morton taking the right wing, with Sir George Douglas. Angus thought that if any outflanking tactics became possible, the seaward side would be more hopeful as to results, and the hard-riding mosstroopers most apt for it.

As they waited, digging and delving continued across the burn.

For a while there was no development. Then, simultaneously the situation changed and on two fronts. For just as the scouts hurried back to report the enemy approaching from behind nearby hillocks, the sound of bagpipes turned all heads in the other direction, backwards. That could only be Argyll's Highlanders. So, reinforcements at last.

Sure enough, over the brae behind came the aid they sought – or some of it – for it quickly became evident that this was by no means Arran's full force but only a part of it, and in two distinct sections, one mounted, the other mainly afoot, the Gordon banners flying over the former, so Huntly's men, the pipe-playing Highlanders of Argyll, the Campbell chief, on the higher ground.

Even as, cheered, they thankfully awaited the arrival of this succour, Angus's people had to turn their heads to gaze eastwards where coming into view were the English, rank upon rank, banners by the score flapping above them. On and on they came into sight, a dire and daunting vision. Digging ceased as men came hurrying back across the burn to remount. What the enemy thought of that music of pipes was not to be known.

Argyll and Huntly spurred forward to consult with Angus, proud chiefs both and tending to look down northern noses at mere Lowlanders, Douglases and suchlike as they might be. But with the enemy in full sight and in such numbers, they did not stand on their dignity.

Angus did the obvious thing, sending the dismounted Highlanders up on to the higher slopes to the right, to reinforce Morton, and Huntly's Gordons to John on the left wing. That man was unsure whether to welcome this, in fact; for the proud Huntly was an earl and might well refuse to serve under a mere knight, be he a march warden

213

or not; so he might assume command, and there might well be trouble with the dalesmen who would not take kindly to Gordons giving them orders. Always the Scots suffered from this sort of clan and district rivalry.

John sought to avoid any possible upset by letting Huntly take up the position his own men had been allotted, and moving them further northwards towards the coastal levels again, on the far left flank. So now Angus's array, of perhaps seven thousand, stretched a long way over the very uneven ground, almost for half a mile.

Somerset, a wily and seasoned commander, was in no hurry. Once his full army was into view and position over at the far side of this fold – that is, save for the detachment back there holding up the schiltrom men in the How Mire – he waited for some time, undoubtedly surveying the ground and its prospects for attack. If the Scots might have been thankful for this delay, in that it might allow further support to arrive from Arran, they were disappointed. None arrived.

There followed a quite unexpected and remarkable event. Huntly, the Chancellor, without consulting Angus, suddenly spurred his mount forward, alone save for his personal banner-bearer, to splash across that burn and ride towards the centre of the English line, there to halt within earshot, and to challenge Somerset himself to individual combat. Let them settle this dispute by hand-to-hand contest, as good knights should, he called. Or if the Englishman felt his years, let him name a deputy. If that also was too great a risk against the Gordon, then ten against ten. Or even a score of the invaders against a dozen Gordons. Needless to say, the Lord Protector laughed the Chancellor to scorn. Huntly, making mocking insults, turned and rode back to the Scots lines.

Thereafter English trumpets heralded action, the entire enemy front commencing to move forward, right and left wings slightly in advance of the centre, to seek to ensure that the Scots made no outflanking moves.

John Maxwell acted also. Thanks to Huntly's arrival and positioning his men, John and his were very much further down the Scots left front than they would have been. He grasped opportunity, and waved his people on, more left-handed still, northwards, heading as it were straight for salt water. The mass of the army awaited the enemy onslaught over the ditched ground and that burn.

The English took a little while to respond to the dalesmen's initiative, their right wing no doubt awaiting Somerset's orders. John had led his people some distance seawards before part of the enemy's extreme right wheeled off, to counter this move, themselves now facing north but not riding fast as the Scots were doing, but seemingly seeking to form a barrier to protect their main body from attack in flank or in the rear. At least John had made an early impact, drawn off some proportions of their foe's strength, and lessening the threat to Huntly.

The dalesmen cantered on, now seeing the shoreline in front of them. They could not go much further, and John swung them round after him, due eastwards now. Over his shoulder he saw the enemy right altering stance also, to continue to face this danger, as was to be expected.

Then he saw something else, out of the corner of his eye, back there. Although the main Scots array stood unmoving, awaiting Somerset's charge over the broken ground, lances at the ready, Huntly did not so do. Perhaps, coming late, he did not realise the value of those pits and trenches. Or it may just have been typical Gordon dash and flourish. At any rate, he set his wing into motion, directly forward at what remained of the English right, seeing it divided thus, in headlong attack.

So the battle had, thus early, taken an unexpected slant.

John headed his men on towards where they had fought previously with Lord Grey de Wilton's detachment, but not so far as to get north of the How Mire hollow, much as he would have liked to rescue the dismounted men trapped there, recognising the priorities of the main battle. Drawing up, he marshalled his force into a line facing south, ready for whatever the situation called for.

In fact it called for more than any barrier strategy almost at once. For Huntly's advance had altered the position of the enemy right which was facing John. If he succeeded in penetrating the rest of that wing, then he would be behind them, and they could be caught between John's people and the Gordons. So their commander changed tactics, at least meantime. The dalesmen were much further away than the Gordons. He swung his company round to face west again, indeed south-by-west, to assail Huntly's flank as he charged down on the rest of the English right wing.

John had to make up his mind quickly. The rash Huntly must be aided, if possible, even if this invalidated the threat *he* was posing to the enemy as a whole. Perhaps it would be for the best, and distract Somerset, with all his right unexpectedly in disarray? Sword drawn and raised high, he brought it down to point directly at the enemy, and dug in his spurs. The dalesmen's shout drowned out the distant skirl of pipes.

They had some six hundred yards to cover to reach their foe, and over rough, uneven ground which prevented any outright charge. They had to pick their way at the best speed possible. Fortunately their mosstrooping horses were sturdy and sure-footed garrons.

At least this less than precipitate approach gave John opportunity to eye the front as well as steer his mount's course. And what he saw developing before him was sufficiently challenging. The Gordons were now in battle, and on two fronts, the enemy right wing reuniting to assail them. Beyond that, to the main battle area, John could not see for the mass of struggling men and rearing horses in between.

What he did see, however, as they neared, was Huntly's great banner, proud above the rest, suddenly disappearing, obviously its bearer cut down, no encouraging sign. John sought to spur the harder.

Thereafter it was no occasion for observing and assessing, for they were into the enemy ranks, thrusting lances and slashing swords. Of course their approach had not gone unnoticed, even though most of the enemy were facing in the other direction, dealing with the Gordons. But some had turned to face this new attack. Into these the dalesmen ploughed their way, smiting.

As such assaults went it was successful, even though no great number of the foe were cut down or unhorsed. The Scots drove on through ranks of the enemy, creating major confusion and upset, and causing those who were concentrating on attacking the Gordons, or some of them, to pull round to defend themselves. John, as his position demanded, was seeking the English leadership, but could not discern it in all the fray. But what he did perceive was that the Gordons, or a proportion of them who were still mounted, were now seeking to withdraw, a fighting retreat but still a retiral. Outnumbered and assailed on two flanks, they gave the impression of being leaderless. There was no sign of Huntly any more than of his banner.

John pressed on with his attack, using to the full the advantage of the chaos his men had already created. But as the Gordons' challenge faded, and escape obviously became their objective, so the enemy became the more able to regain control and to face the new assault. And, to be sure, they still outnumbered the mosstroopers considerably.

Recognising that the situation was now becoming dangerous, John hastily debated with himself, while seeking to avoid and smash down English lances and swords. To continue with his battle here could be ineffectual. He and Huntly between them had disorganised the enemy's right wing, yes; but the main struggle was elsewhere. He might well do more good now by withdrawing from this clash, if he could, and seeking to rejoin Angus, and in so doing possibly posing a threat to the flank of Somerset's central array. He had got that far in his thinking when, through a gap in the enemy ranks, he glimpsed something which made up his mind for him very promptly, another English detachment coming down to the assistance of these he was engaging, Somerset acting the experienced commander and endeavouring to control the entire situation.

It was time to disengage here.

That, to be sure, was none so easy, either in informing all his battling men, or for these to cut their way through the foe and out. They were assisted however by the still partial confusion around them, and lack of effective leadership here displayed.

No doubt many of his followers had perceived the situation and come to the same conclusion as he had, for he found his brother Robert making his way from the rear, which he was sufficiently modest to command, to suggest this very course. In consequence, the disengagement here was accomplished with less difficulty than anticipated, the mosstroopers seeking to mass together and by sheer weight of numbers smash a way through a section of the enemy. Clear, and apparently having suffered few casualties, they headed on for the main battleground.

Before ever they reached it, John recognised all the signs of defeat and victory, the latter, sadly, for the English. The fighting was all on the Scots side of the burn, some of it quite some distance therefrom, indicating major enemy inroads. A great number of fallen littered the ground, and by the way most of these were lying and facing, horses as well as men, they were Scots. Some few were already riding off westwards, clearly their own folk. Up on the higher ground southwards the Highland foot appeared to be retiring in face of the enemy left-wing cavalry. A tight group of banners in mid-fray, some notably showing the stars and red heart of Douglas, indicated that Angus and his lieutenants were still putting up a stiff fight, but it was clearly defensive; and as clearly they were greatly outnumbered. John's heart sank, although he had not been totally unprepared for this.

But he knew more than regrets. He could not, at this stage, change the fortunes of the day, but he could make a diversion and try to help that embattled leadership group represented by the banners, and so save something, perhaps for a rejoining of Arran's force and a new stand. So, waving his people, with Robert's help, into as nearly an arrowhead formation as was possible with such numbers, he pointed sword forward, Wauchope at one side of him, his brother at the other, shouting, "A Maxwell! A Maxwell!"

In all that din and struggle, the cry would never be heard. But with his dalesmen taking up their various slogans behind him, the concerted yelling could scarcely be missed or ignored. As they bore down on the battling masses, heads were turned and some reactions were evidenced, fighting faltering, at least on this flank.

As ever, fiercely charging horsemen had initial advantage over semi-stationary ones, and the dalesmen thundered into the conflict and drove on through. No doubt they rode down Scots as well as English in their furious dash, but that was unavoidable. Momentum did flag, but they pressed on, swords flailing, amidst the clash of steel, the shouts and screams and groans of men, the neighing of frightened and injured horses. The mosstroopers had no more breath for slogan-shouting, reserving their remaining strength for weapon-wielding. This was their third battle of the day.

John, in making for those banners, clustered together whereas the English ones were dispersed, saw the greatest banner of all the field, the leopards of England, well back from the fray, where Somerset, unlike Angus who was in the thick of it, could survey all and seek to control, less knightly and gallant behaviour in a commander but more effective by far. He was no doubt even now seeking to make dispositions to deal with this new development.

The West March charge, although less than headlong now, did manage to penetrate right through to those banners. Angus was there, Drumlanrig, Morton, Argyll and other leaders. No words were exchanged, would not have been heard were they uttered, but Angus pointed commandingly onwards, that is, in the same direction that the dalesmen were facing, due southwards. John understood. They had left a confusion behind them, through which the Scots leadership could ride off, to leave the field; but a similar confusion onwards would help to prevent immediate interference from that side and pursuit. That would make good sense, in the circumstances, however hard on the struggling folk left behind.

So, without pause, John led his tight formation on. Somerset would have difficulty in prompt dealing with that.

Battle was still raging southwards, so that the moss-troopers' flailing advance was no easy process, however determined. The question was – how long to keep it up? John was too preoccupied by what was immediately in front to look behind, but presumably Angus and the others would be disengaging without delay and making off westwards. No need to give them overlong, especially as the rest of the still fighting Scots would see what was happening and no doubt seek to make their own withdrawal, orderly or otherwise.

Unfortunately, or oddly, at this late stage in the day, John received his first wound, a lance-thrust which, glancing off his steel breastplate, found the hinge in the sleeve armour and pierced his shoulder, the right shoulder. It was not a serious injury, but it did cause him to drop his sword. Biting his lip, he pressed on.

But not for long now. He had given Angus time enough. And he had his own men to consider, not to mention himself and his brother. He raised his left arm, casting away the shield that it had borne, and waved it round, westwards, again and again.

No doubt thankfully his dalesmen began to swing off in that direction, still having to beat their way but now through less dense opposition. Ahead lay escape, an end to immediate conflict, whatever awaited them afterwards.

They won free, and could see, beyond other escapers, Angus's party well in front, heading behind the town for the Inveresk area. Glancing back over that painful shoulder, John sought to assess how many of his own men he had lost in the day's actions. It was difficult to tell more than roughly, but the impression was that no great numbers were missing. No doubt some, like himself, had sustained wounds of varying seriousness, but still remained in their saddles.

They pounded on after the leadership group. Behind them, as the Scots remainder melted away, the English appeared to be regrouping rather than immediately pursuing. No doubt they had their casualties to consider also, and much re-forming of sections would be called for, however elated they might be at being left in command of the field, the Battle of Pinkie won.

John's party caught up with Angus and the others at Inveresk, to find a hasty council taking place amidst much anger, recrimination and accusation. Various failures and mistakes were being levelled – at Huntly for his rash initiatives and lack of co-operation with the rest – for which he had paid, it seemed, by being captured; at Argyll's Highlandmen, who seemed to have fought a private battle of their own without concern for the main conflict; and so on. Angus gave an approving nod in John's direction. But the main complaint was against Arran, who, it appeared, had remained with most of his force at the Musselburgh bridge area, this to prevent any force landing from those English ships with their cannon, instead of coming on to back up Angus's main array. And once word of defeat there had reached him, the regent had promptly hurried off, apparently heading for the security of Edinburgh Castle, leaving nobody very senior in command of his force, which had not been long in making off and dispersing likewise, lacking any specific orders. Arran was no warrior, all knew, and had very much proved it, however amiable a character.

Angus, while cursing him, had other things on his mind now, including mourning for his clever brother, Sir George Douglas, amongst the many who had fallen.

More than fault-finding, accusations and mourning were necessary now. Decisions had to be made, and swiftly. It was generally agreed that the leadership should retire to the walled city of Edinburgh meantime, although whether they could continue to hold it against those ships' cannon was another matter. The castle itself could probably hold out, with its strong position on its rock-top and superior artillery. Somerset, when Hertford, would remember that he had failed to take it previously. But large numbers of armed men and their horses would be of no advantage penned within the city's walls, a burden on everyone and little help for the defences. So dispersal for most of what remained of the army meantime, but all to be ready for further orders from Angus, these depending on how Somerset chose to use his victory. Drumlanrig asserted that the Borderland would now be wide open to large-scale invasion and ravage, especially the West March. John and Robert agreed. It was decided that the men from there should return southwards forthwith, the dalesmen insisting on it anyway, along with all other Marchmen.

So, with no time nor place for lengthy debate, the assembly broke up, none happy but almost all able to put the blame on others for this black day for Scotland.

John took the opportunity to have his brother examine his injured shoulder, discovering that, however painful, it was only a flesh wound, and, bound up with a torn portion of his shirting, ought not greatly to trouble him. Others were considerably worse off, he learned, and had to be aided.

John, Robert and Drumlanrig, then, led their people off south-westwards for the Border hills. At least they could claim some credit out of it all. But what was going to happen to Scotland now?

17

That damaged shoulder at least ensured a hero's welcome for John Maxwell at Terregles, the fuss being made over it much in excess of any reactions to accounts of battle and campaigning, or even of warnings of possible enemy threats to their neighbourhood, Agnes almost as preoccupied over it as her husband had been over the first announcement of her pregnancy, modest a laceration as it was. Catherine and Janet were almost equally concerned. Not that the man complained.

Despite, or perhaps because of, all the attention paid, that wound did not seriously incommode him – which was just as well, for he by no means returned to any period of rest and recovery. As warden, he had to seek to organise the West March's defences in case of fresh invasion from Carlisle, or of further assaults by the victorious hordes from the north. Robert helped him in this, and John was indeed thinking of appointing him deputy warden, even though he was scarcely a born leader of fighting men. So there had to be much riding about Dumfries-shire and Galloway, warning, stimulating and planning.

Actually, when positive action was called for, the demand came from elsewhere, the east where, John was surprised to learn, massive English inroads were rife again, in the Middle and East Marches, allegedly a large part of Somerset's army savaging these areas on their way south. Scarcely relishing further warlike challenge so soon after the recent campaigning, any more than expecting the English host to be heading for home so soon as this after its victory, advantageous as it might be for the rest of Scotland, John gathered together a modest force of less-than-eager Marchmen, and headed over the hills for the Tweed.

In the event, although they saw grim signs of enemy savagery and the violation of the countryside, they did not come in contact with any of the English themselves, however much of burning, slaughter and pillage was evident in upper Tweeddale and Teviotdale and Jedforest. Wondering, John made for Ferniehirst Castle, seat of the Middle March Warden, seeking information, and saw plenty of signs of assault and conflict as he approached it. But the Kerr banner of the Sun in Splendour still flew from its topmost tower, and although the drawbridge was up and all defences manned, their Maxwell and dalesmen colours were recognised and their arrival welcomed.

Sir John Kerr, greeting the newcomers warmly enough, declared that he could have done with their arrival and help sooner! It had been a dire interlude. Ferniehirst had been assailed but not taken, although its outworks and castleton destroyed and nearby Jedburgh ravaged again and burned. Fortunately a mixed Scots and French force sent south after the retiring English by Angus, who was now calling himself Lieutenant-General of the Realm, had effected relief of the castle and defeat of this section of the attackers.

Kerr was a mine of information as to the general situation. It appeared that, after Somerset had burned Musselburgh, Dalkeith and Leith, with many villages, and made an attempt on Edinburgh but could not take it, contenting himself with part-demolishing the Abbey of the Holy Rood, he had learned of a plot back in England to unseat him as Lord Protector and to seize the young king, this by Dudley, Earl of Warwick, the father-in-law of the late Queen Jane Grey. Thereafter, deciding his priorities, he had turned his army round, southwards, to return and deal with this situation, hence its savagery in the Borderland as it went. But before leaving Lothian, Kerr mentioned, Somerset had wreaked vengeance of two castles which had given him offence, Fawsyde and

Luffness, the former for seeking to hinder his host before Pinkie, and the latter because Henry Tudor had apparently given orders, before his death, that "Luffness was to be spoiled" for holding up his fleet and the relief of Hertford at Haddington, in the Aberlady Bay incident. The English had demolished most of that castle but had failed to make much impression on the ten-foot-thick walling of the two lower storeys of the keep.

Somerset had left the English Lord High Admiral, the Lord Clinton, and his fleet, to inflict further his will upon the Scots; but after a few days' ravaging of the Lothian coast, the latter had set sail for home, burning Kinghorn and some of the Fife fishing burghs on the way, no doubt considering developments in England more worthy of his attention, in the circumstances.

So, thus soon after their triumph at Pinkie Braes, Scotland was unexpectedly quit of the victors, to the surprise of all. None imagined, however, that this remission would last for long.

Kerr also informed that Huntly had been released by his captors, on payment of an enormous ransom and his promise to do all in his power to further the marriage project between the young King Edward and Queen Mary, which appeared to be still English policy, however little it commended itself to most Scots, who saw it as just another takeover device.

In the circumstances there was no point in John and his people remaining in the Middle March, almost all the enemy now back over the border. Whether there might still be raiding from Carlisle into the West March, in this period of an English power struggle, remained to be seen. All were glad to turn homewards.

In the event, when John arrived back at Terregles, it was to discover the answer to the question of possible West March raiding; also of his faith in his brother to act deputy warden. For during their absence in the Middle March, the English Lord Wharton had led a force of some three thousand from Carlisle into Scotland, presumably some sort of warning gesture ordered by the retiring Somerset. Robert had managed hastily to gather a collection, from round about, to halt this, not before the invaders had taken and sacked the town of Annan unfortunately. No great battle had ensued, apparently, but, orders fulfilled and opposition met with, Wharton had turned and gone back to Carlisle. It had been Robert, Lord Maxwell's first independent command.

The news which filtered down to Terreglès and Caerlaverock that late autumn and early winter, from north and south, was all of the manoeuvrings of the great ones in both kingdoms; devices, statecraft and treachery, but, thankfully, not of demands for armed men. Somerset and Warwick seemed to be playing cat-and-mouse, neither actually into open warfare, although the former retained control of young Edward. Reports suggested that the two factions were fairly evenly divided as to support, the which constituted good news for Scotland. Cross-border hostilities were notable for their absence, save for the endemic private reiving, which never ceased and had little to do with national affairs.

Tidings from the north were also of tensions and power struggles. Angus was seeking to establish himself as lieutenant-general and military leader. There was a move to unseat Arran, after his feeble and mistaken conduct at Pinkie. But this was not to be achieved easily, for the Hamiltons were powerful and Arran's half-brother was the new Archbishop of St Andrews, Primate and head of Holy Church. Moreover the regent himself was next heir to the throne, and should young Mary die he would be the monarch. The suggestion was that the queen mother, Marie de Guise, a strong-minded and able woman, would fill the position adequately, and because of her situation and standing, would be less likely to invite jealousy. Also her influence with her native France, and the gaining of French aid, was vitally important. There was talk of sending her daughter to France for safety, for Somerset had demanded the little queen's delivery to himself before he left for the south, and undoubtedly there would be continuing attempts to grasp the child. Meanwhile she was being sent to the little islet and priory of Inchmahome, in the Loch of Menteith, none so far from Stirling where her mother was based, as a secure haven, in the care of the Lord Seton and Sir David Lindsay, Lyon King of Arms. King Henry of France was now claiming that the little Mary should marry *his* heir, the Dauphin Francis, instead of Edward Tudor, and to back this proposal was sending six thousand more mercenary troops to Scotland, under the Sieur d'Essé, a welcome development. Linking all these moves was Lindsay's suggestion that Marie de Guise should urge her kinsman of France to create Arran a French duke, if he could be persuaded to resign as regent.

All this, however interesting, had little effect on life in the West March, where the priority was in sustaining readiness to counter further English aggression at the same time as getting on with the needful business of living: farming, milling, cattle-raising and marketing, estate and property maintenance and improvement – and some sport, pleasure and entertainment also, to be sure, for life was not to be all duty, anxieties, toil and problems.

Into this category came the wedding of Catherine's father-in-law, Sir Alexander Stewart of Garlies, his third wedding, which took place in the little kirk of Garlies, and which John and Agnes attended. It was a cheerful and noisy affair, much taxing the little church, and indeed the quite large Garlies Castle thereafter, for the bridegroom had no fewer than sixteen sisters, all married and to the lairds of seemingly half of Galloway, and who all came to see their brother make his third match, with their own families. The ceremony was conducted by the groom's second son, John, parson of Kirkmahoe, as lively a character as the rest of his relatives. The Terregles guests were exhausted even next day as they made for home. They agreed that Catherine had married into a remarkable family, while rather hoping that she was not expected to be quite so reproductive.

Young Will was proving to be a baby of character also, early making his mark on the Terregles establishment, usually entirely amiable but when demanding being very much so, and with a powerful pair of lungs. Agnes declared that she did not know who was most trouble to her, her husband or her son, but did not fail in her duties towards either.

Curiously, as those months passed into summer again, and a sort of armistice prevailed with the English, thanks to the Somerset–Warwick vendetta, John found his duties as warden almost more onerous and time-consuming than when he was acting the warrior. This was because the Borderers as a whole, the male ones at least, had more time on their hands for preferred activities, particularly cattle-trafficking – they did not call it stealing – family feuding, woman-exchange and barter, land-boundary disputes and the like. This applied on both sides of the frontier, indeed the actual borderline was all but ignored save in times of national hostilities, and the wardens on both sides were almost as often dealing with the more aggressive offenders from the other March as with their own. John did not see it as his duty to act the law-enforcer over-stringently, at least the nation's laws, for the Borders had their own accepted laws and customs, often with scant relation to the others; but some behaviour could not decently be ignored, especially when specific complaints were made to him, and these seemed to proliferate that year of 1548, his own dalesmen being amongst the most troublesome, possibly because they felt that they had done their fair share of national service and it was now their right to pursue private objectives. This posed problems for John, for who knew how soon he might be called upon to enlist these people's armed support again. Also, he had no desire to be over-hard on Cumbrian malefactors operating north of the divide in case it provoked Lord Wharton, as he now was his English opposite number, to retaliate by making major raids. All had to be finely balanced.

As an example of the difficulties he had only to consider the case of Sir Thomas Carleton. Sir Thomas, of Carleton Hall in Cumberland, was an old hand at reiving and robbing, which clearly he looked upon as something of a hobby and pastime rather than any needful exercise, for he owned broad acres and did not lack riches. And he clearly saw no difference operating in Dumfries-shire and Galloway than from Cumberland and Northumberland. Yet to deal with him sternly, as deserved, could result in serious cross-border clashing, for he was a friend of Wharton's and could, and did, supply the English warden with many lances. So John rather sought to turn a blind eye on Carleton's conduct, so long as it was reasonably modest in scope. But when loud complaint was made from the Scots side, he felt that he had to do something.

Such occasion did develop that late August, when, with the harvest safely in and time on his and his tenants' hands, Carleton evidently felt the need for recreation for him and his. With some three score of his Cumbrian riders, he crossed the Solway sands at low tide from Morecambe Bay and made for the Kirkcudbrightshire shore.

It was unfortunate that he chose that target, and especially the farms of the Auchencairn and Palnackie area, for these belonged to Maclellan of Bombie, one of the most important and proud Galloway chiefs, which Carleton ought to have known. At any rate, at next low water he headed back across the sands for Morecambe with a couple of hundred head of cattle. And the next day Maclellan came storming up to Terregles demanding action and retribution.

John could not refuse or prevaricate, for he could well be needing Maclellan's many men at any time. Moreover, Bombie was a far-out kinsman. He promised to make representations.

There was a custom, indeed a recognised system,

whereby wardens on opposite sides could meet on occasion to discuss mutual problems. John had not so far made use of this, and he wondered whether this was the occasion to try it out – for, after all, Wharton had led the last enemy raid into Scotland, no doubt on orders from Somerset, and had been repulsed by Robert Maxwell. Would he agree to meet, and if so, could any good come of it? It seemed unlikely, but was perhaps worth a trial.

So he sent Dod Armstrong, as messenger, to request an interview, at a time and place to be agreed, but not very hopefully.

But Carleton himself acted first. Presumably well pleased with his earlier foray, he staged another, this time again across the Solway sands but into Dumfries-shire, in the Mousewold and Cummertrees area, none so far from Caerlaverock, and Maxwell land.

This was just too much. Hearing that the Cumbrians were still in the vicinity, John hastily gathered together a sizeable group – he boasted that he could assemble three hundred and fifty men in thirty-five minutes – and went in search of the intruders, who were said to be in the Forehead Ford locality, presumably intending further raiding before returning home.

There followed an interesting and significant confrontation. Carleton, veteran as he was, but outnumbered four to one, quickly perceived negotiation as the preferred option. He made no apologies, declaring that he was only here compensating himself for Scots purloining of his and his neighbours' cattle on sundry occasions; but when John mentioned the so-recent Maclellan raid, he had to admit that perhaps he was over-compensating a little, and civilly offered to hand over the cattle collected on this foray, which gesture John accepted with comparable good manners, although pointing out that these were mainly Maxwell beasts anyway. He took the opportunity to observe that there had been altogether too much reiving and raiding recently, without specifying the culprits, and said that he would have to be having a word with Lord

Wharton about it, for their mutual benefit. Meantime, he would escort Sir Thomas and his people to the border at Canonbie, as was only courteous, in peacetime.

So the two knights rode, ostensibly amicably, to the borderline at the Liddel Water, their respective parties behind them keeping well apart, considerably less sociable. At Canonbie, the Scots lined up at the riverside to watch the others splash across into England, and as the last Cumbrians rode off up the other bank, spontaneously raised a jeering volley of shouts, this admittedly producing a certain amount of fist-shaking from the departing and empty-handed raiders.

Grimly satisfied, John led his people back home, one aspect of his wardenly duties fulfilled.

Two days later he had word from Lord Wharton that he was prepared to meet him, as requested, at Canonbie, in one week's time, if this was convenient.

John guessed that Wharton would not come alone to this appointment, and wondered what numbers he would field, to indicate due authority. He decided that the same party that he had used to confront Carleton would probably be apt, and was content to observe, when he saw the Englishmen awaiting them at the ford, that they were in approximately similar numbers as themselves. Amongst those behind Wharton he could distinguish Sir Thomas Carleton.

The two wardens advanced alone into mid-ford to greet each other, expressions schooled to formal civility. Wharton, considerably the older, said that he had known Sir John's father, and of course Lord Herries, and in return was assured that the Wharton name and reputation was not unknown in Scotland. No mention was made of the previous year's raid over the border, led by Wharton.

Since John had requested the interview, he led off. There had been a number of cattle-thieving forays conducted by Cumbrians of late, he pointed out reasonably, and while a little of this could be tolerated, the scale of it had been increasing and the amounts of stock involved excessive. No doubt there was some similar activity emanating from the Scots side, but of lesser intensity. Perhaps it was time for some exercise of their authority as wardens to limit these incursions?

Expressionless, Wharton inclined his head. What did Sir John suggest?

Some deterrent was probably called for. The threat of some periods of confinement in the cells of Dumfries Tolbooth and Carlisle Castle for over-avid reivers, irrespective of rank or position, might be sufficient to reduce these unfortunate occurrences? He, Maxwell, proposed so to announce and effect. If Lord Wharton would think to do the same, then it was possible that there would be the required diminution of offences and the risk of complaints, unrest and bloodshed, to the approval, surely, of both the English Lord Protector and the Scots regent. How said his lordship?

Wharton stroked his greying beard, then nodded, and said that he would consider the matter, probably favourably.

The two wardens bowed to each other and, reining round their horses, splashed back to their own sides of the Liddel Water, to lead their companies back whence they had come, dignity satisfied, duty done and messages conveyed.

Thus the peace might be maintained, on the West March at least, and the rule of laws, of a sort, upheld.

18

Events on the national scene, in the months which followed, were more dramatic. With the English demands continuing for the young Queen Mary to be sent south into the Lord Protector's care to be duly prepared for marriage to King Edward, Queen Marie de Guise instead sent the girl, now in her sixth year, off to France into the care of that monarch, with the prospect of her betrothal to King Henry's heir, the dauphin, thus cementing the Auld Alliance and warning England of a threat on two fronts should there be further aggression.

Then early the next year a French envoy came with the news that little Mary and her four attendants of the same name, Beaton, Seton, Fleming and Livingstone, were comfortably settled at Versailles and allegedly happy; and at the same time the ambassador brought the royal decree promoting the Earl of Arran to the French dukedom of Chatelherault, the agreed price for his resignation of the regency. He stepped down, therefore, with good enough grace, for he had been scarcely the man for government of a distinctly unruly nation, any more than as a commander of men in the field. The much more strong-minded Queen-Mother was installed in his place, to the approval of most.

Then shortly afterwards the news came from the south of another ducal appointment. Warwick had managed to unseat the Lord Protector Somerset, got young Edward into his hands, later created Duke of Northumberland, and taken over the rule of England. On the whole this development was welcomed in Scotland. Somerset/Hertford had been very much Henry Tudor's man, of a like persuasion regarding the northern kingdom, and his departure from power probably advantageous, since Northumberland/Warwick was not known to have ambitions about Scotland, and his relations with Henry had been stormy, after Lady Jane Grey. He would need time to settle himself into the seat of power, anyway, so that there should be a breathing-space at least.

Somerset, it seemed, was now in the Tower of London.

As far as John was concerned, this period proved to be blissfully uneventful, with no warlike activity demanded of him and local conditions relatively peaceful. The cattle traffic and seizures still went on in a more or less domestic way, but that was normal, and did not call for much in the way of authoritative intervention. And the cross-border raiding was moderate indeed, presumably as a result of steps taken.

John was appropriately thankful, for he well recognised that he had inevitably been neglecting his duties as laird of the extensive Herries acres, and failing to act the good landlord towards the many folk who constituted the patrimony he had taken over from Lord Herries: farmers, drovers, shepherds, millers, spinners, fishermen, woodmen, even brewers and tanners. It was from all these that the Terregles power and wealth derived. Agnes, of course, had sought to do her part, and effectively; but now she had little William to mother, Catherine no longer available to help, and could not spend much of her time riding over quite far-flung lands and attending to problems ranging from unneighbourly behaviour, house-building and repair, flooding and ford-renewing and drainage, to crop and beast marketing and gaining fair prices for hides and wool. All this John had learned to cope with, in some measure, at Caerlaverock. Now he gained much more satisfaction therefrom than from leading mosstroopers in warfare or in patrolling the Marches.

Nevertheless, any illusions which he might have had that this happy state of affairs was likely to continue tended to be dispelled soon after the Yuletide and New Year celebrations, when the new rulers of England proved that they were not wholly unconcerned with Scotland, even though Northumberland claimed that his interest was in religious reform rather than national conquest, thereby of course seeking to win over the Protestant-inclined nobility. At any rate, Clinton, the admiral, arrived with his fleet up in the Tay estuary, presumably with the object of threatening St Andrews, the seat of the archbishop and Primate, now Arran/Chatelherault's half-brother, John Hamilton. He took over Broughty Castle, which largely defended Dundee town, handed over to him by the Lord Gray, a reformer, then occupied the town, under cannon-threat, and sailed up Tay as far as Perth, which was very much a religious centre, with many priories, monasteries, nunneries and hospices, sacking all in the name of reform, his men raping the nuns and calling them whores of Satan. All this undoubtedly to remind the Scots that English claims to overlordship were by no means given up under the new dispensation.

Queen Marie, a staunch Catholic, was not the one to accept all this tamely. She sent up a force under Huntly and other Catholic lords, with additional French troops under d'Essé, and, more importantly, the heavy cannon of de Thermes, and these last pounded Broughty Castle, Clinton's base, into submission, and damaged some of his fleet not quite quick enough to get out of range. The admiral duly returned to his own waters. Probably it was all little more than a gesture anyway, with no intention of prolonged occupation; but the message was clear. Perth and Dundee were left to recover as best they might; and if the archbishop heaved a sigh of relief, he and others were warned that the reform party had powerful friends. John Maxwell recognised that he should make the most of the Borderland's period of remission, for it was unlikely to last.

Actually this demonstration that Northumberland was seeing himself as fairly securely in power at London, and prepared to continue with efforts at the subjugation of

Scotland – partly possibly to bolster his reputation, for he had just lost the English toe-hold across the Channel, Boulogne, to the French, and had had to conclude a treaty of peace with that realm – was to produce an unexpected result. For the shrewd Marie de Guise perceived opportunity. She applied, quoting the terms of that treaty, to young King Edward for letters of safe-conduct through England for herself to visit the King of France, her brother the Duc de Guise, who had taken Boulogne, and her other brother, the Cardinal of Lorraine, who all but ruled the kingdom, ostensibly to see how her little daughter Mary was settling down in her new domicile. In the circumstances such safe-conduct could scarcely be refused, and the three nations were treated to the extraordinary spectacle of the queen-dowager and regent of Scotland travelling in state down through England, being received with due courtesies at Whitehall, and then crossing the Channel to France, all as though harmonious relations prevailed, and Admiral Clinton's ships scarcely existed. And although none could doubt that Queen Marie's main objective that autumn of 1550 was to arrange further support and aid for Scotland from the French, nevertheless, on her return journey, she was entertained at Hampton Court, the late King Henry Tudor's fine palace, by his rather frail and sickly son, now aged nearly fourteen, Northumberland remaining in the background, and Somerset remaining a prisoner in the Tower. The proposed marriage of Edward and Mary did not go unmentioned, but was deftly sidestepped.

Statecraft could have its triumphs comparable with those of warfare.

On her return, the regent called a parliament, to accede to marriage arrangements, but to the Dauphin of France not Edward of England. And at the same time, Marie prudently allowed the reformer lords to propose and pass a number of resolutions condemning the corruption of Holy Church, its gross acquisition of wealth and estates, and the ignorance of many of the prelates, some of whom could not even recite the Lord's Prayer. In fact, no fewer than fifty-seven such motions were tabled, somewhat more than the Queen-Mother probably visualised, but parliamentary motions did not necessarily all result in action.

It was out of this parliament that John was drawn into national, as distinct from West March, affairs again. Robert had sat therein, as Lord Maxwell, and while at Stirling had become friendly with Sir David Lindsay, Lord Lyon King of Arms, to whom he had recounted his brother's successful cross-border negotiation with Lord Wharton. And Lindsay had told Marie de Guise, with the unlooked-for result of John being summoned to attend on the regent at her palace of Linlithgow.

Wondering indeed, and dressed in his best, John, with Robert, set out northwards.

Linlithgow, midway between Edinburgh and Stirling, was always the dowery seat of the wives of the Scottish monarchs, its handsome red-stone palace set pleasingly on a mound above a picturesque loch, on an island of which the Bruce was reputed to have wooed his queen-to-be, Elizabeth de Burgh. John found Queen Marie to be a characterful woman of middle years, not beautiful but quite striking of appearance, with a graceful bearing and a notably long neck. She greeted them in friendly fashion.

The reason for this summons was explained. "I have heard, Sir John, that you are a man who can confer and negotiate as well as lead men in battle. You have proved it, yes?" She spoke with a lilting French accent. "You have already won an agreement with the English milord, Warton, is it? On matters concerned with your western border. Now we may have other use for your abilities. The English have to be discouraged – is that the word? – from the further attack upon us. And it has been told to me that the Border's state and boundaries, and the behaviour of its people, can be used as excuse for the invasion. There are uncertainties, now, as to where the lands meet, in some parts? That should be made in accord."

"There are stretches, Your Grace, which have long been named the Debatable Lands," John agreed. "The borderline is not clearly defined everywhere, especially in the West March. It would be difficult to mark any actual line."

"That may be so. But if the attempt was to be made, in agreement with the English, *d'accord*, it would help to establish peace. There are other matters, yes, to better relations, and so peace. The better tranquillity of all, less of plunder and strife and raid, on both sides. This gives excuse for the English to make invasion. Certain Church lands in Scotland have long belonged to English abbeys and bishoprics, to Hexham, Durham, Lanercost, and such. Still these are claimed by the English, even though they no longer give their duty to Holy Church. This should be made right. Other matters also. So I make intention to ask King Edward to send commissioners to seek to make accord with my own, at some convenient place. I would wish you, Sir John, to be one of the commissioners for Scotland, you with your good knowledge of the Border country and your abilities of negotiation. You will do it, yes?"

"If it is Your Grace's wish and command, to be sure. But I think that you rate my poor efforts too highly, Highness. My speech with Lord Wharton, the English warden, was very brief and of no especial merit, bargaining and warning of a sort, more than any negotiations. I know the West March Debatable Lands, yes. But in other matters I have no great knowledge. And I am very ignorant as to Church affairs and lands."

"Others will deal with that, my friend. The Lord Seton and Sir David Lindsay, the Lyon, will lead the commissioners. And I will have a churchman to speak to that matter. I do not look for great things from this meeting, if the English will agree to have it. But if it leads to more of negotiation, conferring, in place of invasion and bloodshedding, that is a gain, no? I promised as much to the Edward Tudor boy when I saw him in England. So go you and see Sir David. He will tell you more, Sir John."

They bowed themselves out.

They found Lindsay fishing in the loch, with a younger man. Sir David was a pleasant character, as good-looking as he was talented, poet and deviser of masques and plays as well as adroit courtier and chief herald, successor to the sennachies of ancient Scotland, and a worthy one. He told John that this proposed mission was not expected to produce any very direct results, but was more of a signal to Northumberland that parley and discussion were called for, by both Scotland and France, rather than his predecessor's naked steel tactics. The new regent was astute and far-sighted, and able to bring a woman's perspective and valuable touch to the nation's affairs. Clearly Lindsay thought highly of the Queen-Mother.

He said that he would inform John of the time and place of the proposed conference, if the English agreed to it. He would ask the other two March wardens to join them, if Queen Marie agreed, as advisers rather than commissioners.

They left him to his fishing.

It was over a month later, with spring turning into a belated summer, before the call came. Northumberland had acceded to the suggestion of an exchange of views, as he put it; and the meeting would be held at the Norham ford of Tweed, eight miles west of Berwick, in two weeks' time. The Scots party would gather at Kerr's Ferniehirst Castle before proceeding to the rendezvous.

Agnes was quite proud of her husband being chosen to be one of Scotland's commissioners, especially as his fellow-wardens were not. This was something other than leading mosstroopers, patrolling the Marches and wielding sword and lance. She sent him off with instructions to use the wits she was sure he possessed, and who knew what this might lead to?

He found a company of about a dozen assembled at Ferniehirst, under the joint leadership of Lord Seton and the Lyon, these two trusted friends of Marie de Guise, with

239

Douglas of Drumlanrig. Also the French envoy, d'Essé, as a warning presence. The Church was represented by the Archdeacon of Dunkeld and the Prebendary of Dunblane. Supporters included the young man Lindsay had been fishing with at Linlithgow Loch, apparently his assistant herald, William Cockburn, Younger of Skirling, a cheerful individual. The East March Warden was present also; he was now Lord Home, his father having been severely wounded at Pinkie and dying thereafter. The group discussed their remit and tactics for the following day, all recognising it as more in the nature of a diplomatic gesture rather than any real arbitration or negotiation.

With an early start in the morning, they rode the nearly thirty miles up Teviot and Tweed, by Kelso, Birgham and Coldstream, to the Norham ford in the Ladykirk area, in order to be there by the appointed noontide. Here they found a deputation awaiting them, on the English side of the river. These splashed across to salute the Scots and to invite them to come over to Norham Castle to meet the commissioners appointed in King Edward's name.

Norham was perhaps the mightiest of the English border strongholds, formerly belonging to the militant Bishops of Durham, but a royal fortress since the Reformation. It had a dire history as far as Scotland was concerned, ever menacing the East March; and it required a certain amount of resolution on the new arrivals' part to agree to go over and enter its grim portals, where so many Scots had hung. However, it was scarcely conceivable that the English would think of acting with more than verbal hostility on such an occasion as this; and certainly it would be more suitable to discuss their business indoors than on this river bank. So the crossing was made.

Nevertheless, entering the gatehouse arch from over the drawbridge, into that dread fastness, did not fail to affect the visitors.

They found the English commissioners awaiting them in the lower great hall, with liquid refreshment in plenty but smiles scarce. John was interested to discover that Lord Wharton was chief commissioner, with Lord Hunsdon, another veteran, Warden of the East March, alleged to be a bastard of Henry Tudor's youth, and Sir John Forster, a tough individual indeed, Middle March Warden. Also Lord Conyers and Sir Richard Musgrave, a Cumbrian magnate; altogether a formidable group. The fact that all three English wardens were apparently there as commissioners led to a hasty upgrading on the Scots side; it would not do to have two of theirs in any lesser role. The opposition did not appear to boast any clerics.

There was no delay about starting the proceedings, fraternising clearly not on the agenda, with the gruff, all but monosyllabic Wharton taking the lead. Sitting along the lengthy hall table, the Scots consigned to the lower end, he demanded the reason for this visit and what they had come to discuss.

Lindsay, as Lord Lyon, being an officer of state, spoke first, and amicably. He said that they came representing the Queen-Mother, regent of her royal daughter's realm, to seek agreement on various matters outstanding between the two kingdoms. Both would have their respective views and issues; but they might lead off with the moot point which was so relevant to each nation, namely the defining, as far as was possible, of the mutual border between the two, which was very uncertain in parts and apt to lead to misunderstandings and conflicts. Such were probably mainly on the West March. So he would call on Sir John Maxwell, warden thereof, to speak to this first.

Thus early was John pitched into the fray.

Eyeing Wharton, he declared that while all March wardens were very much concerned and aware of this situation and its problems, undoubtedly these were worst in the area of the West March between the Rivers Sark and Esk, commonly known as the Debatable Lands, the country of the Armstrongs, Johnstones, Irvines, Grahames and the like. As they all knew well, many of these folk, being unsure of where the borderline lay, were apt to ignore it altogether, and either paid no allegiance to either realm or chose to support whichever suited them best at various times. This was unsatisfactory for the wardens, and for maintenance of all order. Was that agreed?

Curt nods.

He went on. Two parishes in especial, quite large ones, were the worst for this trouble and confusion – Canonbie and Kirkandrews, between Esk and Sark, with the dales of Liddel and Tarras entering. Scotland and England had both claimed them, or parts of them, down the years, but no March was ever defined. He proposed that now it should be. Here was opportunity to right the matter for the benefit of both kingdoms.

Eyebrows raised, stares and sidelong glances.

John declared that he had considered this long and well. Many of the folk dwelling there were his own dalesmen. Canonbie was somewhat the larger and lay to the north, with its villages of Rowanburn and Overton and Hollows and Harelaw, in the dales of Esk and Liddel. Kirkandrews was to the south, nearer to the Solway and Carlisle and Annan, with Netherby and Penton, Beck and Sarkhall, this Grahame and Bell and Routledge country. His proposal was that the border should be defined, by common consent, down Esk as far as the Crow's Dyke, then west to the Sark and so to the Solway shore, this putting Kirkandrews parish into England, and Canonbie in Scotland. How said they all?

There was a long silence, Wharton rubbing his bearded chin, his colleagues eyeing him. This was very much his concern, as West Warden, and himself owning lands in Arthuret parish and Nicholforest, next to Kirkandrews. John, of course, knew this, and had taken it into account.

"Would your Armstrongs and Johnstones and Elliots, scoundrels all, observe this?" he demanded.

"As much, I swear, as would the Grahame's and Bells and Forsters!" And John glanced at Sir John Forster.

"The riding men care but little for boundaries and limits, as we all know. But this would make it less difficult to control them."

Forster hooted.

But Wharton still scratched his beard. "Glensier Beck and the lower Sark are English," he averred. "Headwaters land of our Beck Burn. The line you named would put them into Scotland."

"These are close to Overton, which none will dispute is Scots, my lord. To twist the March round them would be a folly, and cause the more trouble. The same could be said for Riddings and the Moats, reckoned to be in Scotland, but part of Kirkandrews parish beyond Esk. They would come to you."

"We shall consider it. And on the ground. Hereafter."

With that John had to be content. At least it was not outright rejection. And it had given a worthwhile start to the talking, with something about which to negotiate.

Lindsay, nodding to John, turned to Home. "My lord, you have some matter to speak to?"

"I have indeed," the East March Warden asserted, glaring at his opposite number. "I have spoken of this before to Lord Hunsdon, more than once. His folk from Etal and Ford and Dundo come down Till frequently and wreak havoc in the Merse. They come in large numbers, into their hundreds, no mere reiving. It is not to be borne. It must cease, I say."

"They but pay back raiders from Scotland who come down Redesdale into their lands," Hunsdon cried. "Tell Kerr your lament!" And he pointed at Ferniehirst, the Middle Warden.

"My people but seek what is their own, stolen by your Redesdale and Tynedale ruffians!" Sir John Kerr gave back. "You and Forster put your own house in order, and *then* charge us!"

Lord Seton held up his hand. "My lords and friends, let us mind our business here today. It is not the settlement of disputes between wardens of Marches. That can and

243

should be done otherwise, at your truce meetings. We are here to consider wider matters of concern to the two nations. I myself will raise one such, of importance. It concerns the trade of the realm, both realms. I call on Cockburn, Younger of Skirling, to speak to it."

That young man, usually so smiling and carefree, was looking tense now. "My lords, the Cockburns have wide lands in Lothian and the Lammermuir Hills," he jerked. "As has my Lord Seton. Cockburn itself lies there, fronting the Merse on the southern slopes of Lammermuir. These hills are the greatest sheep-rearing area of all Scotland, its wool one of our main trades. To the Low Countries. It is shipped from Berwick, near to here, down Tweed. Berwick is now in English hands, although its shire in Scotland." He was speaking more fluently as he warmed to his theme. "English merchants from the Cheviots villages are now shipping their wool from Berwick also, instead of from Newcastle and Blyth as before. This to gain the benefit of the higher prices for Scots wool, set by the Staple at Veere. This is wrongous. The wools are different, Blackface as against Cheviot. The Scots suffer. For the price goes down. The staple price is fixed on quality, at Veere. But the English merchants at the Woolmarket in Berwick will not heed our protests."

Somewhat blank stares greeted this. Trade was scarcely of concern to many there, below their lords' dignity.

"Perhaps you should explain further, Will," Lindsay suggested, in friendly fashion. "All may not know of what you speak. The Staple at Veere, see you. This may not be known."

"Yes, my Lord Lyon. Veere is the Netherlands port where the Scots wool is sent and sold. Has been for long. There is a monopoly at Veere. The English wool always used to go to Antwerp and Brussels. The burgomaster of Veere had long held this monopoly of pricing the Scots wool each year – that is, the Staple. His chosen price means a great deal to the Lammermuir shepherds and farmers and their lairds. And the price becomes lower if

244

the wool is mixed in kind and quality. So our people are suffering because of these new additions of Cheviot wool. The shippers know not the difference, and care not. And the price suffers, at Veere."

It was Forster who spoke. He undoubtedly owned land in the Cheviot Hills. "But Cheviot sheep are bigger and better than your Blackface, man!" he declared.

"But the wool is different, sir. Softer, less strong of fibre. Good for other uses. Good for clothing and the like. Lighter. But not for hangings, arras, carpeting, cloaking, where stronger fibre is required. This has been special for Lammermuir always. The Staple is set for it. So this admixture lowers the price set by the burgomaster. We would wish this put to rights."

Wharton flicked an impatient hand. "What is your call then, young man?"

"That the English wool, my lord, goes back to being shipped at Newcastle or other English port, as before, not from Berwick-upon-Tweed, where the vessels all sail to Veere."

"I support this claim," Seton said. "You English can surely strike your own bargains, in your wool as in other matters, without depending on us Scots!" But he smiled as he said it.

That had the opposition bristling, and was meant to do.

"I did not come here to discuss barter and peddling and merchanting!" Lord Conyers exclaimed. "Of greater import are the revenues of Church lands, frequently and wrongously withheld."

"In a moment, my lord," Lindsay said. "We Scots are perhaps more concerned for the well-being of our merchants and farmers and common folk than are you! Let us settle this of the wool first."

Wharton slapped the table. "Enough of this. We shall speak with these wool merchants. Now, to this of the Church lands and rentals. My Lord Conyer?"

That man, older than most there, required no urging.

"I come from Durham," he said. "I was granted former Church lands of Durham bishopric. These include lands in Scotland belonging to that see. I have great difficulty in collecting my rents therefrom. Indeed, some on Coldinghame Moor have not been paid for years. This is robbery and a sin!" He glared at Home, overlord of Coldinghame.

"Sin, you said, my lord?" Lindsay took him up. "I fear that I am a sinner myself, but not over Church lands! However, we have here churchmen qualified to speak on such matters. My lord Archdeacon?"

Master David Meldrum, of the bishopric of Dunkeld, nodded. "The lands held in Scotland by abbeys and sees were granted by pious monarchs and lords and magnates to Holy Church, whether in Scotland or England, in times past, as offerings to Almighty God. But England has swept away Holy Church, and must accept the consequences. Those lands can no longer be claimed by those who have taken them over against the will of the Church. So, my lord, you have no claim . . ."

His unctuous tones were drowned out by very different voices, shouts and growls.

Having expected no less, the Scots waited patiently.

Presently the Archdeacon was able to go on. "However, Holy Church, as Our Lord commands, can be generous. We are prepared to offer you, and other English claimants to such stolen lands, a single payment in moneys as quit claim. The while denying all liability so to do."

The moments passed as this unexpected offer was digested. The men opposite were very much realists, and knew well that the probability of continuing to gain rents from Scottish properties was minimal indeed; and a bird, even if only one, in the hand, was worth many in the bush. Conyers himself could not disguise some interest and satisfaction.

But it was Wharton who spoke. "Who decides the amounts to be paid, priest?"

"The Scots bishoprics and abbeys themselves, my lord.

Only they know the lands and their worth. Accept it, my lords, or . . ." He left the rest unsaid.

"We will inform all concerned, who make claims, of valuation and offers of payment," James Rolland, Prebendary of Dunblane, put in.

"Does any other issue of importance arise?" Lindsay said, to cut short what could have developed into a lengthy bickering.

"Only that I say, *messieurs*, that my friends of religion have been very benevolent. They deserve your thanks, no?" That was the Sieur d'Essé, his first and only contribution.

Nobody appeared to have anything more to say; and no further refreshment or hospitality was offered to the visitors.

Lingering clearly undesired by either side, John had a quick word with Wharton as to when they would meet to inspect the proposed exchange of parish boundaries in the Debatable Land, as agreed. He was told, with a shrug, say in four days' time, meeting at the Tower of Sark, Wharton being no man for hesitation or bush-beating. That was accepted.

The Scots commissioners, after scant parting formalities, rode back into Scotland, the conference, congress, forum or whatever it might be called, having occupied little more than two hours, however significant it might be for Scots–English relations, the first such to have been held for long. They were, on the whole, well satisfied, and John received compliments on having started it off on the right note and with success.

Back at Ferniehirst that night, after a long day's riding, they discussed reactions, progress and likely further developments. Lindsay declared that he was a little concerned that the new Debatable Lands defining should be accepted as authoritative and accepted in the years to come, not just any sort of temporary agreement between the West March wardens. Since Wharton had named an inspection date for only four days hence, he judged that it might be advisable for himself, as Lyon and an officer of state, to be present then, as giving the exchange more warrant on the nation's behalf. John was all in favour of this; and said that Sir David, and Will Cockburn also, would be very welcome at Terregles, if they cared to come back there with him on the morrow. This was accepted.

Next day, then, the party split up, and John and Drumlanrig had company with them on the cross-country ride to the West March.

Agnes welcomed her unexpected guests warmly, and took a prompt fancy to Sir David Lindsay, of whom she had heard of course, notably for his poems and plays, especially his *Satyre of the Thrie Estaits*, a most dramatic and significant entertainment. Moreover, he made excellent company. And Janet found his assistant herald and companion, Cockburn, much to her taste, the attraction obviously mutual. So a couple of very pleasant days were spent at Terregles before the men set off for the Sark.

John was interested to discover, at the Tower of Sark, none other than Sir Thomas Carleton, brought there by Wharton as companion. He was no more happy to see him than Wharton appeared to be to see the Lord Lyon King of Arms. However, Carleton proved to be the more civil of the pair, not difficult to be as that was, and in the tour of the parish boundaries and proposed border redefinitions which followed, he did not prove difficult – although John got the impression, perhaps unfairly, that Carleton would ignore these boundaries and margins anyway, as he had done in the past.

They started off with a disagreement, unfortunately, over that Glensier Beck area, which Wharton wanted to include in England, claiming it as the obvious headwaters of the larger Beck Burn, which actually ran down to Solway Moss and was unmistakably Cumbrian. John countered by saying that if the headwaters argument was pursued, then what of the great River Esk? Nine-tenths of its course was unquestionably in Scotland, and only the last few miles, to its mouth in the firth, in England. That did make some impact, but even so Wharton wanted this Sark Tower area included in his jurisdiction, whereas John was insistent that it was obviously Scottish and always had been. The Irvine owners would never accept it as in Cumberland, and it would be a source of continual trouble. Lindsay supported John. Eventually a compromise was reached by making a large loop southwards of the proposed boundary to include in England the sector of Sarkhall, Corries Mill and Glinger, which scarcely pleased either side but was the best that could be agreed.

After that, although there were opposing views at various points of the two parish lines, there were no major difficulties, for these were in fact largely defined by the Esk, Liddel and Tarras Waters. As they went, the party set up little cairns of stones at decided-upon and significant points, to be replaced in due course by more substantial and lasting markers, Carleton observing humorously that this was probably a waste of time, for if they could be put up, others could put them down or move them.

Eventually they finished up at Sheiling Moss on the Scots side of Esk, and Penton on the English, and parted company, both groups reasonably satisfied, with Carleton, oddly, impressing himself on Lindsay and Cockburn as quite an amiable character, something Wharton would never be. As the Scots turned for home, John knew a certain satisfaction in being able to tell himself that, whatever else, he had established some small part of his nation's territory in perpetuity.

When their guests left Terregles next morning, Lindsay mentioned that he would commend Sir John to the Queen-Mother as an excellent negotiator and representative. He might well be required for further services to the realm. And young Cockburn declared that Skirling, his father's lairdship, in West Peebles-shire, was none so far away that he could not ride it in a day to Terregles, this for

Janet's benefit. Presumably they would be seeing more of that young man.

Left to themselves, Agnes announced that she was fairly sure that she was pregnant again, to her husband's acclaim.

19

The year that followed proved to be one of dramatic events, some dire, some doubtful, some heartening for John Maxwell and his wife, as for other folk. Early in January, Agnes presented him with a daughter, to much rejoicing, whom they named Elizabeth.

Then soon afterwards word reached them that Somerset had been executed for felony; and although this produced no tears in Scotland, it did indicate that Northumberland was now firmly in control in England and might well consider himself strong enough to resume the age-old attempts to subjugate the northern kingdom.

Later, however, came further and still more sensational news from London. The frail young King Edward had died, aged fifteen years, a sad passing which abruptly altered the entire national and international scene. Before he died, Northumberland apparently had persuaded the boy to nominate Lady Jane Grey as his successor, his cousin, whom the duke had married to his own son, Lord Guildford Dudley. This young woman, aged only fifteen, was hastily crowned, but reigned for only nine days; for Henry's daughter, Mary Tudor, by his first wife Catherine of Aragon, marched on London with a Catholic host, unseated the girl, and cast her and her husband in the Tower. So now England had a Catholic queen aged thirty-seven, and Northumberland had gone to join his son and young daughter-in-law in captivity.

This extraordinary sequence of events, all happening in the course of a week or two, almost certainly meant tremendous upheaval in England, and a return to religious conflict, Mary Tudor being a vehement Catholic. What might its effect be on Scotland? Opinions varied. At least it all meant an end to talk of a marriage arrangement between the two realms. Both kingdoms now had queens-regnant, something unknown hitherto, and both named Mary, both Catholic. Henry Tudor would indeed be turning in his grave.

Although all this greatly interested John Maxwell, it did not much affect his personal life, save that, whether as a result of it, or of his Norham meeting, English border incidents had all but ceased meantime. But despite this respite, and the great delights which little Elizabeth provided for the Maxwells, together with visits from Will Cockburn which clearly were going to result in a marriage for Janet, there was worry and distress at Terregles. This was on account of Robert Maxwell, who had fallen ill that late spring, of a sickness which wasted him away in dire fashion, to the heartbreak of his family. He died in July, leaving his young and pregnant wife desolate. He had never been so active and vigorous as John, but his sudden collapse was wholly unlooked-for. Caerlaverock was left to the two widows who, in fact, did not get on with each other.

John missed his brother greatly. He found himself placed in a curious position. For now there was no Lord Maxwell, and he was the heir-presumptive to the title until the Lady Beatrix produced a posthumous child. So the Maxwell clan styled him Master of Maxwell meantime, since it must have a head, which, Agnes declared, added to confusion. For it had been her father's wish, and with the Regent Arran's acceptance, that he should be fifth Lord Herries; and although John had never been called to parliament as such, he was presumably that by rights. So what was he now? That man was quite content to be known just as Sir John Maxwell, Warden of the West March, although he would be requiring a new deputy.

Since this last appointment was a matter of some urgency, he had to do some thinking. It occurred to him that he might be able to use the situation to worthwhile and constructive effect, even though it might well be unpopular with his own clan. The Maxwells and the Johnstones of Annandale had long been at feud, not deadly slaughtering feud, save on the odd occasion among the more obstreperous mosstrooping members, but pronounced enough to cause unpleasantness and, what was more important, some non-cooperation in wardenly activities. If he was to offer the position of deputy warden to the Johnstone chief, this might well heal old sores and at the same time strengthen his own hand in the rule of the West March. Moreover, the present chief's wife was Nichola Douglas, daughter of Drumlanrig.

So, soon after Robert's funeral, he rode off up Annandale the score of miles to Lochhouse Tower, the main Johnstone seat, near the head of that vale just short of Moffat, accompanied only by Dod Armstrong, this being an occasion for tact and a moderate approach.

Lochhouse Tower, as its name implied, stood on the mound of a sort of peninsula jutting into what had once been a loch, really a widening of the River Annan, and was now swampy marshland, a strong defensive position, approachable only by its own causeway-like ridge. Presumably this strength was why the Johnstone chief made his normal dwelling there, for it was by no means the largest of his many houses, which included Elsieshields, Breckonside, Westerhill, and now Castlemilk which he had gained by marriage, his first, for Drumlanrig's daughter was his second wife.

John's approach, then, was readily observable, and in true, tough Johnstone fashion he was met by a hastily mounted group of mosstroopers of no very welcoming demeanour, demanding to know his business.

"I am Maxwell, warden of this March, seeking speech with Johnstone of that Ilk and his lady," John said, although he guessed that he would have been recognised. "I hope that they are at home?"

No answer to that was forthcoming as the group closed

in around the pair, and without comment they were led to the castle.

Lochhouse was a massive square tower of four storeys and a garret, the wallhead surmounted by a parapet and wall-walk, and the angles rounded for improved defence therefrom, all within a high-walled courtyard, itself defended by the usual gatehouse, drawbridge and portcullis. Men gazed down at the newcomers from that parapet-walk as they entered the yard's cobblestones.

If Johnstone had been apprised of the arrival of visitors, he took his time in coming to greet them, and John and Dod sat their mounts there in the midst of their guards, with due patience.

John Johnstone, when he did appear, made no gestures of welcome, but stood in the doorway, expressionless. He was a man of later middle years, stocky, powerfully built, heavy of feature, hair beginning to grey. He knew John well enough, of course, indeed they were related, for his grandmother had been a Maxwell, this before the feud started; but he did not allow that to affect his feud-conscious attitude. John it was who made the conciliatory gesture.

"Greeting, kinsman!" he called. "I come in friendship and regard. I hope that I find you and your lady in health and good state?"

That produced a nod, and a wave of the hand, this last towards his men, who took it as dismissal, dismounted and moved away. The visitors also dismounted, and their horses were led off. Dod remained behind as John walked over to the keep doorway.

Johnstone did not offer to shake hands but, turning, preceded his so doubtful guest to the foot of the turnpike stairway and up it to the great hall on the first floor, which was empty, with not even a fire burning, this still being July.

"So," he said at last, halting. "This visit has no doubt some purpose? I would know what that is?"

"It has," he was told. "A purpose of some importance.

To us both. And to others also, I would judge. An end to enmity and feud. I would ask you to become Deputy Warden of the West March, Johnstone."

The other stared, unspeaking, for moments. "Why?" he said, at length.

"Since my brother died, I require a deputy. The Maxwells and Johnstones are the most numerous and powerful families in the March. It is folly that we should be at odds. Here on the border all leal men are necessary for the realm's defence and well-being. The English have a new and stronger monarch, although a woman, very much Henry Tudor's daughter. We may well have to deal with her. The Johnstone strength could and should be available for that. And for other peace-keeping. Therefore peace between Maxwell and Johnstone should prevail and be seen to prevail. So, I would have you as deputy warden."

The other turned and moved over to a window, to stare out, silent.

John, having made his offer, was not going to plead or add to that. But addition there was, for the door from the withdrawing-room off the hall opened, and a woman came in, considerably younger than Johnstone, and good-looking in a strong-featured way, Nichola Douglas. John had met her at both Angus's and Robert's weddings.

"Did I hear aright?" she asked, frankly. "Deputy Warden is it?" No doubt she had been listening behind the door.

"You heard aright," John agreed, bowing. "My greetings, lady. I would have your husband my deputy."

"That would be good. Excellent, Sir John," she said. "Is that not so, John?" Both men being named John, she had emphasised that Sir.

Johnstone looked back. "You believe so?" he asked carefully. "Second to Maxwell!"

"Oh, I do!" she exclaimed. "Johnstone to the fore again, on the border. And an end to old scores and sores. After all, your grandsire was warden, was he not?"

That was when John's father had been under age, and for once the wardenship not in Maxwell hands.

"A strong deputy is required," John felt that he could add, without seeming to coax. And this young woman's support was to be acknowledged.

Johnstone looked from one to the other, and inclined his head.

Had John won this contest, then? Clearly Nichola Douglas decided that he had.

"The Johnstones will much strengthen your hand, Sir John," she said. "And that Sir Thomas Carleton will not again assail Lochhouse Tower, as he did before, with John your deputy, I think."

That was shrewd, for Carleton had indeed attacked as far north as this, during that first sally, in Johnstone's absence, and created havoc in the neighbourhood, boasting indeed that he would be keeper of Lochhouse for King Edward.

"That insolent braggart!" her husband snarled. "And you were making common cause with him recently, in the Debatable Lands I heard, Maxwell!" That was an accusation. Information got around in the Borderland.

"Wharton brought him," John said briefly. "Wardens have to sup with the devil, on occasion."

The young woman was quick to use that. "But now you will sup with us, Sir John? While you discuss wardenly duties."

Johnstone could do no less than second that, as the visitor was ushered into the withdrawing-room. The issue appeared to be settled.

The older man thawed considerably thereafter, and, thanks to feminine art, all tension disappeared and the men were able to talk companionably and constructively, Johnstone indeed putting forward some suggestions as to the part he and his people could play in the better governance of the March.

When, in due course, John left Lochhouse, he was at pains to convey to Nichola Douglas his appreciation of help received, as well as of the young woman's other abilities and attractions, going so far as to declare that the Johnstone was a fortunate man.

Later, when he told Agnes all about it, she declared that she would have to watch out that too many meetings between the warden and deputy did not take place, at Lochhouse Tower at least.

In September, Janet and Will Cockburn were married, and Johnstone and his lady were amongst the invited guests, to the surprise of many. It was a happy occasion, so clearly a love-match when so many between landed families were scarcely that, and apt to be more concerned with property than affection.

So now John Maxwell had Terregles Castle to himself, his wife and two children; and fond as he was of his sisters-in-law, he rejoiced at it.

The Lady Beatrix bore a son in November, so that there was a Lord Maxwell again, however diminutive. But John would remain Master of Maxwell for many a year, that is heir-presumptive, until this new John – for he was named after uncle and grandfather – should produce an heir of his own.

All this felicitous love, marriage and birth was, sadly, dampened presently by the death of the little Lord Maxwell's grandfather, the Earl of Morton, a friendly and unassuming man to be the head of the great House of Black Douglas. And having no male heir, he was succeeded as earl by a far-out kinsman, Douglas of Lochleven and Pittendreich, who was said to be of a very different character.

PART THREE

20

As it happened, the confusion of styles and titles was resolved when Marie de Guise, appreciative of John's abilities as a negotiator, appointed him to a commission to examine the reforms in religious matters, as far as they concerned temporal affairs, these being proposed by the Primate, Archbishop Hamilton, Arran's half-brother, and which would have to be homologated by parliament hereafter. This was a matter of some urgency as well as delicacy for, with Mary Tudor vigorously seeking to turn England back to Catholicism, the reformist lords in Scotland were worried that the Catholic cause would become more aggressive and assertive here also, in consequence, and were demanding safeguards. In fact, the archbishop was no diehard churchman; indeed many of his prelates called him a backslider and trimmer, only in that position because of his relationship to the late regent and heir to the throne. So his suggested reforms could have a vital effect on the nation at large as well as upon Holy Church; and Queen Marie, staunch Catholic as she might be, was concerned to avoid strife and subsequent weakness in the kingdom at a time when the English might well think to take advantage of it. Hence this committee of reliable and effective members, whatever their religious views, to consider the proposals before they were put to parliament. And to that parliament, John would be called as Lord Herries, at long last.

So John had to travel north to Linlithgow, the fine palace which the queen-regent much preferred to the stern rock-top fastness of Stirling Castle, the traditional royal seat of government. There by the islanded loch, he found an interesting and influential group assembling, including the regent's reliable friends, Lindsay and Seton. He was surprised to find Chatelherault present, tactfully brought in no doubt to appease leading reformers, one of whom John was interested to meet, the Lord James Stewart, a young man of twenty-two years, one of the many illegitimate sons of the late King James, this by Margaret Erskine, therefore a half-brother of the young Queen Mary, austere, stiff, wary, but clearly intelligent and, it seemed, a strong reformer. He was with the Cunninghame Earl of Glencairn, one of the hostages after Solway Moss. On the other side was Huntly, the Chancellor, a leading Catholic, supported by the Earl of Lennox, a shifty but clever character. Apart from the archbishop himself, the Church was represented by Bishop Robert Reid of Orkney, President of the Court of Session, and Henry Sinclair, Dean of Glasgow, an eminent scholar and one of the ablest statesmen in the land, extraordinary brother for the unhappy and rejected Oliver. John was astonished to find himself in such company, and unsure of what he had to contribute to the proceedings.

After welcoming them all, and wishing their deliberations well, Queen Marie left them to it.

Since in theory the meeting was to discuss his proposals for the betterment of worship in Holy Church and its impact on the nation at large, the archbishop led off. He declared that he, like his predecessor the late Cardinal Beaton, was well aware of shortcomings and failures which had beset Christ's Kirk in this land, and had been at pains to seek improvement, with the aid of others, notably the Dean of Glasgow here present. They had compiled a long list of faults, causes of stumbling, omissions and ill-practices, even abuses, which had crept in over the years, all of which they could not go into here. But a summary of the most important reforms suggested, he would rehearse.

Glances were exchanged and eyebrows raised.

First and foremost, Hamilton went on, measures to

counter the ignorance of too many of the clergy, which for long had shamed the land, much of which could be attributed to the long-standing custom of the powerful families of the realm putting their kinsmen and friends into bishoprics, abbacies and other prominent positions in the Church without due training and education. That, needless to say, produced a few frowns. Provision to be made for teaching entrants to the ministry, and indeed occupants thereof, not only at universities and colleges but in cathedrals, abbeys and monasteries, this of scriptural truth, the essentials of worship, divinity and canon law, to amend carelessness in public worship and an end to indecent conduct at services of all kinds by a worthy example to the common folk.

That produced nods of approval all round.

Then measures to be taken to improve the behaviour of the clergy, not only in church. Concubines to be put away, under pain of deprivation of benefices. The dismissal from clerical houses of children born in concubinage, and the deprivation of Church lands, dowries and patrimonies from all such. Prelates not to maintain in their households drunkards, whoremongers, night-walkers, bigamists, blasphemers and gamblers. To dress modestly and live soberly and more frugally, that they might have the more to spare for the poor. No more inordinate luxury at table. The higher clerics to lead the way: for instance, archbishops, bishops and, it was hoped, earls, to have no more than eight dishes of meat at a meal, save at Yuletide; abbots and priors, six; priests and barons, four; monks and burgesses, three. To this end, also, fixed prices for wines and provisions.

All round the table men eyed each other at that.

Then, unqualified persons not to receive holy orders and have the care of souls. A restraining of pluralities of office and the preventing of spiritual censures by the acceptance of bribes. Pardoners and hawkers of indulgences and relics to be put down by the laws of the land. The reformation of abuses in consistorial courts. Heresy to be put down, and speaking against the rites and sacraments to be punished. And all heretical books, poems and lewd rhymes against Holy Church to be diligently sought out and burned . . .

All but dizzy as his hearers were with this lengthy catalogue, that last clause at least served to focus some minds there, notably those of the Earl of Glencairn and the young Lord James Stewart, strong reformers, who both interrupted over the mention of that dire word heresy, which, of course, could be used to cover almost any attitude contrary or deviant to that of the current Church leadership. Their protesting brought counter-objections from Bishop Reid and the Earl of Lennox, and something of an argument engulfed the commission.

But Huntly was Chancellor of the realm, and as such chaired parliaments and had to keep order therein. Now he thumped on the table and demanded discipline. Let them debate these important matters with due care. Had the lord Archbishop further proposals to put forward? – that query all but producing groans.

Whether he had or not, Hamilton clearly decided that enough was probably enough, in the circumstances, and declared that those put forward were the main issues to be considered, as possibly affecting the realm at large, as distinct from the Church itself.

Let them deal with the items in order, then, Huntly said. Then, recollecting that Chatelherault was the senior personage there, added that was unless my lord Duke suggested otherwise. That man, looking alarmed, shook his head.

There was a silence as men tried to remember what indeed had been the earlier issues in that long and involved list of failings and backslidings requiring improvement.

Dean Sinclair helped. "Do all agree that the ignorance of some of the clergy is to be deplored, and the attitudes to learning be improved, teaching at colleges enforced, not only for new priests and novices but to refresh the memory and knowledge of incumbents? This will take

264

time, to be sure, much time to enforce, not least with the training of more teachers. But a start should be made."

"If they teach mistaken doctrine and rituals, where is the gain?" That was young James Stewart, flatly. "Heresy has just been spoken of. What improvement, if the teaching is such as condemns all criticism of Church doctrine as offensive, heresy?"

That was difficult to answer indeed. But Sinclair tried. "The will of this commission, and of parliament, will be considered well, never fear, my lord. And acted upon. Where proper."

Glencairn muttered something derogatory, but most there nodded.

"Then there is the need for betterment of the behaviour of some of the clergy," the dean went on. "Partly this will be improved through the teaching. But rules set out and penalties laid down will be necessary."

"Who makes such rules?" That was Stewart again.

"I do," the archbishop declared. "As head of the Church in this realm. But in consultation with others. And with parliament."

"None could ask better than that," Huntly averred. "What was next?"

"This of table-meats and gluttony," the dean said. "While none would wish to seek to impose frugalities, over-much of rich eating and drinking, aye and drunkenness, is contrary to Christ's teaching, when we have many poor who must feed insufficiently. The Church should set example. But not only the Church. Those who lead the people, the lords temporal as well as spiritual, and all in position of authority, should show the way."

"How would it be possible to impose such limits?" Lindsay asked.

"By prescription, my Lord Lyon. The expressed will of parliament. More we cannot do. Save by example, my friends."

No comment.

"Then there is this of the pricing of meals and

provisioning and wines. Undue wealth is amassed by merchants and traders and the like, to the hurt of all. The costs of such should be limited by due supervision. Local courts to take heed of this matter."

None there disagreed with that, at least.

"This of unqualified persons being admitted to holy orders. That will partly be righted by the better teaching agreed. But there will still be those who are installed in Church positions by lords and others who hold the rights of presentation to office."

There was an uncomfortable silence. Most landowners had had the heritable right to put forward nominees for clerical charges in their respective baronies and parishes, so often a useful destination for younger sons and illegitimate offspring.

"Could parliament rule on this?" Seton asked.

"Parliament can rule on any matter affecting the realm's well-being," Chatelherault put in, his first contribution.

"It could. But *will* it, my lord Duke?"

"A recommendation from this commission, put by the Chancellor, would help," the archbishop observed. "Now, we come to the pluralities of office. Too many prelates admittedly hold many charges, with their revenues – "

"How many do *you* hold, my lord Archbishop?" Glencairn jerked. Not all found cause to frown at that.

"Certain appointments go with the Primacy, and aid its costs. But I am prepared to consider yielding up this or that." He changed the subject. "Pardons and indulgences by the payment of moneys. The sale of relics. These must cease."

There was no disagreement.

"Lastly, the reform of consistorial courts."

All looked at Bishop Reid, the president of the highest court in the land, that of Session.

"I favour that," he acceded. "Too many of these lesser courts, Church and others, exceed their due powers. Consistorial and clerical, yes, but also baronial and heritable. I will speak to that in the parliament."

Since possibly everyone there sitting round that table was entitled to hold baronial courts, with the powers of pit and gallows, not even the eager reformers looked entirely supportive. But none raised voice in the circumstances.

"That is all, then," the archbishop declared, tactfully avoiding the subject of heresy. "How is this commission to make its findings known?"

"I shall confer with my Lord Lyon, the Bishop of Orkney, and inform the regent," Huntly said, with the Chancellor's authority. "Then put it all before parliament. Thank you, my lords." And he pushed back his chair.

So that appeared to be that, and John had not so much as said a word. What had he come for? he wondered. Although it had at least been instructive to see how men considered the state's and Church's interests as against their own.

He learned still more as to how those in power sought to rule the nation, while spending the night in Lord Seton's secondary seat of Niddrie Castle at Winchburgh nearby. Compared with such, he decided, seeking to keep the West March in some sort of order was simple indeed.

The calling of a parliament required a statutory forty days' notice, so that it was almost two months before John went to Edinburgh to take his seat thereat, as Lord Herries, even though he still scarcely thought of himself as that.

Even though he was aware of the business to be discussed, and scarcely looked forward to the debate, he was interested over the preliminary procedures. He was ushered to a seat near the front of the assembly, amongst the lords, where he found a place next to Lord Seton. The great hall of Edinburgh Castle was packed, the turnout greater than usual, which, Seton said, indicated probable trouble, the reformist-minded out in force. The Lyon's heralds were very much in evidence, directing members to their places, and having to assert their authority not infrequently, with folk seeking more prominent positions.

The Lords Spiritual were allotted seating by themselves, over to the left. All were facing the dais platform at the east end of the hall, whereon stood the throne, flanked by lesser chairs, with in front of it the Chancellor's table with his seat, and forms for his clerks.

A trumpeter of the Lyon Court blew a fanfare to indicate that the session was about to commence. Sir David Lindsay himself then strode in, resplendent in his colourful heraldic tabard, and carrying his staff of office. With this he thumped loudly on the floor of the dais, and announced that, by order of Her Grace the queen-regent, this parliament of the realm, duly called, was now in session. The earls of Scotland, such as were not officers of state, would make their entrance.

Into the hall then filed these representatives of the seven ancient Pictish mormaors, or sub-kings, although there were more than any seven now, eleven in this group, including the new Morton, Bothwell, Lennox and Glencairn.

There was a pause, and then to another blast of the trumpet entered the High Constable, the Earl of Erroll, bearing aloft the sword-of-state, followed by the Earl Marischal carrying the first sceptre, then Angus with the second or lesser one, and finally Chatelherault bearing the crown on its cushion. These went up to place their precious symbols of sovereignty on a table behind the throne, and remained standing meantime, flanking it.

The Chancellor, the Earl of Huntly, was announced, and he came to position himself at the frontal table, where two clerks already sat.

There was a pause, and then Lyon ordered all to stand for the entry of Her Grace, the regent, and the trumpeter emphasised this with a flourish.

Marie de Guise entered, with becoming dignity, led by Lindsay who, bowing, aided her up the dais steps and escorted her to the throne, where she seated herself, and he went to stand behind her. All others, save the Chancellor who remained standing, could now sit.

Huntly picked up the gavel from his table and rapped with it. Into the hush he spoke.

"With the due authority of the regent, I declare this session of parliament open. All will observe its rules, customs and behaviour. God save the Queen's Grace!"

That was echoed from all present.

"I call upon the Archbishop of St Andrews to open the proceedings with prayer."

The Primate rose in the clerical benches, to intone his petition to the Almighty to bestow His blessings on their deliberations, for the benefit of their young monarch's realm and people.

The Chancellor resumed. "While parliament will no doubt have sundry other matters to debate and decide upon later, the principal and important issue which has caused the queen-regent to call it concerns matters of reform in Holy Church. She has appointed a commission to enquire into the proposals put forward by the Primate and his associates, and these findings it is now my duty to put before this assembly."

Huntly picked up a paper and, clearing his throat, began to read out the lengthy catalogue of improvements demanded over faults and failings and shortcomings prevalent in the Church at this time, on and on. Not that he was permitted to do so without interruption. Time and again there were cries and interjections, comments and shouts, accusations and counter-accusations, men jumping to their feet, raising protesting hands, shaking fists. The gavel had to be banged time and again on the table to obtain approximate quiet, so that the list might be read to its finish.

Huntly at this stage was accepting no statements or motions. He continued to read from another paper, this time the alleged findings of the commission of enquiry, although John, for one, did not recognise all of them as that, indeed recollecting few actual decisions made at their meeting; presumably these were the summary made by Huntly himself, the Lyon and Bishop Reid thereafter.

These findings, in fact, amounted to agreement that practically all the issues listed did demand some degree of reform, action to be taken thereon. But it was emphasised that not all were the responsibility of parliament, some being wholly for the Church's own amendment, and only those which directly affected the nation's well-being, as distinct from worship and religious observance, being for present decision. Parliament could express opinion on others, for the guidance of the prelates, but had no authority of enforcement. So let members discuss all in orderly and responsible fashion. He would guide them as to sequence.

If Huntly really hoped for order and reasoned debate, he was to be sadly disappointed. From the first item, that of the land's powerful ones putting their kin and friends into prominent positions in the Church, half a dozen protesters were on their feet at once, not all reformers, with others jumping up to refute and shout them down. The Chancellor's useful gavel was promptly in action and continued to be so. No true decisions were possible, for there was no agreement on even motions to put forward, for or against, therefore no voting. The reformers, led by Glencairn and the young Lord James Stewart, but backed by the Earls of Rothes, Cassillis and Eglinton and many others, were more numerous than John Maxwell had realised, and more vehement in their accusations, contentions and demands. The dire word heresy quickly came into play, and was repeated time and again, irrespective of the subject allegedly being considered, on both sides, all sides, since there appeared to be more than two. There was no debate, only charges, allegations, indictments, threats, men all but coming to blows, ignoring the Chancellor and others who urged restraint and discipline. The fact that this was a parliament and legislature seemed to be entirely forgotten by many there.

Presently, despairing of restoring order, Huntly turned to glance back at Queen Marie, sitting tensely on her throne, and then over at Sir David Lindsay, with a gesture. Lyon nodded, and moved to speak to his trumpeter. That man thereupon blew a series of loud blasts, which effectively drowned out all the shouting, and continued to blow until Lindsay held up his hand. Into the comparative hush succeeding, Huntly banged his table.

"This is beyond all bearing!" he cried. "A disgrace and a shame. Unless this folly ceases and order is restored and maintained, I will advise Her Grace the regent that she withdraw from the assembly. And if so she does, then this is no longer a parliament – "

"It is not a parliament, it is the Congregation of Satan!" Erskine of Dun, Superintendent of Angus, interrupted, pointing.

They could have done without that. Immediately chaos re-erupted, almost more loudly than heretofore, with bellows of rage from the reformers, abuse and cursings. Glencairn actually climbed to stand on the earls' bench, to roar that he was proud to be one of the lords of this congregation.

The Queen-Mother rose from her throne and hurried from the hall, Lyon, after momentary hesitation, after her.

In the pandemonium which ensued, the regent was quickly followed by most of the bishops and prelates. Clutching their precious symbols, the officers of state hurried out also, many of the earls not far behind.

The Congregation Parliament, as some called it thereafter, stood most certainly adjourned.

Presumably the Primate's preliminary prayer had not reached its heavenly destination.

John, Lord Herries, bemused, found his way down to the Lord Seton's town-house, where he discovered his host there before him. Presently they were joined by David Lindsay, who declared that he could not do justice to the occasion even in one of his more scurrilous plays. Was this the end of parliamentary rule in Scotland?

Seton did not think so. But it might signal the

end of Holy Church's supremacy, after a thousand years.

Lindsay gently corrected his friend. Five hundred years. After all, the Catholic Church had only been established here in the eleventh century by Queen Margaret, Malcolm Canmore's Anglo-Hungarian wife. For five hundred years before that, St Columba's Celtic Church had continued. Perhaps they were going to revert to it?

John went home next day with plenty to think about.

Swiftly he had more to preoccupy his mind. His sister Margaret's sickly child James, by Angus, had died. And only a little time later Angus himself took a heart attack and died also. Despite three marriages, he left no other children. He was succeeded only by a feeble-witted nephew, son of Sir George who had fallen at Pinkie. The great house of Red Douglas suddenly lost direction and Scotland knew something of a vacuum in consequence.

21

They had not long to wait for repercussions from that travesty of a parliament. A militant protesting group of lords and chiefs and magnates, with even some reformist clergy, set themselves up in an association to press for the establishment of a presbyterian and non-hierarchical form of religious observance in Scotland, and elected to call themselves the Lords of the Congregation, after that memorable accusation, although they omitted the "of Satan". And shortly thereafter, no doubt encouraged by word of this, Master John Knox, a radical reformist priest who had actually been offered a bishopric in England by the Protestant Henry Tudor, chose to return to his native land from exile, which he had endured after being involved with the murderers of Cardinal Beaton at St Andrews, and a term thereafter as a French galley-slave.

His arrival undoubtedly would fuel the flames of revolt.

There were other reactions to it all, notably on the part of Marie de Guise, who clearly was much alarmed. That parliament and what followed caused her, a Frenchwoman, with her daughter in France, and a strong Catholic, to turn to France for help in the rule of her daughter's kingdom, as well as in its defence – which latter had been welcomed. But now she moved in a different way, no doubt unsure of the loyalty of many of the lords, and introduced Frenchmen to aid her in the government of the land, this inevitably creating resentment. She brought in one de Rubay to be Vice-Chancellor, and heeded him more than she did Huntly, who retained the office and style but found himself all but replaced as insufficiently strong.

She imported a Monsieur de Villemore as comptroller, a position of great influence as holding the purse-strings. Also one d'Oysell as confidential adviser and commander of her royal guard. Others less prominent but in positions of power. Resentment swelled.

No doubt arising out of advice given her by these newcomers, the regent decided to set up a standing army such as they had in France. This was hitherto unknown in Scotland, where armies had always been provided by the levies of the lords and chiefs, this providing a useful check, for them, on the powers of the monarch, who had to depend on the goodwill of a majority of his nobles, even though it did allow the more powerful lords to act independently of the crown and encouraged feuding, with some able to field their thousands. Now this was at risk, and opposition was general amongst the nobility. Queen Marie, who had been fairly popular hitherto, and was making an effective regent, suffered a drop in esteem in consequence.

This unrest was coinciding with the rise in power and aggressiveness of Mary Tudor in England, where she was proving to be a true daughter of her father, although reversing his religious policies and putting down the Protestants with a heavy hand, indeed earning the title of Bloody Mary by her drastic measures. It was feared that she might not be long in emulating her sire in foreign affairs also, and turn her attentions to Scotland, ending the period of comparative peace which had prevailed since the fall of the two Lords Protector. The March wardens were advised to be on their guard. Not that they required much warning, for they and their people were ever very much aware of cross-border menace.

John had his own problems on his March. Making Johnstone deputy warden did diffuse tensions with that great clan, but it produced others, for the Johnstones were not long in indicating their rise in status and authority, to the umbrage of other West March folk, dalesmen in particular, Armstrongs, Elliots, Irvines and the rest, so that John had to act the peace-maker, not the usual role for the warden.

At Terregles, however, all was well, and more than well, a joy and a satisfaction, Agnes as rousing and lively a wife as she was a comfort and helpmeet, and the children a delight, even in their naughtiness, for they were as spirited as were their parents. They saw quite a lot of Catherine, who now had a little son of her own. She was strong on the subject of religion, for her husband was a zealous reformer, and she, who had never been particularly interested in such matters before, supported his views strongly. They saw rather less of Janet. Both appeared to be happily married, even though to very different sorts of husband, one the enthusiast, argumentative, temperamental, the other practical and level-headed.

John and Agnes, in consequence, had long discussions on the subject of religious reform, which, apart from Catherine's attitude, was so concerning and dividing the nation. They both agreed that some considerable amendment in Church affairs was called for; but Agnes, perhaps unusually for a woman, was more interested in such matters and felt that more radical change was necessary, taking her own line on this, not Catherine's. She did not go so far as her sister in advocating the sweeping away of the Catholic Church altogether, but held that improvement and reorganisation should be comprehensive, with an end to the clerics' Estate of Parliament and their say in the government of the realm. Religion and statecraft should not mix, she claimed. The Church's duty was to lead in worship of the Creator and to demonstrate His love, not to seek to govern. John, agreeing with that, admitted that he had not thought it all out so heedfully.

Perhaps most of the Lords of the Congregation scarcely saw it all from that angle either, for their claims were as much concerned with the government of the kingdom as with personal worship and behaviour. Indeed it was rumoured that some of the most bellicose had their eyes on the vast Church estates and wealth rather than on religious improvement. Henry of England had shown them the way in *his* Reformation by confiscating the monastic lands and properties; they could do the same. The Church had been accumulating riches for centuries by offering deathbed forgiveness and indulgences to repentant magnates for almost any sin committed, on payment of appropriate donations, usually in land, with the promise of prayer being said in perpetuity for the souls of the donors. Hence the enormous wealth of Holy Church.

So word of reforming zeal came constantly south to the Borderland, where, to be sure, other preoccupations tended to prevail, apart from Alexander Stewart's, Younger of Garlies. And to add to their recruitment, the Lords of the Congregation adopted to their cause the fight against Queen Marie's standing army, and the taxes being announced to pay for it, a subtle move. For here was a policy almost universally unpopular with not only the nobility and landed folk but with all makers and holders of even modest wealth. On French advice, the regent announced an inquisition and nationwide enquiry into the possession of lands and moneys – although not those of the Church – not only of lords and lairds but of farmers, merchants, craftsmen, millers and the like, to ascertain their ability to pay for the army. Fury burst forth. And by cleverly incorporating this resentment into their campaign for religious amendment, and emphasising that the churchmen were not being included in the tax inquisition, the reformers gained a nationwide accession of strength.

Master John Knox was especially eloquent, parading the country.

A great assembly was called, to protest, at Edinburgh that early summer of 1556, at Holyrood Abbey of all places, where Robert Stewart, another of the late King James's illegitimate brood, was commendator-abbot, although not in holy orders – an example of the corruption of the Church in itself – three hundred and more attending. And these issued a proclamation, no less, for the Queen-Mother's and her French friends' instruction, pointing out that, unlike France or England or Spain, this kingdom was that of the Scots, not of Scotland. That the style and title of the monarch was King or Queen of Scots, not of Scotland, as it was of France, England and Spain. And this difference was significant, for it meant that the monarch did not rule the land itself but the people of the land; and from this followed that the wealth of the land was not in the control of the crown, to be assessed and taxed. So the present inquisition and proposed levy was unlawful and must be withdrawn. If not, a parliament would be demanded, which would most certainly reject it. This was a cunning move, however questionable its finding.

At any rate, Marie de Guise and her advisers, unsure of themselves on this subject, withdrew the standing-army project and its taxation. But it all had weakened her regency and her hold over her daughter's nation, and at the same time greatly strengthened the reformist party.

Perhaps Scotland could indeed have done with a standing army that July of 1558, for there was trouble, as long feared, with Mary Tudor's England. Bloody Mary had gone through a form of marriage with the militant Catholic King Philip of Spain, in order to strengthen her anti-Protestant efforts; and since Spain was at war with France, Mary demanded that the Scots links with France be, if not severed, greatly curtailed. King Henry of France's answer to that challenge was to speed up the projected marriage of his weakly son and heir, the dauphin, to young Mary Queen of Scots, and the pair were promptly wed, with tremendous flourish, in the Church of Nôtre Dame in Paris, and the announcement made that any male issue of the marriage would in time become both King of France and of Scots.

This, needless to say, aroused Mary Tudor to wrath, and she threatened to punish Scotland, alleging that this invalidated the provisions agreed at that meeting at Norham those years before, just how was not detailed. At any rate, her threats were taken seriously, for she could call upon the great Spanish fleet for aid, the mightiest in the world, to add to her own.

Threats might have remained merely that, but unfortunately some of the English borderers took them to be a licence to resume their chosen activities, and a quite major raid was made into Scotland from Norham and Wark, over Tweed. John was not directly affected by this, it being in Lord Home's East March, but he took the precaution of readying his Marchmen to be available for action at short notice.

The regent took more definite action, wisely or otherwise. Believing that Berwick-upon-Tweed, in English hands, could be used, with its great harbour facilities, as a base for an English–Spanish fleet to assail Scotland, she sent d'Oysell and a force of French mercenaries to fortify Eyemouth, the nearest Scots port a few miles north of Tweed, and put it in a state to invalidate, if possible, the use of Berwick by enemy shipping.

Bloody Mary was not long in hearing about this, condemned it as blatant provocation, and declared that a state of war now existed between England and Scotland.

The era of approximate peace, it seemed, was over.

There was criticism of the Queen-Mother for this development. Many, including Angus, Huntly, Argyll and Chatelherault, said that it indeed had been provoked by her and her Frenchmen sending that force to occupy and fortify Eyemouth, so near to the English border; and of course the reformers were almost automatically against anything that she did. So Scotland was, as so often, in a state of disunity. John, for one, frequently despaired of his nation.

But word, not of a fleet but of an English land force massing in the Alnwick area of Northumberland, if it did not still the grumbles at least rallied the Scots lords, or some of them, sufficiently for them not to refuse to raise their levies to assemble to face the enemy threat. They mustered on the Burgh Muir of Edinburgh, to ride for the Tweed, a large force. John was sent for to bring his Marchmen to join them in the Ladykirk area.

Somewhat doubtfully, he left Johnstone in charge of the West March and headed eastwards with six hundred men.

They did not get nearly so far as Ladykirk, catching up with the army at Kelso town. And there they found trouble indeed, surprising trouble, surprise that the Queen-Mother was there in person, and that she was facing what almost amounted to treason, mutiny at the least. The nobles, not only the Lords of the Congregation, were refusing to obey the regent's commands.

John was not long in learning the details. Urged on by her French advisers, including d'Oysell who had joined them from Eyemouth, Marie was ordering a full-scale sally over into England, as warning to Mary Tudor and the forces assembling at Alnwick; and the Scots, including Chancellor Huntly, Chatelherault, Argyll and Morton, were refusing to go. They declared that this would be uncalled-for provocation, and would achieve nothing save a worsening of the situation, full-scale and outright war in fact, not just in declaration. This might suit France, but it was not in Scotland's interests. A tense atmosphere prevailed in the abbey of Kelso, where the leadership was lodging, and, to be sure, communicated itself to the rest of the army encamped around the town.

John, although a loyal supporter of the crown, thought that the lords' reasoning was probably justified; but he could not approve of actual refusal to obey. Every effort to dissuade the regent, yes, and to counter the Frenchmen, but not an outright attitude of defiance. Not that John's opinion carried any weight there, especially as his two fellow-wardens favoured the refusal, for their Marches would of course be the first to suffer from English retaliation.

An uneasy night was passed.

In the morning Marie, finding no change in the lords'

resolve, made her own decision. She ordered d'Oysell and the French mercenaries to do what the Scots would not, to make her gesture, cross Tweed near Birgham, and assail Wark Castle, not Norham which was too strong a hold and could fall only to a prolonged siege; and the French had left their cannon at Eyemouth. She would go with them.

This extraordinary decision did not cause the duke – who was still next in line for the throne – Huntly and the rest to waver. But it did present John with a problem. After all, the Queen-Mother had honoured him, made him something of an envoy and commissioner, and he owed her allegiance. Yet none of the other Scots seemed to be going with her and the French force, and his six hundred mosstroopers would be as many as d'Oysell's group, and their going would break the traditional understanding and co-operation between the three wardens. He compromised by announcing that he would personally go with the regent as far as Birgham, with a score of his men, to act as escort and bodyguard in case of English counter-action, the least that he could do. Was this a feeble reaction? he wondered.

Lord Seton at least did not see it so, for he declared that he also would go with them. His friend Lindsay, the Lord Lyon, was not present with the army.

In the event, a few other lords, including Morton, agreed to do the same, but without any sizeable following. Marie accepted their company, but did not enthuse.

It was an uncomfortable party, then, which set out eastwards, leaving the host at Kelso, the Scots group in fact riding behind rather than escorting the Queen-Mother, for d'Oysell and the Frenchmen saw to that. It was all a distinctly sorry episode.

Birgham lay some seven miles down Tweed from Kelso, and Wark Castle, on the English side, two miles beyond. Opposite it, in due course, they could see the stronghold clearly enough on its mound not far back from the river, banners flapping above it. Nothing like so daunting a hold as Norham, some miles further east still, it nevertheless was a strong place, and Seton shook his head over the projected assault, without artillery. How large a garrison it might have, none knew.

When Marie seemed to be intending to ford the river with her Frenchmen, John and Seton, about to try to dissuade her, found d'Oysell himself giving the same advice. He said that there was no sense in her putting herself in unnecessary danger, for there might well be hazard in this, depending on how many men were based in that hold. This was no attempt for a woman. And if they met with strong opposition, the river had to be forded again to win back, which could prove perilous if they were pursued. Reluctantly she agreed to wait.

At least there was no problem about the Frenchmen crossing Tweed at this stage, no enemy appearing to oppose the fording. Yet, since they could see the castle, the watchmen there must have observed them. So that might mean that there was no very large garrison, and that its commander would be content to remain behind its walls. In which case, would d'Oysell's men be able to make any great impact? Possibly not, if it was sufficiently strong a fortalice. But this was, after all, only a gesture, a warning to the English, and the mere threat could be effective.

So the Scots remained behind with the regent, ingloriously only to watch.

They saw the Frenchmen riding up the slight hill towards the castle, and without any opposition in evidence. They saw d'Oysell's force split, presumably to encircle the castle knoll. Then they saw something different, two puffs of smoke appearing against that walling, and the reports of cannon-fire came over to them, not very loud reports but sufficiently significant. So Wark was provided with artillery. And even though this, by the look and sound of it, consisted of only small cannon, nevertheless it altered the picture entirely. The French would have to keep their distance from those walls.

D'Oysell clearly accepted that, for his men were seen to halt and position themselves well back, on both sides. More smoke and bangs. The watchers could not see where the balls were striking, but the Frenchmen did not noticeably move further back, so they had presumably gauged themselves out of the cannon-range and safe. There they waited.

The watchers waited also. Nothing seemed to be happening. If the defenders did not issue forth, what could happen? D'Oysell might be shouting challenges and insults, but without artillery of his own he could do little more. They had not, after all, come prepared to make siege.

Queen Marie fidgeted on her horse as time passed.

Eventually the inevitable took place. After making a couple of circuits of the perimeter, the French party reassembled and turned back for the river.

They came splashing across, d'Oysell shaking his head and shrugging to the regent, who spread her hands. There was no need for explanation. A single defiant cannon-shot from the castle emphasised the situation, however out of range, as they all reined round to head back for Kelso.

At the town no surprise was expressed by the assembled lords at this outcome, no condolences either. Queen Marie quickly retired to the room she had been allotted by the abbot, a woman dispirited and unlike her usual quietly assured self. John knew sympathy for her. He recognised also that this incident would do nothing to enhance her flagging prestige and authority, and this might be to the advantage of the reformers.

The army more or less disbanded and dismissed itself next day. D'Oysell went back to Eyemouth, and John led his Marchmen homewards, a disillusioned and scoffing company.

22

Agnes was pregnant again, and there was great debate as to whether it was with a boy or a girl. She favoured a son but her husband declared that little girls were more fun. Janet, in fact, produced offspring first, in the early spring, and was inordinately pleased with herself, bearing an heir for the Cockburns, who held wide lands in Lothian, the Merse and Peebles-shire.

John had to deal with the first major cross-border raid into his March for what amounted to years, as distinct from more private ventures which went on intermittently, when Sir Stanley Musgrave led a foray into Liddesdale, ostensibly to recover stolen cattle but which, meeting spirited opposition, resulted in much mayhem and the burning of the townships of Larriston, Riccarton and Saughtree. John sent a strong protest to Lord Wharton, with demands for redress, and when this was ignored, led a strong party of his mosstroopers over the border to Carlisle itself, this strictly controlled as to behaviour however heavily armed, greatly to the alarm of the citizens there. The Scots took up position in the central market square between the castle and the cathedral, to wait, keeping his people in hand meantime requiring all John's attention and determination, for they had to remain there, inactive, for over two hours. But eventually Wharton, sent for, did arrive, and with only a small, hastily gathered escort. He was in no position to be as aggressive as he undoubtedly felt, and had to concede, however grudgingly, that Musgrave had exceeded permitted hot-trod limits – that is, the right to seek to recover stolen cattle, even across the border – in burning those Liddesdale townships. He had to promise that due restitution would be made.

They parted on no more affable terms than heretofore, but John's point had been made. The mosstroopers' jeers and catcalls as they rode off northwards were not to be silenced, the townsfolk for their part no doubt heaving sighs of relief.

On the wider scene there were still more dramatic developments. Later in the year, word reached Scotland that Mary Tudor was sick, seriously ill. She had never been robust physically as she was mentally, but reports indicated that this trouble was more than from any mere constitutional frailty. It is to be feared that there was no great concern on her behalf in Scotland.

Agnes brought forth another daughter, to be named Margaret, and changed her mind as to preferences.

When, a few weeks later, came news that Bloody Mary was dead, childless and little mourned in either realm, in her forty-second year, there was actual rejoicing in the northern kingdom. For she was to be succeeded on the throne by Henry Tudor's other surviving legitimate offspring, Elizabeth, daughter of the executed Ann Boleyn, who had up till then been kept very much apart, all but a prisoner. And she was as strong a Protestant as her half-sister had been a Catholic.

The impact of this abrupt change in the power structure in England was immediate in Scotland, and went far beyond mere rejoicing. For now the reformist party, already heartened by progress, saw great opportunity, hoping for aid for their cause from their hitherto dangerous neighbour in the south. Surely the new Queen Elizabeth would wish to help the northern realm turn Protestant? Waverers turned to them, and the ranks of the Lords of the Congregation swelled. The religious aspects of it had no great effect on the Marches, the priorities there tending to be otherwise; but the situation could greatly bear on cross-border relations, hopefully for the better. Marie de Guise's personal reactions could be guessed at, but she was not in a position to make such public nor to initiate any specific proceedings or policies. She kept quiet meantime.

Others did not, in especial Master John Knox. Encouraged by the reformist lords, he travelled far and wide, preaching with fiery eloquence, proclaiming the sins of the prelates, condemning the papacy, and advocating what he called his Appelation, his own doctrine of the responsibility of the temporal power in the nation to protect the subjects from unjust ecclesiastical domination, and sentencing from clerical courts. He asserted that the state had the duty to insist on proper religious teaching, according to Geneva, which he named the most perfect school of Christ. He indeed demanded death for any and all who sought to turn the people away from it. The man was a brilliant speaker and advocate, and made an undoubted impact up and down the land, particularly amongst the lower and less privileged ranks of the clergy themselves, the parish priests. And he was egged on by the magnates who hoped to profit by his efforts, these now including an ever-growing number of the earls and great ones. Notable amongst his supporters was a newcomer to the reformist scene, William Maitland, Younger of Lethington, a brilliant youngish man who had just recently been appointed Secretary of State. This grievously offended Queen Marie, and, removed from that office, he adopted John Knox's cause and company, acting as a link between him and the lords, and accompanying him on many of his forays. Because of his political adroitness and skills – the reason for the regent appointing him to high office – he had become known as Michael Wylie, that is a Scots corruption of the name Machiavelli. His accession greatly aided the reformers.

This campaign of Knox's became so successful and serious that the College of Bishops, despite the Primate's orders to them to keep a low profile in these circumstances, felt constrained to act. They ordered Knox to appear before their court on a charge of heresy. He refused, and at Maitland's urging, wrote directly to the Queen-Mother, stressing her duty as regent to exercise the temporal power, as defined by himself, over Church courts, and indicating the backing of the Lords of the Congregation. Marie did not reply to this, but the bishops did drop their citation to appear before them.

Rumours abounded that Knox and Maitland were being supported from England.

John and Agnes discussed all this frequently. While he thought that Knox was something of a rabble-rouser and a danger to the peace of the realm, she was not so sure. After all, if the new Queen Elizabeth was supporting him, as was said, she must believe that he was more than any rabble-rouser. And Agnes admired that young woman's attitude to religion. She had said that "there was only one Christ Jesus, and one faith; the rest is a dispute about trifles." That more or less summed up her own view. Knox might be a somewhat tiresome zealot, but perhaps a necessary one at this time? Might he not be something of a present-day John the Baptist? Her husband had to admit that she might have something there. But the man's efforts did produce a threat to the peace of the realm – to be told that peace was not everything if it hindered betterment. Perhaps John, in seeking to keep the peace on the West March, was letting it affect his judgment, and making him a peace-at-any-cost man?

Such suggestion was the price he had to pay for having a spirited wife.

Further dynastic news reached them that summer, the death of the King of France in a tournament accident. So now the sickly Dauphin Francis was monarch, and Mary Stewart Queen of France as well as of Scots. This so unexpected occurrence, and its sequel, did not affect Scotland in the way that Mary Tudor's passing had done; but it did mean that the two realms were the more closely allied, and this did have the effect of strengthening the regent's hand. And this in turn caused the reformers to become the more aggressive, Knox reaching new heights of fervour and invective. The bishops felt strong enough to renew his citation to appear before them, for he was still in theory a priest of Holy Church; and when he again refused, they had an effigy of him burned at the stake. With allegations circulating that the zealot, along with Maitland, was in receipt of a pension from Queen Elizabeth, the nation was in something of a ferment. John began seriously to worry about civil war. Scotland had always needed a strong monarch; an absent girl in France did not meet requirements. If only the late King James had married one of his many mistresses, preferably Margaret Erskine, instead of Marie de Guise, then they could have had what was called for, a ruler of some force and power, such as the bastard Lord James Stewart.

Along such lines many were thinking, those last months of 1559.

23

If the preceding years had been eventful and significant ones on the national scene, 1560 surpassed all in fatefulness and teeming incident. Its activities started early for John, in early February indeed, and surprisingly. He received a summons, and in the name of Chatelherault not the Queen-Mother, to meet him and other lords at the Norham ford of Tweed, with the two other wardens, forthwith, no explanations given. Distinctly doubtful as to what this implied, he felt bound to comply, even though his duty was to the regent. The duke was heir to the throne. And one of the lords' names subscribed was Morton's, the late Robert's father-in-law. Agnes said that it looked as though some negotiations were planned with the English, possibly in the interests of the Lords of the Congregation and reform. He should attend, if only to discover what went on.

So it was off, in very inclement weather conditions, on the now familiar journey through snow-covered hills, to Tweedsmuir and down that long river accompanied only by Dod Armstrong, his faithful friend. He called in at Ferniehirst Castle in Jedforest for the night, and found Sir John Kerr ill in bed, a man now of later middle years, and his son Thomas appointed as deputy warden, the wardenship being all but hereditary in the Kerr family, as it was with the Homes in the east and the Maxwells in the west.

John had met Thomas Kerr before, a genial and pleasant-looking young man, whom he judged would make a good warden in due course, and easy to co-operate with. He found the Kerrs as questioning as he was himself over this summons, and wondering whether to attend, especially with the younger man new to responsibilities and uncertain as to behaviour in such matters. He was glad, therefore, of John's lead and advice, and agreed to come along to the gathering of lofty ones at the Norham ford, however doubtful also. He had not been in touch with Lord Home.

When they got to the Norham ford in mid-forenoon, it was to discover only the Earl of Arran, the duke's son, awaiting them, with the explanation that the venue had been altered, at the Duke of Norfolk's request, to Berwick-upon-Tweed, nine miles further, where they were to head. The young man also explained that the meeting was at the request of Queen Elizabeth, to discuss certain matters of concern for both nations, Norfolk being her representative, Hereditary Great Marshal of England. The Queen-Mother, he said, was sick at Linlithgow, and had asked his father to represent her. John wondered whether this was something of a diplomatic illness, and perhaps indicated a reluctance on the regent's part to be committed to any decisions arrived at with the English, until she had fully considered them.

On arrival at Berwick Castle, high above the seaport town and the widening estuary, John was the more questioning. For almost without exception he found the Scots delegation to consist of Lords of the Congregation, Argyll, the Marischal, Glencairn, Montrose amongst them. That Morton had joined them was significant, for with Angus's earldom now held by a mere boy, Morton represented the great power of Douglas. Had he thrown in his lot with the reformers? Home was already present, and told his fellow-wardens that this looked like being a further step in the process of religious reform for Scotland, of which he obviously was in favour.

Norfolk proved to be a strikingly handsome young man, not out of his twenties, but suave and quietly assured. John saw why the wardens had been summoned to attend, for the three English ones were with Norfolk: Wharton, Lord

Hunsdon and Sir John Forster. The two parties eyed each other warily, even though Norfolk acted the coolly amiable host – but very much the host here in Berwick's castle. John reminded himself that it was here that Edward, Hammer of the Scots, had forced what he scoffingly named the Ragman Roll on the Scots in 1296, a shameful document which even Robert the Bruce had to sign, however much he made up for it later.

They were not long in getting down to business, the wine flagons circulating, Norfolk very much leading, with Her Majesty Elizabeth's greetings and good wishes, plus her hope that the true and proper worship of Almighty God would quickly be established in Scotland. But that was as far as geniality went. Thereafter it was a catalogue of accusations, complaints and implied threats. Apparently a large French force had arrived at Leith, at the behest of the regent, to add to the Eyemouth contingent. The new King and Queen of France had announced themselves to be rightful monarchs of England as well as of Scots, this on account of Mary Stewart's grandmother being Margaret Tudor, sister of Henry the Eighth. This was intolerable. The French had also declared that the Protestant religion in England was heretical and blasphemous and must be put down. And it could be that this new French army come to Scotland was to be used in that evil cause. There was more, to similar effect.

John listened, alarmed, and exchanged glances with Kerr. The other Scots looked grave and wagged heads but nowise seemed surprised. Clearly they had known of all this before coming.

Norfolk went on. "Her Majesty requires assurances. First, that the threat of Eyemouth to this Berwick be removed, the French force there withdrawn, a mere ten miles from where we are sitting, and the fortifications thrown up there demolished. Second, that those French, and all others, be expelled from Scotland at the earliest. Third, that a statement be made by the Scots parliament that Queen Elizabeth was recognised as the rightful sovereign of England, and the French claims false, that and the Frenchwoman, de Guise, required to sign it. And fourth, that every effort be made to pull down the Catholic Church in Scotland, and a Protestant regime instituted in its place."

There was silence when Norfolk stopped.

Chatelherault cleared his throat. "We regret all this," he said. "It is against our wishes. And we will endeavour to have the wrongs righted." That sounded distinctly feeble.

Another voice spoke up, much more positively and firmly, that of the Lord James Stewart. "To achieve anything against these French, armed as they are with cannon, and trained in warfare, we will require aid. Likewise, to bring down the popish Church."

"Such aid will be available, in men and moneys," Norfolk said briefly.

"Under what terms, my lord Duke?" Argyll asked.

"Your co-operation in fighting the wrongs, that is all, my lord."

"What assurance have we that once these ends are achieved, all English forces will leave our land?" That was Morton.

"My word, in the name of Her Majesty Elizabeth."

There was another silence. It seemed to be assumed on the Scots side that these English demands were acceptable and indeed beneficial to the reformist cause, which evidently had become favoured by practically all there.

Glancing over at Wharton, across the table, John was bold enough to raise voice. "After that discussion and compact at Norham, which I attended, my lords, English Borderers took the agreement as a warrant to conduct raids over into Scotland, major raids. Can we have assurance that this will not happen again?"

"You have it."

"I am sure that all here will bear witness to your good promise, my lord Duke. Does this stand even though the

291

Catholic Church is not displaced, as not all in Scotland desire?"

"My word stands. But we will hope, sir, that due reform will proceed. And those who doubt will be . . . converted!"

Was there threat behind that?

A certain amount of discussion ensued, but the principal talking had been said, and, on the English side, all by Norfolk. Soon they all rose.

Affability thereafter did not extend to age-old enemies sitting down at meat together. Norfolk suggested that since this ancient hold did not boast quarters adequate to house the distinguished Scots visitors, and the February dark was already falling, arrangements had been made to give them refreshment and beds for the night down in hostelries in the town, which he had ensured were sufficiently comfortable. His clerks would meantime write up the terms of their treaty and agreement, and he would bring the papers down hereafter for the joint signatures.

So that was that. The Scots rode down to the port which had once been Scotland's greatest, one of the nation's original ancient four royal burghs, and where the trouble over the wool exporting had recently taken place; and they were led to various taverns and inns, to the offence of some of them, John and his fellow-wardens to one in the Woolmarket. Most of them had never actually been in Berwick before, for it had been very jealously English-held for long, and no place for the Scots nobility, however vital it might be for sheep-farmers, wool-merchants and the like. The port held a sizeable proportion of Flemish-speaking folk, for the links with Flanders were very strong; indeed their host in their inn was a Dutchman, John questioning him about the Staple at Veere.

They passed a pleasant enough night, almost certainly more comfortable than they would have been up at the castle. If Norfolk brought the treaty papers, if so they could be called, down for signature, these did not come their way; no doubt the wardens were looked upon as mere advisers.

In the morning it was for home, duty done. Had they in fact achieved anything for Scotland? John wondered. Sir Thomas Kerr doubted it, even if Lord Home did not.

Events were not long in developing from all this; indeed clearly the English had been preparing their moves before ever the Berwick meeting took place, for it was only a few weeks before they heard in the borderland that a fleet had arrived off Leith and effected landings against strong French opposition. The invaders were prevented from capturing Leith itself, but came ashore at various points to east and west. The extraordinary situation resulted of French and English fighting each other on Scots soil, while the Scots themselves stood back, in the main, and left them to it. John, for one, could scarcely feel proud of his nation in this pass.

The word was that Queen Marie's illness was far from diplomatic; in fact her condition was said to be deteriorating, which situation conjured up the likelihood of further major problems for the country. Were they going to have the ineffective Chatelherault back as regent again? Or other?

No serious cross-border inroads developed on the West March, at least, although their own folk's reiving activities kept John busy, not least the Johnstones', who appeared to consider that their improved prestige permitted them to ignore even the odd traditional Border laws. Had John been wise in appointing Johnstone as deputy? The man seemed to be unable to control his clansmen.

In May, the Queen-Mother, who had moved from Linlithgow to Edinburgh Castle in order better to try to order Scotland, as it were from her bed, for she was now a direly sick woman, took the unexpected and significant step of summoning the Privy Council and principal lords of the nation to attend her in the castle. John was not one of those called, but heard of it all from others. They had found Marie in her bed and looking but a shadow of her former self. But despite her frailty, she had spoken to them strongly, decidedly. She had said that clearly she was not going to be with them for much longer, and was much distressed at the state of the nation that she would be leaving, torn apart by faction and strife, and with English and French forces battling in the land, the Church in disarray. She had pleaded with the nobles to unite on temporal affairs, even if they could not in religious, but to leave the latter in abeyance meantime to be settled later, and to concentrate on setting the national house in order and in setting up a regency council to succeed her, rather than any one individual. She believed that such council would not have very long to rule, for she had had sure word from France that her son-in-law, King Francis, never strong, was failing sadly and unable to rule his kingdom in consequence, so that his forceful and ambitious Italian mother, Catherine de Medici, was in fact governing the country, and her own daughter, Queen Mary, all but ignored. Mary was now seventeen years, and a young woman of spirit and ability. When her husband passed on, as seemed probable before long, she should come back to her own land and take over the rule as rightful monarch. Any regency council should so urge her. Scotland needed her, and France did not.

When sundry of the lords had raised their voices to comment and question, especially on the religious subject, Marie had closed her eyes and lain back, clearly exhausted. And, arguing amongst themselves, they had left her to her lady attendants.

No nearer harmony and unity, the nation waited.

They did not have long to wait for the next stage, even though it was far from harmony. On 10th June Marie de Guise died; and despite her efforts at paving the way for better government, left chaos behind her.

This irresponsible disharmony was typified by the extraordinary decision of the Lords of the Congregation not to allow the late regent's body Christian burial unless it was by Protestant rites. This, of course, was forbidden by the Catholic hierarchy, and the sad corpse remained in a leaden coffin in a cellar of Edinburgh Castle, amidst bitter acrimony.

Marie had never actually signed that so-called Treaty of Berwick. Now, advised by Secretary of State Maitland, and not wanting Chatelherault to resume the regency, a group, all reformers, met to take at least part of Marie's advice and, calling themselves a council of regency, signed that paper in July. Not that this made a great deal of difference, for the Catholic opposition and the Church ignored it and them. But it did, on the face of it, legitimise the English presence in Scotland, and did the reverse for the French. More to the point, for the nation's well-being, if such could be hoped for, this council called for a parliament in forty days' time. Who would attend this was doubtful admittedly.

John, as Lord Herries, decided that he must, Agnes supportive. *Some* firm decisions had to be taken by somebody, for this leaderless drifting should not, could not, go on. But it would be an even more difficult and fiery assembly than usual – that is, if any of the Catholic party decided to attend.

In the event, there was quite a good turnout, for even though the Church adherents did not recognise the authority of the group which called it, they could hardly fail to realise that a parliament was necessary, some indication of the nation's will, in its present state, to be indicated. Huntly, himself a staunch Catholic, let it be known that he would indeed chair it, as Chancellor, and this undoubtedly helped.

John arrived, then, at Edinburgh Castle, very much aware of that body in the coffin lying below this great hall, to find a fairly large company assembled. And already, well before proceedings started, there were fierce arguments. He noted, sitting beside Seton, that there were very few prelates on the churchmen's benches.

Lindsay the Lyon was faced with a difficult task, whatever his personal views, for to be accurate this was not a parliament at all but a convention; a Scots parliament was only valid if the monarch, or the monarch's duly appointed representative, was present; otherwise it was styled a Convention of Parliament, and had not the same authority. Yet this had to be looked upon as the highest authority available in the land in present circumstances, and Lyon had to strive to make it seem so.

He ushered in the earls, or most of them; then the officers of state, who carried their symbols of sword, sceptres and crown, to lay them actually on the throne itself, instead of the table behind, indicative that no one would be sitting thereon that day. At this stage, from a lesser door at the other side of the hall there entered, without any flourish of the trumpet, the Primate, Archbishop Hamilton, and of the thirteen bishops who could have attended, only two, those of Dunkeld and Dunblane, with no single mitred abbot. A surge of comment, even some hooting, came from the assembly at this so significantly puny representation of Holy Church.

Then Lyon ushered in the Chancellor, with behind him Maitland of Lethington, the Secretary of State, an innovation this. And finally Chatelherault, as heir to the throne, the nearest they could get on this occasion to royal authority. He went to sit beside the officers of state flanking the empty throne. Lindsay declared this Convention of Parliament in session.

Huntly called on the archbishop to pray for God's will to be done in their deliberations and decisions – to much murmuring and growls. The Primate, on this occasion, was notably brief and carefully non-committal in his petition to the Almighty. The gossip was that he had been threatened by his half-brother the duke with imprisonment, even death, if he did not attend and co-operate.

Huntly also was being noticeably careful. Instead of himself leading, he called upon the Secretary of State to open the proceedings.

Michael Wylie, alias Maitland, was actually cheered as he rose to speak. There could be little doubt as to attitudes, preferences and sympathies of the great majority present.

Maitland spoke lucidly, succinctly, far from fiercely, but assuredly. He declared that he was acting for the Chancellor, with his full authority. He announced that they had much business to transact, and urged all to contribute with care and some expedition, on the nation's behalf, for this was a vital and onerous assembly. He would outline the subjects to be discussed, and in the due order in which they should be dealt with. First, the acceptance of the Treaty of Berwick between Scotland and the Queen of England. Second, in ratification of a clause thereof, the expulsion from this land of all French armed forces. Third, parliament's advice of Queen Mary and her husband King Francis that they must neither of them order peace or war in Scotland without the consent of parliament. Fourth, that members of her Privy Council, always renewed under any change of government in the realm, were to be selected by the queen from twenty-four nominees to be agreed by this parliament. Fifth, ratification or otherwise made on the articles of religious reform decided upon at Perth by the Lords of the Congregation and protesting divines in recent weeks, these being entitled the Confession of Faith –

His steady, unemotional voice was here interrupted by a very different one, loud and fierce, from up in the minstrels' gallery where, in the forefront of other privileged onlookers, John Knox stood, arm held high, beard and hair wild, like some Old Testament prophet, and shouted that God's will would be done, or damnation would descend upon all present, upon the nation itself, and deservedly.

Maitland inclined his head with a half-smile, and Huntly forbore to bang his gavel. The Secretary of State went on.

Sixth, all Papal jurisdiction to be abolished in Scotland. The celebration of mass to be banned, on pain of the confiscation of the offender's goods, then, if repeated, death for the third offence.

The noise in the hall at that, mainly cheering, left no doubts as to the feelings of most present, indeed their passion.

Seventh, the dissolving and suppression of all present ecclesiastical sees and authorities, their future to be decided upon by a commission appointed by the council in due course.

Maitland bowed, turned to Huntly, and sat down.

That man, Cock o' the North as he might be, and the most powerful Catholic in the land, waved a hand – indication that the Secretary of State should continue to act his deputy and manage this difficult assembly. With the writing clearly on the wall, he was probably wise, however he felt.

Maitland certainly earned his style of Machiavelli thereafter, controlling that extraordinary session, where the whole direction of Scotland's rule, course, administration and faith was being changed and transformed. What ensued could nowise be called a debate or even a series of arguments, for it was far too incoherent, turbulent and fractious for that, motions proposed by would-be movers seldom to be heard in the din, innumerable members on their feet at any and all times. Some did leave the hall, in disgust or fear, including the two bishops. Knox was on his feet in the gallery almost throughout, waving, pointing, calling. Yet somehow Maitland managed to give at least the impression of being in control, and every now and again made himself heard, to announce that one after another of his seven items had been duly agreed. No voting, as such, at least in the counting, took place, nor was there any need for it, the will of the vast majority entirely evident. Just what this Confession of Faith encompassed John did not learn, nor probably did most there, but it was passed with acclaim nevertheless, like all else.

At length even Maitland had had enough; after all, he and his colleagues had got all that they wanted, and more. He turned, and bowed again to Huntly, who had been sitting expressionless at the Chancellor's table with the

Great Seal of Scotland before him. Now he rose, to bang at last with that gavel for order, and eventually gained sufficient hush to announce that this parliament would now stand adjourned until the morrow, when further details would be dealt with.

There were sighs of relief from not a few there.

But they were not quite finished yet, even as at Lindsay's signal the trumpeter was raising his instrument to blow. For Knox, up there, shouted aloud, and he had the most powerful and penetrating voice. He declared that from now on Scots would worship God in their own chosen way, not at the dictation of that man in Rome. And the Holy Kirk would teach and guide the folk in the ways of truth. To that end there would be another sort of assembly shortly, not as today on matters temporal but in matters of still greater import, spiritual, an assembly of the Kirk of Scotland, to chart the way towards heaven for all believers, and towards hell for the adherents of Satan. Let all take heed!

On that note, plus the trumpeter's alternative blast, the gathering broke up, however noisily, argument and bicker continuing within and outside.

That evening, at Seton's town-house, John announced that he had had sufficient and would not attend any more sessions of this travesty of a parliament. He was for home on the morrow. It was not that he was against reform, but he had not enjoyed this way of gaining it. He himself was contributing nothing, nor was likely to be able to do so. Seton agreed. He would absent himself also, since clearly all the decisions were being made beforehand. David Lindsay, who was with them, wryly admitted that he felt the same way; but unfortunately his position as Lyon demanded his presence at any session. They were fortunate men in being able to choose.

Back at Terregles, Agnes, hearing of it all, was less concerned than was John. She was stronger in her reformist views than he was, and contended that no great improvements in religion, as in all else, were apt to be effected without upset and turmoil. Matters would settle down and better handling prevail. What was vital was that the Church's near-dominance in affairs of state was over, although her husband wondered whether John Knox and his kidney would not seek to put their own oars in hereafter.

Repercussions from that parliament were not long in evidencing themselves, the most troublesome and indeed unexpected being division amongst the reformers themselves after gaining their great victory. The main stumbling-block to unity was the ancient and inbred fear and hatred of England, and the traditional support for the Auld Alliance with France, which last had developed of course to keep the English worried of war on two fronts. Now, after this parliamentary triumph for Protestantism, Queen Elizabeth, the Protestant, announced that she was taking Scotland under her care, and emphasised her approval by sending a first token of aid of four thousand crowns in silver. This unlooked-for donation had a great impact, greater than even Elizabeth looked for almost certainly. For word of it struck many Scots as the beginning of a campaign to gain control of their realm, not by arms and then marriage as that queen's father had attempted it, but by buying it. Not all saw it as a threat, but many did; and the result was a turning again towards France by some in high places. The parliament had agreed to send all French soldiery home; but now it was decided to keep at least some proportion of them, in order to ensure that the English force in Lothian, no longer needed, withdrew to their own country also. So pro-English and pro-French parties appeared amongst the reformist leadership, Scotland once again demonstrating its genius for disunity.

And, as it happened, this had some impact on John's West March, most unexpectedly likewise. Patrick, Earl of Bothwell, had died, leaving a son James to inherit the title, a brash and assertive young man who sought to inherit more than just the earldom and its lands. He claimed that, since the wardenships of the Border were all but hereditary in three families, so the office of Lieutenant of the Borders, held by his father, should also be his. This was not agreed by the council, for although a Protestant of a sort, he made enemies easily, none of the wardens liking his attitude to them; and since he owned Hermitage Castle in Liddesdale, John tended to have most to put up with; he was not given the lieutenancy, then, and he promptly adopted a pro-French line and personally took charge of the French auxiliaries, or some part of them, urging that they should not be sent home. Not only so, but using some of them to reinforce his own Hepburn followers, he actually waylaid and attacked the party which had gone to take over the unsolicited four thousand English crowns, handed over at Berwick; and here again there was some impact at Terregles, for the man in charge of the group was Cockburn of Ormiston, uncle to Janet's husband. So the pro-French party had Elizabeth's silver, and the Lords of the Congregation split the more.

Much dispute followed all this, needless to say. But the pro-English, plus the non-aligned lords, had the majority, at least among the magnates, and gained the day. But even they did not wish to offend France, and they rather cunningly gained a compromise by agreeing that six hundred of the Frenchmen, out of about five thousand, should remain in Scotland, and the rest go home. And they also disposed of the Bothwell problem meantime by sending him to France with them, as a sort of envoy, to help keep the Auld Alliance door open. What happened to the four thousand crowns was a mystery. John had the notion that much of it might well be hidden in the cellars of Hermitage Castle. The lords and John Knox agreed to solve that other problem of the unwanted corpse of Marie de Guise by sending it back to France at the same time.

That was in early December. It had been a very full autumn.

The winter, which started early with unusually cold

weather, was little less eventful. France was in turmoil, with the de Guise and the Huguenots in open warfare and young King Francis taking to his bed, delirious, with catarrh oozing from his right ear. Some blamed it on the weather, for he felt the cold grievously; others quoted astrologers who had declared that he would not live to see eighteen years. Others still said that his mother, Catherine de Medici, was hastening his end. At any rate the unfortunate young man died on 5th October, and Mary Queen of Scots was a widow, and Queen Catherine ruling France in the name of her younger son Charles the Ninth.

Whatever the truth of the matter, it all altered the story not only of France, for there was now nothing to keep Mary Stewart in that country, indeed her mother-in-law was wanting to be rid of her. Bothwell was ordered to urge her return home, and swiftly.

John Knox, typically, had the last word on the subject, as the eventful year of 1560 closed. Referring to young Francis, he declared: "Lo! The potent hand of God has sent unto us a wonderful and most joyous deliverance. The unhappy Francis suddenly perished of a rotten ear – that deaf ear which would never know the truth of God!"

That was not quite his last word for the year, for later in the month the first General Assembly of the Kirk of Scotland was held in Edinburgh, Knox reigning supreme – and at it denouncing Maitland of Lethington, of whose eloquence and cleverness he had become jealous.

24

With Marie de Guise dead and the Lords of the Congregation in effect ruling Scotland, however divisively and quarrelsomely, and with Lord Seton and Sir David Lindsay no longer close to the seat of power, John Maxwell was not called upon to act commissioner in sundry negotiations, and was left to get on with his quite sufficient task of seeking to keep the peace and uphold the laws of the West March, which suited him very well, for he had no ambition to play any more prominent role on the national scene.

Others were more eager so to do, that spring of 1561, in especial three: the Lord James Stewart, Secretary of State Maitland and Master John Knox. Into the power vacuum, with no regent and the monarch overseas, these worked and manoeuvred. But not in any harmony. Knox distanced himself from Maitland, sought to turn other lords against him. And the Lord James, an able man also, deciding that the Kirk was now getting too powerful, as had the former churchmen, threw in his lot with Maitland. Chatelherault, after some dithering, supported these two, while Glencairn, Argyll, the Marischal and even Huntly the Catholic, took Knox's part. The old dichotomy prevailed in the land.

John, all but despairing of good government ever being established, heard of all this but was not personally affected by it, until, in early April, he had a visitor, unlooked for indeed. This was the Lord James Stewart, on his way south to England and en route for France, and putting up for the night at Terregles. At first, John assumed that this was just a convenient halting-place on the way to Carlisle;

but presently he learned that there was more than that to the call. It seemed that his visitor had a mission to Queen Elizabeth on behalf of his and Maitland's pro-English faction, before going on to France to try to convince his half-sister to return to Scotland, which she seemed to be loth to do; and he and his colleagues were worried about Elizabeth's attitude towards those four thousand crowns which had gone astray. She would be almost bound to ask what had become of them, and if she was dissatisfied, no more might follow. There were suggestions that the rogue Bothwell had secreted away most of the money. His castle of Hailes, in Lothian, had been searched, and nothing found. But he owned Hermitage also, in this West March. Had the Lord Herries heard anything?

John had to say that he had not, although admitting that the notion as to Hermitage had occurred to him also. But Bothwell might well have taken most of the moneys with him to France?

James Stewart said no. Bothwell had gone by ship from Leith, and had been escorted to the port by Maitland and others, and had had no large baggage-train. Had Herries any notion of the weight of thousands of silver crowns? Such would be a burden indeed to transport, and would have been obvious on any pack-horse backs. Maitland was quite certain that it had not gone to France with Bothwell. So – Hermitage, perhaps?

Uneasy about this, John was wondering whether the Lord James was intending to go to Liddesdale to try to investigate; but became the more perturbed still when his visitor declared that he must be on his way to England in the morning, but that if he could tell Elizabeth Tudor that a diligent search was being made for the siller it would help his mission to her. And it seemed to him that the Warden of the West March was the obvious authority to go to Hermitage and conduct a search. Needless to say, if the moneys were discovered there, and taken in charge, his lordship would find the Privy Council suitably grateful.

Much concerned over this suggestion, John asked if his

guest realised that Hermitage Castle was the strongest hold on all the border, impregnable, and if the money was indeed therein, then most certainly Bothwell would have given very clear orders to the keeper not to permit anyone to search it, probably not even to enter it. The other frowned at this, and seemed to think that his host was being unco-operative. His lordship must make the attempt at least, and with all his tough and fiery mosstroopers, surely ought to be able to gain access to one or any of the houses within his jurisdiction. He must be able to tell Elizabeth so.

John did not consider that the Lord James had any authority to order him to attempt this, but felt that he could hardly refuse at least to try.

They parted in the morning with that understanding.

Next day, then, John rode for Liddesdale, but not with any large train of Marchmen. He knew Hermitage well, and recognised that if its keeper denied admittance, no force of armed men, without heavy artillery, could gain entry, and even then it would demand major siegery, which he had no intention of conducting. So a mere small escort would suffice.

Hermitage stood, in a branch valley of the River Liddel, on a platform between two streams entering the Hermitage Water, a very strong position, with natural defences as well as man-made, a great soaring pile of four square towers linked by almost equally high curtain walls, and an open courtyard within. As well as its water-filled moat, it had ramparts further back to keep cannon at a safe distance. Its enormously thick walling was almost windowless up to the topmost storey. It had been granted to Hepburn of Hailes, first Earl of Bothwell, by James the Fourth, for aid at the Battle of Sauchieburn, where James the Third had died.

No banner flew over the grim towers as John rode up with his men. But smoke curled up from chimneys, so the place was occupied. Their arrival undoubtedly would have been observed. John had come prepared, with a horn to blow, and Dod Armstrong, who had a vigorous pair of lungs, to do the shouting – for any preliminary talking would have to be at a distance, because of that moat and ramparts.

As near as they could get, he sounded the horn, its ululations echoing from the surrounding hills.

They had not long to wait for answer. "Who approaches the Hermitage of Liddesdale unbidden?" came to them thinly from the gatehouse.

"The warden of this March, the Lord Herries," Dod shouted back, hands cupped to lips. "He requests admittance."

There was no response to that for quite some time, long enough for Dod to try again.

"The Lord Herries, warden, requires admittance to this hold."

Still a pause, and then, "For what purpose?"

"That is between my lord and the keeper here."

"*I* am the keeper of Hermitage, for my lord of Bothwell."

John took over. "Then you, sir, will open for me, Herries, I think," he called.

"For what purpose?" was repeated.

"I do not have to explain my requirements, sir. I am warden here, and have right of entry into any and every house in my March."

"My lord Earl of Bothwell gave me strict orders not to admit anyone to the hold of Hermitage."

"His orders cannot apply to the warden, sir."

"I take my orders from my lord of Bothwell and none other. His I must obey, as his keeper here."

"You refuse the warden entry, then, sirrah?"

"I must do, my lord."

"And that without knowing the reason for my visit?"

"It is not for me to seek reasons. I have my orders."

"I could bring a large force against you here."

"No doubt. But that would not gain entry, my lord." The voice was getting fainter, but no less definite.

"I must assume, then, that you have something to hide. Some guilt." John's own voice was becoming tired with this long-distance shouting.

Another spoke, and slightly louder. "We do not hear you."

John shrugged, and told Dod to tell them that this would not be forgotten, and reined his horse round.

It was, of course, humiliating just to ride away thus, but there was nothing else for it, and this had been all but anticipated. The word of it would be all round the dales in a day or two. All that could be said was that it certainly looked as though Bothwell had something important to secrete there. He had done the best that he could for the Lord James and his friends. He was certainly not going to summon hundreds to make siege of Hermitage.

Agnes had advised him to ignore the Lord James's request. Perhaps he should have heeded her.

They heard on the border of that man's doings, as time went on. How his dealings with Queen Elizabeth had gone was not to be known, but at least they had not prevented him from proceeding on to France. What he would say to Bothwell, if he met him there, was anybody's guess.

All that spring and early summer there were reports of doings in France, not of the Lord James or Bothwell but of still more lofty folk. For the young widow of Scotland had become the target for many matrimonial ambitions. Two kings vied with each other to marry her, those of Sweden and Denmark; Don Carlos, heir to Spain, likewise; even the son of the emperor, and lesser candidates also, to be sure. At home, Chatelherault was eager for his son, Arran, to wed her, so that at least his grandchild might reach the throne. And it was said that Elizabeth Tudor had various suitors in mind, to advance her cause in Scotland. While all this was, of course, concerned with power and politics, it was said that the young woman's own attributes by no means hampered these aspirations, for she was reputed to be beautiful, spirited, talented and yet amiable into the bargain; and she was rich, with the revenue of the duchy of Touraine and the county of Poitou. What her own feelings in the matter were she seemingly kept to herself, while receiving all the suitors or their envoys kindly, at Reims, where her uncles, the Duc de Guise and the Cardinal of Lorraine, made their base. None knew when, and whether, she was intending to return to Scotland, although it was declared that the Lord James, for the Protestants, and Bishop Leslie, for the Catholics, were equally strong in urging it, the latter advising her to sail to Aberdeen, where twenty thousand armed men of the north and the Highlands, presumably largely Huntly's, would be waiting to receive her and ensure her smooth and untroubled ascent to her throne. Her half-brother, however, was reported to be recommending a cross-Channel and overland journey up through England, being greeted by her sister-queen in the process, for the better relations between the two realms. Presumably this had been amongst Elizabeth's suggestions when Lord James was in London.

In the event, Mary Stewart – or Stuart as she was now spelling it, since the French alphabet boasted no W – while returning to her native land, elected to take the guidance of neither, and eventually set sail from Calais, at the beginning of August, with quite a fleet of vessels, including two galleys and four great ships, with escorting craft to the number of sixteen – all this, it was hinted, because she did not trust Elizabeth's navy not to try to intercept her. And she was making for Leith, the port of her capital, Edinburgh, not Aberdeen.

When word of this reached the West March, John was of course interested. But Agnes was more than that. Excited by all that she heard of their young and lively monarch, she was for seeing her, meeting her, not just listening to tales. Surely the Warden of the West March would consider it his loyal duty to welcome his sovereign-lady to her kingdom's shores, and to take his wife with him? She had not had a break from home, save to visit her sisters at Garlies and Skirling, for long. The children would be well enough for a few days, cared for by their attendants. John could not say her nay.

So it was northwards for them without delay, for just when the queen would arrive at Leith was uncertain, dependent on winds and weather. They would make for Lord Seton's town-house in Edinburgh.

There they found Agnes to be not the only female concerned to meet Mary Stuart, and indeed others. For Seton's daughter Mary was one of the queen's close attendants, the four Maries she had had from childhood, and her mother was eager to welcome her back after all the years in France. So she, a Hamilton, was there, as was the Lady Lindsay from Garleton Castle, none so far from Seton Palace, to make a pleasant, indeed stimulating, company. Seton told them that they were just in time, for the report was that the French flotilla had been sighted off Yorkshire's Flamborough Head the day before, and should reach Forth, and Leith, on the morrow, even in this almost windless August weather.

The women made the evening memorable.

In the morning, oddly chill with an easterly haar, or mist off the sea, they started early. As well that they did, for all Edinburgh seemed to be on its way down to Leith, the two miles; lords and lairds, merchants and craftsmen, the ordinary folk and their women and children, those on horseback having to pick their way slowly through the crowds, delay inevitable. But good humour prevailed, everyone in holiday mood. It had been nineteen years since Scotland had seen its monarch, for the child Mary had not been made visible to her people before being sent to France at the age of five, so her father had been the last on view.

Pushing their way through the narrow packed streets and wynds of Leith was still more difficult, and well before they reached the waterside they had to dismount and leave their horses with grooms, amongst innumerable others, actually in a churchyard, the men anxious to ensure that their womenfolk were not jostled.

Quays lined the Water of Leith where it joined Forth, to form the port, and here members of the royal guard sought to keep order and see that only the great ones gained access to the pier-side. As lords and ladies, these newcomers found no problem in getting past.

They discovered much concern prevailing, and cursings at this untoward mist, common enough in November on this coast but highly unusual in August. This was delaying the French ships, visibility down to some three hundred yards. Apparently a couple of barges had been sent out, under the harbour-master, to guide in the queen's galley, which was lying off the haven-mouth, to the narrow entry past the breakwater. They were told that the Secretary of State and the Lord Lyon had gone out in one of these, to make first welcome of the monarch.

John was surprised to see the Lord James amongst the throng of magnates waiting there; he had assumed that he would be arriving with his half-sister. But apparently he had preceded her, for some reason, arriving a few days earlier, by the overland route. There was no sign of the Earl of Bothwell, however. Sir William Kirkcaldy of Grange, keeper of the royal castle of Edinburgh, was standing by to have welcoming cannon fired, but was anxious not to give the signal before the ships were actually in sight. Chatelherault had his son Arran well to the front.

After all the hurry and bustle it seemed a long wait. But at last a tall ship, masts bare of sails but towed by the two barges, loomed out of the mist, and cheering arose. But this was promptly lost in the thunderous crash of cannon-fire, which went on and on, deafening all.

It took more time to edge the great galley in to the quayside, cables tied to moor it, and a gangway run out. A group of women could be seen waiting at the forefront of those thronging the deck, but which was the queen it was impossible to discern. The cannonade ceased at last.

At length, the gangway firmly secured, two men hurried

down it, to stand on the pier and beckon, Lindsay and Maitland. They had scarcely taken up position when one of the young women followed them down, alone, all but at a run, but lightly, gracefully, and everywhere the cheering fell silent as folk gazed.

And undoubtedly the queen was worth staring at, monarch or none. Tall, lissome, superb of figure, she was as lovely of feature and expression as she was of bearing, smiling joyfully although clad all in black mourning for her late husband, save for white at neck and cuffs, her long reddish hair looped up into a white lined coif. There she stood scanning them all from dark but dancing, expressive eyes. Then she raised both arms out towards them in a spontaneous gesture of warmth and caring.

Agnes Herries caught her breath and gripped John's arm tightly. Not that she required to impress anything upon him. The man was staring, spellbound – as indeed were many there.

For moments it was as though the scene was frozen static. Then there was a surge forward of the waiting throng, the great ones at least, an impetuous welcome which had to falter in a few yards as folk recollected due order, precedence and the like. Others were now coming down the gangway from the ship.

The duke, as heir to the throne, and his son Arran, bowing, had to be first to reach out to kiss the royal hand. But the Lord James was not far behind, and, stiffly formal as he seemed, was embraced impulsively and kissed by his half-sister, which surprised not only John there. Somehow that aloof and unsmiling individual did not seem to be one to inspire affection. Did this reveal something in Mary's nature? Some need, perhaps? Hers had been a strange life, all but devoid of close love and tenderness since childhood, however much suit and attention had been paid to her. Did she need this?

Another half-brother came to her, a very different one, Robert Stewart, Commendator of Holyrood Abbey;

most of King James's bastard sons had been made commendator-abbots, although none was in holy orders. This one was genial, hearty indeed, not handsome and said to be unscrupulous; perhaps with that background, he had to be. Mary, not knowing him, greeted him enquiringly. Laughing jovially, he informed her, scarcely mincing his words.

Thereafter there was a long queue of notables to be presented, led by Argyll, who was wed to the Lady Jean, another of the royal offspring. In her turn, Mary presented her de Guise Uncle René, Marquis d'Elboeuf, admiral of her squadron. Reckoning themselves to be far down the list of priority, John and Agnes meantime were introduced to Mary Seton, a dark, fine-featured young woman, not beautiful but good-looking nevertheless. Indeed, as she indicated the other Maries, Beaton, Fleming and Livingstone, all seeking their kinsfolk, it was to be seen that all four were attractive. These had given the queen all the real affection she had known hitherto.

It was Mary Seton who led her father and mother, together with John and Agnes, to the queen, and despite all the previous presentations they were kindly received, with interest shown, Mary Stuart telling Seton how dear a friend his daughter had been to her over the years, and saying that she had heard of Lord Herries and the Maxwells. She did not know the West March, save by name, but would certainly visit it one day. Was it not there, somewhere, that the Earl of Bothwell had a castle? Her speech was good Scots, but with a French accent not unnaturally, and attractive.

Presently a move was made from the quayside as a second French galley was towed in to moor beside the other, and grandees began to come ashore to add to the crowd. Lord James said that the queen ought to go to the nearest large house meantime, for refreshment, that of Andrew Lamb, a prosperous merchant, while his half-brother, Lord Robert, arranged for her journey up to Holyrood Abbey. Clearly there would be no room for all this throng, with more coming, at the merchant's house, so Seton and John and the ladies decided to go back to the Canongate of Edinburgh, where was Seton House. Lindsay had to remain in close attendance on the monarch. Thereafter they could all go down the short distance to Holyrood, to watch the royal arrival there.

As they rode back up Leith Walk, all were loud in their admiration of the eighteen-year-old sovereign, not only her looks but her friendly and approachable behaviour, this young woman so sought after by the crowned heads of Christendom, herself a queen-regnant, as distinct from a queen-consort, the first Scotland had ever had, since the little Maid of Norway, heiress to Alexander the Third, had never got nearer than Orkney before she died. John's extolling of Mary Stuart prompted Agnes to declare her jealousy if this was not modified.

The Canongate of Edinburgh, as its name implied, led down to the Abbey of the Holy Rood; and after brief refreshment at Seton House, the little party walked down past the Tolbooth to the monastic area. Here also they had to pick their way through crowds, for seemingly all the citizenry of the capital who could not face the walk to Leith and back were on their way now to welcome the queen at the abbey below the towering heights of Arthur's Seat.

Wisely bringing three Seton servitors to make way for them, they managed to win a fairly prominent stance in front of the abbot's large house, practically a palace, where the Lord Robert had made a home for his numerous brood of offspring and their mothers, an allegedly riotous but good-humoured establishment.

They had not long to wait before the royal cavalcade came into sight over Moutrie's Hill, a lower shoulder of the Calton, and down Gabriel's Road past the leper hospice into the levels at the foot of the dramatic crags of the lion-shaped soaring hill which King Arthur of the Britons had called his seat. Fortunately the fog had cleared. Before the abbey gate they were met by a choir of singing boys, who ushered them in past a large group of black-robed clergy waiting silently and unsmiling. Amongst these was the unmistakable figure of Master Knox. How would he and his like react towards the firmly Catholic queen?

Whatever was said as Mary Stuart rode up, flanked by her illegitimate kinsfolk – only the males by noble ladies had been allowed to be named James Stewart by their royal father – another long and continuing cannonade drowned it out, this from the castle, Sir William Kirkcaldy clearly determined to demonstrate his loyalty. So, in the din, a move was fairly quickly made into the abbot's house by the great ones, including Knox and some of his ministers. Seton's party had no difficulty in gaining access.

Here they found a splendid banquet spread on many tables in a large hall. So numerous were the guests, invited and otherwise, that most had to eat and drink standing, but no complaints were forthcoming. The queen herself, although provided with a fine chair a little apart, soon rose from it to circulate amongst the other diners, her four Maries at her back. She made a special point, seemingly, of approaching John Knox, of whom she could not fail to have heard; and although John Maxwell and his friends were not near enough to hear what transpired there, they could see that the cleric was all but haranguing her, arms raised to point heavenwards but in no benedictory fashion. Much dismayed and angered at this, they wagged their heads, as did many; but the queen seemed to listen heedfully, saying little, before inclining her beautiful head and moving on. No good augury this.

Presently, with Mary Stuart gone into a withdrawing-room with her brothers and some others, Mary Seton found her way to her father's and mother's side, and was not long in expressing her disquiet over the situation with that man Knox and some of the other Protestant clergy and Lords of the Congregation. It was shameful, she declared, and if this was an indication of future behaviour and attitudes, it presaged serious problems. Her hearers agreed with her. She added that the queen was intending to go hereafter to the Chapel Royal in the abbey church to attend a mass to give thanks for her safe journey and arrival in her kingdom; but this would be a private ceremony, a more public thanksgiving to follow in a day or two; and it was to be hoped that there would be no unsuitable repercussions. Her uncle, Monsignor Francis de Guise, Grand Prior of France, and her chaplain, the Abbot of Brantome, would officiate.

With the queen remaining out of sight meantime, in a short while the Seton group withdrew to their Canongate house again.

Considerably later, Sir David Lindsay called in to collect his wife. He was much upset, for that genial character. There had been distressing scenes. Knox and his fellow extreme reformers had violently objected, to the queen's face, to her intention to allow a mass to be said, declaring this to be now unlawful in this realm, according to the parliament-passed Confession of Faith, as well as an insult to the Almighty. She had been very patient and apparently unruffled, saying that her personal devotions were *her* affair, as they were for others, and only those who worshipped as she did should attend this service. A more general ceremony of thanksgiving would be held in due course. But Knox had insisted that anything such was against the law of the land, and of the national Kirk; and that although she might be monarch by the mischance of birth, she was just one more sinning vassal in the sight of God. Her French uncles – for as well as d'Elboeuf, the Duc d'Aumale and the Grand Prior had come ashore from that second galley – were furious, declaring that this renegade and impertinent priest should be hanged. There had been a terrible to-do in front of the sovereign. But eventually she had composed herself, sought to make peace, and led her French courtiers over to the Chapel Royal, Knox shouting after her that this was now also the parish church of the Canongate. No very large company had actually entered the building for the service, presumably being held in French, Lindsay absenting himself in order to have a word with the Lord James and Maitland. All were perturbed by the way matters were developing, reformist although they might be.

So were Sir David's hearers now. It looked as though Scotland's fair liege-lady was going to have a troublesome reign, trouble for them all indeed. Why did the worship of the loving Christ so often seem to reject His love and seek dominance instead?

John and Agnes returned to Terregles on the morrow, without further seeing the queen.

25

In the months which followed they heard, on the West March, if somewhat belatedly, much that went on around the seat of power – and little of it cheering. The queen was being pulled this way and that, in matters of rule as well as religion, and even allegedly in matters of the heart also. The lack of a resident monarch for so long had encouraged the power-hungry increasingly to take upon themselves rule in the land, and they were reluctant to give this up, especially to a young woman. So men were not only seeking to retain their sway and mastery, even to extend it, but also to influence and dominate the queen, this resulting in open division and intrigue, the Lord James and Maitland against Argyll, Glencairn against the Marischal, Lennox against Huntly, Huntly against them all, he endeavouring to raise the Catholic cause militant now that they had a Catholic monarch actually on her throne, and Knox and the Kirk in consequence becoming ever the fiercer and more inimical to Mary Stuart. Moreover, Bothwell was back from France, via Denmark, and it was said had brought a handsome lady with him therefrom, no less than the High Admiral of Norway's daughter, one Anna Throndsen, installing her in Hermitage Castle, to the offence, since he had not married her, of the King of Denmark. Despite this, Bothwell was making an undisguised, indeed brazen assault on the young queen's affections, for he was a hot-headed character of no subtlety, but seemingly had some essential appeal for women. And this was provoking competition, almost as blatant, with Chatelherault wishing to marry his son Arran to her; and Lennox equally anxious to make *his* heir, the

Lord Darnley, her husband, claiming that this could put a child of such marriage in line for Elizabeth's throne eventually, since she was sworn to virginity, and Lennox's wife was the daughter of Queen Margaret Tudor by her second marriage. The Kings of Denmark and Sweden were said to be still in competition for Mary's hand; but few in Scotland wanted another union of crowns, other than that of England, in time, perhaps.

Agnes declared that the queen did need a strong husband, but not one ambitious for personal power and dominance, poor lass.

John felt himself blessed to be well out of it all, his wardenship problems none so dire, especially now that Elizabeth Tudor's strong if maidenly hand was ruling England and, as she put it, she was still taking a care for Scotland, and discouraging cross-border aggression. Blessed, too, in that Agnes was pregnant again, now in her fortieth year, and so unlikely to bear many more children – and he could do with another son to make two of each sex.

The year 1562 started with more grievous rumours. The queen had made a tour round parts of her domain, starting at Linlithgow, on to Stirling, then Perth and Dundee and finally at St Andrews, which was excellent, and the folk had welcomed her warmly throughout. But allegedly she had performed acts of worship, Catholic worship, in all these, and the reformers had thereafter beaten up her priests, and Knox had denounced her in Edinburgh, saying that she had polluted these towns with her idolatry. She had meantime created the Lord James Earl of Moray, and this alienated the Earl of Huntly, for he had been granted that other earldom, in addition to his own, in 1549. So, in his offence, he resigned his office of Chancellor, and it was bestowed upon Morton. Huntly, Cock o' the North, was now keeping himself to his northern fastnesses, and the queen had seemingly lost the support of the most powerful Catholic in the kingdom.

All this, although much concerning them at Terregles,

hardly affected their life on the border. But another development did. Bothwell, in his determined wooing of the queen, persuaded her to appoint him to his late father's office of Lieutenant of the Borders; and not only so, but added to this style that of Chief Warden of the Marches, a title hitherto unheard of. Here was cause for concern, indeed. Did it mean that the three wardens now were to be junior to another, and he the ambitious and unscrupulous Bothwell?

They did not take long to discover the answer. A peremptory summons presently arrived at Terregles for the Lord Herries to report at Hermitage Castle three days hence, along with the other two wardens.

Almost John was for refusing to accede to this curt command, brought by a mere servitor. But on second thoughts he decided that probably he ought to go, if only to discover Bothwell's intentions. He had no doubt that, if his colleagues from the Middle and East Marches did attend, they would be equally determined to retain their independence. Agnes wished that she could accompany her husband to Liddesdale, for she was much interested to see the Norse lady who was said to be queening it at Hermitage, this Anna Throndsen; but her delivery of child was imminent, and she must not take the risk of the lengthy ride.

John wondered, as he rode for Liddesdale, whether this journey would be any more effective than his last to Hermitage. At least this time he ought to gain access to the castle.

On arrival, with Dod, he saw that he had been preceded by the other two wardens and, unlike himself, they had elected to come in force, for the hold's vicinity was crowded with men and horses in the Kerr and Home colours. Perhaps they had thought to make clear to Bothwell that they were sufficiently strong to resist any overbearing attempts by the earl.

In the event, John found the situation other than anticipated, with the Norse admiral's daughter making herself most welcoming and pleasant to the visitors, and Bothwell, scarcely that, but holding back from any aggressive stance meantime. She was a vividly attractive young woman, handsome rather than beautiful, obviously a positive character, with cascading corn-yellow hair and a full figure. She greeted John heartily, the earl much less so.

He was a thickset, muscular and strong-featured man with a flashing eye and out-thrust jawline. John assessed him as a formidable enemy, whatever sort of friend he might make. At this stage he was leaving reception to the lady, curious behaviour for the man who was reputed to be urgently seeking the queen's hand in marriage.

When Anna left them, saying that she would oversee the provision of a meal worthy of such notable guests, her husky voice heavily accented, Bothwell quickly made his position and attitudes clear. He had requested their presence, he said, to ensure that they might all work together for the better rules and accord of the entire Borderland, as was Her Grace the Queen's express desire, in improvement of the present position where disharmony and pillage so generally reigned. As chief warden and lieutenant, it was his simple duty to see that the royal will prevailed. Did they understand?

The three wardens eyed each other. John, reckoning himself probably to be the senior, at least in years of office, spoke first.

"My lord Earl, we of course respect the queen's wishes, and her care for the folk of the Marches. We acknowledge your own appointment as Lieutenant of the Borders, as was your father before you, a position of some authority over much in the life of the whole area, in such as the appointment of sheriffs and law officers, of the holding of markets and fairs, of the oversight of the councils of burghs and towns, and the like. But . . . we do not recognise the style, nor any authority, of Chief Warden of the Marches. There has never been such appointment. Our positions as wardens could be lessened and weakened by anything such. We cannot accept that.''

The other two made supportive noises.

"It is the royal command, Lord Herries." That was short, abrupt.

"If that is so, then it is made in ignorance of the enduring and ages-old position, my lord Earl. The wardens are each supreme in their three Marches, with fullest powers to enforce the Border laws – which are different from elsewhere – and to protect the borderline from assault. They cannot accept oversight by another.''

"Not even by the crown, sir!"

"Direct orders of the crown, yes," Home put in. "But not by any lesser appointment. The young queen may not know of this.''

Bothwell frowned. "The crown can make or unmake appointments, my lords. It is the fount of all temporal authority. And I have been made chief warden.''

"Then we must see Her Grace, and inform her of the true position," John said.

For moments there was silence, the earl tight-lipped. Then he jabbed an accusing finger.

"Whatever you may say, you are failing in your duties as wardens. Robbery and reiving, rape and assault, burnings and slayings, go on all along the border. These make a mockery of all law and order, and you appear to be unable to check it. Or do not.''

"There is much of strife, yes, my lord," John admitted. "But as I said, the Borders have their own laws, the Leges Marchiarum. You must know that, your sire having been lieutenant before you. These we seek to uphold. Other relevant laws where we can. What are offences elsewhere may not be such here – "

"You say that these so-called laws permit rogues and scoundrelly vagabonds to steal *my* cattle!" the earl interrupted. "My farms of Shaws and Toftsholm have been raided and beasts driven off. By Elliots, I am told. *Your* responsibility, Herries!" His fists were clenched in anger.

"Your tenants have the right to go after the raiders, in the hot or cold trod. To recover their stock and demand compensation. By force of arms. Have they done so, my lord?"

"I do not advise my folk on my land to take the law into their own hands, when it is your responsibility, as warden of this March. The laws of the land must be upheld by its appointed representatives."

That from the man who had waylaid Cockburn of Ormiston's party, to the shedding of blood, and stolen four thousand English crowns, struck John as rich. He wondered how much of the siller was still hidden in the cellars below this hall? He bethought him of an indirect reference thereto.

"You blame the Elliots for the raiding? Is not Elliot of Redheuch your keeper of this castle?"

"He was, but no longer. He was my father's choice of keeper." That was stiff.

"Ah! So there is perhaps more to this than meets the eye, my lord Earl?"

"I know not what you mean! It is not Redheuch, I am told, who leads the raids, but Little Jock Elliot of the Park, a notour ruffian. Redheuch can no more keep order than can you, it seems!" He changed the subject, or at least its direction. "This defiance of the law is not confined to the West March," he said, pointing at the other two. "I hear of the same troubles afflicting Tweeddale and Teviotdale, Jedwater, Lauderdale and the Merse. It must stop. If you cannot halt it, then I will."

"How?" Home demanded bluntly. "It has been the way of the Borders for centuries, ever since there was a border. It may be different in your Lothian. Conditions here are otherwise, on the edge of England. The English crossing always. You hear of it in war, but it goes on all the time, crossings great and small, mainly stealing cattle and horses but burning and ravishing also, not considered warfare, privy endeavour as it is named. Our mosstrooping clans obey their own rules in dealing with this, aye and with each

322

other. And if these are different from the laws of the land otherwhere, so are the circumstances." He paused. "You say that you will halt it. Have you considered, my lord Earl, what these Marchmen's clans can raise against you if you so attempt? If they unite, as they would, especially the dalesmen, you could be facing five thousand of the roughest riders in Scotland!"

That had even Bothwell silent.

John sought to drive the lesson home, and at the same time make it seem less of a threat, more acceptable even.

"These Border laws are not all sword and spear," he pointed out. "They meet conditions here, so close to England. They protect, secure some justice. We, the wardens, have the right to punish masterful and violent theft at our discretion, and can call upon the clans to aid us. We can forfeit murderers' goods for the benefit of the victims' families. We can impose damages on law-breakers, of up to double the cost of their injury, with *sawfey* in addition, that is to make up for expense incurred. We can imprison for false complaints, and over-valuing of alleged loss. We have offences which you do not have elsewhere. Pasturing stock on others' land. The felling of trees likewise. And hunting without permission. Over-swearing, or perjury, before a warden. And impeding a warden in his duty, if three times committed, is punishable by hanging. So, see you, my lord Earl, the wardens' authority must not be lessened or overborne by . . . another."

Bothwell looked from one to the other, those eyes hot indeed. But he clearly recognised that he was not winning in this interview, and that the counter-threats which he might make would be more effectively made from elsewhere. He was probably not displeased when Anna Throndsen appeared in the doorway to announce that the repast was ready to be served, and that they could no doubt debate further as they ate.

In fact they did not do so; there was indeed little more which usefully could be said. The conversation round that well-plenished table was largely of the young woman's initiating, the earl all but silent. She intimated, in passing, that ale had been sent to the waiting men outside, probably insufficient but the best that she could do. The guests at least approved of their hostess.

Feeding over, and with long riding ahead of all, they were not long in taking their departure. They took leave of Bothwell very differently from their farewells to Anna Throndsen.

Back at Terregles, Agnes, interested to hear of it all, especially of the Norse paramour, suggested that Bothwell's trouble with the Elliots could relate to that stolen English money. Apparently Redheuch, their leading man, had been dismissed from the keepership of Hermitage. Could it be that he had appropriated some of the English siller hidden therein, reckoning that the earl would not be in any effective position to recover it? Save by force of arms, which could precipitate all but open warfare on the March. The biter could have been bitten? Which would explain something of the earl's attitudes at their meeting.

John acknowledged that there might well be something in that. But he admitted that he was still concerned over the matter of the queen's appointment of a chief warden. Something must be done about it, for Bothwell would not let it lie.

A call, less than a month later, with Agnes expecting her delivery any day, seemed to offer opportunity to take the vexed matter further. Young Thomas Kerr arrived unexpectedly, his first visit to Terregles, with two announcements. First, that his father, Sir John, long failing, had died. So he was now no longer deputy but full Warden of the Middle March, chief of the Kerrs and laird of Ferniehirst. And second, that the Lord James Stewart, now made Earl of Moray, had been appointed by the queen Justiciar of Scotland south of the Forth, and that he had intimated his intention of holding his first justice-ayre in the Borderland, at Jedburgh, in two weeks' time, and would expect to be housed at Ferniehirst, the royal castle at Jedburgh being unfit for his occupation. And Thomas Kerr thought that here was opportunity to seek James Stewart's influence with his half-sister over the chief warden issue. He was known to mislike Bothwell, and much against that man's wooing of the queen, and would possibly see this as a means of limiting the other earl's activities. If the three wardens could speak with him at this justice-ayre, they might achieve something.

John agreed that this was a worthwhile effort, and said that he would endeavour to visit Jedburgh for the court sessions, which would interest him anyway, as the new justiciar might well elect to hold similar courts at Dumfries, for the south-west area. But for how long might the courts go on? For he was concerned to be with his wife at her childbearing.

Kerr had no idea as to that, for this would be the first justice-ayre to be held in the Middle March since the late king's time; but he guessed that there might well be quite a number of cases to be heard, other than those of infringement of the Border laws, which were the warden's responsibility. Such serious offences against the national laws, beyond the sheriffs' powers, had of recent years been sent up to Edinburgh for hearing.

Fortunately, Agnes had her fourth child two days after Kerr's departure, and with not a difficult birth. It proved to be a boy, as John had desired.

John was at Ferniehirst, then, in good time for the court hearings, indeed before the Lord James, whom they must now call Moray, himself arrived. Home was already present. The trio agreed on their strategy.

They did not press their case right away on that stern individual when he did appear, with two others of his half-brothers, both Lords James, which was confusing, one Commendator-Abbot of Melrose, the other Commendator-Prior of Coldinghame, well looked after with Church lands by their royal sire, and both based in this area. Presumably they were being groomed for useful appointments in due course, Moray no doubt concerned to surround the queen with a circle of colleagues on whom he could rely, as the power behind the throne.

He was not effusive towards his host and the other two wardens; it was not in his nature to be so. But he was as well disposed as could be expected. Bothwell's name was not mentioned; nor, despite being Lieutenant of the Border, was he present for this justiciary court.

The first of two sittings began next day, in the old and bare castle above the town, with Moray directing the three wardens to sit flanking him on the dais, and his brothers nearby, the three sheriffs on the other side. Despite this plenitude of possible consultants, he did not once seek advice nor opinions, a man who most clearly knew his own mind. John was again struck by the thought that if only James the Fifth had married his first nobly born mistress, the Lady Margaret Erskine, instead of seeking a French bride for reasons of state, Moray would now be King James the Sixth and an undoubtedly strong monarch such as Scotland always needed.

The justiciar made little or no preliminary announcements before calling the clerk of court to proceed with the first case.

As it happened, this concerned West March offenders, eight of them, sent in by the shire reeve or sheriff of Dumfries-shire, and all Armstrongs, this without reference to John because their offences were outwith his jurisdiction, not just the stealing of cattle and burning of houses but the abducting of women, after they had had their way with them, whose whereabouts were not now known, but whom they were alleged to have bartered away over the border to English Grahams for due payment. The eight, all in chains, were paraded before the court, appearing defiant.

Moray turned to look at John. "Is this not your responsibility, my Lord Herries?" he demanded. "From your March."

"The first part, of reiving and burning, yes, my lord Earl. But not this of abducting and using women for gain. That is an offence against the realm."

The justiciar shrugged. "You, the accused, Armstrongs all, do you deny these charges?"

Caught red-handed, there was little that they could say. They had already appeared before the sheriff and had been remitted to this higher court, over the English connection. They remained silent, but insolently scornful of any authority.

That was enough for James Stewart. He nodded. "All guilty, then," he said without expression. "All to hang forthwith. Next."

Even the toughest there present raised eyebrows at this so swift dispensing of justice. Perhaps Scotland had not been so unfortunate in being spared this man as monarch after all?

The eight Armstrongs being pushed out, shouting insults and cursings, more or less collided with a new group being brought in, only three of them this time but again from Dumfries-shire and, John noted grimly, all Johnstones. The charge read out was that they had taken the daughter of Maxwell of Kirkblain in lower Nithsdale, used her carnally at the side of the queen's highway, and there left her naked. But this was made to sound almost more heinous in that they had not abandoned the horse on which she had been mounted, a valuable animal. It was thought to have been sold into England. This was a laird's horse ridden by a laird's daughter. Clearly the sheriff had felt disinclined to pass judgment, considering that these offenders were Johnstones and the victim a Maxwell and the Johnstone–Maxwell situation delicate, their chief now being deputy warden.

Curtly, Moray asked if there was any denial of these offences?

One young man spoke up, declaring that Jean Maxwell was a noted wanton, many having had her, including himself one time at Annan. This charge made no sense.

327

"And the horse?" That was rapped out.

No answer came.

"Very well. Guilty. Order, rule and the queen's peace must be kept, even on the West March. All three to hang. Next."

The youngest of the Johnstones was shouting as they were hustled out.

John heaved a sigh of relief when the next case called proved to be an East March one, concerning one Purves of that Ilk, who was accused of treason, no less, in that he traded and conspired with the English. He was not present, having refused to compear. The Berwickshire sheriff himself spoke to this case, frequently glancing over at Lord Home, who looked a little uncomfortable. All there recognised that this charging of a laird, and the head of a family at that, was a serious matter.

"It is a punishable offence in itself not to appear at this justice-ayre, if summoned," Moray observed. "Treason? Name it."

The sheriff, again glancing at Home, declared that Purves frequently visited Berwick town, selling droves of beasts. He owned craft in Eyemouth haven and these unloaded their catches in English harbours. Moreover, Purves was known to have dined at Berwick Castle with the English keeper there. In the last two invasions, his lands had been spared all English attack.

Moray now also looked at Home. He was no fool, and would know that the Purves lands were surrounded by Home properties and that, if found guilty of treason, the offender's lands would be forfeited, and undoubtedly would then be acquired by the Homes, who would certainly themselves trade through Berwick-upon-Tweed on occasion, especially with their wool, although probably not foolish enough to eat with the castle's keeper. Smoothing his chin, he declared flatly that since Purves had failed to appear, warrant should be made out for his apprehension, and he would be brought before the Privy Council in

Edinburgh, to answer a charge of treason, in due course. Next summons.

There were a number of other cases, some of them to do with the illegal netting of salmon, brought by Tweedside lairds. Even Moray could scarcely deal with such by hanging; but branding on the cheek with hot iron would serve, not only to punish but to identify the miscreants to the avoidance of further misdemeanours. The burning of neighbours' harvests and the destruction of mills which forced corn to be ground elsewhere, at a price, were tiresome and time-consuming offences, which clearly irked the justiciar, and only came before him because lairds were involved whom the sheriffs did not wish to upset.

But at length Moray had had enough, and announced postponement of further cases to the day following. Thankfully all retired, even the prisoners possibly, the justiciar and the wardens back to Ferniehirst. Gallows for the unfortunate to be hanged were being erected in Jedburgh as warning to others as they passed. Moray made no comments on his judgments, and John and his colleagues did not think to do so either.

Later, when dining, Home took the lead in broaching the subject of Bothwell's unfortunate appointment as chief warden, pointing out the wrongs and dangers of it, not actually blaming the queen since she would not know of the true situation and ages-old custom and tradition, John and Kerr supporting him. They were careful not to speak ill of Bothwell himself either, although criticism could be inferred. Moray heard them out, with that level gaze of his, and inclined his head.

"I will speak with Her Grace my sister," he said at length. That was all. But his hearers gained the impression that it might well be sufficient.

John had half expected some questioning of their wardenly activities, or lack of them, after one or two of those justiciary cases, but none was put into words. They passed a pleasant enough evening, well entertained both at table and later, with music, by Janet, Thomas

Kerr's new wife, daughter of Sir William Kirkcaldy of Grange, he who keepered Edinburgh Castle and went in for cannon greeting-salvoes; but Moray was not a man for comfortable companionship, and they were all rather relieved when he announced retirement to bed, including his two half-brothers who were considerably more amiable, the Prior of Coldinghame in fact a little drunken, growing somewhat amorous towards his hostess.

It had been quite a memorable day.

In the morning, John took his leave, having had a sufficiency of judiciary sessions, to which he was contributing nothing. Home stayed on, no doubt with good reason, some of the cases forecast to come rather close to his own doorstep.

26

Oddly, whether or not Moray had spoken to the queen over Bothwell, the next they heard at Terregles of that awkward character had nothing to do with the border and the maintenance of laws and order. Quite the reverse indeed. Bothwell was back at court, in Edinburgh, and the land rang with his exploits. Apparently he and the queen's uncle, d'Elboeuf, with the Lord James, Prior of Coldinghame, had distinguished themselves by creating a riot in the city's streets, two riots in fact. Presumably drink-taken, they had broken into a house in St Mary's Wynd, belonging to one Cuthbert Ramsay, in search of a young woman named Alison Craig, daughter of a prosperous Edinburgh merchant, who it was rumoured was being obliging towards the Earl of Arran. Whether they found the girl and lover there was not reported, but the break-in resulted in a violent tumult in the street outside and the trio had to retreat in some disorder. But collecting a larger group of their own, the following night they again sought to get to grips with the lady's and Arran's friends, and a large-scale disturbance broke out, to the effusion of blood, the city guard being doubtful about interfering with such well-born fighters until Moray and Argyll were sent for, who managed to restore order. It all did not do Arran's courtship of the queen any good, which may have been Bothwell's purpose; but nor did it serve to enhance his own credit.

There followed a great outcry over this affair, Moray leading the condemnation. For an earl of Scotland – not to mention a marquis of France and an admiral – Lieutenant of the Border and a member of the Privy

Council, so to behave, was beyond all bearing, at least by some, particularly the Lords of the Congregation. Moray undoubtedly saw it as an opportunity to thwart and obstruct Bothwell's pursuit of the queen's hand, and contrived to have a meeting of the council called, Bothwell however scorning to attend, seemingly sure of Mary Stuart's favour. He had many enemies amongst his peers, and being a Catholic of sorts, the Kirk loudly condemned him. The council decided that he should be summoned to appear before it to answer for his conduct. But, guessing that he would refuse, and more serious and possibly difficult steps have to be taken, even a request to the queen for imprisonment or banishment, it was to be whispered to him that they would be recommending that the Marquis d'Elboeuf should return to France, as overstaying his welcome, and it was advised that Bothwell should offer to escort him thither, and himself remain there meantime. And, whether reinforced by other and unnamed threats, the inconvenient earl had heeded advice given, for once, and he and d'Elboeuf had departed for France from Leith, in some style, the queen seeing them off.

Moray clearly had his methods of getting his own way. And, for the time being at least, the wardens of the Marches could forget problems as to overlordship.

John learned from more local sources that Anna Throndsen had departed from Hermitage Castle, Agnes sorry about that, for she had been looking forward to meeting the lady.

So matters returned to normal on the West March, whatever was the case elsewhere.

It was not long before they learned further of the power struggle going on around the young queen. Moray was undoubtedly leading in this competition but others were competing also, or at least involved in parallel pressures, Chatelherault and Lennox for their respective sons, Argyll and the Earl Marischal both seeking the chancellorship.

Huntly, out of favour, was confining himself to his northern territories but claiming that the Catholic queen should wed his own Catholic son, Sir John Gordon.

This of marriage, indeed, tended to dominate the situation. The realm required an heir, and Mary Stuart was infinitely marriageable. Chatelherault's son Arran, having legitimate royal blood, would be best, a stronger character than his father, if scarcely gallant; but he was a Protestant, and Mary would almost certainly prefer a Catholic. Lennox's son, the Lord Darnley, was sufficiently Catholic, and his Tudor connection important. The foreign suitors, however lofty, could be dismissed, they also being old enough to be Mary's father, and none appealing to a young woman who had already experienced an arranged and less than successful royal marriage.

Moray and Maitland, reformers both, were against Darnley and his father, and of course against Huntly and son. Which left them with Arran to support. Argyll chose to throw in his lot with them. But the word was that Mary was seeing more of Darnley, who was not exactly handsome but almost beautiful, elegant, much more attractive apparently than dour young Arran. The nation, itself all but in love with its young monarch, waited agog. At least Bothwell was out of the way meantime.

At Terregles they were as concerned as were others, especially Agnes, who, although she had never seen any of the contestants, declared that she did not like the sound of Darnley any more than she had liked Bothwell, however different in character they might be. But was Mary any judge of character? Who would be a young queen-regnant! Especially with Master Knox reputedly still haranguing her as spokesman for the militant Kirk.

That autumn all this of rumour, gossip and speculation suddenly took on a much more positive aspect for John Maxwell. A command came to him from Moray, in the name of the queen, to bring a contingent of his mosstroopers to join an army which he was assembling at Edinburgh to go north to deal with

Huntly. And this forthwith. No explanations accompanied the order.

Was it, in fact, a royal command? Or was Moray just using his half-sister's name for his own purposes? As Justiciar south of Forth, James Stewart had no authority to summon John, or anyone else save his own tenantry, in arms against a fellow-earl. But if it was the queen, that was of course different.

He compromised. He collected no very large body of Marchmen. He would take them as far as Edinburgh, and discover the true situation there.

At least he had no difficulty in assembling a force of a couple of hundred dalesmen. With the harvest, shearing and cattle-sales over, these were always happy to be off on any adventures, legitimate or otherwise, especially if booty could be looked for.

They rode to Edinburgh's Burgh Muir, there to find a large muster of men about to move to the north, these under the command of Thomas Kerr's father-in-law, Kirkcaldy of Grange, a veteran warrior. Kerr himself was there, but no sign of Home. Of all places, they were to be heading for Aberdeen. Apparently the queen was up there, having made a tour of her northern domains, before the winter set in, and had somehow fallen foul of Huntly. Just what had happened was not clear, but she, with Moray, Argyll and other lords, felt herself threatened by the Gordons, for all thereabouts was very much his country. Mary Stuart was urgently requiring armed forces for her safety.

That was sufficient for John, although he wondered about Huntly, he being the queen's greatest Catholic supporter. But it was possible that he might have thought to grasp her person while she was in his territories and force her into marriage with his second son, Sir John Gordon, the elder son, the Lord Gordon, being already wed. And Sir John had announced his seeking of the royal hand. He decided that he and the others who had responded to the call, who included the Master of Lindsay and Cockburn of Ormiston – he who had been robbed of the English silver, and was kin to Janet's husband – must take the long road northwards, fully one hundred and forty miles as it might be.

It took the force of some two thousand three full days to cover the distance, by Linlithgow, Stirling, Perth, down Strathmore to the sea at Montrose, then up the coast by Stonehaven to Aberdeen, where Dee and Don entered the Norse Sea. John's mosstroopers could have done it more speedily, but all the company were not so hard-riding as his Marchmen. It was, after Perth, all new country to them, of much interest, and the October weather fortunately genial. The scenery of the background of Highland mountains and then the dramatic cliff-girt shoreline was consistently challenging, whatever the occasion.

That occasion was indeed sufficiently challenging when they eventually reached the granite city, its stonework gleaming strangely. They found the queen ensconced in the Laird of Banff's town-house in Old Aberdeen, there being almost two cities, near to the Don estuary, with Moray, Argyll, the Marischal and other lords. And they were waiting, in a state of alert, for Huntly's next move, and thankful to see the reinforcements from the south, under Kirkcaldy, for Huntly and his son Sir John Gordon had announced that they were going to take the queen into their care, and in this northern countryside they could muster ample men to attempt it.

Apparently there had been a series of incidents in the last few weeks, for Mary had been up hereabouts since July. Huntly had assumed that she would lodge in his grand house of Strathbogie, up in the Huntly area; but this was considered to be too dangerous by the lords, in view of Huntly's marital ambitions, and she had refused, to the Cock o' the North's great offence. She had made a journey further up, to Inverness, to show herself to her Highland subjects; but, intending to lodge in the royal castle there, she had found it barred against her by its deputy keeper, who had declared that he could not admit her without the agreement of the Lord Gordon, keeper, who was absent, eldest son of Huntly. Mary was much put out, but challenged, and offered to wear shield and buckler herself to assert her authority. But the people of Inverness had rallied to her, and the castle had eventually surrendered, and the deputy keeper hanged. Then, further angered over Huntly and the Gordons, she had returned to Aberdeen. And Moray had sent to the south for armed men, for now Huntly was reported to be assembling his own strength. They knew this because his countess had come to the city to plead with Mary for peace with her husband and kindness towards her son; but the queen would not see her, on Moray's advice, and she had foretold trouble. Huntly was officially then put to the horn and declared outlaw; but here, in his own territory, much good that would do.

The newcomers were not given long to rest after their long journey. The very next evening news was brought to the city that Huntly and his son were only some fifteen miles away, in Midmar, with a force reckoned to be of thousands, assembled on the Hill of Fare, north of Banchory in the Dee valley, with others flocking to his banner. Moray, who was very much in charge, declared that, with their army which now amounted to some three thousand men, all horsed, they should sally forth before Huntly's numbers grew larger, as they undoubtedly could, his sway a wide one indeed. This was accepted, the queen deciding that she would accompany the host, not stay in Aberdeen, however much advice she was given to the contrary.

John and the other Borderers were not near the leadership group around Mary as they rode westwards from the city on the gentle slopes of the great Dee valley; but they heard from others that Moray had been in touch with sundry of the lesser Aberdeenshire clans, who tended to be somewhat jealous of the Gordons, seeking to wean them away from any support of Huntly – Forbeses, Burnetts, Leslies, Skenes and the like – with reminders as to loyalty to the monarch and promises of reward. What good this might do remained to be seen.

John was less than happy with the entire situation. He was prepared to fight invaders, the English; but this was civil war, Scot against Scot, largely with religion at the back of it.

South of the Loch of Skene they went, a horsed army. Ahead of them they could see the Hill of Fare, higher than the rest of the north flanks of Dee but no mountain, more of a lumpish series of five summits. There, reports said, Huntly had taken up position, presumably a well-chosen site for a battle, for he would know his own country. His forces would almost certainly be largely hillmen, Highlanders, and therefore unlikely to be mounted; but tough fighters indeed.

As they neared the base of the hill, in the Raemoir area, the leaders halted, and the entire force behind them. The higher ground was, in the main, visible from here, the eastern side of it at least. They had expected to see masses of men up there, but no, only a few small groups were in sight up near the summits. John and Kerr went forward for their orders.

There was much discussion going on around the queen, concern as to where was Huntly's force. Were the reports wrong that he was holding this Hill of Fare? Or was he on the far northern side of the hill, out of sight? That would be a strange position to take up, for reputedly that flank comprised much of gentle slopes and open woodland. Listening to the questioning, John, who was used to operating in hilly areas, made bold to put in a word. He pointed.

"My lords, that is a sizeable burn coming down yonder, centrally. You can see its headstreams up there, high. Then it disappears into a hollow before we see it again, much larger. That hollow must be of a fair size. Difficult to judge from here. But sizeable, yes. Sufficient to hide quite a large force, it may be."

All stared at him. "Is that likely?" Kirkcaldy, the most experienced soldier there, demanded.

"They will not be horsed, belike. That hollow, I judge, is greater than it may look from here. Going by the shoulders of the hill on either side, I say that there would be room in it for a large force."

Some lords present laughed him to scorn.

"Why wait in there, man?" That was Moray.

"A large hollow on a hillside, what we call a cleuch or a corrie, with a burn running through, could well provide bog, marshy soft ground. If there is a sufficiency of that, my lord Earl, horses would be held, sink in, where foot could go more lightly. Bare-shanked Hielandmen in especial! Huntly will know his land and his men. He may wait for us there, on the slopes, with a barrier of swamp in front protecting him."

"Guesswork!" the Earl of Glencairn exclaimed. "No great host could hide there unseen. I say Huntly, if he is at this Hill of Fare at all, is hiding behind the summit ridges. So that if we climb up, he can come over and descend upon us from above."

That produced cries of agreement.

"So, we should go round the hill, not over. Split in two, I say. Round each side. Assail him then on both flanks."

"To divide here would be folly," Kirkcaldy objected.

The queen raised voice. "Should we not send people to discover it? Go round, small parties, to see if the Gordons are on the other side? Wait here meantime."

"We should do that, yes, Your Grace," Moray said. "But if there is anything in what my Lord Herries says, we should know of it. Divided up we could be endangered from a hidden host on the higher ground. Huntly will indeed know his own domains, and will use them to best advantage."

John pointed, and spoke again. "Yonder slight ridge going up on the right. If I took my people up that a fair way, we ought to be able to see down both sides. Into the hollow on the west, and round the hill-skirts on the east."

"Aye, do that, Herries. Send to inform us. We will await your signal."

John rode back to his dalesmen and shouted to them to follow him. Some of them, hill-riders all, might well have seen the situation as he did.

They spurred off, over a small isolated mound or knoll a quarter way up the ridge he had pointed out, but it was still not high enough to see the central course of that burn. So on they climbed, their ridge developing into quite a spine, dropping away fairly sharply on both sides. They could soon see the foothill ground on their right for quite some distance, scattered with trees, but with no sign of men.

Then, quite suddenly, at the best part of a mile up from where they had left the army, the view to the left opened wide. And there, in a great basin of the hillside, were men indeed, hundreds, possibly thousands of men, packed tight, waiting, silent. A little way behind them, as John had guessed, was a belt of reedy, marshy ground, fully one hundred yards of it, through which the burn seeped its way. The Gordons had laid their trap.

Drawing a deep breath, John turned in the saddle to raise an arm to wave and point, his men doing the same. But, almost a mile away, this might well not be distinguished. John sent Dod Armstrong back down to inform.

Now, of course, if they could see, they could also be seen. What was their best course? His two hundred were far too few to charge down on that great force of Highlandmen with any hope of success or survival. To rejoin Moray and the queen? Better to wait up here, perhaps, at least posing a threat; and once they could see what Moray and Kirkcaldy would do, then take whatever action seemed best.

They sat on their horses.

It made a strange experience to wait there, idle, gazing down in the two directions, upon great masses of armed men, about a mile apart, and so very different of aspect, the Highland host necessarily ranked closely, not so far off that their tartans did not make a glow of colour, while back on the lower ground, much more spread out, in troops and squadrons, the mounted cohorts stood, the steel of armour and lances gleaming in the slanting October sunshine, banners high, a gallant sight. On the face of it, the royal host, when it came to action, looked bound to prevail, even though perhaps not superior in numbers. But such assessment would be omitting the important factor, the terrain. Huntly could make the land fight for him. Horsed chivalry was only truly effective where horses could advance in phalanx and charge, not when the beasts sank hock-deep in mire and marsh, but yet where lightly clad men with swords and dirks could run and leap and flit.

The first movement came from the royal side. A detachment moved off half-right, to climb towards that detached knoll which John and his men had surmounted on their way up, but which had not given them the prospect which they had hoped for. As this company drew nearer, the watchers could make out the great lion rampant standard of the monarchy flapping above it. So that would be the queen and some of the leadership taking up a commanding position to oversee the probable field of conflict.

But movement elsewhere diverted John's attention. Down in the hollow, men were running up to those horses tethered above the Highland host. How many it was hard to tell, but possibly about their own numbers, a couple of hundred. What now?

Soon it was apparent. Mounted, this company, steel glinting and with a banner raised at its head, began to ride slantwise across the upper part of that hollow, clearly making towards the knoll where the group under the royal standard had taken stance. And behind the horsemen came a racing band of running gillies, swords drawn. The Gordons had been reputed to intend to grasp the queen's person; now it seemed they were seeking to do so. This move would not be seen from the main royal army, until the attackers almost reached the knoll.

John had no doubts as to his duty and opportunity. That Gordon advance would cut across well below his present position, at an angle if it continued to make for the mound, as seemed almost certain. If he and his charged down upon it, they could take it in flank, cut through it, save the knoll party, it was to be hoped.

There was no time for consideration, assessment. The Gordons had less than half a mile to cover. Whether those on the hillock would see them in time to escape was doubtful. Huntly, or more probably his son, would have been apprised of the situation by those few scouts left up in the summits area, for they could not have seen it from their hollow.

John drew his sword with something of a flourish and pointed it down towards the Gordons. He did not need to make any other command, his dalesmen well able to perceive the scope for action. Round they all reined, and went at the canter downhill, lances couched.

The Gordon leadership, of course, would not be wholly taken by surprise. They would have seen John's company up there, and might have guessed that an assault in flank would develop. There were about five hundred yards to cover, and as John, in the lead, bore down to cut off the other mounted troop, he perceived what the dismounted Highlandmen behind were there for – to deal with him and his, if necessary, distract and assail.

He saw his options and dangers. He could divert, to deal with the footmen. But that would be what Huntly or his son wanted. But if he continued on to attack the mounted contingent, and there was a mêlée of fighting, then his dalesmen would be in dire danger from the running gillies, who could get amongst them, hamstringing and dirking open their horses' bellies and so bringing them down.

John saw no real choice for him. He must halt that assault, on what he assumed must be the queen's position, at all costs, and risk the other. But he could at least seek to lessen the dangers from the running men. A tight arrowhead formation charging through the Gordon cavalry column would break it up, at least temporarily; and if they kept their close grouping thereafter, they ought to be able to turn around and present a solid, sword-wielding mass, disadvantaging the footmen, lances up. Then back against the Gordon horse.

All this decided in his mind was one thing; effecting it was another. To direct a mass of horsemen charging downhill over rough ground into even a very approximate arrowhead formation was by no means easy. The thunder of eight hundred hooves would drown out any shouted orders. It had to be done by signs, pointing and arm-waving. Fortunately his Marchmen were born horse-fighters, and most would probably see the need for some such tactics.

There were only very brief minutes involved before they were into battle. Sir John Gordon – it was almost certainly he, with the fine plumed helmet and heraldic surcoat over half-armour, riding with the banner-bearer at the head of his company – could see that his assailants were not going to be diverted. But he too faced difficulties in turning a headlong advance by hundreds into a sidelong defensive front. He sought to do so, but strung out as the Gordons were, it was less than successful, indeed resulting in some confusion of horses cannoning into each other and men unsure of what was required of them.

At any rate, lances still levelled, the mosstroopers, in roughly a spearhead mass, smashed into the disordered enemy column, overturning and riding down horses and men, into and through, cutting a wide swathe, and at no real loss to themselves, although John himself, the only one not using a lance, actually lost his sword, which caught in the hinge of an enemy's breastplate as the unfortunate toppled from the saddle, and was jerked out of his hand. This was a little humiliating, but it did not affect his strategy. Waving an upraised arm round and round, and pointing, he managed to swing his company about in some sort of tight order, to head back against the broken Gordon column, now in two groupings. He chose to assail the foremost section, not only because it held the leader, but because that pack of foot coming up would be likely to get entangled with the hindmost horsemen.

The advantage still with the attackers, they managed to wreak substantial havoc on the Gordons, but not as much as John would have wished, because the hindmost section rallied and came on to attack their rear. So this small battle became a confusing slash of steel, splintering lances, shouting men and rearing horses. John would have sought to play the leader's part by seeking out and engaging his opposite number, presumably Sir John, only, with no sword, he was scarcely in a position so to do.

Besides, his mind was partly preoccupied otherwise, and he kept glancing round. Those footmen? They were nearly up with them now, and once these got in amongst the mounted ones, with the dirks, they could change all. What was best, then?

He made up his mind. Temporary withdrawal. Get his people out of this smiting affray a little way, and re-form. They had made a fair impact. The Gordon leader would be hesitant to press on towards that knoll with this mosstrooping force at his back. So much would depend on the Highlandmen foot . . .

He wished that he had a horn to blow, to make himself heard, his orders known. He yelled and waved and pointed, but in all the din and clash, men battling for their lives, few heard or noticed – and he himself had to avoid assault.

Then the Gordon leader largely solved John's problem for him. *He* had a horn, and blew it, and also started to wave and gesture. Obviously he too wanted to extricate his men from this tangle. And the horn-blowing drew all eyes, and John's men then turned to *their* leader to see his reaction. So John had their attention for a moment or two, and signed withdrawal, uphill.

So, as it were, by mutual consent, the two groups of battling horsemen sought to draw apart, swiping their way past each other, leaving some casualties of men and riderless horses behind them.

John, as they won clear, saw that they were just in time,

343

the yelling foot, breathless by now as they must be, almost upon them. What effect would that have on the Gordon leader?

Spurring uphill a little way, to regroup, turning, John saw more than he was looking for. Down there, far beyond his immediate foes, the situation was changing. The great mass of Huntly's host was on the move, and forward, over the soft ground, southwards towards the royal army. He could even hear their bagpipes playing.

What did this mean? What had changed Huntly's tactics, abandoning his strong defensive position for attack? Was it something to do with this small action up here? A co-ordinated assault?

Whether Sir John Gordon, if it was indeed him, knew what it meant, he at least reacted. Horn blowing again, he waved his horsemen into some order and, jabbing his sword ahead again, led his company, tighter-grouped now, eastwards still, heading for that knoll, this just as his running gillies came up.

John had to do some quick thinking. Another descent upon that group would probably have similar results, delayed fighting until the foot came up. That would be no great advantage. But if he and his rode along parallel, eastwards also, up here above the Gordons, they would present a constant threat, and surely concern and affect their advance. That would be best meantime probably. He grabbed a sword from one of his dalesmen, to point it over towards that knoll, now perhaps no more than six hundred yards away.

It made an odd situation, two enemy cavalry forces heading in the same direction but about two hundred yards apart, both spurring hard. At least they were leaving the running gillies behind.

Constantly glancing downwards, John saw that the main Highland army was now streaming out of its hollow and downhill towards the royal host. One or two horsemen could be seen amongst them, one presumably Huntly himself.

John looked forward also. He was rather surprised that the group under the lion rampant remained on that hillock-top. He would have thought, in view of the obvious threat posed, that they would have retired, gone back to the main army, for the queen's safety, if indeed she was there. Perhaps they saw something that he could not see from here? Could there be an intervention on the lower ground? Soon he would find out, as the distance between swiftly lessened.

With only a mere three hundred yards or so to go, near enough clearly to see the queen sitting her horse under her standard, the situation suddenly altered again, and radically. The Gordon cavalry on their right abruptly changed direction, swinging right-handed, and rode off downhill, southwards, towards their own advancing army, clearly giving up the assault on the knoll. Why? Astonished, John stared. The running gillies behind were quick to do the same.

Then he saw the reason. A force of cavalry was appearing over a rise of ground ahead half-right, a fairly large company. They could only be royalists, detached to get between the main army and the queen's position, a belated reaction to this Gordon threat. Was it a rescue attempt? Why the queen's party had remained there? Or it could be otherwise – a flanking move, with Huntly advancing, to descend on him from the east and rear? It could be both.

No doubt it was that perception which had sent the Gordon cavalry hastening downhill to warn and aid.

So, thus unexpectedly, John's immediate concern and responsibility was lifted. Relieved, he continued onward the remaining short distance towards that hillock.

There were perhaps four score gathered there with the queen, Moray, all in black, prominent among them, the Earl Marischal also. Something of a cheer arose as the Marchmen rode up, all their activities no doubt having been clearly seen from here. As John came close, bowing from his saddle, it was Mary Stuart who spoke.

"My Lord Herries, we thank you! We thank you, indeed! For your noble endeavour. Your heading off of the peril. Your brave coming to our rescue. Our thanks. We shall not forget it."

"We feared Your Grace endangered. We could do no less."

"Kirkcaldy below was slow in sending yonder company," Moray added, coldly. "We were prepared to retire to the north, there. But the danger is now overpast."

"Thanks to my Lord Herries, brother," the queen pointed out.

The other shrugged, and turned to gaze westwards. "Now we shall see how the battle goes. Kirkcaldy and Argyll should be able to master Huntly's rabble." He looked back at John. "You, my lord, had best take your men down to join that flanking company. You could be of some use there." That was almost curt dismissal. Moray clearly did not like the appearance of needing rescue.

The queen opened lips to speak, but thought better of it. She smiled warmly on John as he waved to his men, bowed, and led them away downhill.

Actually the Marchmen's aid was scarcely required for, if widespread chaos reigned down on the low ground, it was directed chaos on the royalist part and leaderless chaos for the enemy. Everywhere horsemen were cutting down foot, breaking up groups of clansmen, rounding up prisoners. Clearly such battle as there had been was all but over. John could see no sign of a Gordon leadership group, nothing of Huntly nor his son, indeed few if any horsed men at all. His own late foes seemed to have been swallowed up in a complete defeat.

Leaving their wounded to his mosstroopers to tend, John went in search of the veteran Sir William Kirkcaldy, who was presumably in command here. A flutter of banners on a slight rise drew him, but on his way thither he came across Thomas Kerr, minus his men.

And his fellow-warden had news. Huntly was dead,

hence the enemy's sudden collapse. Not slain in battle but having apparently died of a heart attack, a stroke of apoplexy, in his armour on his horse. Overweight and elderly, this campaigning had presumably been too much for the former Chancellor. Sir John Gordon was captured, wounded. Everything was all but over, the day theirs. Had his friend seen any fighting?

It took some time to bring order and direction to the scene, even though the battle itself had been brief indeed. The queen's party arrived presently, and were taken to view the corpse of the Cock o' the North, Mary Stuart eyeing this unhappily, however gloating some of her companions, and crossing herself before turning away, set-faced, this occasioning some frowns. Sir John Gordon was then brought before her, and, wounded and in evident pain as he was, bowed deeply and mustered a smile, declaring that he and his had borne arms not against Her lovely Grace but against her present forsworn, false and impious attendants, from whom he prayed the good God to deliver her.

He was hustled away promptly, with blows, the queen's distress obvious.

With the October sun sinking, and the shelter of Aberdeen all those miles to reach, all who were not allotted the tasks of dealing with the injured, guarding the prisoners and collecting what booty had not already been found – the dead could await burial on the morrow – set off eastwards for the city without much delay, John and his men amongst them. It had been an eventful and surprising day.

Nor were its events over, for that night Aberdeen resounded with celebrations into the small hours of the morning, a strangely divided community, the Protestants triumphant and Catholics and Gordon supporters fearful and lying low. Nor were the two days following less memorable, especially the second day, for it took time to get the prisoners and wounded back and bestowed, and to plan the sequel to the Battle of Corrichie, as it was already being called, Corrichie being the name of that significant if smallish stream, with its great hollow – the corrie of the minor watercourse, in the Gaelic.

Undoubtedly Moray it was who organised the due celebration of victory, elaborate and telling indeed, a lesson for the realm and all doubters. Huntly's body was brought ceremoniously through the crowded streets to the Tolbooth and there publicly disembowelled. Then the prisoners, having been penned meantime in the churchyard of St Nicholas Kirk, to the number of one hundred and eighty, were lined up, in chains brought from the harbour's shipping, and paraded through the town, Sir John Gordon mounted on a mean garron, to end up before the provost's house in Broadgate where the queen was lodged. Gordon's arms were bound behind him, but he held his head high, to eye the stage-like structure which had been set up opposite the provost's lodging, and the chopping-block thereon. As they came up, the executioner mounted the platform, axe in hand.

The Broadgate was packed, the windows of every house filled with watchers, even the roofs being used as viewpoints. Only one first-floor window of the provost's house was not fully occupied.

When Gordon was roughly pulled down from his garron, and of his own volition mounted almost casually to the platform to gaze round him proudly, two figures appeared at that empty window, both in black, one Moray, the other Master Forbes, minister of St Nicholas, who there and then preached a sermon, to the astonishment of not only John Maxwell. As he thundered on against all papists, idolators, recusants and defilers of the Word, just behind could be seen the person of the queen, head bowed.

With the crowds growing restive, and Gordon looking scornful, the preacher, with the prisoner going over to inspect the ominous block, brows raised, wound up his oration with a final blast at the Harlot of Rome, and Moray turned to bring his half-sister forward, her reluctance most evident. With her came the new Douglas chief, the Earl of Morton, a stocky, ungainly but strong figure. Although it was Moray who waved towards the platform, presumably to the executioner, it was Morton who spoke. He shouted, "John Gordon, you are condemned to die a traitor's death. You have taken up arms against your queen and her council. You have broken ward, led revolt, slain the queen's servants and been put to the horn. You now meet your just doom – to the rejoice of all true men!"

In the hush which followed, Gordon did not so much as raise one of his expressive eyebrows.

"Have you nothing to say?" Morton barked.

"Not to such as you," the other answered, clear-voiced. And then, in a different voice. "Madam, your true lover stands before you, to say his farewell. I have loved you well, but methinks you make but a cruel mistress!"

As something of a growl rose from all around, the queen said no word, although she was seen to bite her lip.

"You are the loveliest among women, madam, but your heart, I think, is of stone! I embrace death now, as the warmer lover!"

The shouts of the crowd rose high, fists were shaken, and if Gordon said more, it was not heard.

Moray raised his hand and cut the air in front of the queen. "Enough!" he said, sharply, although only those comparatively near could hear him. He pointed at the executioner. "To your duty, man!"

The gesture was sufficient, even though the headsman probably did not hear him. He tapped Sir John's shoulder.

Gordon bowed towards the queen, shrugged, and without ado knelt down, to lay his head on that block.

The growls and cries of the onlookers died away into a quivering silence.

Flexing his muscles, and grinning his embarrassment, the headsman raised his axe.

Into the moment of silence, Moray's voice came clearly. "Tut, man, the other way round. Have him facing us."

The executioner had to lower his weapon, and jogged Sir John's shoulder with his knee.

Slowly, with difficulty because of his bonds, Gordon rose to his feet, walked round the block, to turn and face that window, to stare, features stern now. Then he knelt once again.

The queen, features working, held out her crucifix towards him.

A smile came on the handsome face, as he bent his head, and the axe fell.

Something like a whimpering rose from a thousand throats, as the headsman repeated his stroke.

Morton turned to support the queen and lead her away from that window. Moray remained, staring.

When it was all over, John and his Marchmen did not wait for the feasting which was to follow, having had sufficient of the granite city and its celebrations, more than sufficient. He found Thomas Kerr to be like-minded, and they went to take their leave of the queen, who looked pale, tense, and gave the impression of wishing that she was going with them, a desperately troubled young woman. She did again assure John, however, that she would not forget his actions on her behalf two days before, and would seek to prove it in due course.

Then it was the long road southwards for the Borderers in their two companies, and in much faster riding than on their northwards journey, John at least thankful to put that entire venture behind him. Whether his dalesmen had garnered sufficient booty to satisfy them was another matter. They said that they much preferred their own kind of warfare, and wondered about that dispensing of justice in these parts, particularly that of the Justiciar south of the Forth, who was now said to have had himself made justiciar of the entire realm.

27

It was well into the new year, 1563, before John was summoned for further duties in the national, as distinct from the local, interest, May indeed. The queen had called her first parliament, to be held at Edinburgh, a very special occasion, at which all Lords of Parliament and commissioners should attend. He was less than eager, having had enough of taking part in the realm's affairs. But he could scarcely refuse, especially as he received *two* summonses. He tended to forget that he was Master of Maxwell as well as Lord Herries, and would remain so until his nephew, Robert's son, was old enough to sit in parliament as lord, and himself produce an heir to the title; meanwhile John had to represent the great family of Maxwell. Also, Agnes was eager to accompany him, to see the queen again.

As usual, they lodged overnight with Lord Seton, in his Canongate house, who, a staunch Catholic, had taken no part in the Aberdeenshire expedition, and was much concerned over the execution of Sir John Gordon and the imprisonment of his elder brother, now Earl of Huntly. Seton declared, like Agnes, that it was high time that the queen married, and if possible to a strong character who, with the crown matrimonial, could help to keep Moray from ruling all, as at present, he having been given, or had taken, most of the Gordon lands, and had himself created Earl of Mar as well as of Moray. With the vociferous support of Knox and the Kirk, no one appeared to be able to stand up to him, this including his young half-sister. Unfortunately Lennox's son, Darnley, whom Mary seemed to think much of, was anything but a strong character, vain and petulant; and Arran appeared to have given up his endeavours.

The parliament was to be held not in Edinburgh Castle this time but in the new Tolbooth, a fine building recently erected by the town council, attached to the south-west corner of the High Kirk of St Giles, Knox's shrine, this so that the people of the city could view all the pomp and circumstance of this notable occasion, take the queen to their hearts and thus further the power and authority of those ruling the country in her name; Moray, Morton who was now to be the new Chancellor, Argyll and Maitland, Protestants all, anxious to play down Mary's Catholicism and make her popularity with the common folk work in their favour.

So the lords and officers of state were ordered to assemble at Holyrood, clad in their best, to ride in state up the almost mile of the Canongate and the High Street to St Giles, behind the queen, John and Seton amongst them. And not only the lords but their ladies, or many of them, including the four Maries, all looking very fine in the May sunshine, Agnes attaching herself to the chattering and good-looking throng. So lengthy was the cavalcade that the leaders were almost up at the Tolbooth before those at the rear had left the abbey.

The queen, preceded by the officers of state bearing the crown, sceptres and sword – seldom had these been carried on horseback – rode in crimson velvet trimmed with gold, the coronation robes, her lovely reddish hair not with its usual silken coif but ringed with a golden circlet, looking beautiful indeed and considerably less troubled than when John had last seen her. The streets were so crowded with onlookers as to narrow them further, which inevitably elongated the procession, allowing the riders to go no more than three abreast. There was cheering all the way up, past the other Tolbooth, that of the Canongate, that originally monastic community having its own jurisdiction still.

Around the great church of St Giles was something of an open square, where rose also the Mercat Cross, and this area was so packed with citizenry and folk come in from the countryside around that the town guard had difficulty in clearing a passage for the royal parade, and in coping with the horses once the riders had dismounted. The queen, smiling and waving graciously, with her official party, was received here by the lord provost and council, and then disappeared into office rooms while the lords and commissioners filed their way into the great council chamber, to be followed in due course by the womenfolk and other privileged spectators such as foreign ambassadors and courtiers, to the visitors gallery overlooking all. John noted, as he was guided to his own place beside Seton on the lords' benches, that John Knox and other black-robed divines were already well to the fore in that gallery. He hoped that, on this occasion, they all might be spared wrathful maledictions from aloft.

It was his first visit to these premises, indeed as it was for most, for the new Tolbooth had only recently been completed, after long building, the town council having been shamed into erecting it to replace the all-but ruinous predecessor which had been a disgrace as the city's official meeting-place, and which could never have housed a parliament. The new premises were certainly a great improvement, spacious and well furnished, with a dais platform, the walls for this event hung with tapestries.

Presently, sitting there, with a choir of boys singing hymns and chanting psalms for their edification, John got a wave from Agnes up in the gallery, beside Ladies Seton and Lindsay.

The usual sequence of events was gone through, even though these premises required rather different entrances and positioning. It was notable that there were no clerics present, other than those in the gallery, the Kirk now having its own General Assembly, which undoubtedly some of the ministers looked upon as more important than any parliament. Many of the former prelates, to be sure, were imprisoned or banished.

Lyon and his trumpeter duly announced the opening

of proceedings, Lindsay declaring that this was a most important and memorable day in the realm's ages-old story, the first parliament attended by the first regnant sovereign-lady Scotland had ever seen, Mary, by the Grace of God, queen. Let all be duly aware of the day's significance, history being made.

The earls then filed in, a very full turnout, even some under-age ones being present, although they would not speak nor vote. Then the new Chancellor, Morton, looking less at ease, indeed bullish, than Huntly had used to do, scowling around him. The officers of state and the earls who bore the honours came next, to place the crown, sceptres and sword on a table before the throne brought down from the castle for the occasion.

Then, after a pause, to a flourish of the trumpet, the signal for all to rise, the monarch entered. Mary carried herself superbly for so young a woman, although she must have been nervous. There was a departure from the usual here, for she was flanked by the High Constable and the Earl Marischal, and close behind her came Moray, looking as grim as ever, he not comforming to the fine-dress observance but clad all in his usual black. His sister was tall, but he towered above her, metaphorically as well as physically, a figure John had begun to look upon as ominous. When the queen went to sit on her throne, Moray moved to stand immediately behind it, indeed hands on the seat back and leaning a little forward. Nothing could have been more eloquent of his position and intentions.

All were about to sit, when a gesture from Lindsay kept them on their feet. He announced, "Her Grace will address this session of parliament." And he bowed to the throne.

Mary rose, and all remained standing when the monarch stood. She surveyed all, a slight frown of concentration on her lovely features, silent for moments. Then, inclining her head, she spoke.

"My lords, officers, commissioners of parliament and friends all, I rejoice to be with you this day, and thank the

355

good God that He has at last permitted me to sit with you all here, and decide for the better state and government of my ancient realm. I have waited for this for long. My royal mother held this throne for me all the years. Now, however unworthily, I must fill it.''

There were murmurs from all around, including something critical from up in that gallery, then someone shouted "God save the Queen's Grace!" And immediately the cry was taken up by all, or almost all, repeating and repeating "God save the Queen's Grace! God save the Queen's Grace!" on and on.

Clearly moved, Mary smiled, the concern and concentration vanishing from her features – and when Mary Stuart smiled, few could remain unaffected.

"You are kind," she resumed, "and I will endeavour with all that is in me to repay your kindness, and to work and act with all of you for the enduring good of my people. And much work and care is called for, as we all know well. The kingdom has been sorely divided, riven, stricken, these years past. Now we must heal it, together. Today, let us make a start, putting behind us the pain and the sorrow, the harshness and the discord, in all the affairs and concerns of my people, of the state and the land and of our faith. For we *are* all one people, one nation, one great family, and we all worship our God, as to how each of us thinks best . . .''

There was a bark from the gallery and a stirring throughout the hall, but she went on in that accented but melodious voice.

"God helping me, and with your guidance, I shall seek the weal of all, peace with other realms, prosperity amongst my people, an end to violence, the support of the nation's laws by and towards all. Sadly we have of late had violence in the north, to my sorrow. But let that be the end of it. Let peace prevail henceforth. Differences to be settled here, in parliament and in all our courts of law, justice and kindly justice to prevail, not the battlefield or in feud and challenge. I saw, in France, where that could lead!''

There were more murmurings, but undoubtedly in the main they were of approval. Even Knox elected to restrain himself.

She half turned, to glance behind her. "I have good friends, good guidance. Notable mainstays and aides. My good brothers, and representatives. We will all work together for good." She gestured at that table. "If my crown means anything, let us hereafter raise it high. Wield the sceptres with mercy. And leave the sword in its scabbard, save as a symbol of our realm's independence and protection, its freedom and justice!"

Cheers were loud and long from the still-standing assembly.

"One last word before I sit, and my lord Chancellor heads your debates, my friends." The queen drew a deep breath, as though she was thankful to have got all that said. She raised a hand to gesture forward. "I spoke of the sword's use for protection only, and justice in the realm. I would point to you all one who has wielded that especial sword notably indeed. I salute him, and commend him to you all. At that sad battle near Aberdeen, he risked life and limb to save myself and my small company, detached from the rest on a small hill that we might oversee the affray. We were endangered by unexpected attack. He rode to our rescue, assailed the foe, with no great following, and so turned away the hazard from us, indeed striking the first blow of that Battle of Corrichie, earning the esteem and gratitude of us all. That was indeed the sword of protection. But it is the same man who has used the sword of justice these many years in the Borderland, firmly but mercifully, wisely, on our West March, where, I am assured, firm judgment, with mercy and understanding, is especially required. My lords and friends, I salute Sir John Maxwell, my Lord Herries, and commend him to you all." Mary Stuart waved a hand, and sat down on her throne.

John stood dumbfounded, staring, overwhelmed in a tide of emotion, unaware of the cheering and the thumps on his shoulders and back by Seton and other lords within reach, scarcely believing what he had heard. Even the smiling queen's hand raised again and pointing in his direction did not really penetrate until a tugging at his doublet by Seton brought realisation that while everyone else had sat down he was still standing, and that Mary was waving him down.

He sank to his bench, recollected, rose again and bowed jerkily towards the throne, realised that Morton was speaking in his harsh voice, so very different from the tones which they had been hearing, and sat down again.

It is to be feared that John Maxwell was all but unaware of what went on thereafter for some considerable time, however especial and important the occasion. In the end it was movement from up there in the gallery which caught his inward-turning eye, and he perceived that it was another female hand waving, Agnes's, signalling her delight. That helped to bring him back to some degree of attention to what was going on, but no very great consideration nor interest. It was in fact Maitland of Lethington asserting the need for another meeting with Queen Elizabeth's representatives. He had just returned from a visit to that English court, and Elizabeth Tudor was proposing her favourite, Robert Dudley, Earl of Leicester, as suitable husband for Her Grace; and this, he urged, with Her Grace's agreement, must be opposed with all determination as unacceptable for the realm's independence. Yet Elizabeth should not be offended, which was important. So careful negotiation was required.

John sat through much talk and discussion on a variety of other subjects, but his mind was not on any of them, until he was thankful to hear Morton declaring that this was enough for their first session and that he was adjourning the sitting until the morrow, when more detailed business would be put before them. It was at this stage that he did at length take notice. Master Knox, up there, with the assembly about to break up, took the opportunity loudly to pronounce his disapproval of all the unseemly show of fine apparel and over-dressing, and the presence of all these flauntingly garbed women around him, an offence to the Almighty on such solemn occasion. The ringing laughter of the said women which greeted this had the unusual effect of drowning out even John Knox's powerful delivery, and he was further overborne as Lyon signed to his trumpeter to sound for the queen's exit.

It took some time for John to join up with his wife thereafter, because of all the congratulations and acclaim to which he was subjected by his fellows. When he did reach her, Agnes threw her arms around him there before all, more words unnecessary.

That man, distinctly bemused, Seton and the ladies led back to the Canongate house in the wake of the royal train.

That evening the queen gave a great ball in the palatial abbot's lodging of Holyrood, that other half-brother's house, to which all the parliament members and their ladies were invited. And not only these, for in her generosity and anxiety to heal divisions, she had extended the invitation to a number of the divines also, including Knox, and, strange to relate, he and others did attend, however frowning upon it all. They could scarcely claim that this was a solemn occasion in the sight of the Almighty and that fine clothing was therefore again unsuitable, but they could and did look much askance at much that they saw, especially at some of the ladies' explicitly feminine attire.

Mary Stuart did not appear for some time, indeed the proceedings seemed to be the concern of the Lord Robert and his multitudinous, peculiar but cheerful household, who made generous hosts, especially with the liquor, to the further disapprobation of the clergy. And when at length the queen did present herself, it was as one in the company of a masque, representing Cleopatra, with an entourage of females, made to look dusky for the occasion, and some of them but scantily clad, coming to visit King Solomon at Jerusalem, this last represented by a throne with a cunningly devised temple of velvet panels. With the young women circling the hall, singing, dancing and plucking lutes, a single male emerged from behind the temple to stand beside the throne, a tall, slender, golden-haired young man, beardless and eye-catching, with sculptured features, high forehead and large hazel eyes, his graceful person very evident in the robe of white silk in which he was partly draped. Seton, at John's side, informed that this was Henry Stewart, Lord Darnley, heir to Lennox.

Cleopatra led her maidens, which included the four Maries, up to this exquisite if less than masculine figure and, bowing before him, offered him a flower drawn from her bosom, which he accepted with a flourish and placed gallantly in his long hair; then taking the queen's hand, led her into a stately dance, to the music of her young ladies, a notable scene, both clearly expert dancers.

To the applause of the company – but not of the divines – after a circuit of the hall, the couple and their attendants paused at the doorway, and Cleopatra was tall enough to lay her head on Solomon's shoulder in a flattering gesture, before all passed from view, leaving behind them much comment and speculation.

Agnes Herries wagged her head. "So that is Darnley," she said. "It is worse than I feared!"

"I cannot say that I share the queen's seeming admiration," John agreed. "Lady-faced, shall we say!"

"Weak but arrogant, I would say. And petulant," Seton said. He pointed across the hall, to where Moray and Maitland stood alone. "Yet those two countenance him, all but foster his cause with Mary. I think that they desire a weakling for Mary's husband, so that they may dominate, Moray in especial. A strong wearer of the crown matrimonial would lessen their influence and power."

"She deserves better than that!" John declared feelingly.

"Have you anyone in mind?" his wife enquired, tapping his arm. "You, who have so greatly won her favour, my brave husband. And who are part in love with her yourself, I think!"

He shook his head, wordless.

Presently, with dancing general, the queen and her ladies came back, clad more fully, Darnley with them. Mary danced with him briefly, then pushed him away, but affectionately, to accept the arm of the English envoy, Thomas Randolph, all smiles and graciousness. Other great ones were queuing for a like favour, including Maitland. But not Moray, who gave the impression of being no dancer.

John had taken the floor with the Ladies Seton and Lindsay, as well as his wife, and was talking with the Lord Lyon when Mary Beaton came up to him, niece of the late cardinal. She touched his wrist.

"My lord, much as I would wish myself to be your partner, I fear that I must forgo that pleasure meantime. Her Grace sends me to summon you."

"Me? Now? The queen . . . ?"

"You, none other. Come."

He followed this self-possessed young woman through the throng to where Mary Stuart stood chatting with Keith, the Earl Marischal.

"Ah, my lord Warden and would-be rescuer!" he was greeted. "I saw that you dance as well as you wield those two swords I spoke of earlier. Come then, and pleasure me, no? My lord Marischal will excuse us?"

"Your Grace, this is, this is . . . beyond all in, in . . ."

She laughed, and took his arm, to lead him on to the floor.

If he had been astonished, all but dumbfounded back there in the parliament, he was still more so now, as he found his arm encircling the lovely and lively person of the Queen of Scots, and the feel of her warm under his hands and against him, as they paced and swayed and swung together. Was he dreaming this?

"You are silent, my lord!" she observed. "Deep in thought?"

"I, I cannot believe that this is happening. To *me*, madam," he got out. "That you so honour me, favour me."

"And ought I not, sir? You put your life at risk to save me from capture. And you served my mother well, on missions, as indeed you have done for myself."

"My simple duty . . ." he began, but she pressed his arm.

"See you, Sir John, I sought a word with you, alone. Thus I can have it. On a matter of some . . . delicacy. You I can trust, I know."

Their dancing now became little more than a mutual, rhythmic pacing, as she spoke carefully, and with so many watching.

"It concerns this of marriage. It seems that marry I must. None let me forget it! And so many seek my hand! Or that of the Queen of Scots, rather? I have already learned the costs of this! In France. I do not wish further lesson! Poor Francis – he had to learn it, also."

John, scarcely realising that he did it, gave his sovereign-lady's person a little squeeze of sympathy.

"My concern is this of Elizabeth of England. She who does not herself wed, would have me marry her admirer and plaything, Robert Dudley. For her own ends, I judge, not mine! Her father sought to win Scotland, first by the sword, then by wishing to marry me to his son. Now his daughter seeks it thus. England will have Scotland one way or another, always. I will not wed her Dudley, whom I have never met, nor wish to meet, and become her puppet!" So I . . ."

The music stopped, therefore the dancing, and partners in the main bowed to each other, and parted. Not so Mary Stuart. She stood still, but holding John's arm, making it entirely obvious that she at least intended to continue their partnership. He saw Moray and Maitland eyeing them, and others, to be sure. The instrumentalists likewise perceived the queen's stance and wishes, and without delay started up again, and the same music as before. Mary closed with John once more, and into action.

"So, my good friend," she resumed, "I wish you to be part of a mission which will meet with Elizabeth's envoys at Berwick, as the secretary spoke of at the parliament. Whether she will send Norfolk again, or another. But I wish you to speak privily with whoever is her chief messenger. Give him my message, whatever that of the others. It is vital that Elizabeth is not affronted, offended. You understand? Displeased she may be, but offence we must avoid, if we may, for the peace of the two kingdoms. My brother and Maitland will be leading the mission, to be sure; but they are, shall we say, more concerned with the nation's seeming weal than with mine! They may well have their own proposals for the English. You, I trust, will convey *mine*, my message."

"But . . . Highness, how can I do that? I am only a March warden, no great one. How will the duke, or other, heed me? And what am I to say that the others do not?"

"They will heed you, John. I will ensure that. See you, here is what you will say, but privily. That I, Mary, seek my loving sister Elizabeth's womanly understanding and aid. That I wish for the closer accord between the two realms. But that I have better proposals to bring this about than by wedding Lord Robert Dudley. Henry Stewart, Lord Darnley, is of royal Tudor blood, Dudley is not. Henry's mother's mother was Queen Margaret Tudor, wife to my grandsire, James the Fourth. I greatly esteem him. And he can bring the two crowns closer than anyone else."

John's head swam – which was becoming Mary Stuart's impact upon him one way or another. Darnley! He was to be the mouthpiece for Darnley, that popinjay! This was beyond all! Besides that, how would he make any impression? Where the others might not? He shook his head, as they paced and turned.

"Your Grace, I am honoured. Greatly. By your trust in me, and regard. But I do not understand. My lord of

Moray, and Lethington, they can do this, surely? They support the Lord Darnley? Know him, as I do not. Why myself? Not them?"

"There is the rub, my friend. Yes, my brother and Maitland seem well disposed towards Henry. But they do not love him. They use him, in order to keep others at a distance. But they would not have him wed me. They seek power, and I am not against that. The realm needs strong hands to guide it. They have, I am assured, other plans for me. But since marry I must, it seems, I would to have my own choice, Henry Stewart. And I would have Elizabeth Tudor know that I intend so."

John felt as though he was scarcely in his right mind, holding in his arms the delectable person of the monarch, feeling her body's pressures and movements, and very much affected thereby; but being asked, indeed told, for this would rank as a royal command, to be sure, to aid in her union to a man, if man was the word, for whom he could only feel dislike, almost repulsion. Yet, could he refuse?

"Highness," he said, in a sort of desperation, "the Duke of Norfolk, or other, will nowise heed such as myself when Moray and the Secretary of State are there, so much my seniors."

"Ah, but they, or he, will, John, he will. When, privily, you show them this." And releasing her hold of him to free her hands, she drew a ring from her finger and gave it to him.

It was a handsome piece indeed, gold, with a little shield on it bearing the lilies of France under a crown.

Taking it, still he wagged his head. "This, this is notable, yes, Your Grace. Could come only from you. But how am I to see the English privily? Speak with them without the others knowing, hearing? I do not see how this may be . . ." John knew that he must be sounding feeble indeed, but this mission being laid on him sounded to him impossible as it was distasteful.

"You must go previously. To Berwick. Before the others

win there. See Norfolk or whoever Elizabeth sends. Tell him my wishes in this of marriage. But say not to speak of it, later, to my brother and Maitland. On my command. You can do that, John? The others will have their own say later, yes. They will speak of other suitors, name not a few. Say that I must have time to consider, this Dudley, to be Earl of Leicester, only one of many. And they will, to be sure, have other matters to discuss, of trade, English pirates, the French Huguenots, and the like."

The music ceased again, and this time the queen inclined her head and moved back. But her hand touched his, the one which held the ring.

"You will do this for me, John Maxwell, and win Mary Stuart's gratitude, her grateful regard?" she murmured. "I will send you word when the meeting is to take place. Keep the ring hidden."

He pocketed it, as he bowed low, and she turned away.

John remained very thoughtful for the remainder of the evening. Agnes rallied him, to be sure, on his prolonged dancing with the queen; but at his almost curt announcement that he would explain later, she eyed him speculatively, but said no more.

Mary retired from the hall soon thereafter, and it was not long before the Seton party took their leave.

In their bedchamber at the Canongate house, John recounted all to his wife, emphasising his unhappiness about the entire affair, although conceding his gratification and surprise that the queen should so choose himself. That he should be selected to further the advancement of the wretched Darnley was galling in the extreme; but he could not have refused. Was it not all an extraordinary dilemma into which he had been cast? What had he done to deserve this? The royal favour, and then this!

Agnes, while agreeing with the unsuitability of Darnley, urged him to look on the bright side. Mary's favour and trust in him was a great matter. Who could tell where it might lead? Not that she desired *too* much involvement in court affairs for her husband, and she would have to keep an eye on him, where their beautiful sovereign was concerned! But the queen's gratitude was not to be belittled, and might prove a notable asset to them and their family. He might even be able to effect some improvement in the Darnley situation, in due course?

That failed quite to lift John's unease.

Agnes at least greatly admired that ring.

The next day's session of parliament was a more productive if less memorable one, much necessary legislation being passed, and some approved that John for one would have not wished, the Lords of the Congregation being very much in the ascendant, and with Morton, as Chancellor, very much one of them, aiding. The queen sat through it all, frequently biting her lip but not uttering, Moray at her back silent also, but to a large extent dominating all, Morton often turning to glance back at him. John had no opportunity for a word with Mary, although more than once she caught his eye. Nor did he see her thereafter.

The following morning they were off for the Borderland and blessed normality.

28

It was two weeks later that a courier arrived at Terregles from Edinburgh, to inform that the meeting with the English envoys would be held at Berwick-upon-Tweed five days hence, on 4th June. No more than that.

John could have done with rather more detail as to when the English and, for that matter, the rest of the Scots delegation were likely to reach there, since he was to see the former beforehand. If Moray and Maitland came the day before, as was quite likely, he might have difficulty in seeing the English privately, as directed. Better if he was there two days early, at least. He reckoned that it was some one hundred and twenty miles to Berwick, two days' riding. But, not to risk anything, he would set off the very next morning. Better too early than too late.

With again only Dod Armstrong as companion, then, he went off in very doubtful frame of mind, despite Agnes's encouragement. They would stop at Ferniehirst overnight, where he was always welcome.

John could not tell Thomas Kerr all that the queen had laid upon him so confidentially, only that he was one of the mission to Berwick. But he did ask the other's opinion of Darnley, and was offered a like opinion to his own.

He reached Berwick next afternoon, to discover the English party not yet arrived, although Lord Hunsdon, who was now governor of Berwick Castle as well as Warden of the English East March, was in residence. His greeting of John was less than warm, but he did reveal that the Earl of Bedford was leading the English mission, with the Bishop of Durham, and was expected at any time. John elected to lodge down in the town inn which he had used on a previous occasion.

It was next forenoon before Bedford and the others came, and John was not long in presenting himself up at the castle again, fearful that Moray and the rest would appear before he had opportunity to undertake his unwelcome task.

When, after a wait, he was ushered into the presence of the English group, it was to find himself being considered doubtfully by four men, including Hunsdon. Bedford was a handsome character of middle years, with a keen glance, the Bishop of Durham rubicund and at least superficially genial, and Lord Conyers, the awkward customer whom John had met before.

Bedford led off. "My Lord Hunsdon says that you seek this interview, my lord, forthwith? Before your fellow-Scots arrive, an odd situation. May we be informed as to the reason?" They were sitting at a table, but no gesture was made for the newcomer to sit thereat.

John went forward, however, and drew out a chair for himself. He was not going to stand before these Englishmen like some felon on trial, or even a petitioner.

"I come thus at Her Grace Queen Mary's express command," he said levelly. "The others will have their own orders and submissions to make, my lord Earl. But I was to see you first."

His hearers, from eyeing him wonderingly, glanced at each other.

"Here is a strange matter, my lord," Bedford said. "Do you Scots speak with two voices, then?"

"As to that I do not know. But what I do know is that Her Grace commanded me so to act. And to prove my authority so to do and to speak, she gave me this to put before you." And he produced the ring, and pushed it across the table towards them.

The earl picked it up, tight-lipped, to consider the lilies of France under the crown, and raised his brows. He passed it to his colleagues. "We must accept this as

368

sure token, I think," he said. "But, why? What is Her Majesty's purpose?"

"Her *Grace* has instructed me closely, my lords." He emphasised the Grace, the Scots term in place of the English Majesty. "She wishes this to be kept privy. As distinct from what her other commissioners will say and propose. This is to be a matter between the two queens, between Mary and your Elizabeth." John sought to marshal his thoughts and words. "She, Queen Mary, appeals to Queen Elizabeth's womanly care and understanding over this of marriage. Your sovereign-lady is proposing the Lord Robert Dudley as husband for our sovereign. For the weal of the two realms. Queen Mary understands her concern, but thinks and feels otherwise. Better a still more close union, through one of your monarch's own blood, the Lord Henry Darnley, son to the Earl of Lennox, whose mother's mother was Queen Margaret Tudor."

There were murmurs from his hearers, and another exchange of glances.

"There are many suitors for our monarch's hand," John went on. "Kings, princes, dukes. You will know of these. But none will advance the mutual benefit of Scotland and England. The fact that Queen Elizabeth proposes Lord Robert Dudley shows that she perceives it. Queen Mary sees Darnley as much the better. And she . . . esteems him."

Bedford stroked his pointed beard. "This may be so, my lord. But why does your queen send secret word by you? When her brother, or half-brother, and her Secretary of State come to meet us here in due course?"

"That is for me to explain, my lords. Queen Mary greatly values the Earl of Moray's and the Secretary's advice and guidance in affairs of state. But in this of marriage, less so. They may have other proposals to put before you. But she, understandably, would choose her own husband. And she believes that another woman, your Elizabeth, will recognise this. After all, *she* is not hastening into marriage, despite many suitors, no?"

That struck home. There was silence.

"So Her Grace would have you inform your sovereign-lady. She wishes to wed the Lord Darnley, and believes that it will advance amity and good relations between the two realms, as your Elizabeth wishes. Much better than the Dudley match, which is well meant but less suitable. She is gratified by Queen Elizabeth's concern, and would have you tell her so."

The bishop spoke. "Mary Stewart is queen. Why does she not tell her envoys this, her other envoys, for them to tell us? Not send such as yourself, my lord?"

"Because they may well have other views, and seek to put what they esteem the realm's good before her own. She feels that this is a matter between two women. Why she chose me, I do not know. But that was her choice."

"How does the Warden of the West March come so close to the queen?" Hunsdon demanded.

John shrugged. "I was enabled to do Her Grace what she considered to be some small service." He eyed them all. "One last matter, my lords. It is Her Grace's desire, her command indeed, that you do not speak of this issue, this of her personal message to Queen Elizabeth, to the other commissioners when they come to you. I will be with them, and we will discuss other matters. You will have your own proposals. But this, between the queens, is privy."

"You are telling us, sir, what we are to say and what not?" Conyers demanded.

"No. I but pass on my sovereign's instructions. This is for Queen Elizabeth's ears alone. Monarchs have their . . . privileges."

There was no comment to that.

"My lord Earl, may I have the queen's ring? And your permission to retire."

In silence he was given the golden token of his authority. He stood, bowed briefly, and went to the door and out.

Thankful to have got that over, John joined Dod outside, and they rode down to the town. That was the strangest task that he had ever had to perform.

The party from Edinburgh arrived next noontide. When John joined them, his colleagues had no reason to suspect that he had been in prior consultation with the English, for there was nothing unusual in his having arrived earlier, coming from Dumfries-shire. But Moray and Maitland looked at him heedfully nevertheless, suspiciously almost, no doubt recollecting that prolonged dancing interlude with the queen, and wondering what it had been for. They were not uncivil, but wary. The other two members of the delegation were unknown to John, save by repute, the Lord Ruthven and Douglas of Lochleven, a kinsman of Morton's.

In the discussion and debate, the accusations and defence, which followed with the English, although illustrious suitors of Queen Mary were named, Darnley was not, by either side. Dudley was not dismissed from consideration, but the Scots delegation, without saying so, indicated that his name would go forward only at the price of Mary being accepted as eventual heir to a childless Elizabeth. Other matters were dealt with, but quite obviously the real reason behind this meeting was the marriage situation of the Scots monarch and its possible repercussions. No mention was made of John's prior interview with the English.

Neither side desiring to prolong the occasion, the commissioners broke up with as little delay as had signalled the commencement.

John, well aware of the doubts of his fellows towards himself, had no wish to accompany the other Scots back to Edinburgh. Yet thither he must go, to make his report to the queen and to return that ring. He reckoned that he and Dod, Marchmen, were almost certainly harder riders than were his fellow-commissioners; and saying nothing of his destination, he took leave of the others there and then below the castle mound, and was not detained. The pair set off westwards, as though for the West March. They would take their own route to Edinburgh.

John Maxwell thereafter taxed their mounts to the full, just as he had taxed himself otherwise those two days. But now he could take and share his secret with the queen, whatever the final outcome – and what a tale he would have to tell thereafter to Agnes Herries . . .

HISTORICAL NOTE

Mary Stuart, lovely, spirited, kind, lacked judgment, at least where men's characters were concerned. She did marry the effeminate, unsuitable but ambitious Darnley, quickly found him inadequate as a husband as in much else, even though she conferred on him the crown matrimonial. But Moray and Maitland, seeking to steer the kingdom, fell foul of him, and Moray had to depart for France. But, another misjudgment, Bothwell was permitted to return to Scotland, and quickly made his own violent impact, especially on the queen, and was reappointed Lieutenant of the Border. Being the man he was, with Morton, he encompassed the murder of Darnley, allegedly with the absent Moray's approval, and thereafter swept Mary off her feet and became her third husband; at least he was not effeminate. But he aroused much enmity, and this developed into civil war with the Lords of the Congregation. After the defeat of Carberry Hill, deserting the queen, he fled to Denmark, presumably back to Anna Throndsen. He died there. Moray returned. Mary had a son, allegedly by Darnley, although there were doubts; Moray, Maitland and Morton had the queen imprisoned in Lochleven Castle, and forced her to sign a declaration of abdication, which she afterwards repudiated. The infant was crowned James the Sixth, with Moray as regent. But Moray was assassinated in 1569 and in due course Morton became regent but was executed in 1581 on his own notorious Maiden. But by then Mary Stuart had been a prisoner of Queen Elizabeth of England for ten long years, after her final defeat at the Battle of Langside on her escape from Lochleven. At that battle, John, Lord

Herries fought at her side, and thereafter pleaded on his knees for her not to throw herself on Elizabeth Tudor's mercy. He remained Warden of the West March until his death in 1594, the longest holder of the office on record.